With special thanks to ...y family and friends who have continually supported me through this journey.

THE STONES OF MOYA

STONE I-
DESTINY SHALL LEAD YOU

MARNIE MERCIER

iUNIVERSE, INC.
BLOOMINGTON

The Stones of Moya
Stone I-Destiny Shall Lead You

iUniverse books may be ordered through booksellers or by contacting:

iUniverse
1663 Liberty Drive
Bloomington, IN 47403
www.iuniverse.com
1-800-Authors (1-800-288-4677)

Because of the dynamic nature of the Internet, any Web addresses or links contained in this book may have changed since publication and may no longer be valid. The views expressed in this work are solely those of the author and do not necessarily reflect the views of the publisher, and the publisher hereby disclaims any responsibility for them.

ISBN: 978-1-4401-7987-7 (sc)
ISBN: 978-1-4401-7989-1 (dj)
ISBN: 978-1-4401-7988-4 (ebk)

Printed in the United States of America

iUniverse rev. date: 2/17/2011

Prologue:

A Chance Meeting with Destiny

The breath of dawn was cold. With determination, I struggled through the narrow bends of entangled demper vine, desperate to reach the outskirts of Hoverdire—the village I had called home from the time I was a small child.

Encircling the township, the maze of vine formed a shield, protecting us from the marauding wolverdogs that scavenged through our land in the winter season. Thorns pulled at my gown, piercing through to my flesh. The putrid smell of rotting foliage that had grown strong over the spring thaw left me thankful the season was nearing its end.

To the east lay the forest of Nevermeed where tall dark sentinels, bursting with new leaf, stood lonely in the mist. Lush shrubbery appeared warm and plentiful as rays of morning twilight broke through the higher reaches. Governed by the Guardians, its depths intimidated many throughout the years. I did not fear the woodlands but rather was drawn to the intimacy of its shelter.

Free from the vine, I looked to the towers where the Guardians of the region stood watch. To my relief, they were abandoned. Shift change was at hand. If I were to make my escape, the time would have to be now. Without another thought, I dashed across the lea, holding tightly to the hood of my cloak in an attempt to conceal my identity.

In the shadow of the timbers, I found what I was looking for: the crumbling archway to the abandoned path of Leere. It was said a great waterfall breached this footway, one whose splendor was not to be denied.

As I carefully stepped through the moss-covered threshold, I was lost in the undergrowth. The path was still visible, though the hands of time had woven over its clarity. I was reluctant to return to the safety of Hoverdire, as I should have done. Instead, I pushed forward through the labyrinth of trees.

I stopped several times to pick wildflowers and twigs to create a crown from the forest's riches—something my uncle had done with me in my childhood. I was not much closer to being an adult now; my years were short lived at fifteen. "The time for you to become a lady, Arianna, is drawing near," my mother often warned. Content in my youth, I chose not to take heed of her words.

My uncle, a gentle soul for his years, was in many ways like a father to me. Our bond was strong. He was short in height and weighted in the belly, which seemed to project his laugh so that it could be heard from anywhere in the village.

I hold no memories of my real father. The true history of his bloodline has never been revealed to me. My mother refuses to acknowledge the past, becoming withdrawn at the mention of it, as though it pained her in ways unexplainable.

When the crown was complete, I placed it upon my head. The faint scent of flora emanated around me, reminding me of our garden kitchen and the ever-lasting comfort the room brought to me.

Distracted by a cluster of birds, I followed them as their jovial choir echoed through the thickets of honeysuckle and briar. I fought my way up the moistened duff to the crest of a peak. Unable to comprehend the splendor before me, I halted. Lying in a bay of stone, the cascade fell like an avalanche of fury as it was forced from its path. Spears of water, repelled from the rocks below, created an array of swirling mist to dance in the open breeze.

Within the thinning trees, the earthen soil gave way to jagged stone. Dense trickles of dew teemed like a satin cloth of water. The smell was rotten, yet fresh, reminding me of the times my uncle and I had shared while gathering sweet berries off the shores of Lake Vanderbrood.

I was about to descend to the lower bank when I heard the snap of branches in the distance. I stood still as the timbers, and my eyes searched the area, only to find a deer foraging for its breakfast in the lush reeds that blossomed from the water-soaked land downstream.

As I climbed to the top of a boulder, I noticed a small puddle grooved into its face. Curious to see the forest crown I had made earlier, I knelt before it. The reflection was muted but clear enough to cast a perfect image of me.

Violets and daisies clung to my burnt umber hair, and the delicate touch of curl held the crown in place. I wiped the dirt from my brow and admired my skin, something I adored, having inherited it from my mother whose beauty was still present in her latter years. "Your eyes have captured the innocence of the fairies," my uncle would tease. I only saw the brown. I both loved and hated my reflection. I was always told of my beauty but never quite believed in it myself.

My cloak, a pale shade of green, had been given to me by the village seamstress on my fourteenth year and was one of my most cherished belongings. I swept off the dead foliage that clung to it as I pulled it around me.

As contentment set in, I could not help but notice the unnatural silence around me. Something was amiss: I no longer felt alone. Feeling insecure, I scanned the area only to find there was no escape that would leave me invulnerable.

Shale began to break from above. It was too late: I had already been discovered—but by whom? Had someone followed me from the village? Had my journey abruptly come to an end? Or was it a stranger?

Fear struck me at the thought. Unsure what to do, I made way for an overhang in the cliff. The moss-covered stone made the passage treacherous. For stability, I reached out for a root that had found its way through one of the fissures, but it too was coated with moss and slipped through my fingers, causing me to lose my balance. Caught in a cleft, my ankle jerked to the right.

I held back the urge to scream as I desperately tried to free myself. With nothing to hold onto, I began to slide down the embankment. As I fell backward, my foot broke free.

In anguish, I sat forward to examine the area. To my relief, there was no sign of a fracture. Even so, I would not be returning home on foot. Chilled by the escaping mist, I slowly pulled myself into the nearest crevice to conceal my location. As I settled in the narrow cavity, I heard the sound of rocks grating from below. The stranger was advancing.

I stilled my breath, preparing for the inevitable. When I looked up, I was immediately taken aback by the man who stood before me.

Potent yet beautiful, his green eyes carried a look I had not seen before on a man's face. He was adorned in warrior's attire, and several holsters were fitted around his muscular torso and legs. A quiver of arrows was secured to his back and held his lengthy bow in place. Thick long locks, autumn leaf in color, fell freely past his broad shoulders. Despite his common traits, there was something different about him. His ears—they were pointed at the top, like those of characters in a children's story.

"Who are you?" I uttered as tears began to trickle down my cheeks. "What do you want?"

"Come," he said as he held out his hand. "I wish you no harm."

Although wary, I inched my body toward him; my options were few. Grasping my hand, he helped me from the depth of the rock face. I winced as the weight of my body was forced onto my ankle. Noting my injury, he pulled me into his arms. As he leapt from one boulder to another, I was carried to the safety of the forest bed.

After examining the wound, the man pulled some hazelroot from the riverbed. As I watched him with intrigue, he took notice and smirked, eyeing the crown of twigs upon my head. Embarrassed, I quickly removed it.

He dampened the root and placed it gently on the swollen areas of my ankle. With his free hand, he pulled a piece of cloth from around his neck and secured the root in place.

When his work was done, he took rest next to me. His presence was strong, yet genteel, drawing feelings from me I had not yet experienced. He reached into his satchel and pulled out a brick of cheese and a loaf of bread for us to share. I wanted to speak, only I lacked the courage.

"You are from the region born to Man's Blood," he said with a raised brow. Before I could respond, he continued in his gentle demeanor, "What brings you on the path that leads to the Elvish land of Maglavine?"

"There are no such things as Elves!" I sputtered in disbelief. "You speak of stories told in myth alone. I mean ..."

"Your people speak of us in myth!" His eyes widened with a chuckle. When I looked to him with confusion he rolled his eyes. "I can assure you, there is no folklore strong enough to erase the past our two people have shared."

Embarrassed yet again, I blinked. "Forgive me. I only know what I have been—"

"Save your excuses," he interrupted as he began to pack his belongings. "It is dangerous in these woodlands. Man's Blood or not, I wish no harm to come to you."

He then glanced over his shoulder, in the direction of my village. "I will see you to the forest end, to a place where you will be easily found by your people." He paused before continuing, "I will assume it is Hoverdire from which you came."

"Yes." I nodded. "If you do not mind my asking, how is it you know of the place?"

"Leave your questions," he said as he gathered me into his arms. "Your only concern should lie with my getting you back there safely."

Secure in his hold, I chose not to confront him. Instead, I took time to memorize his face. Despite the innocence of youth that accompanied his demeanor, there was a great strength within his eyes, leaving me to wonder of his age. There was no doubt he was older than he appeared, if the myth of eternal life proved true with his people.

"What do they call you, sir?"

He paused as though to question the need for any politeness. "They call me Darwynyen."

"My name is Arianna." I smiled. "That is, if you care to address me again, sir."

He released a heavy breath and then kept silent.

Disheartened, I decided to push him no further. It was obvious he did not wish to share in a dialogue; thus, we continued forward in silence.

When we reached the forest's end, he placed me on a fallen tree near the fields. "It is here where I shall leave you," he said as he scanned the horizon. "You may wish to call out once I have gone." He turned, taking his direction back to the forest.

"Wait!" I begged. In the face of his departure, I had to know what would become of this chance meeting. "Would you not like to announce yourself as my rescuer and set the stories of our folklore straight?"

He stiffened and returned to me briskly. As his face neared mine, our eyes met as one. My heart took on a pace that echoed with every beat, and I thought I was going to faint. "There will be no answers revealed today nor tomorrow. Things must stay as they are!"

When I did not answer, his stare deepened. Powerless to breathe, I broke from his gaze. To my reaction, he turned cold.

"My life is in another region. I do not wish to entangle it with yours."

I felt pain as he spoke. It was not in my ankle, but in my chest. Before I could respond, he continued, "I will ask you to never speak of me to anyone, not even those closest to you."

His request bewildered me. "But why?"

"Because you will set events in motion that are not yet to be."

Feeling the weight of his words, I nodded, knowing deep down there was no use in trying to reason with him. Besides, without him to bear witness, my proclamations would only be accepted with laughter.

When my eyes began to tear, he turned to leave. As I watched him go, I could only hope things would not end in such a manner. "Wait!" I cried.

He ignored my plea, disappearing into the shrubbery.

The passing hours felt like an eternity. Eager to be found, I called out to distant riders while flailing my arms. When my attempts proved vain, I glanced back to the trees in hopes that the Elf called Darwynyen would return for me.

I yearned for him, the man I knew so little about. Our encounter, although brief, had somehow left me changed, leaving me to wonder why our meeting was to end so cold. Even so, in repayment of his debt, I would respect his wishes and not speak of him.

Through the faltering light of dusk, I caught view of the Guardian riders as they raced along the forest wall. To my good fortune, they had found me.

"I am here!" I waved frantically.

As they neared, I could see the disappointment on their faces. This was not the first time they had been forced to search for me. Noting my ankle, the lead rider gathered me onto his horse. Without words, we rode off in haste. With thoughts of Darwynyen, I looked back to where he had left me. He was nowhere to be found.

When I was returned to my home in the village, I was deluged with question after question, not only by my mother but by the Guardians themselves. I answered all I could without revealing the help I had received from my Elvish stranger. Although my interrogators were suspicious and unsatisfied with my broken truths, the incident was soon forgotten. My life eventually returned to normal, to that of a poor villager whose sole purpose stemmed from basic farming and sheep herding—a life too meager to keep me idle. Somehow, I knew I was meant to do more. I could only hope that one day soon my true path would be revealed to me.

Throughout my years in Hoverdire, I often thought of Darwynyen, the Elf who rescued me one spring morning. In time, when my restrictions no longer bound me, I frequently revisited the place where we had met in hopes of finding him.

But he was never to return.

Chapter 1:

The Life to Come

It was a morning like no other. I was to witness the last sunrise in the only place I had ever known. The day had come when I was to leave Hoverdire to return to a role that was taken from me as a child. No more would I live the life of a commoner, a life I had somehow grown accustomed to.

To the north, beyond the newly planted fields, I could see a coach making its way through the fields. It was accompanied by a full escort of the King's Royal Guard on horseback, holding their banners proudly.

In their approach, the guard's commanding nature was not to go unnoticed. Rays of sunlight splintered on their silver helmets, breast plates, and shoulder plates. Each bore a shield of stature that was etched with markings I did not recognize. Their weaponry made it clear these men were strong and brave enough to risk their lives should anyone have the courage to challenge them.

When they halted, the man leading the small accompaniment removed his helmet and nodded to my mother with recognition. I was staggered by his appearance. He was rather young to hold such a charge.

Clean shaven and somewhat handsome, his face gave him a trustworthy exterior. His blond hair was uncommon in this region, forcing many to stop and stare. He was short in height and broad in the shoulders and had a slightly bowlegged walk.

"My ladies," he said with a bow in his approach, "I am General Corbett. I lead this escort. We are here to ensure your safe journey home." As he spoke, his eyes ran the course of my body. I took a step back in disgust. Undaunted, he took my mother aside to speak with her in private.

In their absence, I retreated to my thoughts. Three days had passed from the time the royal footman had appeared at our door. At first, when he had spoken of my father, I had experienced a sense of joy. It was when he had continued that the reality had become hard to face.

My mother had been jubilant. "Oh, Arianna, the truth will finally set us free!" As I recalled the look on my mother's face it made me shiver. "No longer shall we live as peasants!" The latter of her words came with a look of greed I had not before witnessed.

Then I remembered the letter. Still stunned by its markings, I pulled it from my sleeve.

> Dear Child,
>
> Many years have passed since the time I was forced to part with you. You must understand I was given no other option. Your life depended on my action. Although danger still looms, I now ask you to take your place by my side.
>
> Your role ahead may be demanding. Upon your return, you will embrace your royal duties with pride.
>
> Do not fear the future. I will share with you the challenges your new life will bring.
>
> Your Father, Velderon, King of Aarrondirth

2

As I folded the letter, I wondered about my father. Although the excuses for our separation seemed plausible, was the turmoil in our land so great that he had no choice but to relinquish us?

Knowing I would soon be faced with the answers, I decided to assume no further. Instead, I would focus on the journey at hand. After waving to those who had gathered to bid us farewell, I turned to the soldiers. To my surprise, they were throwing our belongings onto the back step of the coach with little regard, leaving me to wonder whether these were the first signs of what was to come.

The sun was well into the sky when we set out. A slight breeze kept to the air, leaving the day crisp and refreshing. Our coach, crafted out of wood, bore the royal seal on each door. The interior was lush, made with fabrics I had not seen before.

I felt my mother's hand on my arm. "Arianna, stop fidgeting. The journey ahead will be a long one. I will not have you—"

"But, Mother," I pleaded, "the seats provide little comfort."

"Do not blame the cushioning," she snapped. "This road is rarely traveled, my dear."

I put my hand to the frame when the coach began to sway. "Why did my father send us so far?"

"To keep us safe." Her eyes narrowed. "Forget the past. You must only focus on the future." She reached for a blanket. "When we reach the mountains, the weather will turn. Keep yourself warm. I would not want your father to find you ill on our arrival."

I turned to the window, knowing by her tone it was best to leave the conversation for another time.

As I glanced over the landscape, I thought back to the past, three seasons precisely, to the day that had forever changed me. It was a time when my childhood would be lost forever, where I would begin to transform into a woman—the time I had met the Elf Darwynyen. Although our encounter had been brief, I was determined to hold on to anything that reminded me of him. Days after my rescue, I had questioned my uncle on Elvish folklore. To my delight, he bore many stories, stories that seemed to hold in truth.

"Oh, Arianna," I could remember his gentle voice as though it was only yesterday, "the Elvish clans hold many mysteries, tales that have long since been forgotten."

He spent hours speculating on their enduring youth and the arrogance that came with it. While flipping through a stack of books he kept hidden under his bed, he elaborated on their extraordinary abilities when it came to archery. "Their precision with a bow is remarkable," he said with a sigh, pointing to drawings of them in perfect poise. "No one of our blood could ever match them."

Through his words, I desired to learn the skill of archery, for Darwynyen had worn a quiver of arrows on his back the day we had met. And though I never actually witnessed his skill, I felt certain he was a master of it.

It was my uncle who had persuaded my mother about its teachings. Even so, she had sworn us to secrecy, knowing it would not be welcomed by those in our village whose duty it was to protect us.

After learning the skill to the best of my ability, I yearned for more. My uncle suggested the sai. "The sai is a great weapon of choice and an advantage for a lady, being you can hide them under your gown."

Unfamiliar himself with its defensive application, he had spared no time in finding us a suitable mentor. To ease his conscience, he declared on several occasions, "Not much to hold our attention in Hoverdire. What better to have than a hobby?"

On my seventeenth year, he surprised me with a proper set of sai along with matching sheaths, "A lady should never be seen with such weapons of death. It would be best to keep them hidden under your gown, my dear."

Tears filled my eyes when I recalled the day not long after. I had awakened early that morning in anticipation of our final lesson where my skills in the sai would be tested. When I found him, he had already grown cold: death had taken him in his sleep. The local healer could offer no explanation other than perhaps he had had a weak heart, something not uncommon for a man in his years.

Fighting the tears, I felt the recurring turmoil of his passing. I had never gotten the chance to tell him how much I loved him and how empty our lives would be without him. He had always taken such good care of us, despite my mother's differentiating mood swings.

With the reminder of her, I turned from the window. She was sound asleep. Alone in her company, I lifted my dress to examine the sai that were secured within the shin holsters my uncle had given me. Still polished from the morning I had received them, they gleamed as I ran my fingers down the grips.

When my mother shifted, I sat back. She would not approve if she found I had not left *all* my weapons behind.

† † †

Several days passed before the summits of Alcomeen were behind us. Despite the warmth of the sun, a whisper of the crisp mountain air still lingered, reminding me of the near treacherous path we had just taken to get here. Before us, sweeping fields extended from the remaining highlands. The creeks were laden with ice crystals that had been carried down from the summits to dance in the trickling currents.

In the peace of the day, I wondered about the times ahead. What luxuries would my new home in Aarrondirth bring? Our cottage in Hoverdire was meager but quaint, containing only three rooms. My mother and I had shared the larger of the two bedrooms. My uncle had slept in the other that extended into the large garden kitchen. My mood saddened when I again thought of his passing.

"Halt!"

When I heard the general's voice, I moved to the window.

"See to the women!" he commanded as he rode by.

I was about to unlatch the door when the one behind me opened. The youngest of the men in our accompaniment stood waiting. His ginger locks swayed gently in the breeze.

"We are to take rest," he said as he placed his hand under my mother's. "You may wish to make use of the water."

She nodded, taking leave from the coach.

After a well needed stretch, I noticed my boots were sinking in the muddy road. It must have rained some time in the night. As I slid my feet on the neighboring grass to clean them, I noticed a log encroaching on a nearby creek and made toward it.

The young officer followed. "Do not stray too far."

"Where would I go?" I knelt to unlace my boots.

"I only caution you," he said, glancing over his shoulder in a northerly direction, the way of the road. "We are close to the Marshlands of Gobbler, the place of the forbidden people."

"Forbidden people?" I stood with a frown. "Where is this marsh? Can you see it from here?" I looked over the fields we had yet to travel.

"No, you will know of our arrival when we pass through the gates." His hand fell to his sword as his voice became stern, "As for its people, they are thieves and murdering sorts, those who have fled execution from the laws of our land."

Stunned by his words, I searched the area. "Then why do we take this road?"

"Because," he said with a shrug, "there is no other road to take."

I released a heavy breath. "I see."

"What is it?" He moved closer, as though to observe me better.

"I see now the great lengths my father took when he sent my mother and me away."

"I know little of that time. When your deaths ... I mean, when your father sent you away, I was only four years of age."

"Our deaths!"

His face took on a look of distress. "I did not—"

"Tell me what you know!" I demanded.

"Your father," he said, looking over his shoulder again, but this time toward the accompaniment, "he had no choice. If his plan was to work, the people would have to believe you dead. How else could he ensure your safety?"

He paused as though to search for his next words. "You will find the answers you seek upon your arrival in Aarrondirth. Do not ask me to share more. I have said too much already."

"Very well." I changed the subject. "What is Aarrondirth like?"

"It is a majestic city, encompassed by the greatest of towers." His eyes lit up. "No one would dare risk defeat should—"

"No," I interrupted as I searched his eyes, "I was asking of my father, of his rule."

"Then you ask what I do not know." His jaw tightened. "No one has seen him for years."

"Whatever do you mean?" My mouth fell open. "He is the king, is he not?"

"We should not be discussing these things," he said, turning away.

"Wait," I said, taking hold of his arm. "Why do you recoil?"

"The general would not like me speaking with you."

"Please," I pleaded, releasing him, "I beg you!"

He led me back toward the creek. "It is rumored that your father prepares for battle. It has been alleged that the Sorcerers of Morne have reunited in an attempt to find the last of the hidden stones."

"What stones?"

"The Stones of Moya," he replied. "There are said to be three. Once joined, they will unleash a power greater than anyone could possibly imagine."

"And these Sorcerers?"

"They work to turn the stones against those who have chosen a life of freedom. They have no good intentions."

"Your words are gibberish." I scowled in annoyance. "You conceal the truth with stories not even a child would believe!"

"I assure you my words are of no lie!" His voice deepened, "You will see for yourself soon enough!"

I continued in my defense, "*If* you speak the truth, then *where* will this battle take place?"

"Up North," he said as he knelt to the water, "in a region known as Cessdorn. It is a desolate land that lies beyond the regions of Man's Blood, a place were no one with common sense would dare to roam."

He paused before continuing, "Do not concern yourself. The Man's Blood will make their stand, putting the Sorcerers' ambition to rest."

"If you say so," I said, kicking off my boots in defeat. "Is it all right if I wade in the current?"

"Of course." He stiffened his stance. "I will protect you."

I rolled my eyes. "What do they call you?"

"They call me Gin." He smiled, which brought a sparkle to his green eyes.

"Gin? What kind of name is that?"

He ran his fingers through his ginger locks with exaggerated movement. "I am not sure of its origin."

"Oh," I said with a smirk, "I will assume the name was given to you by someone other than your mother."

When his cheeks became flush, I took notice of him. Despite his words of warning, he seemed different from the others, who all seemed less kind than my mother. It must have been his youth or the freckles on his fair skin that gave him his innocent appearance.

"Men" the general called, rearing up his horse, "it is time we moved on!"

Disheartened, I looked to Gin, "But I have not had a chance to test the water!"

"Come." he reached for my boots. "It is not in good taste to argue with the general."

Although disappointed, I took my leave toward the coach.

† † †

My body tensed as we passed through the desecrated gates of Gobbler. Overgrown with weeds and shrubbery, their years of abandonment were obvious. When I allowed myself to look past the rust, I could see the faint presence of the gold they had once been painted. Beyond the gateway, reeds of green spread throughout the water-soaked land. Crickets danced in the reeds, keeping in tune with the toads as they grunted to one another in conversation. Isolated in the thick overgrowth, the smell was moldy, almost putrid. Unlike the rest of our travels, I felt certain our journey through this part of the region would linger as I would be on constant watch for these evildoers that Gin had spoken about.

Shortly after passing the gates, the coach came to a sudden halt. Curious, I opened the window. It seemed we had stumbled across two wayfarers. Because of their common nature I assumed the general would allow them safe passage.

"Why do you travel this road?" he demanded, moving his horse to block them.

"We make our way to the southern coast," the shorter of the fellows replied.

"Are you not aware of the king's orders?" he snapped. "No one of Man's Blood is permitted on this roadway until the next falling of the sun!"

The larger of the gents put his hand to his chest. "But the day of the falling sun has already passed, my lord."

"Are you questioning me?" The general pulled out his sword.

"No," the man said, falling to his knees. "Please, I beg you to forgive our ignorance."

"I cannot!" The general eyed two of his men.

"Wait," I called out, leaning through the window. "General! What are your intentions?"

"Silence her," he said, turning to Gin.

As Gin approached, two soldiers led the men into the reeds. "Arianna," he said, blocking my view, "I know you find our tactics ruthless, but the power of evil grows strong in this region." Steadying the reins on his horse, he forced my stare, "Because your return is of paramount importance, we can leave nothing to chance."

I heard the men again beg for their lives and then an abrupt silence.

"Oh, Gin, I cannot bear it."

"Pay no attention," my mother said, putting her hand on my shoulder. "Let the men do their work!"

Tears began to trickle down my cheeks. "No, Mother, I will not stand—"

The horses, as though sensing something, shook the coach.

"What is happening?" I asked, turning to Gin.

"There is a tree barring the road ahead!" a soldier shouted.

The general appeared. "Stay in the coach!" he commanded.

Before I could respond, he rode off. Gin pushed the window shut and then kicked his horse to follow.

I searched the area as the coach edged forward, "Mother, what are we to do?"

"Keep quiet, child," she hissed, turning to the window.

Lost for words, I sat silent beside her.

When the coach reached the tree that blocked the road, the guardsmen pulled out their axes.

"Clear the path!" the general commanded.

As they began their work, a horn sounded. Moments later, I heard men's feet pounding the dampened soil around us.

When they broke through the reeds, I gasped. These were not men, but creatures so horrifying that one's worst nightmares could not bring them to thought. Their fiery eyes glowed from within their beryl-like skin. From every direction, the creatures hurled spears, and those near the coach attacked by sword. Although determined, the creatures lacked the skill and armor of the guardsmen. As the men took their lives one by one, I had no pity for them; instead, I reveled in their defeat.

"Do not give chase!" the general shouted.

Hearing his words, I searched the area. To my surprise, the creatures had begun to flee. I unlatched the window. "Is it over?" I asked, looking to the men nearest the coach.

"Quiet!" The general appeared at the front of the coach, putting his finger to his mouth.

I nodded, knowing that if the creatures were to return we would not get far—not with the fallen tree still before us. I shook my head at the thought, then I examined the bodies that were scattered along the ground. To my relief, most carried the face of our attackers. In hopes of finding Gin, I opened the door to offer my assistance.

When the general saw my intentions, he rode over. "Stay in the coach!" he growled. "We cannot protect you when you are in plain sight!"

I was about to respond when I noticed the cut on his left cheek. The wound looked deep. "You carry a wound," I said, extending my hand to examine it.

"It is nothing," he said, wiping the blood off with his hand. "I will see to it later."

When the horn sounded again, it distracted us both. "Get back into formation!" he yelled, turning his horse. "This battle is not over!"

As the men assembled, the creatures made their return. This time, there were archers. Their arrows struck the guardsmen with precision. Blood hit my face when I moved to secure the door. As I wiped my brow, I looked toward the greenery for a hope of escape. In the distance, I saw what appeared to be the creatures' leader atop a boulder. He was pointing his staff to the reeds and giving direction to those below. In his other hand, he held a spear. When he caught my stare, he became enraged, hurling it toward the coach.

From the driver's seat, I heard a wail. The spear must have struck its mark. Seconds later, I saw a shadow pass by the window. It was the driver falling to his death. With no one to hold the reins, the horses shot forward.

The coach struck the tree with force. Then it rolled backward before again plunging forward, forcing the wheels over the broken limbs of the trunk. After a final heave through the remaining debris, the horses, alerted to their freedom, broke into a run.

Separated from our protectors, my mother and I were left to fend for ourselves. "Mother," I cried, "what are we to do?"

"We are doomed, child," she said in a panicked voice, grabbing me by the arms. "Those creatures will not stop until our blood is on their hands!"

"No," I said with determination, breaking free of her hold, "we are going to get out of here."

"How, child?" she asked. Then she let out a scream as a branch struck the coach, breaking the window.

"We will jump," I said, trying to pull her from her seat. "There is no other way."

"No," she said, closing her eyes, "they are out there! Let the horses steer us from danger!"

I edged my way to the broken window. We were moving with great speed on a path with no end in sight. If she would not jump with me, I had no choice but to commandeer the coach myself. Through the cracks in the pane, I caught view of the driver's step.

"Cover your face, Mother." When she nodded, I wrapped my fist in my cloak and dislodged the remaining glass.

Free of shards, I leaned through the opening, "I will need your help, Mother!"

"You must not leave me!"

I stepped on the bench. "I have to get to the driver's seat." I lost my footing when the coach hit a rut.

"Child?" She used her hands to stabilize me.

"I will be fine." I anchored my feet between the cushions, sliding the remainder of my body through the opening. "Take hold of my ankles."

"You will not reach the steps," she said, shaking her head. "They are too far."

Annoyed, I spoke harshly, "Take hold of me until I tell you!"

In her grasp, I ran my hands along the bordering rail of the driver's seat. She was right: the toeholds were out of range. I had no choice but to pull myself upward by my own strength.

"Now, Mother," I shouted through the rattling of the coach.

When she released me, I drew my foot forward, bridging it on the lantern hook near the step. Unprepared for the shift of weight, I began to lose my grip, and weakness overwhelmed me. Unwilling to give up, I gave my arms one final tug. To my relief, it was enough.

Through the hammering jolts, I managed to take a seat. The reins, to my dismay, were dragging on the ground before me. There was no way for me to obtain them. Out of options, I again looked out over the land.

"Arianna!"

I slid to the end of the driver's bench when I heard Gin's voice.

"Hold still," he said, raising his arm. "I will slow the horses for you!"

He took hold of the lead horse, and we finally began to slow.

"Thank you," I cried.

He ignored me, raising his hand. I followed his stare, to find the others approaching.

"Secure the coach!" the general shouted. At his words, the men broke into formation, taking their place along the coach.

When we came to a stop, it was apparent to me and to all those around me that I had taken an unnecessary risk. I should have known the guardsmen were to follow. It was then that I gave into the tears that had haunted this journey from its beginning.

Gin helped me from the coach. "It will be all right," he said, putting his hand to my back. "We are nearly home."

I nodded, looking to the general. His eyes were full of rage. To avoid a confrontation I took refuge with my mother.

Six men had lost their lives in the battle, and the remainder smelled of exhaustion. Many bore injuries that needed tending. Unable to aid them, I worried about their strength.

As we pushed onward, I could not help but contemplate the creatures' motive. There was no doubt their attack had been well planned. Were they sent by the order of another or was our meeting by chance? Was it riches they sought, or were they out for blood? Unsure of these answers, I decided to let them go until we had safely arrived in Aarrondirth.

Restless hours elapsed before we found freedom from the Marshlands of Gobbler. Before us were the Great Fields of Aarrondirth. The land was lush in its capacity. At a glance, it appeared that the rolling fields were made of emeralds. In the distance, I could see the towering city of my birthplace.

"Lead the coach forward!" the general called, rallying his men. "Our journey has finally come to an end!"

My mother, recovered from her weakness, sat across from me in proper posture. To support her, I smiled. Perhaps in time I would learn to share in her enthusiasm.

As we traveled through the massive city gates, shadows fell from the monumental architecture that appeared as if out of a dream. Buildings made of sandstone and plaster crept high above one another in a competition to touch the sky. People looked from their windows and doors as we made our passing.

My mother waved to the common folk who ran alongside the coach. Overwhelmed, I could not partake in the action. With no more than a fleeting look, I considered the seriousness of the role I was soon to take. Were there strengths within me that would allow me to one day assume a throne that had long past forsaken me? Terrified by my thoughts, I pushed them aside. Although my life in Hoverdire seemed trivial in light of my return to Aarrondirth, I could not help but hold onto the memories of the one place that had given me a deep sense of security.

The coach slowed when we neared a barbican. I assumed it was the entrance to the castle. As the weighted doors slowly opened, I was struck with a vague perception of familiarity. I had seen this place before.

A large courtyard embraced the fortress that stood taller than all others. Built on the peak of a hill, the castle stood proud on its motte. Four towers graced each corner of the outer structure. Several turrets encompassed the inner keep and parapet. Winds erected the flags on the rooflines. Each bore the royal shield of our lands. When I glanced back to the rampart, I noticed the wall walk carried a minimal amount of guardsmen. Only half the posts were manned, leaving me to wonder why the castle had been left with so little protection given Gin's warnings of war.

In the center of the courtyard, a stone bridge spanned a gentle flowing stream. Trees and foliage surrounded the banks. Swans poised in superiority drifted in their mirrored reflections. The beauty of the lea was stunning. It allowed me to forget for a moment why I was here, and thoughts of joy filled my heart.

"This is your home, child," my mother said, taking my hand. "Do you approve?"

"It is far more than I expected." I replied, falling back on the bench.

She smiled. "The main entrance is just beyond the stables. Your—"

When the coach came to a sudden standstill, we moved to the window. A man appeared at the door. "My Queen, your king awaits you."

With a gentle nod, she took his hand. I followed her lead. The long journey had finally come to an end. Tears welled in my eyes. As I blinked them away, a man standing at the vestibule caught my attention.

"My King," my mother said with a bow. When he nodded, she ran up the stairs to embrace him.

Cold in his demeanor, he brushed her aside. "Leave me to greet my daughter."

Taken aback by his odd behavior, I glanced over him. The years had not been kind. Crevasses of age had taken to his skin, notably around his eyes. He was tall and lean with a lengthy beard that concealed his angry face. His lifeless silver curls clung to his ashen garb like dead foliage in an autumn breeze.

In his descent from the vestibule, he met with the general. They spoke for what seemed like an eternity. Unsure what to do, I turned to my mother. Her eyes were empty, and she appeared to be gazing right through me.

"Arianna," my father said, extending his arms to embrace me. His hold on me was short and uncomforting. As he pulled away he spoke, "So, this is what has become of the heir to Aarrondirth." He looked to my mother. "For what reason does she appear to me as a peasant!"

I was shocked by the disappointment in his eyes. "Why would you expect anything more," I uttered.

"I see you carry no manners," he said, shaking his head. "We will soon see to that!"

Two women appeared from the entrance.

"Take my wife and child inside," he commanded. "See to their every need."

"Yes, my lord," the women said, bowing their heads in succession.

"General," my father said, raising his hand. "Let us continue our conversation in the study."

Taking his leave, he did not look upon me again. It seemed in our years apart his affairs of state had become of greater importance than that of his own family.

I was about to call after him when the younger of the ladies approached and knelt. Her long sandy blonde hair was braided down her back. A broad nose extended from between her gentian eyes. Like the other woman she wore a dark red dress with the royal seal on the front. Unsure what to do, I looked at her blankly. She smiled and then raised her hand, placing it under mine. As she directed me toward the castle, the other woman addressed my mother as "Queen" and led her in before us.

The main foyer was immense. Marble statues lined the path to the staircase. Halfway up the rise, the stair broke in two. My mother veered to the left. She seemed to know her way even though she hesitated with every step. We followed in silence. I dared not speak to her, unable to comprehend what she was going through.

When we reached the mezzanine, it opened to another great room. Large chandeliers hung from trusses two stories above. Narrow tables lined the outer walls, allowing the faltering sun's reflection to dance upon the inner tapestry. "This is the ballroom, Your Highness," the girl offered.

I nodded as we continued our ascent.

When we reached the next level, my mother took her leave down a small hall to the north. Two large doors ended the corridor where guards stood at attention. I guessed the room to be hers, the one she and my father had shared prior to our departure.

"This way, Your Highness," the girl said as she turned, leading me up yet another staircase.

The next level opened to a small foyer that extended to three corridors, each leading out in their own direction. The one to the right mirrored the entrance where I had just left my mother, only smaller.

Upon our approach, the guard bowed. "My ladies."

When we nodded, he pushed open the wooden doors. As they gave way, I stood in awe of what appeared to be my new bedchamber.

The girl released my hand. "My name is Edina. I will be your lady in waiting. If you wish for anything, you may pull the sash beside your bed. I will hear your call from there." She turned, and I followed her stare to find a small door on the opposite side of the entrance. "You must be exhausted from the journey, Your Highness. I know it has taken you many days to get here."

I entered the room as I responded, "If it is my understanding that we will be spending much time together, I will ask that you call me by my given name, Arianna."

She seemed to relax to my gesture. Her contentment brought me a sense of ease I had almost forgotten. "Of course, my lady," she said, bowing gently.

I was about to correct her when two servants appeared with large ewers of water. "Bring them in here," Edina said, directing them to the bathing room. Struggling with the weight, they stumbled behind her in compliance.

While they prepared the bath, I took the opportunity to explore my new abode. Three great windows extended across the east wall. The other wall opened onto a balcony. Several pieces of furniture were positioned throughout the area, and arrangements of flowers stood upon most. The fresh aroma was welcome, relieving some of the room's stateliness.

"The water is not warm enough," Edina said, emerging from the bathing room. When the servants ignored her, she followed them from the room. In her absence, I took a moment to place my sai safely under the bed.

"Your Highness?"

I stood suddenly, concealing my deed. "Yes?" I turned to find her at the doorway.

Her eyes scanned the mattress. "Your bath is ready. Its warmth is not what I preferred but—"

"I am sure it will be fine," I said quickly and brushed past her as a means of distraction.

As I undressed, she began to brush my hair. Feeling uncomfortable, I took a step back. "Edina, you need not wait on me. Chores of a personal nature I would prefer to tend to myself."

"Your Highness," she began and then paused, "I mean, Arianna, I am your lady in waiting. It is my duty to see to your every need."

Her face took on a look of worry. "Am I brushing too hard?" she said, testing the bristles on her palm. "I will lighten my pull if you so desire."

"Of course not," I replied. "I recoil because this all seems unnecessary."

In response to my remark, she set down the brush and moved to leave, but she hesitated as she neared the door. "Please, Your Highness," she said, holding out her hands in exclamation, "if I cannot do my work, the king will have me removed."

Feeling ashamed of my actions, I looked down at the floor. "It was not my intention to upset you. I know you are only striving to complete your duty. If you give me some time to adjust, I am certain we will find some common ground."

She knelt. "Thank you."

I nodded as she left the room.

When I heard the latch strike the door, I sighed in relief. Finally, I was alone, something I had longed for in our recent travels. In the peace of the room, I drifted into thought. The sudden changes in my life were hard to comprehend.

This was my first bath in a tub. Although I had seen many, we could never afford one ourselves. We always took to the stream to tend to our grooming. My uncle told me it was the life's blood of the village and to never take it for granted. I always enjoyed the playful currents that held the crispness of an autumn breeze. But when I grew older, I was embarrassed to unclothe in the open, fearing the boys near my age would follow me to steal glances.

Saddened by my memories, I had to let them go. Instead, I would gaze into the future—to my father. What had become of him? He frightened me with his malcontent. I could only hope his demeanor would soften in time and that he would love me in the ways I desired, in the ways my uncle had once shown me.

Finished with my bath, I searched the area for something dry to wrap myself in. There was nothing in sight.

"Your Highness." A knock came to the door. Before I could respond, Edina emerged with drying cloths and attire. "I brought you a robe and sleeping gown," she said, placing them on a hook near the tub. "As for the rest of your clothes, your father has insisted that we burn them."

"Burn them?" Was I that unacceptable in my old attire? Was that why my father had treated me so coldly?

"Yes," she replied, picking up my soiled gown. "You are to see the royal seamstress as soon as you have dined."

I nodded with little emotion as I reached for a drying cloth.

Dressed in my new cotton evening gown, I made way to the balcony. The view was astonishing. I could see all there was to the northern countryside. To the right, a turret opened to a descending stair. Curious, I took the opportunity to see where it led. In my descent, I soon reached the next level. From the archway, another balcony extended to what I guessed to be my mother's quarters, being the layout was identical to mine, only larger. The steps continued downward. Following them to their conclusion, I came to an old wooden door. When I tested the handle, it was locked.

Out of breath on my return, I took a moment to regain my composure. In doing so, I noticed a narrow archway between the castle wall and the turret. It appeared to lead to another balcony. In eagerness, I made my way toward it. Again, the view extended as far as the eye could see, but to the east this time. Four gigantic mountains broke the horizon. Their jagged summits far surpassed those I had grown accustomed to in Hoverdire.

When a crisp breeze tugged on my locks of damp hair, I shivered. I was about to return to the warmth of my quarters when I remembered the locked door at the bottom of the turret stair. Peering over the ledge, I quickly found its location. It was the only door bound by a lock and chain on the main terrace below.

"Curious," I mumbled.

"Your Highness," Edina said, appearing at the turret, "would you prefer to dine outdoors?"

I shivered again. "I would only catch a chill if I remained out here."

She nodded and extended her hand.

I found dinner prepared and waiting on a small table near the window. When I sat, she turned to leave. "What do you call the four gigantic peaks to the east?" I asked.

"Those are the Four Sisters of Vidorr," she said, glancing toward the windows. "It is said that Miders rule that land, though none of our time would admit to such things."

"Why?" I frowned. "What are Miders?"

"I am not really sure," she replied. "It has been many years since our land broke with those who were not of Man's Blood." She glanced over her shoulder as though she feared someone might overhear our conversation. Her actions reminded me of Gin's.

"Is there something wrong?" I stood.

"No," she said, moving to the door. "Enjoy your meal, Your Highness."

Before I could respond, she was gone.

Confused, I again took my seat at the table. Something was amiss. Gin's apprehensions I could understand, but Edina's were suspicious. Was she hiding something, or was she reacting out of fear? Unsure of the answer, I began my meal for, if nothing else, I was famished.

After eating what I could of the fresh chicken and minced vegetables, I left in search of Edina. Rather than pull the sash, I made way to her door. When I knocked, she appeared with haste. "Your Highness," she said with eyes wide, "is the sash broken?"

"I saw no need to summon you in such a manner," I said, extending my hand. "If we are to visit the seamstress together, I thought it best to gather you on route."

"Of course," she said as she directed me down the foyer to where the stair had opened to the alternate corridors. "The seamstress, Marion, occupies the last room on the left." She pointed to the hall on the right. "You shall find her there."

I turned to face her. "Are you not to join me?"

"I would prefer not to," she replied, her eyes wandering to the guard.

Although perplexed by her actions, I nodded. "If you have other matters to tend to, then please, do not let me keep you."

She bowed her head. "If you do not summon me on your return, I will collect you in the morn."

To conceal my frustration, I turned and made my way down the corridor. When I reached the door, I hesitated. Something in Edina's manner had left me uneasy. I was about to turn around when the door opened with haste.

An old woman stood impatiently at the threshold. "What do you want?" she kept a tight grip on the handle. "Why are you here?"

"My name is Arianna." I took a step back, intimidated by her odd behavior.

"I see," she huffed, as though annoyed by the intrusion. "Come in. There is plenty of work to be done."

Unnerved, I took a moment to observe her. Time had whittled away at what was left of her sunken body. Remnants of her black hair were layered with silver, leaving her fair skin to appear satinlike.

"We do not have all night," she said, tapping her toe.

As I stepped through the threshold, I took notice of the room. Many fabrics lay strewn upon a table below the window, where the remainder of daylight had gathered. The unused bundles were stacked on a rack to the right. To the left was her living quarters. The area was slight, fitted with a bed, wardrobe, and washing table. Near her bedpost was a tarnished metal mattress warmer, her only means of heat in a room with no fireplace.

"Take your place on that stool near the window," she directed. "I will need to measure the length of you."

With a slight nod, I did as she asked.

"Keep still," she said, putting her hands to my waist to steady me. "The sooner we are done, the sooner you may be on your way!"

Despite the urge to confront her, I kept my poise obediently. I thought it best to leave her to her work, in hopes that she had more skills as a seamstress than she had with her manners.

When the last of the measuring pins were in place, she again addressed me. "I will have two dresses tailored for you by dawn. You may return to claim them when you awake." I felt her hand on my back, "The rest of your gowns will be delivered in the coming week. Mind your wardrobe."

I was about to respond when she ushered me through the door. "Good night, Your Highness."

I could not believe her rudeness. Thankful to be out of her presence, I took my leave. I needed to address more important things at hand.

Despite the intimidating presence of the guardsman, who had remained at my door despite the hour, I knocked on Edina's.

Moments later, she appeared, "Your Highness."

I spoke quietly to avoid the guard's attention. It was enough that I could feel his eyes upon me through the narrow slots in his helmet. "My time with the seamstress is over. Before I retire, I want you to take me to my mother."

"I cannot, Your Highness," she said, taking a step back. "The king's instructions are for an early night."

"I thought you were at my beck and call," I snapped.

Her hands opened in exclamation. "Not before the King."

"Very well." I turned to the guard.

"He cannot help you," she pleaded. "Be wise and return to your quarters."

"Why?" I frowned.

"I have said all I can." She closed the door.

Frustrated, I wanted to scream. Before the guard could deny me, I brushed past him and down the stair.

I knocked as hard as possible at my mother's door to be sure I was heard, assuming her quarters to be far grander than those I had received. The door unlatched.

"Your Highness," her lady said with bow, "the queen is not accepting any visitors."

"Not even her own *daughter!*" I put my hand to the door when she moved to close it.

"Your Highness—"

Before she could continue, I pushed her aside. "Where is she?"

"Please," the woman begged, "you are not supposed to be here."

From the foyer, I saw my mother gazing out one of the windows. I turned to the woman. "You are excused."

She nodded hesitantly.

As I made my way through the sitting area, I took notice of the room. It was drab and musty. Unlike my quarters, there was not a flower in sight.

"Mother," I spoke softly as not to alarm her.

She turned abruptly, startling me. "Did you not hear?" Her eyes widened. "The king wishes us to retire early!"

"Yes, I heard, but I needed to see you." I took her by the shoulders, "I require some answers, Mother!"

She pulled away from me. "Things have changed, my child. So much so that I do not have the answers you seek." Tears began to trickle down her cheeks. "You must go to your quarters before your father arrives. Please, do not make any trouble tonight. We will speak in the morning."

Stunned by the fear in her eyes, I nearly lost my footing. "Good night, Mother," I said softly as I slowly turned to take my leave.

Returning to my quarters, I ignored the guard when he pushed open the doors. As I sat down on the bed, the outer latch snapped. I stood, half expecting Edina. When there was no movement, I tested the handle. It was locked.

In my newfound imprisonment, I could not help but reflect on the day. It was impossible to escape the ill feelings brought on by my mother's peculiar behavior. I could only hope she would ease my concerns in the morning, as she had promised.

† † †

The hour was late when a noise disturbed me from my sleep. In a moment of confusion, I leapt from the bed, having forgotten where I was. When my head cleared, I set out for the balcony to investigate. The doors remained open from earlier. A gentle breeze brushed the curtains into a delicate dance.

As I stepped outside, I was greeted by the most beautiful array of stars. The moon, full in its capacity, bathed the castle with a delicate luminosity. Comforted by its familiar glow, I jumped when I heard glass breaking from below.

"Why are you doing this!" my mother cried. "What has happened to my loving husband?"

Out of respect for their privacy, I should have left, but I could not tear myself away. I slowly stepped toward the ledge.

"You have neglected your responsibilities, woman!" he replied. "Why has my daughter returned with the mannerisms of a peasant?"

"How could you expect more!" she screamed. "You left us with nothing!"

I heard a smack. "You will take complete instruction over Arianna, starting tomorrow. I expect her to be ready for her duties in two weeks' time."

"Why ... why do you rush things?" she stammered.

"Arianna is to wed the general after the next moon cycle, to cement his loyalty to me, the king."

I was about to cry out when he continued, "Until then, it will be asked that she settle the nerves of the people." His voice softened, "I fear their hearts have turned cold to me."

"The general?" she gasped. "Why the general? Certainly there is someone more suitable."

"Do not question my authority, woman!" His voice was beginning to crack. "It is best for your health to do as you are told. Many things have changed … things I can never speak of." He cleared his throat. "Never meddle in what is to be. Make no mistake; your daughter will marry Corbett. The decision has already been made."

"The decision has been made," I thought. Obviously, these nuptials were planned long before my arrival.

"A decision by whom?" my mother asked. When she challenged him, I feared for her safety.

"I warned you not to question me, woman!"

When my mother cried out, I knew it was by his hand. "If you choose to disobey me on this matter, I can assure you, you will not like the consequences as they will be beyond my control!"

"Consequences"? I frowned. *"Beyond his control"?* What consequences could supersede the rule of the king?

It had grown quiet. I was unsure whether my father was even still in the room. Devastated by what I had learned, I had no more time to worry about my mother.

What was I to do? I could not marry that horrible man. And why? The people of Aarrondirth would surely not want the rule to fall to him.

Were these consequences intertwined with the plans of my prearranged marriage? Was there another person pulling my father's strings?

In any case, I was glad I had overheard what I had. It would take time to find the real truth behind this façade.

† † †

Rest did not come easy. Time seemed to move slowly until the sunlight crept through the open windows. With little energy to spare, I pulled on the sash. There was no point in evading the inevitable.

Moments later, Edina appeared with a smile. "You are up early, Your Highness."

I sat reluctantly. "What am I to do?"

She tensed as though she knew my words referred to something far deeper than the daily routines I was now speaking of. "Is everything all right, Your Highness?"

When my eyes began to water, she sat to face me. "If you wish to speak in confidence, I can assure you it will go no further."

Although her words seemed genuine, I decided it best to conceal my emotions until we could establish a bond of trust. "Thank you," I managed a smile. "Would you please see to my dresses?" I did not have the patience to deal with Marion myself. "I wish to be ready when my father summons me."

"Of course." She stood with a look of disappointment. "I will be back momentarily."

I nodded, wondering whether her reaction stemmed from my lack of candor or that I had asked her to visit the unabiding seamstress. Deep down, I knew it extended from both.

She returned shortly thereafter with two gowns in hand. One was gold in color, and the other was a pale shade of green, similar to the cloak I had received from the village seamstress in Hoverdire. "Your father has asked that you wear this one today," she said, placing the gold dress on a hook near the wardrobe. "This afternoon, he will formally announce your return to the people in the city."

Stunned by the latter of her remarks, I looked at her blankly.

Undaunted, she began to adjust the sleeves. "Although the final touches were only added last night, this dress was crafted long before your arrival."

"What do you mean by "announce"? I questioned, trying desperately to regain my composure.

"You will see soon enough." She took my hand. "Let us get you dressed. I will need to tend to your hair. Your father was specific in his instruction."

Unable to comprehend the day ahead of me, I did not resist her. "Very well," I sighed. "Do what you must."

Without a response, she began her lengthy duties. After endless amounts of tugging, primping, and discomfort, Edina finally led me to the mirror. "Do you approve?"

Her hard work had turned me into someone I did not recognize. "I do not know what to say," I uttered.

"I will return momentarily." She left the room.

Intricate braids were intertwined in one another. With the loose strands pulled away from my face, my brown eyes shone like copper. The dress's fabric shimmered as I swayed back and forth. Embroidery graced the upper body and inner layers of the skirting. Satin leaves fell from my shoulders. Upon them were the royal seal of Aarrondirth. For the first time, I felt like a lady, a part of my newfound life I would not take for granted.

Edina returned with a case. "Your birthright lies inside this box." Her eyes brightened. "You have worn its contents once before, as a child." She paused in thought. "Yes … it was on the day you were given the title, 'Princess of Aarrondirth.'"

I looked at her with interest. "How do you know such things?"

"All the people of Aarrondirth are aware of that day," she said with a smile. "It was the day new hope was bestowed on the city. Later today, when the announcement is made, you will see—"

"For yourself," I nodded as I finished her words. "Do you know what the times were like before the day of my birth?"

Please," she said, looking over her shoulder toward the door, "we have little time."

By her sudden withdrawal, I was convinced she knew far more than she spoke of. "Keep your secrets then!" I snapped.

When she took a step back, I regretted my reaction. In the end, I could not expect her to trust me when I could not give her the same courtesy in return. Even so, it felt like something of great importance was being kept from me. "Forgive my rudeness," I said, releasing a heavy breath. "Are you going to show me what is in the case?"

"Of course," she said, pulling open the lid.

To my surprise, positioned upon a satin pedestal sat the most magnificent tiara.

"It is beautiful, is it not?" She smiled as she placed it on my head. "You look stunning."

A thin gold band caressed my forehead, and in the center of my brow hung a single tear of pearl. "It represents eternal life," she explained, securing the piece in place.

"Arianna!"

When I turned, I found my mother at the door. She smiled when she caught my attention. She was dressed in similar attire, that of an extravagant gown. I relaxed, for I did not want to endure this day alone. As she neared, I looked for the remnants of the blow she had received from my father. There was no discoloring in sight.

She danced across the room. "Your father will be proud, my child!"

I was disgusted that she could act so cheerful after what I had overheard last night. Selfishly, I tried to antagonize her. "I heard voices from your quarters last night."

She halted. "What did you hear?"

I answered carefully. "Nothing really. Is there something you would like to tell me?"

Worry overtook her face. "Why do you ask?"

"No reason," I replied with a shrug. It seemed best not to reveal too much at this point in time.

She turned to Edina. "I wish to be alone with my daughter."

Edina nodded and then left the room, pulling the door closed behind her.

She hesitated before taking my hand. "My child, please do not cross your father." Her hold tightened. "You must do all that you are asked or trouble will come to us both!"

I was about to confront her when a knock came to the door. "Enter!" my mother commanded.

When the guard opened the door, an older woman stood with her hands on her waist. I could immediately sense the kindness in her grumpy ways. "I am here by order of the king," she announced. "He has requested your presence in the dining hall." Before we could respond, she turned to leave. "He does not like to be kept waiting!"

"Come." My mother took my arm.

"Evelyn," my mother addressed the woman near the stair, "I see you have managed to hold your position within the castle." She glanced to me before continuing, "I do not recognize most that reside here now."

The woman appeared sullen. "My Queen, most were cast off when the news of your sudden death broke. How I managed to stay on is well beyond me."

"My child, this is Evelyn," my mother said, smiling, "the castle stewardess. All duties first pass through her. If you are displeased with any matters regarding your new home, this is who you speak to."

"Nice to have made your acquaintance," I said, bowing my head.

My mother frowned. "When did you learn to speak as a lady?"

"Not all is lost, Mother." I lifted the hem of my gown as we descended the stairs. "I know it is hard for you to believe, but I *have* learned much from you over the years."

When her eyes lightened at my gesture, I decided I would make a better effort when it came to my father and his expectations. Despite her faults, I did not wish her to endure further harm by his hand. Besides, I would need to appear eager if I wanted to find the key to the answers behind my forthcoming nuptials that I so desperately sought.

Once on the landing, we were led through an archway that opened to yet another corridor to the north. A faint echo of pots and pans clanked in the distance, leading me to believe we were near a kitchen.

"The size of this castle will never cease to amaze me," I gasped.

"You will get used to your surroundings in time, Your Highness," Evelyn said with a wink as she led us through a small set of double doors. "This is the dining hall."

I slowed my pace. The lack of windows, being the room was in the heart of the main ward, left the room dull and daunting. When I gained focus, I noticed light splintering through two larger doors at the opposite end of the hall. Four long tables filled the interior. On their surfaces sat large marble centerpieces and several candelabras.

"Woman!" my father shouted. "How dare you bring my wife and child through the servants' entrance?"

When I heard my father's voice, I found him seated at the end of one of the long wooden tables. "I do not know why I keep you on!" he snarled.

Startled by his cruelty, Evelyn apologized. I could see that my mother wanted to defend her, but she kept silent, pulling the strings of tension even tighter.

As we walked the aisles to greet him, I noticed several paintings along the wall. Most were of men, but some were of women. I wondered who the faces belonged to. This, however, was no time to be asking useless questions.

My father stood at our approach. "Please, take your seats."

I was about to greet him when I noticed the additional table setting next to mine. "I have asked General Corbett to join us." He raised his brow. "I thought it would be nice for you to get better acquainted, my dear."

My body tensed, "Whatever for?"

"It is not your place to answer me with a question!" He glared at my mother. "The discussion is closed. He will be joining us momentarily."

In realization of my contempt, I apologized. "Forgive me, Father. I did not mean to upset you."

He seemed to relax at my gesture. "Are your quarters suitable?"

In an attempt to lighten his mood, I replied sincerely, "Yes, Father, I could not be more pleased. Thank you for all you have done in preparation for our return." I then thought of my mother's quarters, and how unkempt they were. I dared not ask of this; it would not only anger him, but he would know I was there when I was not supposed to be.

"I see you have worn the gown I requested." He smiled greedily. "You are sure to make a great impression on the people."

"I could not agree more!" a gruff voice concurred, one that was not soon to be forgotten.

When I turned, I was taken aback. The ruggedness the general had borne on the journey was all but washed away. The cut on his cheek had begun to heal. For a moment, I almost found him attractive, although the feeling was much less than I had felt toward Darwynyen.

He noticed my stare. "Do not pity me," he said, putting his hand to his cheek. "The wound is a trophy of my loyalty to your father, the king."

I nodded. "I am glad to see it is healing nicely."

His candor surprised me. Perhaps I had grown accustomed to his coldness, though that may have just been his way. After all, being the leader of my father's army would require a strong nature.

As he took his seat, he addressed us all, "Please excuse my lateness. My duties carried on longer than first expected." When my father nodded, he continued, looking in my direction alone, "I hope you have settled in nicely, Your Highness, and that the journey has not left you too distressed."

"Thank you for your concern," I replied, "but I can assure you that what lies ahead is far more distressing."

At my remark, he glanced to my father, who took the lead in changing the subject. "We should begin our meal. There is much to be done today. Time should not be wasted."

After we had finished our meal, I sat complacent.

As the servants removed our plates, my father stood. "The people of Aarrondirth will gather in the courtyard at midday. Once the announcement of your return has been made, you will address the crowd." When I gasped at being reminded of the announcement, he looked at the general with concern. "Come, we have much to show you," he continued, extending his hand.

Without any questions, we followed him up a narrow set of stairs that began in a reception hall outside the dining area. After ascending one level, we arrived at a small foyer that connected two corridors, one leading south and the other west. We took neither path, instead moving through an archway in the immediate area.

"This is my study," my father said as we entered the room. "You will never enter this room without the company of General Corbett or me." His voice deepened, "Do you understand?"

"Yes, Father." I nodded as I took notice of my surroundings.

Dust had collected over the years, leaving the study with a sense of abandonment. A large round table was fitted in the bay of windows to the east. Bookshelves lined the walls on each side.

My father directed us to an easel where a drawing hung. "This is a map of the castle." He pointed to the parapet above the main doors. "This is where we will make the announcement."

Terrified, I choked on my breath.

"What is it, child?" he said with a frown.

"I have not spoken publicly before." I looked down. "I would not know what to say."

At my response, he began to chuckle. "You will say what I tell you," he said, handing my mother a scroll.

As she took it, I cleared my throat. "You have written my words?"

"Of course," he said with a sneer. "Did you believe I would let you speak for yourself?"

"I …" Unsure what to say, I looked at my mother.

"Do not worry," he said, moving to a smaller window on the southern wall. "I will be by your side the entire time. Come," he continued, motioning to me.

I nodded as I made my way to join him.

"Before you is the courtyard," he explained with his hand on my back. "You see, the people have already started to gather."

When one of the onlookers pointed in our direction, he pulled me away. "Do not let them see you. Your appearance is to be made in the grandest of entrances."

Overwhelmed, I took a step back.

"Leave us," he ordered, eyeing my mother. "Take my daughter on a tour of the castle. The general and I will meet you in the gallery once we are finished."

My mother took my arm, leading me from the room. "Of course."

When the latch struck the door, she sighed in relief. "Come, child, let us do what your father has asked. Perhaps a tour of the castle will ease our nerves."

"Very well," I replied. "I could use the distraction."

Once in the main foyer, she took our direction east to the kitchen. The massive room was bustling with activity. The bakers had obviously been working very hard. The aroma of freshly baked goods filled the air. When the scent of cinnamon caught my attention, I looked toward the stove. Upon it I found my favorite—apple pie. My mother had never bothered with pastries, unlike our village seamstress who had always had a piece waiting for me on my arrival.

When we exited the kitchen, she led me across the hall to the servants' quarters. The substantial area was all but empty. This struck me as odd, knowing the sheer size of the fortress would command the upkeep of many servants. I then remembered our arrival, and how the wall walk carried few guardsmen. Was my father in debt? Were these some of the repercussions of the consequences he spoke of last night? Whatever the cause, my interest was growing by the minute.

"This area used to be the heart of the castle," my mother said, circling the room. "I do not understand how your father has managed with so few to administer his commerce."

I was about to question her when she shook her head. "I do not have the answers you seek, child."

Although I wanted to confront her, I decided to wait for a more appropriate time.

North of the dining hall, we entered a gated passage that opened to a terrace. As I glanced over the land within the inner ward, I was again swept away by its beauty. From the rich green pasture grew thick hedging plants that encompassed an old majestic fountain. A statue of a warrior, speckled in moss, stood prominently in the middle.

My mother took my arm in hers. "This way, my child." She led me up a set of stairs to the small foyer I had seen the previous night and the location of the turret door that led from our quarters. Unguarded and out of view from the upper walls, its location was suspect, especially when it came to our safeguard.

"This door," I said as I halted, "what is its purpose?"

"It is for our protection," she replied. "If the castle is ever under attack, this is where we would find our escape."

I frowned. "But it is not guarded?"

"No." She smirked. "It is not supposed to be obvious."

"Oh." I nodded as she led me to another stairway.

At its top was a small guarded antechamber. Upon our arrival, the men fussed with the keys. When the latch broke free, she led me deep into the keep, the heart of the castle.

The passage was dimly lit. Doors secured with locks and chains lined the walls. "Beyond these doors is your future, my daughter. These rooms are filled with the family's wealth!" She turned to me and took both my arms. "Someday, this will all belong to you!"

Besieged by the underlying significance in what she had said, I kept silent as we moved on. The hall veered to the east where it led downward to a dimly lit corridor near the main foyer on the west side. In our approach, the guard moved to block our path.

"No one is to pass in this direction!" he said with a sneer.

"We were given permission to tour the grounds!" my mother insisted.

"By order of the king, you are not allowed to pass." He slammed his pike into the floor. "Trouble me no further!"

When the man spoke of "the king" my mother backed off immediately. "Let us not anger your father. All that lies this way is the dungeon and defense rooms that our people use in time of war."

I nodded as I stole glances of what appeared to be another abandoned wing of the castle, something I found very disconcerting if we were preparing for war as Gin had warned.

My mother ushered me into the main foyer where we ascended the stair.

"Mother," I asked hesitantly, "are we going to be all right?"

She halted. "I guess you will learn the truth eventually." She seemed reluctant with her words. "Your father is not himself. It seems our time apart has taken its toll on the love we once shared."

Although the conversation was not taking the course I had hoped for, I continued, "So you did share in love at one point then?"

"Yes." Her eyes began to water. "Or so I would like to believe."

"Mother," I said, taking her hand, "please, I did not mean to upset you."

"Take no heed," she said, wiping her tears. "Come. We should begin your instruction."

Despite the urge to reach out to her, I again kept silent, following her to her quarters.

After what seemed like an endless lesson in mannerisms, a footman appeared at the door. "Hurry! Hurry! The king awaits! The courtyard is full. It is time to make the announcement!"

"Mother," I said as I stood up, "I cannot do this!"

"You have no choice," she replied, handing me the scroll. "We must not keep your father waiting!"

Taking heed of the undertone in her words, I moved to the door.

When we arrived at the gallery, my father was pacing the room. "What has taken you?" he huffed.

I felt my mother's hand on my shoulder. "We were in lesson," she snapped, "as you requested."

Nervously, I began to twist the scroll. At my reaction, he released a heavy breath. "Do not fear the people, my daughter. You will be welcomed, I assure you."

"But—"

"Child!" he stammered. "You must be strong. The impression you make now carries great weight on our future!"

"Yes, Father," I replied.

"If there is nothing else, let us begin." He motioned to the two heralds on the balcony.

At the sounding of the horns, he moved to greet the crowd. "Welcome, my people," his voice echoed through the courtyard. "Your loyalty has been duly noted!"

The mob grumbled.

"Although the days before us are plagued with uncertainty, today is a day to rejoice!" He paused as though to observe their reaction. When there was little, he continued with vigor, "My wife and daughter have returned to take their place by my side!" Before they could react, he continued, "I understand that my motives in their departure brought many of you to your own conclusions over the years. Regardless, you must understand that I was unable to risk their fate until now."

His words seemed hollow, leaving an ill feeling in my stomach.

"I hold the deepest affection for my family," he said, putting his fist to his chest. "Going forward, I will cherish every waking moment I have with them, as I know you will as well!"

Knowing his proclamation to be a lie, I wanted to stop him in his words—if only I had the courage.

"I would first like to announce my daughter, Arianna, Princess of Aarrondirth!"

I froze in fear when he beckoned me.

"Come, child," he growled under his breath.

As I claimed view of the awaiting crowd, my head began to spin. There were hundreds of them. Although most of the people were of a common nature, there were a few of the more prominent families in the back, who for some reason seemed to carry a look of distrust about them.

Impatiently, my father motioned for me to begin. I nodded as I unraveled the scroll. "Thank you people of Aarron …" I paused. The written words began to blur, and I was finding it impossible to concentrate. When I looked at my father, he was tense with anticipation.

Without a thought, I dropped the scroll and stood strong. "I would first like to thank you for joining us on this grand occasion." I raised my hands, "It brings me great joy to stand before my people once again!"

The crowd began to roar. Unsure how to continue, I emulated my father. "The time has come for us to stand together, to face the troubles that have plagued our land, troubles I intend to see through no matter what the cost!"

The crowd again roared. When I glanced to my father, I was taken aback by the look of appeasement on his face. He gestured for me to continue.

I hesitated, shameful of the misrepresentation I was now to present. "I would now like to take a moment to thank my family, who stood with me throughout the years. Who encouraged me and gave me the strength to carry forward." I stiffened my stance, "With this strength, I will do nothing but embrace the times ahead, when I am better able to serve you."

As though pleased, the crowd began to chant my name.

"Enough!" My father beckoned to the heralds.

At the sounding of the horns, the crowd settled. "I now introduce my loving wife," my father stood aside, "Brianna, Queen of Aarrondirth."

My mother entered the balcony with a glow I had not seen before. The gallant crowd hung on her words of strength and honor. When she had finished, my father made the final announcement. "In a tribute to my wife and child, a celebration will be held this eve at the falling of the sun." He pointed toward a theater on the western bank of the stream beyond the courtyard. "Your return will be most welcomed!"

At a last sounding of the horns, the people began to disperse.

After their retreat, my father led me inside. "How dare you disobey me in such a way!"

I replied with resolve, "I apologize, Father. I was unable to concentrate under the pressure."

Unsure of his response, I backed away. To my surprise, he smiled cunningly. "In any case, you did well, my child. A born leader you are!"

"I could not agree more," said the general, bowing his head.

"Come," my father said as he nudged him. "We have much to discuss."

When I moved to follow, he turned. "Not you, child." Then he glanced at my mother. "You must finish with your instruction."

She nodded, and we watched them take their leave.

† † †

The minutes awaiting the celebration passed as hours. Unable to concentrate on the table setting before me, I shifted in my seat.

"Does my company bore you?" my mother asked as she put the fork she was holding down on the table.

"No, Mother," I answered as I adjusted the sleeves on my gown. "My mind drifts …"

"You are anxious for this eve?"

I nodded. "Yes. I am unsure what to expect."

"I see," she said, closing the book on her lap. "I suppose we have done enough for one day.

Relieved, I moved to the window.

Below, servants were adding the final touches to the inner lea. Several tents had been erected near the stream. To the left of the theater stood a massive banquet table covered in an array of food, evidence of my father's extraordinary efforts in his charade. If the people only knew how we lived on the other side of the rampart, of how cold their king truly was, they would probably no longer accept him. In my thoughts, I remembered the crowd and of how silent they had been during his speech. Perhaps, they did not respect him after all.

"Come," my mother said, taking my hand. "We should prepare ourselves for the night ahead."

I followed her into a small room that was concealed by a worn velvet curtain. "This is my dressing room." She tried to conceal her saddened eyes. "It used to be filled with the most beautiful of gowns."

Like the rest of her quarters, the area held the same abandonment. A few dresses hung in the back. Dust had gathered on the mending table and chair. As I brushed the cobwebs, aside my mother handed me a case. "My child, in this was my wedding present," she said with a smile. "I would like you to wear it this eve."

Stunned by her offering, I opened it with haste. "Mother," I gasped. "It is most beautiful." The gold necklace shimmered in the light. Rubies adorned the outer rim, giving it a stately appearance.

She took it from the box and placed it around my neck. "Wear it with the dignity I once did."

Proud that she had given me an important part of her life, I squeezed her hand. A tear fell from her eye. "Come, my child, we must wait for your father in the foyer."

Escorted by the royal guard, my mother and I were led from the main door of the castle. Heralds lined the path, holding banners decorated with the shield of our land.

General Corbett met me near the bottom step of the edifice. We did not address one another nor share any discourse. My father and mother did the same.

The courtyard before us was filled with a variety of people. Most were engaged in conversation and fare, while others rejoiced in the music of our heritage. Various entertainers stood among the crowd. Their gift in illusion forced many to stop and stare. A few of the general's men were sparring with the common folk for fun, demonstrating their skill in warfare.

With our approach, a horn sounded, bringing everyone to a standstill. The people bowed as we passed.

When we reached the theater, my father addressed the crowd. "As your king," he said, extending his hand with regal authority, "I officially open this celebration. Let the festivities begin!" During the applause that followed, we were escorted to a long wooden table to the right of the stage. Once my father was seated on his throne, two servants pulled out the chairs on either side of him. Noting our cue, my mother and I sat obediently.

As I watched the crowd indulge in the merriments, I longed to join them. Somehow, I knew my father would not approve.

"Bring us our food," he said, eyeing the servants. "Tonight we shall *all* eat as kings!"

From behind us, Evelyn and her workers appeared with plates.

"Summon the jester," my father commanded, swallowing a measure of wine.

Moments later, a man appeared atop the stage.

"My King!" he said as he began to juggle. "You have chosen none other than the best to entertain you."

"We shall see," my father snickered.

Undaunted, the man opened a chest that sat in the center of the empty stage.

With anticipation, I turned to my mother. As we shared in a meaningful smile, I took notice of my father. His dark eyes bore through me. Unnerved, I looked away, giving my focus back to the people.

In the passing hours, it seemed my father was beginning to enjoy himself—or perhaps it was just the wine. Eager to mingle with the people, I decided to risk his anger.

When I stood, the general barred my path. "Where do you think you are going?"

Annoyed, I turned to my father. To my surprise, he only shrugged. "I see no harm."

I smiled, pleased that he would put his trust in me.

"Corbett," he said with a smirk, "escort my daughter around the grounds for her safety."

My jaw dropped in surprise. I was no child! I could manage myself!

"Certainly, My King," the general replied, offering his arm to me.

A knot formed in my stomach. What was I to do? Realizing I had no choice in the matter, I nodded and placed my hand on his forearm. "Thank you, sir."

As we walked through the crowd, I could not help but steal glances at him. He appeared proud to be at my side. If his intentions were honorable, how could I refuse him?

My breath caught at the thought. How could I even consider such things when my heart belonged to another? Although longing for Darwynyen seemed pointless in the crossroads of my new life, not even time could break his hold over me.

The event was drawing to an end. In a subtle manner, the heralds began to extinguish the outer torches. When the people began to disperse, I searched for a means of escape, if nothing more than to be free of the general's endless stories of bravery and valor. In the surrounding company of his men, I backed away slowly. To my relief, he had not taken notice, caught up in the tales of his exploits. Even so, I had to be swift, knowing my absence would not go unnoticed.

As I glanced over the remnants of the crowd, I heard a voice from behind. "You there!"

I turned to find a lad who looked to be about my age. He was a commoner, with meager clothing, matted hair, and a broken tooth.

"Come," he said, ushering me into the sheltering trees.

Curious about his motives, being they seemed harmless, I made my way in his direction.

As he entered the shadows, I lost sight of him. I was about to retreat when I caught view of his chubby exterior near the stream. I approached with haste.

"What do you want?"

He put his finger to his mouth, concealing the broken tooth. "Quiet, or we will be discovered!"

"Do you know who I am?" I stiffened my stance.

"Of course I do," he said, looking over my shoulder. "You know nothing of your father's evil toils, do you?" Before I could respond, he continued, "Is it your intention to follow his rule?"

"What is it you speak about?" I pulled him close to a tree in an attempt to keep us better hidden. "I have only just returned and know nothing of the times."

"I—" he began, but we both turned when we heard the motions of people drawing near. "I must go," he continued and then he disappeared through the brush.

In fear of being discovered, I left in the opposite direction. The trees began to close in on me. "General," I called out.

When there was no response, I retraced my steps back toward the stream. A whispering breeze took hold of the leaves, allowing the trickles of moonlight to reveal the outline of a man. He was standing under the cover of a tree. My heart quickened. It was hard to see his face within the hood of his cloak. Even so, I was convinced he was looking directly at me. On his right hand, I could see the sparkle of a red gem on his ring finger. When he clenched his fist, I took a step back. "Who is there?"

"I wondered where you had gotten to."

I turned to find the general. In his approach, he glanced over the area. "You must excuse the young warriors," he said, smiling. "They revel in the stories I tell, as you may one day."

I glanced over my shoulder. The man was gone. "I think it best we return. I find these woods very intimidating."

"Do not worry, Your Highness." He sneered. "My men guard this lea. There are no foes among us."

When I shivered, he put his hands on my shoulders. "What is it?" He scanned my face. "You look as though you have seen a ghost."

"Please," I pleaded, again glancing over my shoulder, "let us return to the festivities."

"What are you hiding?" he said, putting his hand to his sword. "Is there someone out there?"

"No," I replied, securing my arm in his. "There is no one there. I am only tired. The day has been long, and I wish to retire."

"Of course," he said with a nod, despite the suspicion in his eyes. "If it is your wish, I will see you back to the castle."

"Thank you," I replied.

† † †

Weeks had passed. Upon completion of my formal instruction in the mannerisms of a lady of the court, my father set about arranging several social engagements for my mother and me to attend. Today would be the first of many days when I would be allowed the privilege of taking leave from the castle.

As our coach traveled through the bustling city streets, I took notice of the people in their day-to-day activities. Carts lined the roads and alleyways. Vendors stood beside them, bartering with impatient patrons. Wagons filled with supplies were hindered by the pedestrians maneuvering between them.

I felt my mother's hand on my arm. "Arianna, are you all right?"

"Yes," I said, turning to face her. "Why do you ask?"

"The hospital," she said with downcast eyes. "Did you not find it distressing?"

I thought back to the faltering structure. "No," I replied, shaking my head. "It might not be what we had hoped, but I have trust in the dedicated healers."

"I suppose you are right." She nodded. "They seem to be managing."

When the coach began to slow, I returned to the window. Outside, a beautiful fountain sat in the center of an open square. "Where are we?" I asked.

"We are at the mainstay," she said with a smile. "The city's place of commerce."

"Oh." I frowned, thinking of the roadway where we had first arrived from our travels from Hoverdire. "I assumed the road that opened from the city gates was—"

"No," she interrupted, shifting to the door when the coach came to a halt. "That road leads to the castle alone, allowing those at the barbican to observe the migration in and out of the city."

"My ladies," a guard said as he opened the door, "your final appointment for the day awaits."

My mother extended her hand, allowing him to escort her from the coach.

When I realized where we were, a knot formed in my stomach. What purpose would take us to a jeweler? Could it be that my father was preparing me for my coming nuptials? I knew it was not uncommon to have an arranged marriage, but nothing he had done in this matter made sense.

"My Queen," a man said as he bowed at the door. "Please, I welcome you inside."

"Thank you," my mother responded as she entered the establishment.

Having no other choice, I followed.

The waiting area was larger than I had first expected. Several settees were placed with precision throughout the room, permitting a customer to sit in comfort at any of the elaborate displays.

"I will not keep you long," the man said, directing us to a glass casing filled with an array of women's jewelry.

As I glanced over the charms and bracelets, he continued, "Have you thought of a ring?" He led his hand across the upper rungs near the back.

Stunned, I turned to my mother, "For what?"

The man took a step back. "Has she not been told?"

"Excuse us," my mother said, stiffening her stance.

"Of course," the man replied as he exited to the back room.

"A ring for what?" I scowled.

"Forgive me," she said, biting her lip. "I thought your father—"

"Did you not think I—"

"Child," she stammered, "if your father chooses to buy you a gift, you must not deny him."

"Gift?" I gasped. "Is that why we are here?"

"Of course." She searched my eyes. "What did you believe to be the reason?"

I released a heavy breath to conceal my emotions. "I apologize, Mother. I was mistaken."

"Very well," she said, gesturing to the man. "Let us continue."

He nodded and returned to open the case. "You may choose from the middle rung, Your Highness."

"Thank you." I began to examine the precious stones before me.

As I tested one on my finger, I thought back to the general. How could I marry such a man? No, my heart was for one alone.

I then thought about the boy in the lea. If only we had not been interrupted.

"How about this one," my mother asked, pulling out a loop of peridot.

"Yes," I said as I placed it on my finger. "It is perfect. Thank you, Mother." Overwhelmed by the recurring thoughts of the general, I turned to the window as a means of escape.

"Child," my mother reprimanded, grabbing my arm, "mind your manners."

I nodded and then gave my attention to the man. "Thank you for your time, sir. The ring is beautiful."

Before he could respond, I made way for the door.

"Wait!" he beckoned.

In my desire to leave, I replied harshly, "I beg your pardon, sir?"

"Please," he said, extending his hand. In it he held a gold bracelet with a vinelike engraving along the rim. "I would like to offer the princess a gift, for her company."

Embarrassed by my rudeness, I managed a smile. "Thank you," I said, taking hold of it with a gentle nod. "You could honor me more if you would give its cost to the people."

"I do not understand, Your Highness."

"We just came from the hospital," I said, glancing at my mother. "Although they manage somehow, they require bandages and medicine." I paused. "Perhaps on your next sale of this bracelet, you would offer them the proceeds?"

"Your Highness," the man said, furrowing his brow, "are you certain?"

"Yes," I said, returning his offering. "Nothing would please me more."

"Then consider it done," he said, bowing his head.

Satisfied, I made my way through the door. As we approached the coach one of the people caught my eye: it was the lad from the night of the celebration. He was entering one of the city's taverns on the opposite side of the square.

"What is it?" my mother asked, taking my arm.

"Nothing," I said, shaking my head. "I thought—"

"Come. Your father will be expecting us."

I nodded and stepped into the coach.

As we pulled away, I looked at the tavern. The boy was no longer in sight, but even so, his presence still lingered. His words bore through me. What had he meant when he spoke of my father? There was no doubt things were amiss within the castle, but to label the king evil was nothing less than treason. Why would the boy take such a risk? Either way, I would not be able to confront him under my father's watchful eye. My only hope seemed to lie with the general. Perhaps if I befriended him, he would give me the answers I sought.

Distracted by my thoughts, I jumped when the guard opened the door to the coach. "My lady," he said, extending his hand, "your father awaits you in the dining hall."

"Where is the general?" I asked, placing my hand on his forearm.

"He is in the horse's keep," he replied as he led me from the coach.

"Thank you." I looked at my mother. "I will follow shortly."

Before she could respond, I dashed off toward the stables.

I found him addressing some of his men while the ferrier shoed their horses.

"General?" I called, raising my hand.

With a quick wave, he dismissed those around him. "Your Highness, can I assist you with something?"

"Yes," I said with a smile. "If you are not too busy, I thought you could take me on a stroll this eve."

"A stroll?" He appeared perplexed by my request. "Why?"

"I grow bored," I answered with a shrug. "There are few to speak to in this castle."

"Oh." His eyes brightened. "If that is the case, I will meet you on the northern terrace at the falling of the sun."

"Thank you." I turned to leave.

I had only taken a few steps before I halted. It felt wrong to deceive him. Would it not be better to allow our relationship to blossom naturally?

I only contemplated the question for a moment. No. I needed some answers.

† † †

As I stood in the faltering sun with its light trickling on the flowing leaves that danced around the old fountain, I began to wonder if the general would keep his word and meet me as promised.

If he declined my invitation, would it be by my father's hand? There was no reason. In light of our coming nuptials, the king would surely endorse such initiatives. As for the general, was he truly loyal to the king, or was it power he sought? If it was the latter, was he deceiving my father, or was my father deceiving him? Or perhaps I was the deceiver?

"Your Highness."

When I turned, the general bowed. "I apologize. It was not my intention to keep you waiting." Unlike most days, it was apparent he had spent extra time on his grooming.

"There is no need." I smiled. "I know your charge is demanding."

"Shall we?" he asked, extending his arm. "Let us begin our stroll."

I nodded, taking hold of him. "Is the skyline not beautiful this eve?"

"Not as beautiful as you, my lady," he answered, tightening his grasp.

Uneased by his remark, I changed the subject. "So, how long have you served my father?"

"Many years," he replied, leading me toward the fountain. "The king is an honorable man. I would serve no other."

"I would not know," I said, looking down. "I have not had the opportunity to spend much time with him."

"He is a very busy man," he said with a wink.

"I know," I sighed.

After an uncomfortable silence, he continued, "You must have been stunned when you found out your true identity."

I slowed my pace. "Yes, my mother kept her secrets hidden well."

He was surprised by my tone and turned to face me. "Did you not welcome the news? It almost sounds as though you preferred your life in Hoverdire."

"No," I answered, looking deeply into his eyes, "I am happy here."

When his demeanor softened, it seemed an appropriate time to gather more information. "Did you ever find those horrid creatures that attacked us?"

"No," he said, nudging me into motion. "When my men returned to engage them, they were nowhere to be found."

"What were they?" I asked, shivering at the thought of their blood red eyes. "I still wake in terror of their return."

"There is no need," he reassured, putting his hand on my back. "You are safe here. I will protect you."

"What is it my father has you do?" I asked, embracing his hold in an attempt to ease him further. "I have seen no sign of a coming war."

A glimpse of anger flared in his eyes. "Entrusted by your father, I will not divulge such things, not even to you."

Taken aback, I turned to face him. "I only inquire in preparation for the day when I become queen."

He countered in a condescending manner, "You should not trouble yourself with such things. Your only concern should lie with the dangers before you!"

Unsure about what he meant, I took a step back.

"What I mean is ..." he stammered, appearing anxious, "there is much time before you are to bear the burden of queen. Do not let it trouble you now." His hands opened in exclamation, "I am sure you have plenty of other things to focus on with your new duties and such."

I nodded in agreement, wondering what he meant by "the dangers before you!" As I absorbed his words, a chill ran through my body. Was my life in danger? Was the lad at the festivities right in his warnings, or was the general referring to something that linked back to the attack in the marsh?

"Where is Gin?" I asked, looking back at the castle. "I have not seen him since my return."

"Gin?" He frowned. "Why do you ask of him?"

"No reason," I said hesitantly.

"Gin is gone. You will not see him again."

"Gone?"

"He has been sent north." There was coldness in his voice. "He was weak and could not handle the roughness of battle. Gin's duties will not go beyond that of a scout."

"Oh," I replied. "I did not realize."

When he declined to respond, I felt certain he was hiding something. I shook the thought. Perhaps his disposition stemmed from my friendship with the boy.

"Do you mind if I have a word?"

I turned to find my father emerging from the shadows on the terrace. Had he been watching us all along?

"Father?" Assuming it was my cue to leave, I nodded, making my way from the fountain. "Excuse me."

"No," he said, taking my arm at the crest of the stair. "It is with you whom I wish to speak."

"Very well, My King," the general said, bowing obediently. "I will meet you back in the study."

"Come," my father said, leading me to a bench on the terrace. "Sit, child." He kept his stance.

"Thank you, Father." I sat, looking up at him.

"So, I must ask you of your feelings for the general." Before I could respond he continued, "I have noticed that you have been spending more time with him. I can only hope you have grown compliant by his ways."

I thought it best to lie. "Of course, Father."

"Good," he said, releasing a heavy breath.

I could see in his eyes that he was about to tell me of the nuptials. "There is something I wish to tell you," he uttered.

"Yes, Father." I managed a smile to conceal the fact that I already knew of his intentions. Not only did I owe it to my mother, but I thought it would be best to keep his trust until I could better understand his motivations.

"You have come to the age …" He paused. For the first time, he seemed almost awkward in his ways. "As your king, I have taken the liberty of arranging your marriage."

Obediently, I nodded. "Father?"

"I have chosen for you the general."

I looked down to conceal my reservations. "Not to offend you father, but why the general?" When his eyes darkened, I resumed, "I know he is an honorable man, and though we have grown close, I thought I would be betrothed to someone with more of a royal background."

"The sooner you accept the decision," he answered with a raised his brow, "the better it will be for all concerned."

I bit my lip with anticipation. "May I ask when?"

"In a fortnight," he replied. "Before the next coming of the moon." He paused, taking a step back. "If there is nothing else, I will give you some time to reflect on things."

I nodded as he took his leave.

When he disappeared through the gated passage, I fell back on the bench. What was I to do? Or more to the point, what *could* I do? If I defied my father, there was no doubt my mother would be the one to suffer the consequences. That was something I was not willing to risk in her weakened state. Even so, was it in me to allow these nuptials to follow through, especially when the general himself carried deceit in his words?

Knowing I was to get nowhere with my previous plan, I had no choice but to take the lad's warnings more seriously. My only means would be to confront him. To do so, I would have to find a way out of the castle.

† † †

The hour was late. Unable to settle my nerves, I made way for the balcony. A storm was brewing in the distance. Despite its might, it was no greater than the turmoil within me.

As my mind raced over the past weeks, I could not help but feel a sense of disconnect. Although there were many pieces of the puzzle before me, the pattern itself was hard to place. First, there was the attack in the marsh. Then the suspicion behind my forthcoming nuptials. And not to forget the lad who risked everything to approach me, which was followed by the cloaked man.

When a bolt of lightning broke the skyline, I could not help but take notice of the turret. "The door," I uttered. "I could—"

"Your Highness?"

Startled, I turned in haste. "Edina! Forgive me. I was not expecting you."

She stepped from the doorway, pulling her night robe tightly around her. "Are you having trouble finding sleep?"

I looked to the sky. "It is not the most pleasant of nights." Before she could respond, I moved through the door. "Perhaps I could use a warm drink, something to settle my nerves."

"I have some herb tea in my room," she replied, turning to leave. "I will return momentarily."

"I will go with you," I said as I followed her. "I could use the distraction."

"There is no need." She halted. "I am—"

"Please," I begged, "do not deny me. There is no need for you to recoil. As you know, we once shared the same past."

"Very well," she said, extending her hand.

Her room was quaint and brought me a sense of comfort. It reminded me of the home I had left behind in Hoverdire. Several family mementos were placed upon the furniture around her bed. Fresh-cut flowers were poorly arranged in a vase next to the window. The common nature of the surroundings seemed to tear away at the protective barrier I had been building since my arrival. Relieved, I decided to risk everything to form the bond of trust that I had apparently been yearning for.

"Edina," I began, wavering in my moment of weakness, "may I ask you for the confidence you once offered?"

"Your Highness," she replied, lightly tapping on her mattress in a gesture for me to join her, "as I said before, I am here for you. Your trust is mine."

Second guessing my decision, I decided to first get to know her better. "Before we continue," I said, changing the subject as I sat, "will you tell me of your life?"

She shrugged. "There is not much to tell. Like you, I spent most of my life on the other side of these castle walls. My mother was employed by the mainstay bakery up until two years ago, and my father—" She blinked as though her words pained her.

"Edina?"

"There was an accident in the armory."

"Forgive me." I sat back. "I did not mean to upset you."

"You did nothing of the sort." Her eyes fluttered. "We manage. Along with my wages here, my brother earns a living playing music. Between the two of us, there is enough to cover the losses."

"Do you …" I paused. "Do you have a husband?"

"No," she replied with a smile, "but I am soon to wed."

"To whom?" I asked.

"His name is Stuart." Her cheeks became flush. "We have known each other since we were children."

"I envy you." I recoiled at the thought of the general.

"Why?" she gasped.

"You hold a life I could only wish for."

She nodded as though she knew the meaning behind my words. "Your father …" She hesitated. "I apologize … it is none of my business."

"No," I said, standing up, "continue, please!"

"I was only going to say that he has a temper," she said. Her words gently forced me back to the bed. "In many ways, his manner frightens me."

"I know," I sighed. "His actions are nothing less than perplexing."

In the uncomfortable silence that followed, I decided it was time to reveal my true intentions. "My marriage has been arranged," I blurted. "It too will take place in the coming weeks."

"To whom?" she questioned with a hint of doubt.

"You must not tell a soul," I warned.

She put her hand to her chest. "As I said, you can trust me."

I nodded and grit my teeth. "I am to marry General Corbett."

"No." She shook her head. "You must be mistaken."

"There is no mistake." I took hold of her pillow for support. "I was informed by my father this very eve."

"The general," she huffed. "Why? Not only is he not of royal blood, he holds little favor with the people."

"What do—"

"Wait!" She moved to the door.

I watched her peek through the message hole before returning. "We must keep conversations such as these a secret."

"Of course." I closed my eyes in realization. "I now understand your reluctance before. Why my simple questions brought you to worry."

She nodded. "Speaking freely in this castle does not go unnoticed."

I released a heavy breath. "Will you tell me what you know of the general?"

"To my regret, I have little to offer." She rejoined me on the bed. "Although there has been speculation, his origins are unknown."

I was about to speak when she continued, "Over the years, your father has gone to great lengths to keep his business as his own. As you know, he trusts few."

"But why?" I threw up my hands in exclamation. "I see no reason!"

"Many believe that he prepares for war." She gave the door a fleeting look. "With that, trouble will certainly follow."

"What do you mean?" I furrowed my brow.

"To be truthful, I doubt many will follow him. Most wish to see his reign come to an end."

"What else do you know?" I could feel my body tense.

"Arianna, please, try not to look so troubled." When I did not answer, she blinked again. "What is it?"

"A soldier, one of those who escorted me here, mentioned these words of war you speak of."

Her eyes widened. "One of Corbett's soldiers spoke in candor to you?"

"Yes." I nodded. "And now he has disappeared."

"Disappeared?"

I stood. "I must find out what is going on."

"If there is something I might do, then let it be asked!"

"What if helping me leads you to danger?"

"What of your life could bring us to danger?" she asked bluntly.

I responded in a stern tone, "If I tell you there is no going back."

A look of certainty came over her face. "Your Highness, my family has believed in you from the day you were born. I swear to you, I will do anything needed to see you through these troubles that beset you."

It was then, when I felt complete trust in her, that I began to reveal the bizarre happenings that had occurred since my arrival.

As she filtered through my words, I offered my proposal. "I plan to escape the castle."

"How?" she questioned. "Are you to seek the lad?"

"Yes." I lowered my voice. "The turret door from my balcony is unguarded."

"And *how* far do you expect to get from there." She rolled her eyes. "Besides, the door is locked."

"The lock is old." I moved to her writing table. "Nothing an ink feather and oil will not fix."

"All right." She stood. "How will you get through the main gates?"

My body sunk. "I do not know. I—"

"Leave that to me," she said, crossing her arms. "All you need to worry about is getting there unnoticed."

"How … What?"

"We can discuss the details in the morn." She eyed the door. "You should probably retire."

"Of course." I turned. "We would not want to draw any suspicion."

She took my hand, forcing my stare. "Before you retire, I must again assure you of my trust, Your Highness. The people of this city want nothing more than to see you on the throne. If I can assist you in getting there, consider it done."

I nodded and took my leave.

† † †

For the first time since my arrival, I awoke with a sense of purpose. Putting my trust in Edina had, if nothing else, given me hope. Even so, it was best to keep up my guard, especially where my father was concerned. If he were to find out my intentions … I shook off the thought.

As I finished dressing, a knock came to the door. "Enter!"

Edina appeared in a timid manner. "Are we alone?"

"Yes." I took notice of the scroll under her arm. "What have you brought?"

"A map of the castle." She unraveled it and placed it on the dining table near the window. "I found it in the library."

I was about to ask her about this room when she pulled some clothing from under her gown. "Here," she said, holding a tattered frock to my shoulders. "The guards will not recognize you if you are in disguise." She unfolded the cloak. "Make sure you draw the hood when you near the barbican."

"Could you have picked something more hideous," I said with a laugh.

"Trust me, it will do perfectly." She tossed the outfit under the foot of my bed. "If you are questioned, tell them that you are new and that you work for Evelyn in the kitchen." She glanced over her shoulder. "Because of the shift changes, they will have no cause to refute you."

"What if they do?"

"Speak in a foul nature," she replied as she rolled up the map. "If you disgust them, they will want to be rid of you."

"Understood." I reached for a tiny jar of cooking oil. "I stole this from the kitchen last night."

"Good." Then she paused and looked at me with disapproval. "You snuck out of your quarters?"

"Yes." I crossed my arms defensively. "I knocked on my door halfway through the night, claiming to the guard that I had a sore stomach." I smirked. "After pleading with him, he allowed me to make way to the kitchen.

"Why did he not summon me?"

"I asked him not to bother you," I replied. "I *can* be persuasive when needed."

She shook her head. "You should not be taking unnecessary risks."

I looked down. "You are right. I was only trying—"

Before I could continue, she grabbed the oil, making way for the balcony. "We should oil the hinges now."

I nodded and followed her to the turret's archway.

As we descended the stair, she pulled out the cork of the bottle. "The door hinges to the inside. I know this because it was intended that way. It bars any intruders from the royal family if the castle should be breached." She continued when we reached the bottom, "We shall remove these pins." She dropped some oil on the hinges. "And open the door backward."

Astounded by her cleverness, I smiled. "You are brilliant! I could not have done this without you."

She raised her brow. "I know."

When the hinges were saturated, we both ran up the stairs.

Once inside the room, I embraced her with intense elation. "I cannot believe we are doing this?"

"Doing what?" My mother frowned from the door. "I have been waiting for you in my quarters." Her hands fell to her waist. "Are you not to join us for breakfast?" Then she paused before continuing, "I had not realized that the two of you had gotten so well acquainted."

"We are not!" I spoke out defensively. "We were just—"

"There is nothing wrong with confiding in your lady in waiting," she said with sincerity. "Many great friendships have transpired in such a way." Not waiting for a response, she turned to leave. "Are you coming then?"

"Of course, Mother." I followed her from the room.

Before exiting, I looked to Edina. "See you tonight!"

† † †

It was well after midnight when Edina found her way into my room. I leapt from the bed with anticipation. "I thought you would never arrive!"

"Am I late?" she asked, pulling the bottle of oil from her pocket.

"No, of course not." I released a heavy breath. "Do not mind me. I am only anxious."

"So am I," she said, glancing over her shoulder toward the door. "We have little time. I told the guard I was only checking in on you."

Already dressed in the outfit she had brought me earlier, I followed her to the turret stair.

When we reached the bottom, we began to remove the pins that held the hinges of the door tightly in place. The task was tedious, not only were our hands chilled by the crispness in the air but the oil was sticky.

"I cannot pry it free," I cried.

"Here," she said, handing me an iron knitting needle.

"What am I to do with this," I snapped.

"Use it as a makeshift strike!"

I nodded and placed it under the top of the pin. "Use more oil," she instructed as she handed me the bottle.

"Can you pour it?" I asked as I began to push on the pin.

"Yes, but be quick!"

I was about to give up when I felt the pin begin to loosen. "It is working!"

"Let us do the other one," she said, kneeling to reach the bottom pin.

Without another word, I followed her lead.

Only minutes passed before the hinges broke free.

As the door inched back, a crack of light appeared from the foyer. Overwrought with stress, I searched the surrounding area. There was no one in sight.

"Check the antechamber to the keep," she said in a strained voice as she braced the weight of the door.

"There is no need." I pulled the hood of my tattered cloak close. "I shall find my way from here."

Before she could respond, I made haste toward the gated passage that connected to the dining hall. Staying close to the wall, I found it with ease. With a gentle nudge to the latch, I was on my way to the kitchen.

To my relief the room had long since been abandoned. With no one to hinder me, I made way to the fireplace. To complete my disguise, I needed to rub some soot on my skin.

When my hands were blackened, I returned to the corridor. As I made way to the servants' entrance, my heart began to quicken. There was no turning back. I had come too far. I paused to still my breath and then sped through the doorway.

"Good evening, sir," I said as I dashed past the guard. Expecting the worst, I closed my eyes.

"Good evening," he replied.

From the corner of my eye, I saw the general tending to his horse at an open paddock. When he stood back, I thought he had seen me. I looked to the ground and hastened my pace. To my good fortune, I was not the focus of his attention. Instead, he called to a stable boy.

Relieved, I continued through to the courtyard. All that was barring my path now was the barbican.

As I approached, I lost my mannerisms and began to trudge, "I am donen for the night, sir, and will be returnin' in the morn." I muttered as I walked past the guard.

Before I could exit, he stopped me. "Who are you? What was your business in the castle?"

Stricken with fear, I stuttered my words, "I w-was h-hired this afternoon, sir. I be here to clean the kitchen. The house master, Evelyn, was not 'appy with the untidiness of the new cook." I paused before continuing, "My name is Mildred, passed on to me by my great grandmudder, sir."

"Enough rambling!" he shouted. "Be on your way, woman!"

I nodded obediently and made my way through the threshold.

When the wall walk was out of sight, I took a moment to collect my thoughts. Edina and I had missed something, something I could not—

"Where are you going, lass?"

I turned to see a few drunken lads peering from an alleyway. Intimidated, I broke into a run toward the mainstay.

I slowed in my pace when I ran out of breath and the square came into view. I headed west past the fountain. Testing my memory, I soon found the tavern I was looking for. As I approached, I could hear the faint murmur of the crowd inside. Men and women stood around the door. Embraced in their own desires, they paid no attention to me as I maneuvered between them.

The entrance was dimly lit, and I nearly tripped on the inner threshold. As I regained my composure, I took notice of the room. It was tightly packed, and the presence of spirits and conversation filled the room. To gain a better view, I ascended the stair to the mezzanine.

"Well, aren't you a pretty little thing!" A drunken old man staggered toward me from a table near the back. "Can I buy you a drink, lass?"

"No thank you," I replied. "I was just—"

"What is it, love?"

"I should not be here," I said and turned to leave.

As I pushed my way through the crowd that had gathered at the crest of the stair, I bumped into the lad. "What are you doing here?" he snapped with widened eyes. "Are you trying to get us both killed?"

"Young Edric," the old man said, appearing from behind. "A lucky man you are." He puckered his brow. "You know better than to leave a pretty lady in here on her own. Not wise, not wise!" He turned to me with a silly smile then stumbled off.

"Your name is Edric?"

"I will not ask you again," he growled. "Why have you come?"

"Please," I said, glancing over my shoulder, "do not draw attention."

At my words, he grabbed my arm, leading me through the mob of people to a stairway behind the bar. "Go up these stairs," he ordered. Then he gestured to the bar man in passing. "I will not be gone long."

The man huffed in annoyance.

"What are you—" I began.

"Do as you are told." He raised his brow. "It is your intention to stay hidden, is it not?"

"Very well." I was about to turn when I noticed the cloaked man. He was leaning on an archway near the door. Panicked, I pulled at Edric's shirt. "That man! In the cloak! He was watching us the night of the—"

"Who? Where?" He searched the area.

When I moved to direct him, the stranger was gone. "He was there, I swear!"

He turned to me impatiently. "Are you sure you are not seeing things?"

"Of course not!"

"Could he be a spy of your father's?" he asked, nudging me up the stair.

"I do not know." I hesitated at the landing. "Perhaps I should just take my leave."

"No," he said, directing me down a corridor at the top of the rise. "What is done is done."

I tried to settle my nerves as he led me through a door. "These are my quarters," he said, ushering me to a stool near his bed. "Make yourself comfortable."

"Thank you." I glanced over the room. A sloped roofline, fitted with a narrow window, finished the scanty area. Between his wardrobe and bed sat a night table filled with keepsakes. "Does your family live here?"

He smiled in a proud manner, revealing his broken tooth. "Generations of my kin have called this city home. This tavern has sustained our name for over a hundred years now."

I pulled my hood back. "It comforts me to know your roots lie close to Aarrondirth."

He crossed his arms in a condescending manner. "So, what have you learned since I last saw you?"

"I have learned nothing," I replied. "That is why I am here."

"If you are being watched, could it be by the general?" He moved to lock the door.

"I do not believe so." I shrugged. "If it were him, would he not have taken action by now?"

"Agreed," he conceded. "In any case, how did you get here?"

"Is it not obvious?" I smirked. "I left the castle disguised as a servant."

"You have taken a great risk," he sighed. "Even so, I would suggest the use of less soot next time. Your people may be poor, but they still have their dignity."

I wiped my brow with my sleeve, "You are right. In the future I will try to be more observant."

"Can I ask how you found me?"

"I saw you the other day," I replied, "from the royal coach during one of our social engagements."

He lifted a half-empty pint glass from the table. "So, what do you want?"

"What do you mean?"

"You want to know the truth about your father then?" He took a measure of ale. "Are you certain?"

"Yes." I bit my lip. "I need some answers before—"

"Before *what?*" He frowned.

"Please," I said, meeting his stare, "tell me what you know."

He brushed his fingers through his woolly brown hair. "I have ties to a secret society whose name I cannot reveal." He began to pace the room, "They have watched over your father, Velderon, from the time of his succession."

He paused for a moment. "Did you know that he came from a place that to this day is unknown?"

"Unknown?" I uttered.

"Yes," he nodded. "His arrival in Aarrondirth was suspicious. Out of nowhere, he arrived to claim he was the lost brother of the king."

"I do not understand."

"The king of that time, Alameed, lost his brother as a child," he replied. "At the peak of every moon, they would go hunting in the fields. During a winter expedition, they were ambushed. Only one of the princes returned."

"What happened?"

"We have little time." He turned to face me. "I will share the details with you later." When I nodded, he continued. "Guilt ridden, the king accepted your father at his word and declared him Prince of Aarrondirth."

"Do you question my father's proclamation?"

"If you would hear me out ..."

"Very well," I said, biting my lip with anticipation.

"It was then that all began to change." He rested his foot on the bedpost near my stool. "Weeks later, the king, Alameed, discontinued his engagements. Some claimed he had lost all interest in life."

"Was my father not to counsel him?"

"Of course not." He sneered. "He had other plans. Not even a year was to pass before he had taken a wife, one of great social standing, your mother, Brianna. The new couple was admired by many. They attended every social occasion in replacement of the king. Eventually, people began to accept him, trusting his claim about who he was." He looked at me and smiled, "When you arrived, all adored you. You were the first child born to the family in many years."

I looked at him questioningly, but he continued before I could speak, "A year and a half from your birth, the king came to a mysterious and untimely death, being ever so early in his years."

He stood by the bedpost. "Does it stir you that you may not be of royal blood?"

"Why would it?" I looked down, half embarrassed. "I have lived a life such as you until only a few weeks ago."

"Are you not consumed by the luxuries brought by your new role?"

"There are few luxuries to be found," I replied. "Despite what you see from the outside, the castle is being run with minimal staff."

"I see." He set down his glass. "Then let us carry on." His eyes began to wander, "The king was discovered in his quarters, poisoned from a root uncommon to these regions—a root that your father coincidently claimed caused *your* death." He stroked his chin. "Which is odd … would you not agree?"

"Are you accusing my father of murder?" I stood. "He might be capable of many things but—"

"How else could he claim the throne?"

"Was no one to protest?" I asked, returning to my seat.

"Of course," he huffed. "But the royal family was too late. Once he had the throne, he had them executed for treason."

"Have your claims been proven?" I scowled.

"If you prove worthy," his voice deepened, "you may ask the sole survivor yourself one day!"

"Survivor?" I uttered. "Who is this person?"

"Forget your questions for now." He took a seat on the bed. "I know these words are hard for you to accept, especially because the source has yet to be revealed, but you must let me finish."

"Please," I gestured.

"With no one to challenge your father, he soon began to deny the people. When his servants began to gossip about his newfound interest in magic, he had them dismissed, claiming it was out of safety for his family. Weeks later, he brought in new blood from the north."

"Is that when he met the general?"

"Yes." He nodded. "And though he was young and inexperienced, he would soon become your father's loyal companion."

"What of my mother?" I asked.

"From the accounts, she kept up with her engagements." He finished the last measure of his ale. "She was devoted to her duties."

"What happened next?"

"Despite your mother's attempts, the people began to waver." He cleared his throat. "Soon after came the announcement of your death. Using grief to his advantage, your father redirected the people's suspicion toward the Elves, blaming them for your demise. He was clever in this as there already stood a rift between the two people."

I interrupted him at the thought of Darwynyen. "Will you tell me of the Elves?"

When he looked at me oddly, I turned from his stare.

"With no one to stand in his way, your father began recruiting his now elite royal guard. The small army was led by the young—"

"General Corbett," I finished his words. "Is there anything to substantiate this sinister story?"

"Have you ever seen a Crone in the midst of the castle?"

"No." I stood again. "Why do you ask?"

"A girl once claimed to see your father in the company of one a few years back." He clenched his fists. "When rumors spread that your father had turned to the dark powers, the girl went missing."

"Did you know her?"

"Forget her." His eyes grew cold. "It is believed that this Crone aids your father now. Beware, should she make herself known to you in the castle."

I could not believe the crazy words he spoke. "Have you had a few too many brews this evening?"

"The Crone exists," he snapped. "She has come in hopes of finding the last of the three stones."

"Do you speak of the Stones of Moya?" My thoughts drifted to Gin.

"Yes." He searched my eyes. "How do you know of them?"

"From a soldier I met on the journey home." I raised my brow. "He was going on about Sorcerers and war."

"Save your sarcasm," he said, moving to the door.

"No," I pleaded and returned to my stool. "Forgive me."

He released the handle. "Do you not see? If your father finds the stones … No, there is no way for them to unlock the last of the riddles."

"What riddles?" I asked.

"The Men of Moya are the ones who created them." He clasped his hand to his mouth.

I knew then that he had revealed the secret name. I was about to laugh when he glared. "Should I go no further? You have taken little heed in anything I have said."

"No," I insisted. I finally held some interest.

"The riddles are puzzles. They lead the bearer to five specific areas in our land. Five different men of Man's Blood chose the locations. The riddles themselves were crafted by the Elves, written in an ancient dialect. The structures where they can be found were built by the Miders. Once they were complete, the Little People created traps intricate enough to slay anyone foolish in their attempts to try to out maneuver them."

"Where are the other two stones?" I puckered my brow.

"It is said that the Sorcerers escaped with them at the peak of the last battle."

Overwhelmed by the information, my attention diverted to my thoughts. Could it be true? Were my father's deeds as evil as Edric had claimed? In my heart, I knew his intentions went far deeper than I was at first to believe.

"Edric, come out!" We both jumped when the door began to rattle. "I must have a word!" a man shouted.

"Not now!" Edric replied in an angered tone. "I will be down in a few minutes!"

There was no response. When we heard footsteps down the corridor, Edric sighed in relief. "We must go." He took hold of his empty pint glass.

"But you have not yet finished!" I pleaded.

"There is nothing more I can tell you." He paused. "Before we part, know this: many have claimed to hear digging below the motte of the castle. If this is true, your father's men have found their way through the last of the riddles. The stone may no longer be out of their reach."

"What am I to do? I thought you said the riddles—" I stood in realization of what I had overlooked in my departure. "You cannot leave. I have no way back!"

He moved to face me. "Are you saying you have no means of return?"

My eyes began to tear. "I knew I was forgetting something."

"I do not believe this!" He put his hand to his brow. "Very well, you may stay here for the night. In the morn, once shift change has passed, I will return for you. From there, you will have to lie your way back into the castle."

I nodded, taking hold of his arm. One question still loomed in my thoughts. "Why is it ..." I hesitated in fear of his answer. "Why do you think my father did not poison us if the evil words you speak of are true?"

"I do not know," he replied. "Perhaps, he did hold love for you. It would take a cold man to murder his own."

"What do the Men of Moya believe?"

He looked at me with resolve, "They believe it was your father's infatuation with the magic that led to your exile. Our laws are clear. If he was found to have taken on a Crone, he would have been executed on charges of devilry." He moved through the door. "I will leave you to your thoughts.

In his absence, I lay on the bed, absorbing his words. If my father had exiled us to conceal his dealings in the magic, I had to wonder why. This stone seemed far from his reaches—or was it?

Should Edric's proclamations prove true, the time had long since passed for my father's redemption. It was clear there was no love in his eyes when he looked upon me. A part of me wanted to test these boundaries, evoke his emotions. Deep down, I knew the cause would be wasted.

CHAPTER 2:

THE CLOAKED MAN

When Edric left the room, he made his way down to the pub where he found the cloaked man awaiting him at the bar.

"What have you told her?" the man demanded.

"Enough," Edric replied.

"You fool," the man growled. "You bring upon us great risk." He grabbed Edric by the shirt, dragging him from the inn. "What if she tells her father?"

"She is not like her father," Edric countered.

The man slipped into the shadow of a narrow passage next to the inn. "You better hope you are right."

"I carry little doubt, for she—"

Come," the cloaked man interrupted, his eyes surveying the area. "We must tell the others of your escapades." He disappeared down the passage.

With a sigh, Edric followed.

Chapter 3:

Men of Moya

I awoke to a knock at the door. When I opened my eyes, I found Edric at the foot of the bed. His face was concealed by the weak glimmer of sunlight.

"Are you all right?" he asked.

To conceal the fact that I had succumbed to little sleep, I rose sternly. "Yes, of course. And you?"

"I will be a lot better when you are back within the realm of the castle!" he huffed.

As we made our way down the corridor, he hesitated. "I almost forgot ... I retrieved the gateman's name. They call him Charlen. If you should come to any trouble, speak to him as though you have already made his acquaintance." He smirked. "He spends most of his evenings filled with spirits in the pub and would not risk the embarrassment of not remembering you."

"Thank you." I pulled the hood on my cloak close. "When will I see you again?"

His body stiffened. "I spoke to the men last night. They feel you should involve yourself no further."

"Why?" I spoke in anger.

"Do not fret." He nudged my arm. "In the end, I was able to change their minds. That is," he continued, crossing his arms, "if you are able to see yourself free of the castle once again?"

I looked down. "What if I am unable to get back in?"

"You will." He took hold of my chin. "Believe in yourself, and the rest will come easy."

I took his hand and pushed it away from my face. "When will this meeting take place?"

"You must return this eve," he replied. "I will meet you at the Fountain of the Mists, the one that sits in the center of this square. Once the men are certain that no one follows, you we will be signaled." His eyes wandered for a moment. "Do you agree to these terms? Once you have taken this path, there is no turning back."

"What would I turn back to?" I asked. "My whole life seems to have been but a lie."

"I suppose you are right," he replied sympathetically.

With nothing more to say, we left the room.

Outside, the city was readying itself for a new day. While vendors prepared their carts, patrons with baskets in hand stood waiting; taking little notice of us in passing.

When we neared the barbican, Edric spoke aloud. "Have a good day, my cousin!"

I took his hand, squeezing it. "See you tonight."

He nodded and disappeared through the crowd.

I made it through the gates with little trouble, using the same story as before while addressing the guard in his name, as Edric had instructed. Like the others before me, I kept my head down and walked quickly along the road to the castle. Thankfully, I blended well with the commoners, which allowed me to slip through to the back entrance unnoticed.

When I arrived at the turret door, I tried to pry it open. "Edina," I whispered.

"I am here," she replied, levering its weight so that I could pass.

As I squeezed through the opening, a tear fell from my eye. "Edina, I am so very sorry. I forgot—"

"You are here," she said quickly as she pushed the door back in place. "That is all that matters."

I dithered for a mere second and then ascended the stair. With no one in sight, I quickly dressed in the gown Edina had left out for me.

"What happened?" she asked as she began to tend to my hair.

"I found him," I sighed.

"What did he say?" She turned me to face her.

"I must leave again tonight." I bit my lip.

"Are you to start a romance with him?" She glared.

"No." I shook my head. "There are people he wants me to meet."

"I see." She again took hold of my hair. "That should be an easy task for you, now that you are able to see yourself free of the castle."

I was about to respond when a knock came to the door. A guard appeared. "The King wishes your presence in the study."

A shudder of fear coursed through me. "Whatever for?" I asked.

"You ask what I cannot answer." He replied, rolling his eyes.

When Edina had secured my hair in a bun, I turned to her. She shook her head in warning.

"Very well," I said resignedly before looking to the guard.

He bowed his head and ushered me through the door in an undaunted manner. His carriage put me at ease for a moment, until I realized his position would give him little knowledge of the reason I had been summoned in the first place.

Fearing the worst, I hesitated with every step. Was it possible he knew? If I had been discovered, there was no doubt most of the repercussions would fall on my mother, something I worried about in her delicate state. Should I find her and flee to the city?

Caught between uncertainty and trepidation, I tried to calm myself. Perhaps, he had asked me to his study for another reason.

As I descended the stair to the main foyer, my mother appeared in an impatient manner. "Have you not been told child?" she stammered. "The King has requested your presence in the study."

"I know," I said, hastening my pace. "I make my way there now."

When she nodded, I stopped to embrace her. "Mother," I whispered, "I forgive you for not showing me the love I have always desired. I want you to know that I care for you deeply."

"What has gotten in to you, child?" she replied sternly, pulling away. "This is not the time to be sharing such things."

Hurt by her response, I brushed past her.

Upon my arrival, I found my father gazing out the southern window, the one that overlooked the courtyard. He seemed content for the first time.

"Father, you asked for me."

He turned to face me. "Yes, my child. Please enter." He motioned me to the table, while closing the door. "I wish to speak with you."

I nodded, taking a seat.

"So …," he hesitated, "is there something you wish to tell me?"

"No, Father." I choked on my words.

"I was told you tried to refuse my gift the other day?" He stood to face me.

"No," I replied, displaying the ring. "I would never refuse a gift from you, Father."

"But you tried." He paused. "I was also told that you left your quarters the other night. Why?"

"I was not feeling well." I put my hand to my stomach to conceal the shock of learning how much I was actually being watched. "I needed some milk."

"That is what your lady in waiting is for, to see to your every need."

"I know," I replied. "Only I am not used to such customs."

"Very well." He returned to the window. "We are soon to make the announcement of your nuptials." His hand caressed his beard. "I fear the people will need time to accept your fate."

Confused, I interrupted before he could continue, "Why would the people need time?"

"Again you question me!" he shouted. "Leave me this instant! I cannot stand the sight of you!"

Terrified by his reaction, I ran from the room. When I reached the foyer, I stopped to wipe the tears.

Although it was painful to accept, it was confirmed: my father did not care for me. The reason he had summoned us back was clear. He feared the people, and needed me to calm them. He must have picked the general as my husband to keep me at bay, to make sure I did not meddle.

As I shook the thoughts, I noticed the archway to the defense corridor. For some reason, the guard was not at his post. With anticipation, I scoured the area for any sort of presence. All was quiet. With little to lose, knowing now that my father still needed me, I crossed into the threshold that had been restricted to me from the time since my arrival.

After passing several doors covered in cobwebs, I arrived in an open hall. To the left, I could see what appeared to be the defense area. Two guards were talking beyond the archway. To the right, the corridor continued in a downward slope.

I glanced again at the guards. They would not stand idle for long. With opportunity in my favor, I dashed through to the neighboring corridor before they could take notice.

The stone floor soon became dampened clay. The torches that lit the narrow passage had burned low. A slight upward draft took hold of their flames and taunted my every step. In the distance, I could hear the faint clanking of hammers. At the thought of

Edric's words, I hesitated. Was he right? Was my father searching for the stone?

Through the droplets of water that filtered through cracks in the stone above, I caught view of a staircase that seemed to lead deeper into the bowels of the castle. Although I dreaded what I might find at its end, I began in my descent.

I must have descended a hundred uneven stone steps before the corridor began to open. The sounds of hammering had grown intense and echoed up the chamber. A sour odor filled the air that I did not recognize.

At the end of the final turn, I halted, unable to comprehend what stood before me. It seemed impossible that such a place existed under the motte of the castle.

Bridges made of wood spanned over a gaping hole in various directions. Each bridge connected to a cave that was full of debris. Droplets of water trickled from the stalagmites above, dancing in a delicate rhythm as they fell in between the mining carts suspended by pulleys and onto the rocks below. Two large gargoyle statues hovered over the entrance to the main bridge. Thick chains secured them to the cavern walls, and the pedestals beneath them were placed in cut stone for stability.

Startled by the sound of movement behind me, I slid into a cleft that opened between the pedestal and the cut stone facing around it. Someone was descending the stair.

"Fasken!" a man shouted from the bottom stair.

I recognized the voice immediately: it was the general.

He walked over to meet with someone on the larger of the bridges. "Have you finished your search of the northern region?"

When I claimed view of the pair from the opposite side of the statue, I nearly screamed. It was no man he spoke to but one of those creatures from the marsh.

"No, Your Eminence," the creature hissed through its jagged teeth. "But we are close." It wiped the froth from around its mouth, "You must let us search the southern reaches," it begged.

Its fiery eyes widened. "I am certain the stone will be found there!"

"No!" the general growled. "The southern reaches must be left to last. If we are discovered down here, we do not have the armies required to handle a rebellion." He paused before continuing, "I grow tired of explaining this to you. Until we have the power of the stone, we are at risk of being defeated. We must go unnoticed!"

"What of the child?" The creature's eyes narrowed.

"She suspects nothing," he replied smugly. "Velderon keeps her at bay."

His hand fell to his sword. "I should have killed you for your deceit."

"Why?" the creature cried.

"If your attack in the marsh had gone as planned, the Men of Moya would be the least of our problems."

"It was the Hynd who gave those orders," the creature challenged. "Shall I pass your grievance on to them?"

The Hynd? I thought. Who were these people? Could it be they were the ones behind the consequences my father had spoken about?

"The Hynd know nothing of these times," the general said, shaking his head. "They were foolish in their attempts. Arianna's return has given the people hope, a perfect distraction. There is no doubt she is a cause for distraction ..."

The creature countered, "You speak as though you desire the girl for yourself, my lord?"

"Do not push me, Fasken! the general replied angrily. "I warn you!"

"Perhaps you are right," the creature conceded. "She may be more valuable to us alive should a bargaining tool be needed."

The general nodded. "Bringing us back to the Men of Moya. The people do not shun them as they once did. I fear they grow close to revealing us!"

"Worry, worry," the creature cackled. "The society in its years has never posed a threat." It held out its hands, pleadingly. "Certainly they have grown stronger, my lord, but they lack the conviction to see any of this through."

"I do not care for your thoughts," the general snapped. "Now tell me, what has been done with the spies we captured two nights ago?"

"We are holding them in the southern cavern," the creature said, looking over its shoulder toward the caves. "They have yet to reveal whom they serve, but their strength grows weak as the Crone works her magic."

I tensed at the mention of the Crone.

"Good," he said, taking a step back to turn. "Now make haste in your search. We do not have much time. The sooner we are on our way back to Cessdorn, the sooner we can set out in creating the armies we require for the months ahead!"

They finished their conversation with laughter as the general retreated up the stairs.

As I struggled to comprehend their words, a part of me felt an odd sense of relief. Despite everything, I finally knew the truth. My only hope would be that the Men of Moya would help me right the injustices of my father's rule.

When the creature was no longer in sight, I slid from under the overhang. As I made my way up the stair, I realized I had no means of escape. The general's visit had ensured the guards would be back at their posts.

I turned to the bridge. The path seemed dodgy. If I were to come across the Crone … I tensed at the thought.

Contemplating my route, I noticed a ridge behind the statue that followed the outer rim of the open cavity. The girth was slight but extended enough to see me through to the caves that opened off the gaping hole to the right, where, if nothing else, I would come across an alternate exit on the northern side of the castle's motte. With little choice, I again slid along the pedestal to make way.

Holding tight to the wall, I edged my way along the rock face. Debris began to break away near an outcropping. I took a step back. Unwilling to take the risk, I slowly turned. As I struggled to reach the statue, my foot gave way.

My knee hit the soil hard. When I fell backward, I reached out for a rope that hung from one of the pulley carts above. To my relief, the latch on the pulley was locked, and the rope had not released. Satisfied that it would hold my weight, I slowly began to push myself from the wall with my feet. When I gained enough momentum, I leaned to the left. After several attempts, I was nearing the opposite side of the ridge. As I struggled to find a foothold, my hands began to burn.

I was about to give up, when I thought about the people. I had to do whatever I could to protect them from my father. With my last burst of energy, I managed to swing farther than the last time and was able to secure my fingers in one of the narrow fissures in the wall. From there, I pulled myself to the safety of the ridge.

Further down the path, I found a crevice wide enough to fit my body through. Relieved, I quickly made way.

The stone inside the crevice was uneven and tested my ankles. It was hard to see in what remained of the torchlight. When I slipped on the dampened rock face, I slowed and used my sense of touch to guide me.

When I came upon a cave, the hard rock gave way to earth. Mounds of dirt were piled in various locations, making it obvious why it had taken years to find the stone. If it was buried in one of the fissures, the creatures would have no choice but to take care, should they wish to avoid a cave in.

"Nahahhaha!"

The cackling startled me. It was the Crone, I was certain. Terrified, I ran in the opposite direction from where it had originated. My route did not seem to matter, I was lost and there was nothing to be done about it. When I reached a narrow cavity, I halted. There was no way out except a small hole in the lower base of its wall. I fell to my knees. Vine had weaved over the other side of the opening, making it hard to break through. I was about to give up when I saw a crack of light.

My eyes burned, struck by the piercing rays of descending sunlight. As I wiped the tears from my cheeks, I inhaled the fresh air.

Realizing the hour and that I would soon be expected for dinner, I searched the area to find I was no longer inside the boundaries of the castle. Green pasture extended as far as the eye could see to the west. When I looked up, I could see the wall walk, well out of reach from the rock face I had just squeezed through.

What was I to do? There was no way for me to gain access through the barbican. What if I chose not to return? I could seek Edric instead and tell him of what I had learned. No, that would only force my father into action. My only option was to go back to the castle. The only question was how?

With little time before I was sure to be noticed missing, I began to run along a path below the wall walk. As I tore through the thicket, the ground began to soften. Ahead I could see a stream filtering through an old arrow loop.

As I fought to keep my footing, I examined the area. Just below the water, I could see the end to the crossbars. The stench was foul and burned my nose. There must have been a sewer trench nearby.

One way or another I had to enter the stream, but what questions would I receive if I returned to the castle soaked in gutter water? Besides, the thought of immersing myself in raw sewage sickened me. I again looked to the city. No, I resolved. There was too much at stake.

Despite my reservations, I slowly entered the water. Stones and reeds made the path slippery. Thankfully, the weight of my dress kept me grounded.

Holding my breath, I swam under the crossbar. When I reached the other side, I could not help but gag. The trench was in front of me, draining from a conduit that extended from the castle. Desperate, I swam for cleaner water.

When I came up for air, I looked to the wall walk. Two men were standing by one of the towers. By their idle stance I knew I had gone unnoticed. Thankful, I pulled myself along the bank to a more sheltered part of the stream.

"Help!" I cried.

"Who goes there?" One of them put his hand to his brow.

"It is me, Arianna." I waved. "Help me! I have fallen in the water."

Rushing to my aid, they ran down a stair that accompanied the wall walk. "Your Highness," the other man said, holding back the sword that was secured to his waist belt as he knelt down. "Let us assist you."

I nodded and extended my hand.

He stood on a boulder and lifted me free of the water. "What happened, Your Highness?"

"I lost my footing on the creek bed." A shiver escaped my body. "Before I could recover, I fell in. Please," I begged, "do not tell my father. It will only embarrass him."

They looked at one another with uncertainty and then shrugged. "Come," the older of the two said, holding out his forearm. "We will see you back to the castle."

"Thank you," I replied with gratitude, knowing they could corroborate my story. "I would appreciate your escort."

When we entered the castle, the younger of the guards yelled out, "We need assistance here!"

"No," I cried out, turning sharply. "I can make my way from here!"

"What is this?" My father appeared from the dining hall. "Where have you been, child?"

"I—" I looked to the guards. "I was wandering in the western end of the courtyard by the stream. I guess I lost track of time and—"

"Leave us," my father commanded, dismissing the guards.

As they bowed in retreat, the general appeared. "Let me handle this," he said, stiffening his stance as though to prove his intent to my father.

"Very well. She is your problem now."

"So," the general said, raising his brow, "you were walking in the courtyard, you say."

"Yes," I replied as I attempted to straighten my dress. "When I tried to reach for a flower lily, I fell into the stream."

"Strange," he said, searching my eyes. "I looked for you in the courtyard earlier, but you were nowhere to be found."

"Oh." A knot formed in my stomach. "Perhaps we just missed one another." I paused. "Come to think of it, I thought I heard someone calling my name, but I excused it for the wind. I guess I did not wish to be disturbed. Forgive me. I did not know it was you."

Despite the suspicion in his eyes, he nodded. "I suggest you make your way to your quarters and change." His eyes ran the course of my body. "We will wait for you in the dining hall."

"Do not keep us waiting," my father said, glaring angrily. "I will not have my dinner spoiled on account of you."

I bowed obediently and ascended the stair.

When I arrived at my quarters, I found Edina pacing the room. "What happened to you?" she said, rushing over. "You are a mess!"

"I am in a hurry," I replied as I unbuttoned the sleeves on my gown.

She was about to question me, but I shook my head. "I have little time. I am expected at dinner.

"I understand," she replied.

"Is there any water in the tub?" I looked toward the bathing room.

"Yes," she said, holding out her hands, "but it is cold."

"I do not care." I tore off my dress.

After a quick wash, I made way to the dining hall.

When I entered the room, my father slammed his goblet to the table, "It is nice of you to finally join us."

I held back my anger as I moved to take my seat. "I apologize, Father." I nodded to my mother. "It was not my intention to keep you waiting."

When she ignored me, staring blankly at the table, the general stood to offer my chair. "It is good to see you have fully recovered from your unfortunate incident, Your Highness."

Evelyn appeared with the dining cart. "My King, I beg your forgiveness. The chicken has been kept warm, but the potatoes are—"

"Are you telling me my dinner is ruined," my father snapped.

"It will be fine," my mother interjected. "Please, allow us to eat."

My father took a measure of his wine. "Serve the food. My wife and child are hungry."

Evelyn nodded and gestured to the other servants.

To avoid conversation, I kept my head low and made no eye contact. It was obvious that the general and my father were growing suspicious. In addition, I found it difficult to be in their presence or even that of my mother. Their actions disgusted me.

How could my father put his own needs before those of the people? Moreover, how could my mother sit idly by allowing him to push forward with his agenda? The question begged if she was even aware? There was no doubt she had not been herself lately. Perhaps she was struggling with the guilt.

When she dropped her knife, I looked to her.

"Is there a problem?" my father asked, raising his brow in her direction.

"No." She tried to regain her composure. "Please excuse me."

"Very well." My father took another measure of his wine. "You are excused."

My mother nodded. "Thank you, My King." Without another word, she left the room.

"Women," my father huffed.

The general turned to face me. "Your Highness …" he began hesitantly.

I blotted my mouth. "I am done if you wish me to—"

"No," he interrupted awkwardly. "I understand you are aware of our coming nuptials."

"Yes." I tried to manage a smile.

He reached for his goblet. "I would like to make a toast to my coming bride." He stood and faced me. "Arianna, you make me the happiest of men. I am proud to know I will be spending the rest my life with a woman such as you."

"Here, here!" my father spoke in a dull tone.

Reluctantly, I took the general's hand. "Thank you." I met his stare. "I am pleased for our future as well."

"Arianna." My father frowned. "Is there something that troubles you?"

"No." I gave the general a fleeting look. It seemed my disapproval had not gone unnoticed. "I am happy."

I paused to mock a yawn. "It seems my mishap in the stream has left me somewhat exhausted."

"Perhaps you should retire," my father said, releasing a heavy breath. "You will need your rest for the coming days."

"You are right," I replied, placing my napkin on the table. "Will you please excuse me?"

My father nodded. "You are excused."

When the general assisted me from the chair, I bowed my head, "Good evening, sir." Before he could respond, I rushed through the door.

As I ascended the stair, I thought about my father. Although I had grown accustomed to his changing moods, he seemed more agitated than usual. Were his plans being hindered by the Hynd? By the words of that creature, it seemed they too had a stake in the stone. Perhaps the Men of Moya would know of their intentions. With that in mind, I made haste to my quarters.

† † †

At the setting of the sun, I had the guard summon Edina. As I waited for her, I knelt by the bed in search of my sai.

"Your Highness," Edina said, appearing at the door.

"Close the door," I said, returning to my feet with the sai in hand.

When the latch struck, she turned. "What are those? Do you carry weapons?"

"Yes," I replied. "These are my sai, the weapon I am skilled with. Tonight, I will not leave the castle unarmed. Things are far worse than I had expected."

She glanced over her shoulder. "Where were you today?"

"When I left my father this afternoon—"

"Has he learned of our—"

"No," I shook my head. "Allow me to speak."

She nodded. "Forgive me."

I began to strap the holsters to my shins. "I found my way into the defense rooms this afternoon."

"How?" Her eyes widened. "That area is always guarded."

"Not today." I looked down. "I know it was a great risk, but I was upset. With no one to hinder me, I made way."

"What did you find?" she said, her mouth falling open.

"A gigantic cavern below the surface." My eyes began to water. "Edric was right. My father is searching for the last of the stones."

"The Stones of Moya?" she uttered.

"Yes." I frowned. "Do you know of them?"

"My father ..." she began, closing her eyes in realization. "We always thought him foolish in his words."

I took her by the arms. "You must tell me what you know!"

She pulled away abruptly. "I know little. He would only speak of an orb, saying it fell from the sky. When its location was discovered, many took it as a bad omen. It had supposedly broken into three flawless sections upon landing."

"It came from the sky?"

"Yes." She sat on the bed. "When evildoers from the North united the pieces, the stones produced great powers. It gave them the ability to mount an army of Trolls."

"Trolls," I gasped, holding my breath. "Do these beings have fiery eyes?"

"I believe so." She nodded. "Why?"

"These Trolls …" I hesitated, frightened by my own words, "they work in the caverns as we speak."

"Are you certain?" She cringed. "What if they … things grow too dangerous? We must cease—"

"There is too much at stake!" I stammered. "We must finish this!"

"The people will not believe you," she cried. "I am finding it hard to comprehend myself."

"But now is the time!" I insisted. "I heard the general himself declare my father's armies weak."

"What if they find of your deceit?"

"It must be risked!" I met her stare for a moment before undressing, "If we do not act, my father most certainly will." I moved to the foot of the bed. "These men I meet tonight should have the answers I seek."

"Do you not hold any waver?"

"Of course I do." I pulled the servant gown over my head. "Let us make way to the turret." I took hold of the cloak.

Although hesitant, she followed my lead.

As I slid through the opening, Edina took my arm. "Be careful," she warned. "I expect to see you back here in the morn."

I nodded; disappearing into the darkness.

As before, I made my way through the gates with little trouble. When I was free from the prying eyes on the wall walk, I broke into a run. It was not in my interest to keep Edric waiting.

When I reached the fountain, I only found a few drunken men along its side. Engrossed in song, they did not take notice of my approach. Confused, I halted. Was I in the right place? I was about to turn when I saw the cloaked man. He was standing in an alleyway near the jewelers. Startled, my heart skipped a beat. Was he following me? By his demeanor it seemed unlikely. Still, his constant presence was becoming a concern.

"Be on your way!" Edric shouted, walking briskly from the inn. "You have disturbed my mother from her sleep!"

"My apologies, Edric," one of the men said, raising his glass. "Come, lads. It is best us are on yours way home," he mumbled drunkenly

I chuckled when one of them stumbled, nearly falling. His companions took him by the arms and led him from the fountain.

Edric turned. "I was beginning to think you had forgotten."

"No." I pulled the hood on my cloak close. "I had a bit of a—"

"Come," he interrupted as he led me to the edge of the fountain. He glanced over his shoulder to the opposite side of the square. "Make yourself comfortable while the men make sure you were not followed." He sat, and his voice had deepened when he spoke again, "We cannot proceed until they are certain."

I wanted to tell him of the cloaked man, but when I turned to find him, he was gone. Besides, by his reaction my last time at the inn, it seemed best not to. Instead, I began to clean my hands of the soot. Unsure of what to expect from the Men of Moya, I wanted to appear strong in my demeanor.

Seemingly invigorated by the night air, currents of water forced their way through the veins of the statue. Torrents fell to the basin, forming a swirl of mist that reminded me of the Falls of Dean.

As I dried my hands, a whistle echoed through the square. Eric stood in response to the signal. "Come. It is safe."

When I followed his stare, my stomach tightened. It was the cloaked man, but he was not where I had last seen him. He awaited us at a narrow passage near the inn. It took me a moment to realize what was happening.

"I ... he," I stammered, turning to point. "That man ... he is the one—"

"Arianna," Edric said, taking my arm impatiently. "We have little time. They will not wait on us."

I nodded, knowing the revelation was of little consequence, and followed his lead. At our approach, the cloaked man stood aside, allowing me to pass.

"We must be swift," he said. "The others have already made way for the den."

I felt his hand on my back. His touch gave me an odd sense of assurance, something I had forgotten in the past weeks.

"Where are you taking me?" I asked.

"Quiet. This is not the time," he said bluntly. "Turn left past the coal bins."

Not wishing to upset him, I silently took his direction.

We traveled through several abandoned corridors before arriving at the rear delivery port to the city bakery. The cloaked man tapped what was apparently a coded knock on the door. As we stood waiting, he remained silent.

Moments later, a man appeared. Without a word, we were ushered down a flight of stairs to the basement. The smell was sour yet sweet, the remnants of what had recently been baked upstairs. I loved the aroma. It reminded me of my home back in Hoverdire.

As we descended, I noticed several men at a table. They stood on our arrival.

"Is this the lady?" one questioned.

"Yes," Edric replied.

The room was plain. No windows graced the exterior walls. An open door at the back led to the supply room. Atop the flour sacks I could see bedrolls and rucksacks. When I turned to make way to the table, I froze. For a moment, I thought my eyes were deceiving me.

"Who … what are they?" I gasped.

"Has the girl never seen a Mider?" one of them chuckled.

Unsure what to say, I glanced over his body. He was half boar and half man, which gave him a domineering appearance despite his short stature. His long roan hair was tangled in thick chucks. A ring of gold pierced the flesh between his nostrils.

"What happened to your legs?" I uttered. "You … have too many!"

"Do not be jealous!" the creature replied as his hooves struck the paving stone. "It is not my fault you only have two."

"I am sorry." I shook my head in disbelief. "I was—"

"Do not fret, my dear." His dark features warmed within his sunken skin. "We will not harm you."

I looked to Edric for support. He smiled and turned to the cloaked man. "Are you not to reveal yourself?" he asked.

When the shadow left the man's face, I was stunned by his beauty. Long dark locks fell from his shoulders, and his emerald green eyes danced in the glow of the light.

Edric frowned at my reaction. "What is it?"

"Nothing." I took a step back in embarrassment.

"My name is Madigan," the man said, bowing his head. "I lead this group."

Before I could respond, he continued, "These men." His eyes scoured the room. "Represent the different regions of Aarrondirth and beyond." The men bowed their heads. "It is our sworn duty to watch over the last of the stones and to protect it at any cost."

Anger swelled in his eyes as he revealed a ruby ring, the same one he had worn on the night of the celebration. "Unlike you, I am the last survivor of King Alameed's descendants and the true heir to the throne of Aarrondirth."

I turned to Edric in shock. "Is he the one you spoke of?"

Edric nodded.

"Your father, in his greed, had my family murdered. We descended from Alameed's first and only cousin, Faris. Many of them were only children."

He released the buttons on his shirt and pulled it open. "His guardsmen, however, were clumsy in seeing the task through." At the sight of the scar running down his chest I winced. "To my good fortune, they did not check to see if I was still breathing before they left!"

"Save your blame!" Edric scowled. "You know as well as I that she was not part of her father's deeds!"

"Even so," Madigan replied, as he turned to face Edric. "She should know of the blood spilled by his command?"

Edric raised his hands in apprehension. "Forget I spoke."

Madigan released a heavy breath. "I apologize if I frightened you, but you must understand the depths of the situation."

The rest of the men stood idle as they observed the exchange.

I knew that I needed to respond, so I summoned my strength. "It is all right that you feel the way you do. I too am sickened by my father's deeds." I looked down. "If nothing more, you should take comfort that you will not have to live with the guilt."

I stiffened my stance. "That is why I stand here now. I do not intend to falter, only to succeed. My father's reign must come to an end!"

Madigan leaned on the back of a chair. "If so, what do *you* have to offer?"

"I have learned much today." I replied, crossing my arms. "Do you care to listen or shall we continue speaking of things beyond our control?"

"Enough!" The Mider who had first addressed me approached. "They call me Dregby. I speak for the underworld of the Miders." He forced a harsh smile, displaying the gold in his teeth. The practice must be a custom of theirs I assumed. "Welcome, child."

"Thank you." I glanced back to Madigan.

"Very well." Madigan gestured to his men.

After his men nodded in acknowledgment, I was directed to the main table.

"We should get started." He glanced to the stair and took a seat. "It seems the Elves have declined our invitation."

At Madigan's words, my heart raced. Did these men have dealings with the Elves?

"So, Arianna," Dregby began to circle the room in a slow gait, holding to the sheath that held his pickaxe in place, "what is it you have learned?"

I was about to respond when a knock came to the door.

"Perhaps I spoke too soon." Madigan motioned one of his men toward the door.

"Who is it?" I asked breathlessly. Could it be? Could the day have come? No, I shook the thought.

Moments later, footsteps rattled the stair. As the small accompaniment of men cleared the landing, I lost my breath. The last newcomer to appear was Darwynyen. It was as if time had stood still. He had not aged from the time I had last seen him. His dark autumn leaf locks fell gently from his hood as he pulled it to his shoulders. When his green eyes fell upon me, forgotten emotions swept through my body.

"Who is she?" he asked with a frown.

"Her name is Arianna," Madigan said, extending his hand. "She is the formerly exiled daughter of Velderon."

"Why is she here?" he snapped, throwing his cloak to a chair. "Have you all gone mad in our absence?"

The pain from our last encounter resurfaced. Why was he being so cold?

"Darwynyen!" The elder of the Elves glared, untying his cloak. When he turned, I took notice of the intricate braiding that gathered his long silver hair down his back.

"Forgive me," Darwynyen conceded, looking directly into my eyes.

I could feel the color rush to my face, and the room faded away as I came under his gaze. I felt powerless to move or speak while his attention was on me.

"If Madigan has welcomed you, then so shall I."

The elder Elf turned to face me, and the spell I had been under broke as Darwynyen's eyes released me. "My name is Morglafenn," he said, putting his hand to his chest. "We represent the Elvish regions of Tayri and Maglavine."

His gentle demeanor allowed me the courage to speak. "It is nice to make your acquaintance." I said with a halfhearted smile.

After my response, he focused on the others. "If we have been discovered by the daughter of Velderon, I am sure there is much to discuss."

"Yes," Madigan said, offering him a chair.

When the group all turned to me, I hesitated.

"Does she speak?" Darwynyen chuckled.

"Leave her be!" Edric snapped.

"Arianna," Madigan said, eyeing Darwynyen, "please, tell us what you know."

I nodded and did my best to compose myself before speaking. "After meeting with Edric yesterday, I was able to find my way into the defense area of the castle."

I was about to continue when I noticed Darwynyen's stare. His eyes had softened as though he saw a glimmer of the young girl he had rescued at the Falls of Dean. Trapped again in his gaze, I looked down.

"Darwynyen?" Madigan chuckled, "I know she holds beauty, but this is no time to fall in love."

"I …" He paused. "What are you asking?"

"It is not like you to swoon over those … She carries the blood of Men." He raised his brow. "Has the time come for you to stray from your kind, or have you just run out of women in Maglavine to choose from."

When the room broke out in laughter, Darwynyen recovered. "I am glad you are finding such humor in this, Madigan. Is Shallendria not giving you the love you desire?"

Again the men laughed.

"Leave her out of this!" Madigan snapped.

Despite the urge to learn more of their conversation, I was eager to share my findings and sat forward. "I found a staircase at the end of a corridor that led away from the castle's defense area." At my words, the men settled to listen. "It led to a vast cavern below the motte where I found Trolls." I shivered at the memory. "They were working feverishly in search of the stone."

"I knew it!" Madigan stood up abruptly.

Dregby looked at me. "By your words, I will assume they still seek its location."

"Yes," I sighed. "At least, from the time I last saw them."

Madigan slammed his fist on the table. "If only we had acted sooner!"

"How?" Darwynyen stood to reason with him. "We have not had the men to fight."

"Darwynyen is right." Dregby crossed his arms. "Furthermore, we were not certain of his actions until now. Our spies have never returned."

Morglafenn took my hand. "Did you see any prisoners?"

"No." I shook my head. "But they are there. I overheard—"

"They still live." He turned to Darwynyen and nodded.

Remembering the general's dialogue with the Troll, I stood. "Is it not apparent from my findings that their army is weak? Would that not be the reason why they have stayed hidden in their work?" I shrugged. "Maybe little time has been lost. Perhaps if we strike now, we can put a stop to this madness before the stone is found."

"She is right," Dregby said, putting his hand on his sheath. "We should prepare for an attack!"

Morglafenn responded with prudence, "Let us not act too rashly. It will take some time to get the necessary arrangements in place."

I intervened, wanting to take part in what was to be, "How will you gain access to the castle?"

"There is no need." Madigan glanced to the others. "We know of another entrance at the bottom of the west hill."

"You must allow me to assist you. I can lead the attack from within."

When the room went silent, I continued, "I hold skill with the sai. A skill my father is unaware of."

"You risk too much!" Darwynyen stammered.

Madigan countered, "Yes, but she knows the castle better than any of us. So, if she *is* skilled ..." He looked at me for confirmation. "Which I will take it that you are."

I nodded sternly.

"We should take advantage. Besides, she will not be expected to fight, only to lead us through to the caverns."

Darwynyen clenched his fists. "If she is to take part in this battle, it should be alongside me!"

Confused, I searched his eyes.

Morglafenn stood. "What has gotten into you, Darwynyen?"

"Nothing," he said, returning to his seat.

When the room settled, I spoke again, "There is something else." I bit my lip, unsure of their reaction. "There is a Crone." I gave Edric a fleeting look of acknowledgment. "She dwells in the castle, a companion of my father's, if you will."

"A Crone!" Dregby cringed. "Are you certain?"

"Yes." I tried to shake the echo of her laughter, again looking to Edric.

"She speaks the truth." Edric nodded. "My family has believed in her existence for years."

The men glanced at one another with apprehension.

"Let us not worry about the Crone until she shows herself." Madigan moved to a cabinet under the stair. "She is only one, and we are many. If we catch her by surprise, she will not have a chance to work her magic."

The men began to grumble. To distract them, he pulled out a map. "Let us focus on the battle. There is still much to be decided."

"Do you know of the Hynd?" I paused. "I heard the general—"

"The Hynd." Dregby chuckled. "Is a broken term for the Sorcerers of Morne."

"Oh." I blinked.

"Interesting," Morglafenn said, raising his brow. "So, your father has sought an allegiance with those whose hearts are stained with darkness."

"Forget the Hynd!" Madigan set the map on the table. "Our motivation only lies with the stone."

When the men nodded, Madigan looked at me with annoyance. "Is there anything else?"

"No." I shook my head, realizing that I had said too much already. Fear was a useless motivator. Madigan was right; we needed to focus on the coming battle alone.

After hours of deliberation, our plans were solid. We would attack in five days time, which would allow Madigan to get the men in order and to recruit anyone he could from the city. My role would be to see to the castle gates and to lead the battle from within. To avoid suspicion, I would not return until the eve of the third night when I would confirm what I had accomplished.

As I broke from thought, I noticed a spear of light from the supply room I had noticed on our arrival. "I should be on my way," I said, rising to my feet.

Madigan glanced over his shoulder. "I see morn is upon us."

"Arianna," Morglafenn said, taking on a look of warning. "You *must* take extra caution. The people of our times have forgotten the past. It will be hard to turn them without proof."

"There is no doubt my task will be difficult," I agreed. "Either way, I am glad we are soon to take action. Marrying the general would only—"

"The general!" Darwynyen's eyes widened. "Why? Never mind! Has he touched you?"

"Darwynyen!" Madigan reprimanded, glancing to Morglafenn. "Why do you ask such things?"

"No reason." He released a heavy breath.

"If there is nothing further, I will be on my way." I tried to see Darwynyen's eyes, but his gaze was focused on the table.

"Be safe, Arianna." Madigan nodded.

When I reached the landing, I heard footsteps from behind. With reluctance, I turned. To my disbelief, it was Darwynyen. At his approach, my legs began to waver. He took me by the hand.

"I do remember you." His words seemed to trouble him. "I know by my actions, you thought I had forgotten." His hold tightened. "But now, with all the uncertainty, I cannot let you leave without telling you how I have carried you with me over the years. From the day we met …"

"No one has stirred me as you," As we spoke the last words together, my eyes began to tear. He smiled at my reaction as his fingers ever so lightly touched my face.

"What goes on here?" Madigan appeared at the foot of the stair.

Darwynyen turned in haste. "We cannot let her go back to the castle. I will not allow it!"

Morglafenn approached and stopped next to Madigan. "Darwynyen, have you gone mad?"

"If you must know," Darwynyen responded, "she—"

"She is the one." Morglafenn finished the sentence as he slowly ascended the stair. "The one that has stirred you all these years."

"Yes," he replied. "Now that the truth has passed between us, I cannot abandon her to the perils of her father!"

Madigan joined Morglafenn on the stair. "What is happening here?"

"There is no time to discuss these matters," Morglafenn said, pointing to the breaking light on the door. "She must be on her way."

"No." Darwynyen shook his head.

"Darwynyen, you must release her," Morglafenn reaffirmed. "If we stir too soon, more will lie at risk!"

"He is right," I said, pulling up the hood on my cloak. "If I do not return, there is no telling what my father might do. Besides, I am of better use to you if I am inside the castle, where I can observe him and the general more closely!"

"Yes, but if he should find that you have deceived him, he will take harm to you." Darwynyen turned to the others. "That is a risk I am not willing to take!"

"Darwynyen," Madigan pleaded, "I feel for you, my friend. There is obviously much to be told of this story. Even so, there is little chance that danger should fall to her now."

"I will be fine," I whispered. A part of me wanted to take hold of him and never let go. "There is no such fate that would lead us to one another only to take it away so briskly." I pulled from his grasp. "Please, let me go. Dawn is drawing near."

"Very well." He raised the latch on the door. "Promise me, if your father suspects you of anything, you will return immediately, no matter what the cost!" He finished his words while looking at the men.

"I promise." I smiled, giving my attention to the men at the bottom of the stair. "I shall see you in three days' time."

When they nodded, I squeezed Darwynyen's hand one last time before taking my leave.

CHAPTER 4:

HEART SET ABLAZE

Darwynyen, although reluctant, returned to the table. "I believe we have made a mistake in letting her go."

"No." Morglafenn shook his head. "You are allowing emotion to cloud your judgment."

"I do not wish to speak of her again," Darwynyen responded. "Leave me to my thoughts."

"Come," Morglafenn said, ushering him into the supply room. "We should settle this now."

"If we must." Darwynyen stood to follow.

Morglafenn gestured to Madigan. "Excuse us."

Madigan reached for a bundle of maps. "Take your time."

As Morglafenn shut the door, he spoke, "My next words may take you aback."

"What?" Darwynyen frowned.

"Your mother," Morglafenn replied, "has already warned me of this day."

"I do not care to hear of my mother's words," Darwynyen snapped, half kicking one of the flour sacks. "Now that fate has brought Arianna and me together once again, I will fight my feelings no longer!"

Morglafenn smiled gently. "I am not asking you to fight your feelings, Darwynyen. If she is the one you desire, then so be it."

Darwynyen looked down. "She carries a great burden with her. I hope she is as strong as she appears."

"I feel she is," Madigan spoke from the door. "I admire her strength already."

"Madigan." Morglafenn turned. "We only asked for a moment."

"I apologize," Madigan replied as he edged his way into the room, "but I feel I have the right to know what is happening here."

Morglafenn spoke for Darwynyen. "He will reveal his emotions when he is ready. Now is not the time."

"Whatever." Madigan rolled his eyes. "If your conversation holds little importance, will you at least assist with the preparations?"

"Of course," Morglafenn sighed.

When Madigan turned, Morglafenn put his hand on Darwynyen's shoulder. "You must not lose hope. I feel certain you will see her again."

Darwynyen cleared his throat. "We will not speak of her again. From this moment forward, we will focus on the coming battle alone."

Morglafenn nodded and followed Darwynyen from the room.

CHAPTER 5:

WITHIN THE WALLS

I accomplished little over the beginning of the week. After the morn of my return, my mother and I were forbidden to leave the castle, a decree so ordered by my father, the king. In addition, the guards and soldiers seemed to all but vanish. I believed that my father must have summoned them to search for the stone, which led me to believe that they had grown close in finding its location.

The announcement of my nuptials had been delayed for another week, making it apparent that my mother and I were soon to be of little value. Still, one thing my father did not take into account was my determination, and though my resources were few, I had Edina.

"Gaining an alliance within the castle is proving to be difficult." Edina said, reaching for one of my pillows. "Most of the people in your employment are from the Northern regions. With no ties to Aarrondirth, they cannot be trusted."

"I know." I turned to face her on the bed. "But if we do not come up with something soon, I will have failed the Men of Moya."

"Do not worry." She fluffed the pillow before resting on it. "We will figure something out."

Then a thought occurred to me, and I leaped from the bed. "Of course! The answer has been in front of us all along."

"Arianna?" Edina puckered her brow.

"Evelyn!" I began to fix my dress. "She has been with the castle for years."

"Does that not prove her loyalty to your father?" She sat to face me.

"Not necessarily," I replied. "I once witnessed a conversation she shared with my mother when they spoke in common."

"That does not mean you can trust her," she huffed.

"Regardless, I see no other option." I moved to the door. "The hour is early. I will approach her now before dinner."

Before she could protest, I left the room. There was no one in the kitchen on my arrival. I was about to leave when I heard raised voices from the livestock paddocks out back. Curious, I made way to the open door.

"Is it your wish to see me beheaded?" Evelyn shouted, waving her hands in the air.

"No, House Master," the butcher replied, steadying the goats as they muscled around his feet. "You must know that venison is hard to come by in this region. Furthermore, livestock has been sparse since the market wars. These goats were all I could find!"

She released a heavy breath. "Then I guess there is nothing more we can do, now is there."

I giggled at her annoyance. Startled by my blunder, she turned. "Arianna … I mean, Your Highness, I am sorry for the fuss. I hope I did not disturb you."

"No." I smiled to ease her.

She turned back to the butcher. "Bring the goats to the east pen. We will sort this quandary out later."

With her stern direction, the butcher gathered the goats and made way.

"Evelyn." I glanced back through to the kitchen to make sure we were still alone. When there was no one to be found, I continued, "May I have a word?"

"Of course, Your Highness." Her eyes widened. "Have I done something that displeases you?"

I shook my head. "Is there somewhere more private?"

She took on a look of suspicion, "Why?"

I took a step back. "I was … I—"

"Speak, child." Her tone was blunt. "I assure you, there is no one in ears' hearing of these paddocks, for they could not stand the stench!"

"Very well." I nodded with a moment's hesitation. "I know you have been employed by my father for several years now." I looked at her with resolve. "I know you are not like the others; you do not come from afar."

"Yes, my lady," she spoke with caution. "Is there something you require?"

I took a deep breath before replying. I risked much in her confidence. "Do you hold any loyalty to my father?"

"Of course, my lady." Her eyes took on a look of fear. "Why do you ask such things?"

From the manner of her words, I did not believe her loyalty to be true. "My father, he has been involved in dishonorable deeds. I have found many things to prove this since my return."

"Your Highness," she said, taking me by the arms, "why are you telling me this?"

"I require your help," I replied. "There are men who wish to see my father's reign come to an end. If you are willing, it is my intention to help them."

"Your Highness." She carried a look of pride. "I knew you did not carry the same heart as your father." Her eyes brightened. "Tell me what it is you need."

Relieved, I took her hands in mine. "I knew I could count on you! I knew by the loyalty you have shown my mother."

She tensed. "Your mother is not well. I have seen it in her eyes."

"I know. "My father's anger has taken its toll." I changed the subject, knowing we had little time. "That is why we must put a stop to his wrath."

I again looked over my shoulder. "The men I speak of have planned a rebellion. It will take place three days from now. We must seek an alliance within the castle and seize the gates when the time comes."

"I know of what it is you speak." She paused. "I too have ties to this group."

Shocked, I stood in awe. "What are you saying, Evelyn?"

"My husband, Amstead, has assisted them for years." Her tone deepened, "He has warned me of the rebellion. In fear for my safety, he does not wish my involvement."

Disheartened by her words, I looked to the ground.

"My lady, do not take my words to heart." She squeezed my hand. "I have longed to assist in their work and intend to help you in any way I can!"

I looked at her with conviction. "Are you certain? I do not wish to cause trouble with your—"

"Nonsense!" she exclaimed. "Amstead may be my husband, but he is not my keeper!"

"Thank you." I smiled.

"I swear, Your Highness!" She bowed her head. "You will not find the milk sour again. In the meantime, I can offer you some moistened oat."

When I frowned, she moved to the side. "I see you have returned with the carrots, Brise."

I turned to find one of the cooks.

"Yes, House Master." he nodded. "I will chop and prepare them now."

"Make haste in your work!" She ushered me toward the cellar. "Once I have seen to the princess, I will assist you."

He turned and made his way to one of the tables, dropping the sack of vegetables on a wooden chopping board.

Confident by his mannerism that he carried no suspicion, I followed Evelyn into the cellar. The room was cold. I put my arms to my chest to keep warm. "We should end our words now," I pleaded. "I will return later."

"No," she countered. "We must use this opportunity while it is at hand."

I nodded and glanced over the room. The area was dark and musty, lit by a single oil lamp. Assortments of cheese and vegetables were strewn casually about the shelves. Buckets were stacked behind the door, and measuring cups were half buried in the grain that lay open to the air. Speckles of old grain lay stuck to the earth, evidence of frequent use.

She closed the door and reached for a scoop. "I will approach my cooks when you leave. They despise your father. He is always mocking their food." She handed me a bowl, "I also know one of the gatemen; Kalvern is his name. I keep company with his sister. Being he is from Aarrondirth, he has never been truly accepted by the others." When my bowl was full of oats, she returned the scoop. "Each will serve a purpose. Moreover, their trust is unquestionable."

"You speak as though you have kept these thoughts for a while." I searched her eyes.

"Perhaps," she agreed, reaching for a small pitcher of cream. "It was my intention to be prepared should my husband and his companions grow desperate."

A wry laugh escaped me. "You are full of surprises, Evelyn. What else did you have in mind?"

She looked to the ground. "I am afraid that is all I can offer at this time."

Regretting my question, I took her by the arm. "I apologize, Evelyn. I did not mean to dishearten you."

"You did nothing of the sort." She poured the cream over the oats. "Now come, before we draw suspicion."

I nodded as she reached to unhinge the latch. "I will ask you to meet me again tomorrow, before I am to return to the den.

From there, we can discuss your progress." I bit my lip. "I only wish I could do more."

"You will, my child. The people will need your reassurance when the time comes." She pushed open the door. "In the meantime, stay vigilant and be patient. Our motivation is deep. I am confident it will be enough to see us through."

"Thank you, Evelyn." I shivered in the warmth of the open air. "I will speak to you soon."

"And you, my dear." She moved to join Brise at the table. "Enjoy your oats, my lady."

I took a spoon from one of the canisters and left the room.

† † †

A day passed, and next one brought good news. After a brief meeting with Evelyn, I found that she had spoken to Kalvern, the guard at the barbican. Although he was wary, he had agreed to aid in the rebellion. Her cooks had also accepted the ploy. They would state that they needed to stay past their shifts to clean the cellar. When alerted, they would start a fire at the rear kitchen door to distract those on the parapet and towers. They would then dispose of the guard at the servants' entrance, allowing the Men of Moya to gain access.

Edina and I would ambush the men who were posted in the defense area. While we awaited the others, we would search the armory for extra weapons.

The plan seemed sufficient. I admired Evelyn's cleverness and looked forward to the coming eve when I would see the Men of Moya once again.

Glancing over my room, I felt helpless. If only I could do more. I wanted to find my way back into the caverns to check on my father's progress, but knowing I would never get past the guards, I decided to take a chance and explore his study instead. He took frequent visits to the room, and I wondered about his business there. With that in mind, I leapt from the bed.

The main areas of the castle were again abandoned. With no one to hinder me, I quickly walked through the main hall to the reception area where I found the stair leading to the eastern wing of the castle.

Halfway up the rise, I heard a presence from behind. It was him. I was certain. Unsure what to do, I quickened my pace. When I reached the foyer, I ran to an open door near the end of the east corridor.

Holding my breath, I watched as he emerged from the stair and unlocked the study. Only when he moved through the archway did I follow.

Peeking from the threshold, I saw him pull a book from the middle shelf on the northern wall. To my astonishment, it triggered a mechanism that released the shelving from the wall. When he disappeared through the opening, I entered the room with caution. A salty odor began to fill the air. Placing my sleeve to my mouth, I knelt to look through the small opening that remained.

Although my view was restricted, I could see my father gesture to another before taking a seat at a table to the back of the room that appeared to be her living quarters.

"It is good for you to have come." From the woman's shrill voice, I knew I had stumbled across the Crone. "There is much we need—"

"Have you spoken with the Hynd?"

"Yes," she cackled. "They are pleased to know we are close to finding the stone." She paused. "They too bear news."

"What is it?" he growled.

"They have captured the Siren who holds the key to the Dungeons of Naksteed, the lost realm where the fire-breathing dragons are imprisoned," she said intensely. "They make way as we speak. Once the beasts are free, they will work steadily in our favor, bringing down those who condemned them so many years ago."

"Brilliant!" My father laughed.

"They also brought words of warning." Her voice deepened. "Your daughter ... they feel she will soon deceive you!"

My father slammed his fist to the table. "Why must they always question my plans? Their little attack in the marsh nearly cost us all!" His voice began to break under the stress. "The Hynd know nothing of these lands. They put far more jeopardy in our hands than they will ever know!"

"Calm yourself, Velderon," the Crone hissed. "You must take heed in their words for I too have felt deceit in her."

"She knows nothing of what is to come." He held out his hands in exclamation. "I will not end her life until we have obtained the stone. If nothing else, she will prove worthy as a bargaining tool."

Bargaining tool!, I huffed once again at the thought.

The Crone put her hands on my father's. The sight of the warts and boils made me gag. "Regardless, you should watch over her more closely."

"Agreed," he said, rising from the chair. "I will return later."

When he moved toward the door, I froze for a moment before darting to hide behind the long drapery that hung from the bay window. If I were to be discovered, there was no doubt the outcome would be disastrous.

Hidden in its folds, I watched my father return the bookshelf to its rightful place and take his leave from the room. Seconds later, the lock struck the latch. I was trapped.

My predicament left me vulnerable, more so than that day at the Falls of Dean. This time, I would not be rescued by a handsome stranger, nor would the Guardians be searching for me.

Unsure what to do, I made way to the small window on the southern wall that opened to the courtyard. To my relief, I found that it was directly above the main balcony where I had addressed the city people. Unlatching the pane, I crawled onto the ledge. When the bookshelf rattled, my body stiffened. Thinking that I would rather fall to my death than face the Crone, I jumped.

I struck the stone hard. As I fought for breath, I looked to the upper parapets. No one was in sight. Relieved, I ran across the balcony to the royal gallery.

Pacing the room, I fought to settle my emotions. Despite the risk, what I had learned would prove valuable. I needed to focus on the positive. Not only had I overheard their plans, it was confirmed that I still held value to my father, giving me time and assurance to see the day through. The only thing left to worry about was my mother. Could I leave her to face the rebellion alone? No. She was not well enough. With that now weighing on my mind, I made way to her quarters.

I hesitated before entering her room, even though there was no one there to stop me. I had not seen her for days and wondered about her state. If I were to warn her of the rebellion, would her fear of my father overpower her will to survive? In desperate need of the answer regardless of the outcome, I pushed open the doors unannounced.

I found her alone, sitting on the bed. She appeared to be lost in a daze, staring down at the mattress. As not to startle her, I spoke quietly in my approach, "Mother, I have something I must speak to you about." I took notice of her soiled gown and unkempt hair.

"What is it, my child?" She asked, looking to the window.

"I have great news." I took her hand. "You will soon be free of my father."

"Yes, of course," she replied with a smile.

Confused, I searched her tired eyes. "Did you not hear me mother?"

"Why have you come?"

"Mother." I squeezed her hand. "We are going to get out of here."

"Why would we want to do that?" She frowned.

I shook my head in disbelief. "Because your husband, my father, has turned evil!" My chest tightened. "I have met men outside the castle on two occasions. They wish to see his reign come to an end. It is my intention to assist them."

She looked at me blankly. "What are you talking about, my dear? You have not met others outside the castle, nor is your father evil. He may have changed in his ways, I agree, but it is the hardships of ruling this land that has soured his mood, nothing more."

By her response, I immediately regretted my confidence. Fear sped through my body. I had no idea how troubled she truly was. In her weakened state there was no way to predict her actions. Hoping that she would forget our conversation altogether, I turned to a different subject. "How are you feeling mother?" I brushed the soiled wisps of hair from her face. "I have not seen you for days."

"Do not worry on me." She released my hand. "We should be speaking of nothing more than the arrangements for your coming wedding."

"Mother!" I stood before I could implicate myself further. "I think it best that I be on my way."

When she nodded, tears welled in my eyes. Had she finally snapped? There was no rationality in her words. Perhaps I should have checked in on her more often. Guilt stricken, I decided I would do whatever I could to save her.

"Mother," I said, taking a step back, "do not fear. You have my word that you will not endure this alone."

Unresponsive, she stared back into the mattress. My promise had gone unnoticed.

With nothing left to say, I left the room.

† † †

The hour was at last drawing near. Night was soon to be upon us. As I pulled the servant's attire from under my bed, I realized this would be the last time I left the castle under the garb of another. Freedom, it seemed, was soon to be upon me.

My heart quickened at the thought of Darwynyen. Was it possible our destinies were now to be shared? It seemed trivial that we would find each other under such uncertain circumstances and not in the ways that I had dreamed. Even so, I knew I did not want to be without him.

Lost in my thoughts, I jumped when the doors crashed open. The general's men entered with a look of vengeance. Overcome with terror, I ran toward the balcony, but I was quickly overcome. Two of the guards grabbed me by the arms and threw me to the floor.

"What do you want?" I screamed. But they did not respond.

"It seems you have been up to no good, Your Highness." The general snickered in his approach, like a predator stalking his prey. "Your time has come." He halted and turned to the guards. "Bring her. The king awaits!"

One of them pulled me by the hair until I stood. "General," I cried. "Why are you doing this?"

"You will know soon enough!" He replied as he gestured to the men.

As they dragged me across the room, I looked at my bed, appalled by my weakness. Why had I chosen not to take action, to defend myself with my sai? I buried the thought; this was no time to hold regret.

I was led through the corridors to an unkempt part of the castle in the southwest wing. The men were brutal, wrenching my arms when I struggled to break free. "Where are you taking me?" I winced.

"To a place where no one will find you," a guard chuckled.

At the end of a narrow hall, we ascended a stair to one of the towers.

Halfway up the rise, I was shoved into a room. My father stood waiting. "Bind her to a chair."

As the men secured my bonds, he knelt to meet my stare. "So, you have taken the path of deceit I see." His eyes narrowed.

"What have you learned, my dear, that has brought you to this treachery?"

At his manner, I found it hard to speak, "I do not—" I began and then looked down.

"I am waiting, child." He took hold of my chin. "I know you have left the castle, and I intend to find out why." His eyes lightened. "Make it easy on yourself, and you will not have to suffer."

My heart sunk at the thought of my mother. She must have gone to him after our discussion. I should have never trusted her.

Before he could continue, she appeared at the door. Bound in rope, she fell when the guards released her. As she muttered to herself, my father snatched her by the hair. "You should not put your trust in those who have lost their minds!"

"Mother," I cried, "how could you?"

"You should end their lives now," the general said as he entered the room. "We no longer have use for them."

"No!" my father shouted. "My daughter *knows* something!" His brow rose. "If she has been meeting with people outside the castle, we must find out about their intentions!"

"If it is your wish." The general bowed. "Then so be it."

"I know the words will not come easy for you, my child." His hands caressed his beard. "I will give you some time to think on things." He motioned to the guards. "Lead her to the top of the tower for the night. When the cold has bore through her, she will be more yielding to my demands. If not, she will watch her mother die!"

The general moved to interject, but my father turned to him with rage, "Do not question my actions! You do not bear the knowledge to comprehend my will."

"My King, I must—"

Before he could continue, my father slapped him across the face. "Get back to the caverns. See that the work is hastened. Our time in Aarrondirth is coming to an end!"

The general put his hand to his face. When he turned to leave, my father looked to the guards. "*Well?* What are you waiting for?" he shouted angrily.

At his words, the men cut the restraints. "Up to the tower, Your Highness!"

As one fought with the tower's trapdoor, I pleaded with the other who was restraining me, "Please, I beg you. You must release me!"

"Why would we do that?" the man sneered.

The latch released. When the other guard pushed open the door, a chill swept down the corridor. "Shove her through," he snapped, bracing the weight. "We do not have all night!"

As I was forced into the open air atop the tower, I cried, "Please, do not do this!"

Without a response, they dropped the door. The striking of the latch followed shortly after.

I sat idle, stunned by what had just happened.

What was I to do? I had no choice but to keep silent when it came to the Men of Moya. Even so, could I live with the guilt of my mother's demise? Despite everything, she was innocent. It was my doings that had brought us to this.

At the thought of the men, I stood to look over the city. In vain, I began to wave my arms in hopes that one of them would see me, but realizing I would only put them in danger, I dropped them. I would rather die than see my father interfere with our plan.

As I knelt to shelter myself from the wind, I could only hope that Darwynyen and Madigan would not concern themselves with my absence and continue with their plans. Not only would their success bring down my father, it would bring Darwynyen to me. To keep my heart from breaking, I could do nothing but believe I would see his face again. Perhaps, if I could stall my father for time, I would live to see the battle through. The only question, was how?

CHAPTER 6:

EVELYN

It was late into the night when Darwynyen and Madigan approached the barbican, concealed in their cloaked attire.

"Where could she be?" Darwynyen spoke softly despite his mounting frustration. "Something terrible has happened. I can feel it. I can feel her!"

"Try not to worry, my friend." Madigan scanned the wall walk. "She is strong. She will find a way to carry on."

"Yes, but for how long?" Darwynyen countered, stepping into the torchlight.

Madigan grabbed him by the arm and pulled him back into the shadows. "As long as she has to!"

Darwynyen broke from his hold. "We should attack now! Most of the men are in place."

"No," Madigan shook his head. "We will attack the day after tomorrow, as planned."

"You are right," Darwynyen replied, his voice filled with doubt. "There is too much at stake."

"We should leave." Madigan turned. "It is not safe here."

Darwynyen looked over the castle one last time before conceding.

As they made their way through the abandoned streets, two figures appeared from the darkness. Darwynyen moved to slip into an alleyway but Madigan had halted.

"Wait," Madigan whispered. "It is Amstead and his wife, Evelyn." As the couple approached, anger crept into his voice, "Why are you here?"

"They have seized Arianna," Evelyn cried. "They hold her in the southwest tower!"

"Have you seen her?" Darwynyen tensed. "Is she all right?"

"She lives," Evelyn replied, taking hold of her husband's arm.

Darwynyen turned to Madigan. "We must do something!"

"No," Madigan insisted. "Arianna is smart. She will find a way to survive."

Before Darwynyen could respond, the group saw men approaching from the distance.

"Be on your way!" Madigan demanded.

Amstead nodded, pulling Evelyn with him into a neighboring alleyway. Madigan and Darwynyen watched the men a moment longer before following after.

CHAPTER 7:

THE PLOY

The colors of dawn had split the skyline when I awoke. I was ever so cold, as my father had promised. As I awaited the guards' return, I began to fear what I believed to be inevitable. Would my father stay true to his word and kill my mother, or would he seek another means to extract information? Either way, there was too much at stake to save her, no matter how much the thought of her death pained me.

When the hinges on the trapdoor rattled, I stood.

"Do not fight," the guard warned, bracing the weight of the door.

"Please." I knelt at the opening. "You must let me in."

The guard emerged and took me by the arm. "Come. Your father waits."

Before I could respond, he led me unsteadily down the stair.

When we entered the tower's room, I found my mother tied to a chair. She was again muttering to herself. My father stood to her side, looking smug. "Are you ready to speak, my daughter?"

"Release her!" I demanded. "She is not well."

He chuckled as the men secured my hands around the back of my chair with rope. "Did you enjoy your new quarters?"

To deny him in his taunting, I kept silent.

"Speak!" he shouted.

I stiffened my shoulders in an attempt to deceive him. "I will tell you what you want to know, but you must first assure me that you will release both me and my mother."

"You are not the one making the demands here. In any case." He shrugged. "I see no harm ... if your words prove worthy."

His demeanor sickened me. "I do not believe you. You will not keep your bargain, regardless of whether or not you find the stone." I glared. "That is what you seek, is it not?"

"So you know of the stones," he huffed wryly. "What else do you know about my toils?"

"I no longer believe you are who you claim to be," I scoffed.

"Why is that?" He crossed his arms.

"I have been warned by the people of this city." I shifted in my bonds. "It has been said that you have taken this throne under a veil of lies. That you are nothing more than an impostor!"

"How can you be certain?" he questioned. "Perhaps the Men of Moya have poisoned your mind."

"Do you refute their accusations?"

"Thank you for proving my suspicions," he smirked. "I knew it was them of whom you spoke."

Shaken by my blunder, I blinked. "Does it matter? They will see you to your end, one way or another."

"Believe what you will." He pulled a medallion from his chest. "But I am who I claim. I was the rightful heir to this throne long before I had taken it. You see?" He dangled the medallion in front of me. Upon it was the seal of the Alameed family: a sword in the center of two dragons. "This seal bears the truth of my heritage."

His eyes darkened. "When I discovered my past, I was consumed with hatred and tormented by my father's lack of courage when it came to seeing through to my rescue. His lack of action condemned me to a life of slavery!"

I was about to interrupt when a knock came to the door. A guardsman entered. "We found these weapons under her bed, sire."

His eyes examined them. "Are those sai?"

"Yes, my lord."

"Interesting." He knelt to take hold of my hands. "Are you trained in weaponry?"

"Yes." I recoiled, unable to bear his touch.

"Perhaps we should test your skill." He chuckled. "Feed you to the Trolls?"

Unsure how to respond, I kept silent as he moved to the window. "Take the sai to my study. My daughter will no longer be in need of them."

When the guard nodded, my father turned. "Be gone!" he shouted. "Do not trouble me further! If another knock comes to that door, it is you who will bear the brunt of my anger!"

Terrified, the man bowed and took his leave.

"So," I began hesitantly. Shaken by his rage, I risked much in leading our previous conversation forward, even though I had few other options. "You blame your past on another, even though you were never to know the reason."

"There were no reasons." He circled my chair. "My father's weakness was unforgivable." His fingers caressed his beard. "In my bitterness, I sought revenge. To my delight, my brother was no more of a man, carrying the same weak disposition as my father. Poisoning him came easy. With no one to stand in my way—"

"You set out to murder your own family." I closed my eyes, unable to stomach the thought. "Despite their innocence?"

"How do you know of this?" he growled.

"Does it matter?" I met his stare. "As I said, the people of this city are on to you. Your reign will soon be at an end!"

He laughed. "You know so little of what is happening. Believe me when I tell you that this is only the beginning!"

Another knock came to the door.

"What is it!" my father yelled.

When the guardsman entered, my father pulled a knife from his belt and flung it into the wall near his head.

Fear stricken, the guard bowed. "I am sorry, my lord, but we have word that the Elvish prisoners are about to speak." He took a step back and extended his hand in courtesy. "The general thought you would like to be present."

"Of course." My father clasped his hands. "I would desire nothing more." Then he turned to face me. "Do not get too comfortable, my dear. We will finish this later."

Before I could respond, he followed the guard from the room.

"Mother." I shifted my chair to face her. "Can you hear me?"

She did not respond.

Desperate, I tried to free myself. The rope was tight, and the fibers pulled at my skin. If I could only see how the knot was tied, I might be able to undo it. I released the tension and tried to stand. If I moved carefully, I might be able to slide my arms up the back of the chair.

As I slid my body upward, I lost my balance and fell to the floor.

"What are you doing, child?"

The strength in my mother's voice startled me. "Mother." I fought against the restraints to face her. "I am trying to get us out of here!"

"What can I do?" She shifted in her chair with resolve.

"Nothing!" I gasped. "If you were found assisting me, father would—" I broke off my words. There was no need to further frighten her in her state. I was pleased enough to know that she could comprehend the situation.

"Good you are, child." Then her eyes went blank. Before I could respond, she had fallen back into a daze.

Dismissing any hope of my mother's assistance, I tried to straighten my chair. After several failed attempts, I heard the latch release on the door.

"Child!" My father ran over and took me by the hair. "You are wearing my patience thin!"

I began to cry. "Please, Father. I am sorry. I was only trying to look after my mother!"

"Save your lies!" he shouted, reaching down to erect my chair.

When I was righted, he returned to the window. "Do you have something to share, or should I end your life now?"

Despite his threats, I had no choice but to continue to push him. "I would first like to finish our last conversation." I did my best to appear to pout, hoping to get him to talk by encouraging his ego. "Will you not share a few more of your truths?"

"Clever you are, trying to stall for time." He turned with a smirk. "Do not worry, there is much left in the day to find your friends." Then his body softened in a curious manner. "What is it you want to know?"

"I wish to continue where you left off," I replied. "When you saw to the death of your family."

"Very well." His words came undaunted. "When I had gained control of Aarrondirth, I grew bored. My passions led me to magic—white at first. And though I learned swiftly and was good in the trade, I wanted more. It was then that a Crone approached me, making promises no man could resist. After delving deep into the dark magic, there was no turning back. To ensure my survival, I could not have my wife or child betray my secrets. I had to be rid of you. The laws of this land are clear when it comes to the teachings in magic."

He moved from the window. "It is to your good fortune that I lacked the spine that I hold now. It was an impossible task, bringing death to my near family as I had done to the others. Instead, I had you exiled."

He rubbed his hands together. "Free to do as I pleased, I sought the acceptance of a ring of Sorcerers in Morne, who in turn revealed to me the myths of the stones. From there, a bond of trust prevailed. Thereafter, we collaborated on the means to seek the last of the stones that, until recently, had lain safely hidden in our lands."

He paused. "Believe me, this was no easy chore. Whoever made those riddles did well in their work. I lost many of my men and *years* to this task."

I felt his hand on my shoulder. "That is where you come in, my child. You see, I had hoped to never see you again, but as the people grew wary, I had no choice but to create a diversion."

He again paused. "I think you have learned enough!"

Desperate, I decided to risk angering him. "From what I overheard, the Sorcerers, or shall I say, the Hynd, do not trust you! They feel you are weak." My stare on him intensified. "So much so, that they took to attack us in the marsh!"

At those words, he extracted the blade from the wall. "You hold the key to my next actions," he warned, grabbing my mother by the neck.

"All right!" I screamed. "But first, let her go!"

"Why do you keep them alive?" the general asked, appearing at the door. "We no longer have use of them."

"Stop your moaning and listen," he spoke smugly. "This should be interesting."

The general crossed his arms. "If you insist."

"Speak, child!"

My only hope was for my plan to work, so I had to continue in my attempt to stall him. "They stay in a basement on Putnam Street." I picked a place on the opposite side of the city where we had stopped once to fix a wheel on the coach, a place I well recognized. "It is where the man who tends to your horses lives. Buckley is his name."

I paused. "I cannot remember the exact way. I was only there once."

"You tell lies." His eyes darkened. "You told your mother you were in the city twice!"

"You are right." I nodded in apprehension. "My first meeting took place in a tavern."

"What are the men's names?" he demanded.

"I do not know." I looked down. "They held little trust and would not reveal their identities to me." Then I returned his stare. "I could, however, recognize them … if I were to see them once again."

"A wise choice you have made." He turned to the general. "Get your men together. Make way to their den."

"She is telling you lies!" The general shook his head in disbelief. "If she is working with the Men of Moya, she would never turn them in!"

My father grinned. "You obviously do not understand the bonds a mother and daughter share. Besides, if she is lying, she will watch her mother die in front of her upon your return." He continued before the general could respond, "Do not question me, as I have warned you. Go now before I anger further!"

"I will return shortly," the general replied irritably, stomping from the room.

My father turned. "You better hope we find what we are looking for or this time with your mother will be your last!"

In fear of his threats, I kept silent as I watched him leave.

When the door struck the latch, I turned to my mother, hoping that she had emerged from her daze. Maybe with her help we could find a way out of here. "Mother, can you hear me?"

She lifted her head in acknowledgment. Her eyes were red from crying. It saddened me to look on her for what could be one of the last times. I could not bear the thought. It tore me to pieces. I began to cry as she spoke, "I know I have wronged you, my child. I have no excuse. You have done all you can for me."

Tears streamed down my face. "Why, Mother?"

She coughed, struggling to continue. "I am proud of you, my dear. Your courage overwhelms me."

I looked to the ground. Her words had come too late. "If only you had stayed quiet," I uttered.

"My sweet girl," she gasped, "your father was there yesterday. He followed you up the corridor, keeping outside the door when we spoke." She began to choke on her words. "I do not blame you. You were only doing what I should have done weeks ago, if only I did not lack the strength you so heartily possess."

Stunned, I felt the overwhelming pain of guilt. "Oh, Mother, I am so sorry. I—"

Before I could finish my apology, she had lapsed back into one of her dazes. "Mother?" I pleaded. "Do not—"

My words gave way, knowing there was nothing more I could do but wait for the end of our imprisonment with dread.

† † †

The door burst open. My father rushed in with a rage in his eyes that I had never seen before.

"So." I felt his hands grasp my throat from behind. "You have chosen to deceive me yet again!"

He paused. "You realize you have left me with no other choice."

"I see you have come to your senses," the general said as he entered the room.

My father regained his composure. "Get it over with."

I tensed as the general took a knife from his boot. "With pleasure, my lord." He grabbed my mother by the hair and pulled her head back, exposing her neck.

"No!" I cried.

My father took me by the hair. "Tell us where the Men of Moya are!"

"Never!" I shouted.

The general put the knife to my mother's neck with anticipation.

My mother opened her eyes. "I love you, my daughter."

"Speak, child!" my father screamed.

My body went numb, dreading what would be the outcome of my response. "You know I cannot do that, Father."

He turned to the general and nodded.

I cried out in horror as the blade swept swiftly across her neck. She made no sound as death claimed her. Seconds later, her body went limp. It was over. She was to breathe no more. In agony, I watched the blood as it trickled to the floor around her.

My father knelt down to me. "It did not have to be this way. You brought this upon yourself."

When I did not respond, he stood and addressed the general. "Untie her. Leave her dead body on the floor." His eyes circled the room. "Let my daughter mull over what she has done. Hopefully the next hours will give her some clarity, for I would hate to see anyone else die so needlessly."

He moved to the door, "In the meantime, grab her lady in waiting. Detain her until this eve."

"No!" I cried. "She is innocent!"

"In saying that," he warned, "I will give you the chance to make the right decision."

"Your Eminence!" A Troll rushed through the door. Ripe with anticipation, its fiery red eyes burned bright.

At the sight of him, my father broke into a rant, "I thought I told you to never leave the caverns!"

"But we found it, Your Grace!" It wiped the froth from its mouth.

My father staggered, as though weakened by its words. "You found it?" he uttered.

"Yes, Your Eminence," the creature cackled. "My minions dig it out as we speak!"

With a look of greed, my father rushed through the doorway. The general turned before following. "Do not worry; we have not forgotten about you!" Before I could respond, he sped down the stair.

Realizing the magnitude of their discovery, I looked at my mother, whose body grew cold on the floor. My silence had proven futile. Her loss was without purpose. My father had found what he was looking for. In misery, I cried inconsolably. With the stone in their grasp, I wondered if they would return to finish their work as the general had promised, or would they make way to Cessdorn unhindered?

The question seemed pointless. All I could think of was my mother. A part of me wished I were in her place.

CHAPTER 8:

TO BATTLE

Madigan had observed Velderon's discreet and ongoing searches throughout the city and smiled when he thought of Arianna. "She is most clever in stalling her father." He chuckled.

"What are you going to do?" Darwynyen halted from his pacing. "Will you not even send out scouts?"

"I have done so already." Madigan stood up from the table. "I will ask you to sit, my friend."

"I cannot." Darwynyen shook his head. "There is too much at stake."

Madigan ushered him into the other room. "You are sparking doubt in the others. The men see worry on your face and grow anxious."

Darwynyen turned to him in anger. "I will not calm! Every minute that passes leaves her life to more risk!"

Madigan countered, "You must keep faith that she will survive!"

Darwynyen calmed at his words. "I cannot help but feel that something terrible has happened."

"But you still feel her." Madigan put his hand on Darwynyen's arm. "Hold to that!"

"I have only just found her," Darwynyen pleaded. "I could not live with the guilt if she—"

"Darwynyen," Madigan urged, "Please, tell me of the story you share."

"There is not much to tell." Darwynyen looked away. "I met her briefly in another life. She was not who she is today. I rescued her from an injury I had caused. From that day forward, I have thought of little else but her."

Madigan smiled. "That is called love, my friend. When you make its true acquaintance, it never releases you. It binds you for all eternity."

Darwynyen blinked. "My true emotions have yet to reveal themselves. Even so, my yearnings are too strong to deny. My very soul demands that I see her again."

"And you will, my friend," Madigan sighed.

"Madigan!" a man shouted. "We have visitors."

"Is there news?" Madigan darted from the room to find Evelyn and Amstead at the foot of the stair.

"Yes." Evelyn nodded. "I know it was dangerous to come." She looked at her husband.

"What is it?" Darwynyen asked from the doorway.

"Arianna." She paused. "I was dismissed from my duties this afternoon. I fear Velderon has found the stone. If they have … Arianna will no longer be of use to them."

"My wife," Amstead interjected, "has seen to Kalvern at the gates. If it is your will, we can attack tonight." He looked down. "I would hate to see anything happen to—"

"Madigan." Darwynyen took him by the arm. "We must move forward with this battle!"

"No," Madigan spoke with resistance, "we must keep to our plan."

"The time is now." Evelyn stepped forward. "Not only do we have Kalvern, but my cooks were ordered to stay on to prepare food for Velderon's travels. They will set a fire tonight, distracting the guards."

She looked away with apprehension. "I may have overstepped my bounds, *but they are expecting you.*"

Although reluctant, Madigan conceded, "See to the men."

Darwynyen looked to his Elvish companions. "Let us gather our kin. Make way to the gate!"

As the men quietly armed, Madigan pulled Darwynyen aside. "When you have secured Arianna's safety, make way to the caverns. You will be needed there."

Darwynyen nodded. "Of course."

Madigan turned to the others. "Are we ready then?" He sheathed his sword. "Dregby is assembling his forces to the west of the city. We will have no time to alert them. If we should falter, they will have no choice but to lead a second attack tomorrow."

When Madigan saw worry on their faces, he continued, "Aim steady. Fight hard. Trolls are weak in battle. Success will be ours. I will meet you at the end to celebrate our victory!"

With his words, the men's confidence was restored. At ease, they talked amongst themselves.

Madigan looked to Darwynyen one last time before ascending the stair. "In the caverns, my friend."

Darwynyen nodded sternly. "Come." He motioned to his men. "The barbican is ours for the taking!"

† † †

With discretion, Madigan led his men over the lower bank of the western hill, the hill that connected to the motte of the castle. Below, where the cavern opened, trolls worked steadily in preparation for their departure.

"Evelyn was right. They must have found the stone." He reached for his dagger. "At no cost are we to see them flee. Fight like you have never fought before!" When the men nodded, he signaled to those near him and made way into the darkness.

With shadow in their favor, the frontline troops assembled upon a ridge above the opening. Before they could be discovered,

Madigan pounced from the crest of the shaft, and his men followed. They took the Trolls by surprise and skillfully cut their throats without incident.

When the trolls had been dispatched, Madigan gestured to his men while alerting the others with a short burst of whistles. As they advanced, he proceeded into the cavern. "Do not follow until you are signaled."

Madigan crept close to the walls to stay hidden, and he soon had a good view of the Trolls' activities. Frantic in their preparations, they filled wagons with supplies in a cavity beyond the threshold. As he moved to report back to his men, one of the Trolls approached. Not yet ready to attack, Madigan hid within a crevice as the Troll neared. As the creature made its passing, Madigan grabbed him from behind and pierced the back of its throat with a dagger. His actions did not to go unnoticed.

"We are under attack!" a Troll shouted. It ran straight toward Madigan, covering the ground with surprising speed.

Madigan swung his dagger, hitting the creature in the eye. "Good of you to notice," he grumbled. "Make way!" he called to his men. "Men of Moya, to battle!"

† † †

When Darwynyen reached the gatehouse, the streets held a serenity of calm. Unaware of the coming siege, the men on the wall walk sat idle. Darwynyen signaled to the other Elves. As they crept through the shadows, he pulled up the hood on his cloak.

"Who goes there?" a guard yelled from the wall walk. "Hold! Do not—" The man fell to the ground, pierced by a dagger. One of the men had come up behind him as Darwynyen had acted as a distraction.

Darwynyen whistled to his archers. Darting from the cover of darkness, they released their arrows with haste. Unprepared, the men on the wall walk fell quickly.

"Come! It is I, Kalvern," a man shouted. "The gateway is open."

Darwynyen led his men through to the castle. "Thank you." He bowed his head. "We could not have done this without you."

Kalvern glanced over his shoulder. "No worries, the rest will be left up to you."

Darwynyen nodded in understanding before following after his men. As they approached the main stable, they saw two men dressed in kitchen attire. They waved their arms in panic as Darwynyen drew near. "The guards are in the kitchen," one cried. "We set a fire to distract them."

"Go," the other shouted. "You must hurry!"

Darwynyen pulled two daggers from his waist belt and made way to the servants' entrance. As he walked the corridor, he could hear the guards shouting from a room to the right. Using the distraction to his advantage, he stood in the doorway. "Is there something I can help you with?"

The guards' faces held a look of shock when they realized their predicament. Darwynyen's companions crouched in the doorway and fired their arrows with precision. Darwynyen hurled his knife, piercing one in the face. The man fell quickly. Those who remained surrendered. To secure them, Darwynyen had his men lock them in the inner cellar. The group then headed to the interior of the castle.

The foyer was empty when they arrived. "Follow this path." Darwynyen extended his hand. "It should lead to the defense area." He looked to the upper mezzanine. "I will meet you there shortly!"

The Elves nodded and followed his direction while Darwynyen took to the stairs. In his ascent, he came across a servant woman. "Tell me the way to the southwest tower," he demanded.

"Do not hurt me!" the woman begged.

Annoyed, he grabbed her by the arm. "How do I get to the southwest tower?"

"Take the corridor to the west of the ballroom. Halfway to its end, turn right. You will find the stair there."

Without a response, he released her and made way for the tower.

CHAPTER 9:

RAGE

Distraught and somewhat numb, I took little notice when my father and the general made their return.

"Are you proud of yourself?" my father sneered. "You have forced my hand for nothing. Your mother's needless death is by no fault but your own." He circled her corpse. "Nonetheless, our task here is complete. We have found the stone and are making the preparations for our departure as we speak."

"I despise you!" I growled.

There was a look of satisfaction on his face as he responded, "Well, my dear, it is time we moved on. I just wanted you to know that you have failed in whatever it was you set out to do." He gave the general a fleeting look. "Do what you will with her."

"It has begun!" A guard appeared at the door. "We must flee!"

"You silly fool!" my father shouted in impatience. "I told you not to disturb me!"

"The castle has been breached!" the man wailed. "The caverns are overrun!" Not waiting for a response, he disappeared down the stair.

Undaunted, my father rolled his eyes. "I will leave you to deal with my daughter." He moved through the threshold. "Make haste in your retreat. I will see you before long. You know the place."

When my father disappeared, the general turned to me with a malicious grin. "Time is at an end for you, my love." He pulled out his knife. "Still, I would hate for you to leave this world never knowing a man's touch."

"No," I uttered, realizing his intentions.

"But you deserve nothing less." He cut the restraints that bound me to the chair.

"Please," I begged. "No!"

Ignoring my pleas, he picked me up and placed me on a table near the window. I resisted when he leaned into me. "Please, I beg you!"

"Quit fighting and relax!" He began to pull the buttons on my dress. "You will be taken, one way or another."

Overpowered by his strength, I loosened my body. I would need to find another way out of this.

In a rough manner, he began to kiss my neck. My body tightened when his coarse hands fell to my legs. When I looked up, I saw a lantern on the table and within reach. I grabbed it and hit him on the side of the head.

Dazed by the blow, he fell back for a moment. It was not to stop him. Intent returned to his eyes. "Is it going to be that way then?"

I nodded, holding to my strength.

"You wench!" He pulled me from the table and put his knife to my throat.

I was about to give in completely when I heard a voice in the corridor. "Arianna, where are you?" It was Darwynyen.

"I am here!" I cried.

The general dug his blade into my skin. "Quiet or it will end for you now!"

At the sound of approaching footsteps, he turned me to face the door, using me as a makeshift shield.

Darwynyen appeared with his bow aimed in readiness. "Let her go!"

"And who by the gods are you?" the general sneered.

"You are dead no matter what you do," Darwynyen scanned the room, "Remove yourself from the girl!"

"I think not." The general stiffened his stance. "It is I who has the upper hand here. Should your arrow meet its mark, I can assure you I will take her with me."

"Is it that I frighten you that you hide?" Darwynyen taunted. "How about I place down my bow? That way you may die as a man, rather than a coward."

When I met his stare, he nodded. "Arianna, I swear, this will be over soon."

The general loosened his hold. "You know one another?" He regained his poise. "Very well, if you wish to die before her, then so be it."

Darwynyen slowly put his bow to the ground. "You are running out of time."

"You do not frighten me, Elf!" The general pushed me aside.

As they moved toward one another, I crawled to a corner. Darwynyen pulled a dagger when the General held forward his blade.

"Fight me," the general said, thrusting the weapon erratically.

Darwynyen out maneuvered him with ease. "What is this?" He threw a chair to the side. "I was told you were one of the best."

Enraged, the general kept swinging. "Fight me!" After countless attempts, his strength began to waver.

Taking advantage, Darwynyen swung his knife and sliced through the healing scar on the general's cheek.

Stunned, the general he took a step back. "You had better do better than that!" He wiped the blood from the wound on his sleeve.

Darwynyen nodded. "I intend to."

At those words, the general darted forward. Darwynyen grabbed him by the wrist when he overextended himself and pulled him around to his knees. Without hesitation, he sliced through the general's neck, as the general had done to my mother.

Defeated, the general fell to the floor, gasping for air. Darwynyen nudged him with his foot. "Know in your death that you have failed in life."

After the general took his last breath, Darwynyen turned to me. The tense anger left his face. "Arianna." He rushed over and knelt. "It is over. You are safe."

Noticing the state of my clothing, he began to dress me. "Did he …" He hesitated as though fearing my response.

I shook my head. "My mother." I pointed to her body. "They murdered my mother!"

He took hold of my chin. "Let me take you away from here." Not waiting for a response, he gathered me into his arms and swept me from the room.

As we descended the stair to the foyer, Edina appeared from one of the corridors. "Arianna!" She rushed over. "What happened? Are you all right?"

"She is not," Darwynyen spoke sternly. "Who are you?"

"I am her lady in waiting. Your men have only just released me from the dungeons." She turned. "They make way to the caverns!"

Darwynyen set me on the bottom stair and addressed Edina, "Watch over her."

Edina nodded. "Of course."

"I need to join the others." He stood, and with a look of compassion, he said. "I will return for you as soon as I can."

When I nodded, he grabbed hold of his bow and ran toward the defense area.

CHAPTER 10:

A SIEGE AT HAND

Darwynyen arrived to find the cavern consumed in battle. Arrows filled the air as the Elves fought for ground. Trolls threw spears from the higher reaches while the general's men attacked with swords. Eluding his opponents, he edged his way across the main bridge. When the Trolls began to retreat, he tensed his bow and aimed for those in the higher reaches.

Once the area was clear, his companions joined him. As they advanced into the caves, he saw Madigan emerge from one of the shafts. "Madigan!" He rushed over. "Have you found the stone?"

"Not yet." He raised his hands in frustration. "It seems Velderon has already secured it!"

Darwynyen turned to his men. "Continue in your search!" We cannot allow Velderon to escape!" When they dispersed, he put his hand to his chest. "Arianna is safe."

"If we do not find the stone, your rescue will be in vain!"

"No." Darwynyen shook his head. "We will put a stop to this now."

"For all we know." Madigan wiped the sweat from his brow. "Velderon has already gone."

"I do not believe so." Darwynyen glanced over his shoulder toward the main bridge. "I have only just seen to the death of his trusted companion."

"The general?"

"Yes," he replied. "And if he was still here, Velderon must be as well."

"Then let us seek him out." Madigan raised his sword.

When they heard screams in the distance, Madigan grabbed Darwynyen by the arm. "I will search the lower regions. There are many ways leading out. Make your way in that direction." He pointed northwest. "That is where the Trolls have fled to thus far!"

Before they parted, Madigan turned, "Be careful, my friend. There are many places to hide down here."

Darwynyen nodded and headed northwest.

The passage before him was abandoned. Bodies of the dead, mainly Trolls, were scattered about the ground. Dampness kept the air musty and foul. In the distance, he could hear the moans of fallen men. Despite his empathy, he could not stop to aid them. As he brought his dagger to a wounded Troll who was crawling on the path, he heard men approaching from behind.

Wary of their presence, he fell back as they neared. Seconds later, shadows appeared on the walls. In hopes that he had stumbled across Velderon, he pounced. "Not another step or you will meet your death!"

The small company halted. "Who are you to order me, the king?" Velderon sneered.

"You are no King," Darwynyen growled.

"Kill him!" Velderon shouted.

At his command, the Trolls brought forward their weapons. As they encircled him, Velderon pulled the stone from his garb. "Naek na faad!"

A spell was at work. Moments later, an amber glow surrounded the king. "Your Elvish skill will prove futile against the powers I now possess."

Darwynyen released an arrow, but to his dismay it bounced from Velderon's aura. "You cannot hold your spell forever!" he taunted as he took down the Trolls around the king with his blades.

"You have no power here!" a wretched voice echoed through the corridors.

Darwynyen turned to find a most hideous sight. "Who are—" He hesitated when he realized it must be the Crone. Her thin hair was colorless and desiccated. Boils and warts covered her neck and hands. Her back was deformed; the hump left her stance uneven.

"My, are you ugly. It is no wonder Velderon kept you hidden!"

"There is no reason to be impolite." She turned to Velderon. "Make way, Velderon! I will see to him."

Darwynyen fired an arrow. She swayed it with her magic. Before he could fit another to his bow, she directed her staff. "Fanakdonu!"

A bolt of light struck Darwynyen with force, pushing him backward. Recognizing the spell, he struggled to counter its paralyzing effect.

"Do not fight me," the Crone growled. "Your Elvish powers are no match for mine!" She again turned to Velderon, who stood watching the encounter. "Be gone, Velderon!"

Velderon released the spell of protection. "I will leave you a horse. Find me when you can!" He sped from the area.

Unable to stop him, Darwynyen persisted with his attempt to defy the spell's power.

Enraged, the Crone waved her staff. "Pathetic you are!" The spell intensified. "Ha!" Her tongue swept across her broken teeth. "Do not fret. I will not make you suffer."

"What the—" Madigan appeared from one of the corridors.

From behind, a fatal arrow struck the Crone, set off by one of Darwynyen's companions. When she fell dead, the spell dissipated. Regaining his strength, Darwynyen gestured to the

Elf. "Kendrick, Velderon makes his exit to the west." He pulled an arrow. "We must be swift!"

The men broke free of the cavern only to find what remained of the previous battle. Velderon was nowhere to be found. "He has escaped!" Madigan thrust his sword into the ground.

Darwynyen turned to the Kendrick. "Thank you, Kendrick. I would not have survived her magic without you."

"You are most welcome." The Elf nodded.

"This is no time for pleasantries," Madigan snapped. "We have failed!"

"Madigan." Darwynyen took him by the arms. "We will find him! He will not get far on his own!"

"Help us!" Morglafenn called from the mouth of the cave. "These men are near death!"

Distracted from their defeat, the men turned. When they saw the Elvish spies clinging to Morglafenn's shoulders, they rushed to aid them.

"Bring horses!" Madigan shouted.

Moments later, two men appeared. "Over here. Hurry!" Madigan looked to Darwynyen, "Where were they a few minutes ago?"

As the men approached, the group moved with urgency. Kendrick and Morglafenn lifted the Elves onto the horses.

"Take them back to the den," Madigan ordered.

As they rode off, he turned to the cavern. "We must see to the wounded."

Without words, the men followed his lead.

CHAPTER 11:

AGONY GIVES WAY TO LIGHT

It felt like an eternity, awaiting the return of Darwynyen. When he appeared from the defense corridor, I cried out. "It has been hours! What happened?"

He knelt to face me. "It is all right."

I clung to him with desperation. "I feared you had—"

"No." He wiped the hair from my brow. "It is over. You are safe."

"Arianna." Madigan approached from behind. "You must tell me of your father's plans? Do you know where he has fled?"

"Leave her." Darwynyen stood. "She has been through enough. Not only was her mother slain in front of her, the general tried—" He broke off the rest of his words. "I doubt Velderon would be foolish enough to share any his plans with her."

Madigan nudged him aside. "You need to tell us of anything you have learned."

"Give her some time to regain her strength!" Darwynyen snapped.

"We have no time!"

"Madigan is right." Morglafenn appeared through the main door of the foyer. "We must scour this castle immediately."

"There is a secret room in the study," I uttered, "on the fifth level to the east. If you pull one of the books on the midshelf of the center bookcase, a door will open." I looked down, "That is all I know that can assist you."

"Go!" Madigan ushered his men up the stair. Before leaving, he knelt. "I am sorry for your loss, Arianna. You have proven yourself brave."

He stood to face Darwynyen. "I will search the study. When we are finished, I will meet you back at the den."

"No." I took his hand. "The castle is now yours. You must keep it from this day forward."

He looked at me oddly and then retreated up the stair.

Darwynyen took hold of me. "Where are your quarters?"

"I will show you the way." Edina extended her hand. "If you have no objections, I would like to draw her a bath, sir."

"Your gesture is kind." He managed a smile. "But the bath must keep until later."

When she nodded, he gathered me into his arms. As we passed through the broken doors of my room, Darwynyen halted.

"This is where they took her." Edina's eyes began to water.

"Perhaps we should find another room." He turned.

"Yes." Her eyes brightened. "I know just the place."

We ascended two levels before arriving at a door that opened to the outer crown of the inner keep. From the shadows of night, I could see a cottage-like structure built into the northwest tower. "This is where the custodian to the keep is intended to dwell." She paused. "I found it after—"

"Thank you, Edina," Darwynyen interrupted, moving to the door. "Let us get Arianna inside."

The room was quaint. Several windows graced the west wall. A bed made for one was placed in a nook that was fitted with two night tables. At the far corner was a bathing tub and wardrobe. To the left was a small circular table with two chairs. To its right, a desk was covered with scrolls and maps of the castle. Dust covered most of the furniture, making its abandonment obvious.

Darwynyen placed me on the bed. "You may return for her later."

"Of course," Edina replied, taking her leave.

When the door struck the latch, Darwynyen removed his weapons, placing them on the floor. "Your pain will lighten in time." He embraced me. "I will be here to see you through this."

Safe in his hold, I could contain myself no longer. As I began to weep, he eased me to the pillow. "Take rest. I will not let danger come to you."

I nodded and closed my eyes.

Shaken from the most terrible dream, I sat up flustered. "Where am I?"

"You were dreaming." I felt Darwynyen's hand on my back.

"Oh." I turned to face him. "I thought …" I looked down.

"It is all right." He pulled my chin to meet his gaze. "I am here for you."

"I know," I replied. "I am thankful that you found me."

He gave the room a fleeting look. "I only wish I could have gotten to you sooner."

I brought my finger to his lips. "You did all you could." I fought the tears. "When you left for the caverns, I feared you would not—"

"I am not that easy to kill." He smiled with sincerity.

"There are no words to explain how I feel for you." I wiped the tears as they trickled down my cheek.

"You are right." His hand grazed my cheek. "Words do not come easy. Even so, this bond we share is too strong to deny."

Before I could respond, he kissed me on the brow. When his lips touched my skin, the torment began to diminish, and warmth took its place. Unwilling to let go, I placed my arms around him. Please." I met his stare. "Promise me you will never leave me again."

"I …" He hesitated.

I understood the measure of my request. There was no doubt the day was soon to come when he would leave me in search of my father.

"Never." He smiled.

By his response, I knew the promise was little more than a means of comfort.

"I should check on the men." He stood, reaching for his weapons. "I will gather some food on my return."

I nodded.

"Try to get some rest. I will wake you when the next morn is upon us."

Although I feared the thought of being on my own, I knew not to stop him. "Do not forget the path here." I smiled.

"Not a chance." He winked.

When the latch struck the door, I fell back on the bed. As I pulled the cotton blankets around me, I inhaled the aroma. The musty scent reminded me of my room in Hoverdire. Still, sleep would not come easy.

Darwynyen stood in the foreground of my mind. I was torn between my grief and the unremitting desire to be with him. Were my thoughts of selfish nature? How was it possible I could love and hate so reasonably?

Regardless, I had no choice but to focus on the future. Where was my life to lead me next? Would I be hated for my father's deeds? Despite his seemingly legitimate claim to the throne, one thing was for certain: I did not want the charge. Besides, Madigan was better suited as king than I would ever prove as queen. Only one question lingered: what should I tell Madigan? Nothing. I did not have the endurance to prove my case either way, especially if he chose to challenge my authority. If only my mother … At the thought of her, I rose from the bed.

As I ascended the tower stair, I was deluged with flashes of her death. Near the landing, I halted. The putrid smell of death penetrated the air, making it obvious her corpse had long since been forgotten.

Dawning light broke through the windows, leaving the room dull and almost eerie.

"Mother." I knelt to her with guilt and futile desperation.

"Arianna?"

I turned to find Darwynyen standing at the door.

"What are you doing here?"

"I had to see her," I cried.

"You should not put yourself through this." He took my hand. "My men are seeing to a box as we speak." He tightened his hold. "Once the arrangements are made, you may say your good-byes in celebration of her life."

Not waiting for a response, he lifted me to my feet. "Please, let me take you away from here."

I could not resist his command, knowing his words stemmed from concern alone. Before leaving, I took one final glance at my mother. "I hope you have finally found peace," I whispered.

When we reached my quarters, Darwynyen sat me on the bed. "You must understand that your mother's death does not lie on your hands. Your father was ruthless in his cause and would have killed you both if the opportunity arose."

As I absorbed his words, I felt an overwhelming sense of hatred. "I will find him you know." My body stiffened. "I will end his life as he did my mother's!"

"Do not speak such things." He met my stare. "Give yourself time to grieve."

Unable to respond, my eyes began to tear, and he embraced me. "There is something I must tell you," he uttered. "Before long, I will make my journey back to Maglavine to seek the guidance of our queen. Her powers of foresight will see us through—"

"What does this mean?" I interrupted, in ill comprehension.

"Please." He pushed my hair back. "Let me finish."

"Forgive me." I released a heavy breath.

"I will not go on this journey alone." He smiled. "You will join me in place of Morglafenn. It is our queen's desire to counsel you."

"I cannot leave!" I pulled away. "I must first tend to my mother!"

"Arianna," he sighed, "I would not deny you your grief." He continued in a soft but firm tone, "We will not leave until you have said good-bye to your mother, but we will leave nonetheless."

"If it is your wish," I conceded, "I will do what you ask of me."

"Do not fear." He pulled the covers around us. "Take rest. Allow me to first mend your wounds. We can discuss things further when you awake."

I nodded, taking comfort in his warm embrace.

† † †

Unlike Darwynyen, I was unable to find sleep. Instead, I watched the delicate rays of sunlight as they found their way through the west windows. The light brought me an odd sense of ease. As I shifted the covers, I took a moment to observe the being who had somehow become a part of me.

He was handsome in his ways, but unlike most men of Man's Blood who held more of a brooding nature, his beauty did not conceal the honor that bore through him. By traditional standards, it would be improper for us to be sharing the same bed, but I did not care. As I removed a strand of hair from his cheek, I inhaled the aroma of his body. I could almost taste him. When his dark eyelashes fluttered, I pulled back. Peaceful in his slumber, I did not wish to disturb him.

With a sigh, his breath deepened. Content, I continued to gaze upon him. Although my wounds were deep, his presence seemed to fill the void. To gain a whisper of his touch, I ever so slowly placed my mouth to his. Before I could feel him, he woke.

"I was just …" I smiled, half embarrassed.

He smirked as though aware of my intentions. "Feeling better?"

"Yes," I replied. "The pain is not so deep."

"Good." He slowly stood with a muscled stretch. "So you know, Elves do not sleep as your people do but rather use the time to align our thoughts. That is how we find rest."

"Oh," I said, again embarrassed.

"We should make our way to the kitchen. With any luck some food has been prepared."

I recoiled uncomfortably. It would be difficult to face the others in light of my father's deeds. Besides, I was still uncertain of Madigan's intentions. If he saw me as he did my father, could I live with the indignity?

"What is it?" He frowned.

I spoke in trust, "I feel awkward facing the men."

"Why?" he asked.

I looked away in my response, "Some may look to me with hatred now that my father's intentions have been revealed."

"Whatever for?" He took my hand. "If it were not for you, things would be far worse now." He paused. "I did not mean to lessen the death of your mother."

"No." I shook my head. "You did nothing of the sort."

"Then join me." He lifted me from the bed. "You have nothing to fear."

"We shall see." I squeezed his hand. "Madigan made it clear on our first meeting of his ill feelings toward me."

"Ill feelings?" His eyes widened. "You have done nothing but restore his conviction. If you had not stumbled upon us, his toils would have only deepened. He may be strong and direct, but he is just and honorable enough to see the errors in his judgment."

He nudged me to the door. "Now come, so you can see things for yourself."

I nodded and followed his lead.

As we walked the corridors, I was thankful that no one stopped to stare. Most in passing took little heed, busy with their new duties. When we entered the kitchen, I saw Edina by the stove.

"Edina!" I ran to embrace her. "It is most good to see you."

"Arianna!" She pulled away enough to face me. "How are you? I was just warming the water for your bath."

"Oh, Edina," I sighed, "there is no need for you to wait on me further."

"Nonsense!"

I turned to find Madigan at the archway. "This castle is still in your command, Your Highness." He eyed Edina. "Nothing has changed. By her request, your lady in waiting is still in your service."

Unsure what to say, I turned to Darwynyen.

"He does not make the decisions around here—you do." Madigan bowed his head. "If you will have me, I wish to embrace you as a sister. How could I refuse the people of this city? They have held trust in you from the time of your birth."

Tears filled my eyes. "Thank you, Madigan. Nothing pleases me more than to know you hold no ill will toward me."

"How could I?" he gasped. "Despite your father's deeds, you have proven yourself more than worthy."

"My father ..." my voice faltered, "his escape has left nothing in our favor."

"Do not despair, as I had done previously." Madigan gave Darwynyen a fleeting look and moved to take my arms. "There is still hope. Not only do we hold command of Aarrondirth but we have found a weapon, one to use against him."

"What is it?" I frowned. "Did you find something in his study?"

"Yes." He nodded "We found a portal. If our assumptions are correct, it should open to the realm of your father's conspirators."

"It does." I stiffened in realization.

"What do you mean?" He released me. "Speak, Arianna. You must tell us everything!"

I clenched my fists. "Before my capture, I followed my father to that very room. During his conversation with the Crone, she mentioned her communication with the Hynd. They have captured a Siren that holds the key to the fire-breathing dragons of—"

"Naksteed," Darwynyen interjected. "Do you speak of the Dragons of Naksteed?"

"It cannot be." Madigan staggered backward.

"Morglafenn." Darwynyen turned with anticipation. "Shallendria must be warned." He left the room quickly.

"Who is Shallendria?" I asked, following him to the reception hall. "You spoke her name at the den."

"She is my cousin," he replied. "Morglafenn summoned her from Maglavine when we discovered the portal." He ran toward the back stair that led to the eastern wing of the castle. "If we are to utilize her powers, we must ensure that she arrives safely!"

Before I could respond, he had disappeared.

"May we speak." Madigan extended his hand toward the northern terrace.

"Should we not see to Darwynyen and Morglafenn?"

"They can wait." He led me down the corridor. "There are other matters that are of equal importance."

Curious about his request, I conceded.

"The people …" He ushered me to one of the benches near the turret door where our conversation would go unnoticed. "Some decisions must be made." His eyes fought to keep my stare. "Aware of the rebellion, they grow wary of what is to come." He paused in an awkward manner. "Before they are led astray by rumors and common talk, they must be addressed."

"I agree." I nodded. "What are you to do?"

"Me?" He shook his head.

"Yes," I replied. "I told you before—the castle is yours."

"You cannot mean the words you speak." He stood.

"I do," I insisted, standing to face him. "You know as well as I that my father was an impostor."

"But we have no proof," he argued. "Regardless of what has happened, you are bound by your duty. If—"

I silenced him, "I swear to you now, I hold no desire for the throne."

"But why?"

"I am no leader, Madigan. Nor do I wish to be."

He took a step back. "But the people have already begun to gather in the courtyard, expecting you to address them."

"Let them gather," I snapped.

"Arianna." There was doubt in his eyes. "Are you certain you have thought this through?"

"Madigan, you must understand that my heart no longer lies in Aarrondirth. I wish to share in a future with Darwynyen. In doing so, I must resign my role as queen. You know as well as I that the people would never accept him."

"If you give them time—"

"No." I took hold of his arm. "You must not ask of me such things. The kingdom is yours. Please, do not fight me!"

"Regardless of your decision, your role must not be relinquished. In their eyes, you are still the princess of Aarrondirth. It is your place to see this through."

"What if they …" I blinked. "What if they want me dead?"

He released a heavy breath. "You are not to blame for your father's deeds."

"I am not well," I stammered. "My mother is dead! You must give me time to grieve!"

"I am sorry for the loss of your mother." His voice softened, "She was loved by many."

A tear fell from my eye. "If only she were here."

"She is not." I felt his hand on my arm. "It is you who must stand in her place."

"Very well," I sighed. "I will appoint you king."

"Again, I must ask: are you certain of your decision?" He put his fist to his chest. "As you are aware of my lineage, I will not decline your appointment."

"Yes," I replied with conviction. "The charge is yours."

"Then so be it." He nodded with the same conviction. "I will have the heralds make an announcement, informing the people that you are soon to address them. I will also have my men call upon the city councilmen; they should be present as representatives of the people. If you will prepare your words, I will have you summoned to the gallery at the falling of the sun."

"I will be there." I wiped my tears with my hand.

"There is much to be done." He turned. "I will leave you to your thoughts."

He rushed off before I could respond.

I returned to the bench, gazing at the statue on the fountain as if it were a silent mentor. Was I making the right decision? Although my father's claim held substance, did I hold a desire to the throne? No. My time here was done. There was no future for me in Aarrondirth that would see me with Darwynyen. I would rather follow his path than be without him. Before I could do so, I needed to say good-bye to my mother.

"Arianna?" Edina approached from the gated passage that opened from the reception area. "Madigan said you were in need of me."

"Edina." I bit my lip. "You need to take me to my mother."

"Do you believe it wise?" she asked with concern. "You must give yourself time to grieve." Her eyes lightened. "I know they plan to make an announcement soon. Would it not be best to for you to say your good-byes in the support of others?"

"No," I turned. "If you will not take me, I will find the way myself."

"Wait." She took my arm. "If it is your will, you shall not go alone."

"Thank you," I replied.

While still hesitant, she escorted me inside.

When we reached the second level, I saw a draped encasement in the center of the ballroom. "Is she there?"

Sun was filtering through the windows, casting a colored reflection on the velvet material. "Mother?" Images of her death swept through me.

"The city mourns for her." I felt Edina's hand on my back. "I am so sorry for your loss."

"Thank you for your comfort." The smell of death began to overwhelm me. "I must have a moment."

"We have found a prisoner!" a man shouted from the foyer below. "Find Madigan!"

"What goes on here?" I made my way to the landing.

The guards bowed. "We have found another in the dungeons, Your Highness. He must have gone amiss in our searches yesterday." The man who spoke paused. "Forgive us. We will disturb you no further."

"Leave Madigan to his work." I ran down the stair to address them. "Where is this person?"

"Come." He nudged his companion aside. "We will take you there now."

The state of the dungeon left me weak. Thoughts of torture and pain filled my mind as we passed an assortment of blades and whips covered in dried blood that hung from various hooks along the outer wall.

"He is in here!" The guards ran to the end of the hall.

Edina blocked my path, "We should call upon Madigan."

"No." I pushed her aside. "I must see who it is."

When I reached the cell, I stood in disbelief. "Gin?" I knelt to face him. "Gin, can you hear me?"

"Where is he?" He winced, holding a hand to his chest.

Although I was confused by his question, there was no time to waste. "Quickly." I stood. "Take him upstairs."

"Do you know this man?" one of the guards questioned, looking to his companion.

"Yes." I gave Gin a fleeting look. "Take him to one of the guest quarters immediately."

By my command, the men set forth in their duty. Edina and I followed. We directed them to one of the rooms on the third level.

"Lay him on the bed," I removed the blankets as they put him in place.

Edina felt his brow.

"What are you waiting for?" I turned. "Go fetch a healer!"

The men bowed their heads and left the room.

"Come." I gestured to Edina. "We must get him out of his clothes. They are spoiled and will only cause infection."

She nodded and took hold of one of his boots.

His body was covered in bruises. He had taken a beating few would survive.

"Gin, can you hear me?"

When there was no response, I put my hand to his brow. "He is warm, too warm."

"I will fetch some water." Edina made way for the door.

"Arianna," Gin mumbled, "is that you?"

"Yes." I took hold of him. "Who has done this to you?"

He struggled to open his swollen eyes. "The general," he replied. "On the eve of our return he had me arrested for treason."

"How did you get these wounds?" I asked.

"His vengeance was deep." He choked on his words. "When time would allow, he would return to beat me at his leisure."

I began to weep at the consequence of my actions. I should have never befriended him. "I am so very sorry, Gin. I did not know."

"Do not blame yourself." He squeezed my hand. "You were not aware of his—"

He broke off his words and sat up with a frantic look on his face. "Where is he?"

"Rest, my friend." I reached for the blankets I had tossed earlier. "He cannot harm you now."

Edina appeared with a bucket of water. "It has been boiled. If we are lucky it will stunt any infection."

"Where are the guards?" I snapped. "Why have they not brought the healer?"

"I will go and see." She turned in a humble manner.

"Wait!" I blinked. "Please, you must excuse my actions. I—"

"Say no more. I will return shortly." She left the room.

Welling with frustration, I was about to scream out when the latch released on the door.

"Edina?" I stood. "Did you—"

"Yes." She led an elderly man into the room.

"Come." I took the man by the arm. "My friend needs your help."

The man placed his case on the table. "What goes on in this castle? Many people speak of a rebel—"

"Save you questions," I ordered. "See to your duty!"

He sighed with annoyance. "What is his ailment?"

I pulled the blanket down. "He has been beaten. You must use your medicine to heal him!"

He took a step back. "Who would do such a thing?"

"Does it matter?" I snapped.

"Arianna." Edina took my arm. "Let us leave him to his work."

Infuriated, I stomped from the room.

Edina followed, closing the door behind us. "Who is this man?" she asked.

"He is a soldier I befriended on my journey home. His name is Gin."

"I see." She blinked. "Can he be trusted?"

"I would think by his current predicament that the answer would be yes." I could feel my body tighten. "Would you not agree?"

"It was not my intention to offend you."

At observing her defensiveness, my body weakened. "You did no such thing." I put my hand to my brow. "Forgive me."

"There is no need." She leaned against the wall. "Let us hope the healer is able to help him."

"One can only hope." I leaned next to her.

When the door opened, the healer emerged with a look of concern. Edina took me by the arm when I shot forward. "Is he to be all right?"

"Perhaps." The man wavered. "You will need to watch over him. Dry his wounds with salt. Keep a cool cloth on his brow." He paused. "The next few hours will be critical. If he should slip into a deep sleep, there is nothing more we can do for him."

I looked to Edina. "Will you fetch some salt?"

She nodded. "I will return shortly."

"Thank you." I turned to the man. "I would appreciate your discretion in this matter."

"If it is your wish." He secured his satchel. "Should your friend's brow cool, the worst will be over. You will know when the time comes. After that, he should heal quickly."

He lowered his head, "If there is nothing more."

"You are excused." I ushered him to the stair.

He placed his satchel under his arm as he descended.

Despite the urge to seek Darwynyen, I returned to the room. From the shadows, I could see Gin's trembling body. I moved to the table to light a lantern.

"The healer said you are going to be fine." I tried to keep an optimistic tone. "Nonetheless, my friend, you must keep fighting."

His only response was to mumble.

"I brought the salt." Edina brushed through the door.

"Keep quiet." I put my finger to my lips. "He needs his rest."

She handed me a ladle. "You should have him take some water."

I nodded, knowing she was right. As I sat, I lifted his head. I held the ladle to his lips. "Gin, you must drink."

Before he could respond, I let a few droplets of water into his mouth.

"Enough," he coughed.

"Perhaps we should allow him to rest." Edina moved to the door.

"You may go." I secured his blankets. "I will stay."

"Do you wish me to call upon Madigan?"

"No. I will speak to him later." I paused. "But if you should see Darwynyen, please tell him where to find me."

"Of course." She nodded. "I will make my return later in the hour."

"Thank you." I knelt to the bed.

I could feel her presence for a moment before the latch struck the door.

"Please," I begged, "you must live. Too much tragedy has crossed my path as of late."

He began to stir, as though lost in a dream.

To ease him, I ran my fingers through his auburn locks. "Sleep, my friend." Fighting the tears, I vowed to do whatever I could not to lose him, as I had my mother.

"Why do you weep so deeply?" he uttered. "I will heal of these wounds."

"It is not only you I cry for." I wiped the tears. "My mother." Unable to face him, I put a cool cloth over his eyes and brow as the healer had suggested. "She was taken from me by my father's hand."

"I ..." He again choked on his words. "I am sorry for your loss. I did not know."

To stay his concern, I changed the subject. "Let me test your warmth."

He took my hand when I lifted the cloth. "You are a strong woman, Arianna. I thank you for all you have done."

I smiled in an attempt to hide the grief. "The cooling cloth seems to be working. If you find rest, we may be able to avoid …" I paused.

"Do not fear." He pulled the covers closer. "My wounds, unlike yours, only lie on the outside."

I admired his strength. "If you feel well enough, perhaps you will take more water?" I asked, reaching for the ladle.

"Perhaps." He dithered for a moment before conceding.

When he passed into sleep, I moved to the window. The sun's glow had made its presence known in the west. Eve was upon us.

"How is he doing?" Edina quietly made her way through the door.

"He has improved." I sighed. "Despite the healer's warnings, I believe the worst is over."

I turned. "Have you seen Darwynyen?"

"No." She shook her head. "They have all gathered in the study. I could keep on here if you care to find him."

"I would rather stay." I returned to the bed. "I would ask you to find some food, if it is not a bother."

"Of course." She nodded. "You have not eaten today."

"It is not for me," I replied. "But I should probably take some.

Wait!" I stood. "I am supposed to meet Madigan in the gallery. I should have been summoned already!"

"Then leave your friend to me." She knelt to grab another cloth from the bucket. "I will see that he is taken care of."

"Thank you." I rushed from the room.

Chapter 12:

The Eye

In the hours that had passed, Darwynyen had spent his time in the study with Morglafenn as he prepared the portal for Shallendria's arrival.

"I fear I have done all I can. I must continue in my studies." Morglafenn stood back from the portal, taking one final look at the eyes that floated within their casings. "Unfortunately, I do not hold Shallendria's skill in magic and cannot retain the gaze of the eyes—there are simply too many of them."

"Then save your strength." Darwynyen followed him from the room. "Is her arrival not soon to be anticipated."

"Indeed," Morglafenn sighed. "There has never been a time when we have needed her more. Should the Sorcerers gain control of the dragons, Velderon will be the least of our worries."

"Have you found success?" Madigan appeared at the door.

"No." Morglafenn replied. "But many of the spells that will be necessary have been prepared."

Madigan turned his attention to Darwynyen. "Where is Arianna?"

"I cannot say." He shrugged. "I have not seen her since I left her with you."

"Then she is nowhere to be found." He glanced over his shoulder. "She was supposed to meet me in the gallery some time ago. The people await our arrival."

"Did you try the dwelling atop the keep?" Darwynyen moved to the door.

"She is not there." Madigan blocked his path. "There is something you must know."

"What is it?" Darwynyen glanced back to Morglafenn.

"She has relinquished the throne," he replied. "I am soon to be the ruler of this land."

"Why?" Darwynyen's mouth fell open. "Are you certain she was clear in her intentions?"

"Of course!" Madigan's tone turned defensive. "I have not taken advantage."

"Perhaps she does not wish the burden," Morglafenn interjected. "Not long has she held the charge. With all that has happened, her desires may now lie elsewhere."

Darwynyen looked down to hide his doubt. "I hope her decision was made with clarity."

"She was adamant," Madigan snapped. "Moreover, as you very well know, the throne *has* and always will be rightfully mine."

"You are right," Darwynyen conceded. "I will question you no further."

"Nevertheless." Madigan took a step back. "I still must find her."

"Why?" Darwynyen smirked. "You appear stately enough. Can you not move forward without her?"

"No." He adjusted the collar on his shirt. "Things must be done as they have always been done."

Darwynyen ushered him through the door. "If that is the case, leave us to our work and go find her."

"Now is not the time to mock me, my friend." Madigan trudged from the room. "You are not the one to face the people without her."

Chapter 13:

Madigan's Succession

With little time to spare, I did not allow the memories that now tainted my previous quarters to hinder me. Instead, I quickly moved through the area where the general's men had captured me to my wardrobe. After moments of searching, I found the gown I had worn at the first announcement with my father. I pulled it from its hanger, deciding that familiarity would be my best weapon against the people, who I feared would blame me for the death of my mother, their queen.

Once dressed, I ran to the gallery. Madigan was nowhere to be found. In his place, a small assembly of the city's councilmen had gathered.

The jeweler who I had previously met approached and bowed. "Your Highness, we were summoned by your request. Are you ready to make an announcement?" He paused in an antagonistic manner. "I am sure there is much to be told if Madigan has requested the king's crown."

"Leave her." Madigan appeared from the corridor. "Arianna, where have you been?"

"You call her by her given name," the man scowled.

"Do not speak to him in such a manner." I glared. "He is soon—"

"Arianna," Madigan began, looking to the balcony, "for the last time, are you certain of your decision?"

To prove my resolve, I stood to face him. "Yes." I adjusted his collar. "Do not fear. The people will see through to your strength, as I did the moment I saw you."

He released a heavy breath. "Regardless of the outcome, I will not release you of your duty." His eyes grew serious. "You still hold a place in this kingdom."

"We shall see." I managed a smile.

When the heralds sounded their horns, he met the gathering crowd. "You have come because you hold despair about our future!" His voice deepened. "I will ask you to disregard your ill will. Times have changed! From this day forward, you will no longer follow the path of a ruthless king!" He turned. "I give to you Velderon's successor!"

Although hesitant, I moved to meet him. Like before, many of the people were common folk. Those from the more prominent families again stood to the back, though this time their look seemed to stem from concern rather than suspicion.

"Do not fear, my people!" I raised my hands. "Our future has been secured!"

When the applause dissipated, I continued. "It is now, in the face of my mother's death." The crowd gasped. "That I relinquish my forthcoming role as your queen. As you bear witness, I turn my charge over to Madigan, the last descendant of the Alameed family and the next in line to the throne."

"But why?" someone shouted. "Do you speak the truth? Does a descendant of Alameed's live?"

"Yes." I gave Madigan a fleeting look. "The truth has been spoken. He is the son of Alameed's first cousin Faris." I stiffened my stance and turned to the herald who held my father's crown on a satin pillow. "Because his blood flows through my veins, I will beg you to embrace him as your king!" I paused. "You must trust in him. He will lead us to victory, no matter the cost!"

"Where is your father?" another asked.

"He has fled the city," I replied. "Deceit has clouded his path."

"If he is a traitor, why should we follow you?" a woman asked with a scowl.

"You follow me no more," I spoke sternly. "Give your allegiance to Madigan, as I have requested."

"Who is he to take your place?"

"He is your king!" I held out my hands. "Is it your will to question me?"

When the crowd grew silent, I lifted the crown from the pillow and placed it on Madigan's head.

Madigan cleared his throat and turned to the people. "As your king, my first action will be to secure our lands. Too long have Velderon's guardsmen kept us idle! Alliances that have long since been forgotten will soon be mended!"

He put his fist to his chest. "The people of this land must reunite if we are to face what is before us!" When the crowd began to grumble, he continued. "A myth you have all spoken has been proven true: the last stone of Moya has been found!"

"You will lead us in the words of myth!" one cackled.

"Do not take my words lightly." He glared. "We will prepare for battle, nonetheless!"

"Why would we fight?" a young man questioned.

"The choice is neither yours nor mine!" Madigan countered. "There are forces here at work that few of you are yet able to comprehend. Either way, our battalions are soon to return from the outer regions. Once again, we shall stand united!"

Elated by the latter part of his statement, the crowds began to chant his name.

Madigan silenced them. "This is no time to rejoice!"

"But our sons are soon to return!" an old man shouted.

When I saw the rage in Madigan's eyes, I intervened, "They will be called upon to serve. The times ahead are uncertain. It is now that we must turn to the man who can lead us!" I put my hand to Madigan's shoulder. "King Madigan is his name!"

"Prepare yourselves," Madigan said, leaning hard on the ledge. "We must be ready when the time comes!"

"Why?"

"Because the dragons of Naksteed will soon be upon us!" He took a step back as though regretful of his words.

"Dragons?" An old lady stood forward. "Were they not banished?"

Madigan clenched his fists. "Dragons or not, we have enough to worry on. Should the stones be united ..." He shook his head in defeat.

"What will become of Arianna?" another questioned.

"Arianna will continue on in my counsel," he replied. "She will not be far, should you need her."

He took my hand with vigor. "The day after tomorrow, we shall honor her mother, Brianna, our beloved queen, in her passing."

The crowd began to disperse. "Wait!" he shouted. "Any of you able to bear arms must report to the gatehouse. You will be directed from there!"

When the people took little heed in his words, he stomped into the gallery. "Why must they be so ignorant?"

One of the vendors approached him with caution. "You forget yourself, Madigan ... I mean, My King. The people are simple. They do not require details, only assurance and leadership. The stories of the past have long since been forgotten. You must give them time to adjust!"

"Time!" His eyes widened. "We have no time! We must prepare now!"

The man looked down. "Is that not what our armies are for?"

"Get out of here!" Madigan shot forward.

I took the vendor's arm. "Come. I will escort you out."

"Of course." he dithered, obviously frightened.

As I led the man and his companions from the gallery, I glanced back to Madigan. He was pacing in an erratic manner.

I could only hope he would soon adjust to his new commission, forget his commonalities, and acquire the behavior of a true king.

CHAPTER 14:

A Moment's Loss of Hope

Exhausted, Morglafenn closed his book of spells. "Where is Shallendria?" he huffed.

"You must rest, my friend." Darwynyen led him from the secret room. "It has been hours and *still* you push, knowing your attempts are futile."

"You are right." Morglafenn nodded. "We should leave our work for now."

He paused. "Perhaps you should seek Arianna."

Darwynyen fought a yawn. "Perhaps."

"Go to her now." Morglafenn sat at the table. "I will take a moment's rest and then continue in my reading."

"You will be no good to us if you are weak." Darwynyen raised his brow.

Morglafenn began to caress his neck. "Even so, I must further my study."

"I will not pretend to counsel you." Darwynyen winked. "For you are the mentor, not I."

"Go," Morglafenn insisted. "There is a new road for you to follow."

Darwynyen sighed. "I fear we shall soon see where that road leads." Before Morglafenn could respond, he left the room.

When he arrived at the dwelling upon the keep, the room had clearly been abandoned. "She must be at her mother's box," he uttered. Securing the latch on the door, he made way.

As he descended the last of the stairs, he looked into the ballroom. To his surprise, the room was empty. Would she be in the tower? He shook the thought. There was no logic in this reasoning. Perhaps she had taken rest in the room that was given to her by her father. With that in mind, he returned in the direction from which he had come.

At the top of the rise, he halted, taking notice of the archway. It was cluttered with an array of tools and cut wood.

"Do you seek Arianna?" Edina appeared from her quarters.

"Yes." He nodded. "Where is she?"

"Have you not been told?"

"Told what?" he demanded.

"I left word with the guard outside the study. He said you were not to be disturbed."

"Where she is," he growled.

"She … she stays in a room down the hall," she stammered, flustered by his demeanor. "She looks over a friend."

"Who is this person?"

"His name is Gin," she replied. "He was found in the dungeons this afternoon." Her eyes widened, "She is only there to aid him! He was hurt and—"

"Where is this room?"

"Take the corridor to your right." She extended her hand. "He rests within the first door to the left."

Without a word, Darwynyen turned and made way in the direction Edina had pointed.

CHAPTER 15:

JEALOUSY

Jilted from my sleep, I jumped from the bed when the door broke open.

"Quiet!" I snapped, believing it to be Edina.

When my eyes gained focus, my heart skipped a beat. "Darwynyen." I quickly fixed my clothing when I saw the look in his eyes. "I have been waiting for you."

"Have you?"

I ushered him from the room. "What is it? Has something happened?"

"Why are you here?" He glared. "Who is this man you care for?"

"He is a friend," I replied. "He was found in the dungeons this afternoon."

"What do you mean by *friend*? How can you give your trust so easily?" He took me by the arm. "What do you know of him?"

I pulled away. "I met him on my journey home."

"Are you telling me he works for your father?"

"Not anymore." I crossed my arms. "He is not like the others."

"Does Madigan know of this?"

"Not yet." I looked away. "He has enough to contend with."

"I know." He took my chin. "He has told me of your decision."

"Oh." I blinked. "Are you disappointed?"

"There is no reason to be." He met my stare. "It is you who has to live with the decision." His eyes searched mine. "I can only hope you are able to settle with it."

"I have only done what I thought to be right." I looked away. "In saying that, I will ask that you not question me."

He eyed the door. "My only concern lies with your companion."

"Save your concern," I sighed. "There is little we can do at the moment anyway. Gin is in no capacity to cause harm."

"For now." He took a step back. "Perhaps we should retire. You are exhausted. I can see it in your eyes."

"No." I took hold of the door handle. "I promised him I would be here when he awoke."

When I saw the disappointment in his eyes, I tried to reassure him. "Gin, despite our short time together, has become like a brother to me. I will not abandon him until he has regained some strength. Please, try to understand."

"Do what you must." He turned. "I will await you atop the keep."

Shocked by his manner, I let him go. It seemed pointless to argue. Besides, I would not leave Gin, no matter what repercussions might follow. I owed him that much after the misery I had led him to.

Chapter 16:

Shallendria

The sun, obscured by mist, revealed the outline of a rider approaching from the east with haste. "A rider draws near!" a guard shouted. "Alert the king!"

Minutes later, Madigan appeared at the tower. "Where is she?" he moved to the ledge.

"Who?" the guard questioned.

"Shallendria." He turned. "See she is found safely through the gates."

The man lit a torch, sending a signal to those at the barbican.

Madigan broke through the servants' door with anticipation. "Shallendria!" He raised his hand at her approach. "I am most grateful to see you."

"What is the hour?" She dismounted her horse. "How much time has been lost?" She pulled the hood on her cloak, allowing her long flowing locks to rest on her shoulders.

"I dare not ask, but how did you get here so quickly?" He looked to the sky. "We were not expecting you for several hours."

"Are you not pleased by my arrival?" she smirked. "You forget, my horse is the best. He carries the last blood of the Unicorn. His relentless strength promised to see me here as swiftly as his legs could carry me." She pulled a strand of hair from her face. "Forget the common talk; he requires water and food immediately."

Madigan turned. "See to the mistress's horse."

When a stable boy ran over, she handed him the reins, "Guard him with your life."

The boy nodded. "Certainly, my lady."

"Come." Madigan beckoned. "You must see to the portal. By the words of the Crone, it seems the Sorcerers of Morne have obtained the key to the dragons of Naksteed."

"I know." She followed his direction. "Morglafenn has already warned me."

"I can only hope they have not found a way to out maneuver us."

"We shall see," she replied.

He nodded as he led her to the study.

When she entered the room, Shallendria put her hand to her chest. "Is this where the Crone dwelled?"

"Yes." Darwynyen rose from his chair. "In that chamber over there."

"My cousin." She moved to embrace him. "It is good to see you."

"And you." He pulled away. "I do not mean to be rude ..."

"Of course." She pulled a book from her satchel. "Let us get started."

"Morglafenn has already prepared the spells for you." Darwynyen lifted a stack of writings from the table.

She ignored him and made her way through the threshold. "It is the portal of forbidden eyes," she gasped.

Darwynyen came to her side. "Morglafenn has been working on it for hours. Despite his attempts, he could only get two of the eyes to align."

"That is because he is not strong enough to manipulate this kind of magic."

"Are you?" Madigan met her stare.

"Your question will be answered soon enough." She knelt to an iron frame that hung from the wall where the eyes sat waiting in their encasements. "I will ask you to stand back. When I awaken the eyes from their slumber, their gaze must fall on me alone."

"I am not sure I am comfortable with this." Madigan knelt to meet her. "Let us seek Morglafenn."

"There is no need," she huffed. "The portal will only answer to one."

"She is right," Darwynyen interjected. "Let her get started."

"I hope you know what you are doing." Madigan raised his brow.

Shallendria ignored him, turning to her spell book. "Stand back."

Hours passed. Shallendria, weakened by the magic, began to tremble.

"You must take a minute's rest." Madigan put his hand to her shoulder.

"Do not interrupt me again!" she snapped. "If the portal had been opened, you could have lost me forever."

Madigan stood abruptly and glanced at Darwynyen. "Forgive me. I did not know."

"Take heed in her words," Darwynyen warned. "The magic must never be taken for granted."

Unable to argue, Madigan released a heavy breath. "If disaster has been avoided, perhaps we should use the opportunity to refocus." He attempted to avoid the odor that hung in the air with his sleeve. "Perhaps a bit of fresh air will ease the mood. There is no doubt the Crone who inhabited this place was not of the cleanest nature."

"It is the remnants of her magic that stifles you," Darwynyen snickered. "Nevertheless, you are right, my friend: the air *is* no doubt foul."

Shallendria stood. "Forgive me. I did not mean to snap."

"It is forgotten." Madigan led her from the room.

As she inhaled the fresh air, she spoke, "So, who is this girl, Arianna?"

"She is the daughter of Velderon," Madigan replied. "She risked her life to give us the information needed for the rebellion."

"I see." She blinked. "And where is she now?"

Madigan frowned. "She is in the castle. Why?"

"It is not important." She gave focus to Darwynyen. "You look tired, my cousin. What have you been doing with your time?"

"Working on the portal." His eyes narrowed. "Is there something you wish to ask?"

Madigan interrupted, "What is your interest with Arianna?"

"I should return to the portal." She turned, avoiding further eye contact. "Too much time has been wasted."

Madigan gave Darwynyen a fleeting look before following her back into the room.

After a final review of her spell book, Shallendria knelt to the portal. "Nokced noramad noramand." At her command, the eyes began to stir in their glass casings. Her tone deepened, "Noromad noromad! I command you!"

Splinters of light divided the room. "Nokced, focus your gaze upon me!"

At her words, the eyes began to settle in the casings, each gazing in the same direction. "Show me through to the other side. I command you!"

A vision materialized around her. "Noromad, noromad, clear this vision before me!" she shouted.

When an alternate setting appeared, she winced. "Darwynyen, I believe I am at the altar of Cessdorn."

"Are you alone?" He glanced to Madigan.

"Yes." She used her hands to guide her as she fought with the spell. "There is no one here."

"What do you see?" Darwynyen questioned.

"The altar has been left for ruin. Time has whittled away the Arms of Asking. No longer do the stone spires hold their majestic throws."

"What are the 'Arms of Asking'?" Madigan puckered his brow.

Darwynyen took his arm. "It was said that when the Sorcerers found the stone, they built an altar most desired by those who followed in the magic. Four gigantic arms encompass the structure." He paused. "They reach for the sky, as though to plead for the powers of twilight."

"I see a table near the slab of offerings." Shallendria moved through the vision. "There is a map. It is a drawing of the northern regions." She again fought with the spell. "I believe it is their plan of attack."

"Who are you?" The voice struck her hard. "Speak or you will pay with you life!"

"Set me free at once!" she demanded.

Madigan began to panic. "What should we do?"

"Nothing!" Darwynyen did not break the stare he held on his cousin. "She is strong. She will break free as soon as she is able."

Before Madigan could respond, Darwynyen silenced him. "Do not distract her. It will only make things worse!"

Madigan took a step back.

"What is it you seek?" the voice echoed. "Tell me now!"

"Never!" Shallendria cried.

"What is it you seek? What is it you seek?" The voice hounded her.

"Darwynyen." She frantically rubbed her temples.

He was about to grab her, when he saw the face of a wretched old man. "Who are you?" the man growled.

"I am Shallendria of the Elves." She stiffened her stance. "Forget your quest! Our armies will soon be upon you."

"You hold no power here," he cackled.

Before she could respond, the vision intensified. White light tore through her like a razor and evaporated as she screamed. She collapsed on the floor.

Madigan broke into a state of distress. "Is she to be all right?" He knelt to her.

"It is over." Darwynyen looked down for a moment. "She must take rest."

"I have failed you," she uttered.

"No." Madigan gathered her into his arms. "You saw the workings of their plan."

She put her hands to her brow. "I must connect to Aldraveena."

"The queen can wait." Madigan responded as he carried her from the room.

"Wait!" She whispered something in his ear.

Madigan turned. "Shallendria has brought a message for Arianna. Bring her to my quarters when she is able."

When Darwynyen nodded, Madigan took her from the room.

CHAPTER 17:

Misgivings

Unsure of the time, I moved to the window. A new day was upon us. As I massaged the sore muscles in my neck, I released a yawn.

"There is no need for you to stay." Gin shifted under the covers.

"How are you feeling?" I smiled.

"Better." He reached for the ladle, and I moved to assist him.

"If you are hungry," I said and glanced at the door, "I would be happy to get you some food."

"That would be most kind." He wiped his chin.

I turned. "I will make my return shortly."

"You can have it sent." His head fell to the pillow. "I have had enough of your fussing."

I narrowed my eyes. "If I did not know better, I would say you were trying to be rid of me."

"Perhaps." He winced. "Is it working?

"Very well." I moved through the door. "I will allow you some time on your own, but I will not be gone for long."

After seeing to a meal for Gin, I made way to the northern terrace. As I took in the warmth of the sun, I thought of

Darwynyen. I could only hope he had not misjudged the situation and grown cold to me. If he had, I would have no choice but to make it up to him. I had no intention of staying on in the castle any longer than was needed.

As I sat on a bench, I noticed Madigan lost in thought on the eastern stair. Curious about his contemplation, I made my way over to him.

"Madigan?"

"Arianna." He turned. "Has Darwynyen found you?"

I shook my head. "I have not seen him."

"Shallendria has arrived." He looked away with an uncertain expression on his face. "She takes rest in your mother's quarters. I hope you do not mind."

"It is your quarters now," I replied. "The sooner we adjust the—"

"Of course." After an uncomfortable silence, he continued. "When you are able, she wishes to meet with you."

"Why?" I took a step back. "Is it in regards to my father?"

"I am not sure." He shrugged. "Perhaps we should go there now."

"I would prefer to find Darwynyen first." I bit my lip. "If you do not mind."

When he nodded, I slowly backed away. "I will leave you to your thoughts."

"Wait!" He stood as he called after me. "I understand that my men found a friend of yours in the dungeon."

"Yes." I blinked, remembering Darwynyen's suspicion. "I meant to tell you, only I had not found the time." I stiffened my stance. "He is of no threat. You should carry no doubt in that. If so, I would have sought your counsel immediately.

"Who is he?" He frowned.

"His name is Gin," I replied. "I befriended him on my journey home."

When I saw the protest in his eyes, I continued, "I have embraced him as a brother. He was the first person to show me kindness when my life took a change."

"How can you be certain of his trust," he questioned, "if he was in Corbett's service?"

I smiled to sway his concern. "Corbett did not like him. He is of a kind heart, unlike the others. To hinder our friendship, the general had him locked in the dungeon upon our arrival. He barely survived!"

"If you have chosen to trust him, what counsel could I offer?"

He took my hand. "Still, I will need to speak with him." When I tried to pull away, he tightened his hold. "Will you take me there now?"

"He sleeps," I replied sternly. "I would prefer not to disturb him until he has regained some of his strength."

"Then summon me when he wakes." He released me. "I will not keep him for long."

Frustrated, I put my arms on my waist. "Madigan, what is it that troubles you?"

"My only concern lies with you." His eyes began to wander.

"There is no need," I huffed. "I have not been led astray, I promise you."

"We shall see." He turned and took his leave.

In his absence, I returned to the bench. A part of me felt hurt by the lack of trust that both he and Darwynyen seemed to share. Even so, I would not abandon Gin, regardless of his service. Unlike me, he had no one else in the castle to turn to.

As I again absorbed the sun's warmth, I realized that I had begun to work through some of my grief. Having to care for another had, if nothing else, brought me a sense of purpose.

"Your father kept quite the fortune!"

When I turned, I saw Dregby approaching from the keep. "You have returned." I stood. "It is good to see you."

Absorbing his words, I paused. "What is it you found behind those locked doors? I was never given the opportunity—"

"The wealth is immeasurable." He grinned. "I am sure Velderon was quite distraught over having to depart without it."

I sensed a bit of greed in his voice. "I carry doubt about your surmise." I hesitated at the thought of my mother. "He seemed to value the stone above anything else."

He slowed his gait. "I apologize, Arianna. I meant no disrespect."

"I know." I managed a smile. "It was not you who led him astray."

"Nor was it you." He met my stare.

I nodded solemnly. "Will the fortune be enough to see us through?"

He smirked. "There is no need for you to concern yourself, my dear."

I almost changed the subject but could not help myself. "I will assume by your words that your people find contentment in riches."

He broke out in laughter. "Yes, of course, my dear. What else is there?"

"Well, I am not sure," I replied, "but I think family and love are of high value, for a start." I closed my eyes. The words had brought my thoughts back to my mother.

I felt his hand on my arm. "Do not worry, child. You have a new family now."

He winked. "I best be off. You have company."

I followed his stare to find Darwynyen.

"I have been looking for you all over." He held out his hands. "Is everything all right?"

"Yes." I stood to greet him. "Everything is fine." I glanced to Dregby, who took his leave without further words.

Darwynyen nodded to Dregby as he passed and then turned back to face me. "My cousin, she wishes to meet with you."

"It is too soon," I appealed. "I am not ready to make new company."

"But you must," he demanded. "She has brought a message from the queen of our lands. We must find out what it is."

He paused. "Besides, I would like you to meet her. She is very dear to me."

"Very well," I conceded to his wishes. "Are you to accompany me?"

"You would find me nowhere else." He led me to the gated passage that connected to the dining hall. "Do not worry; she will not keep you for long."

I nodded and followed his lead.

When we reached the small foyer, I halted. Despite my concessions to Madigan, I felt somewhat betrayed that a stranger took comfort in the room that used to be my mother's. Was it fitting for anyone to assume her accommodation prior to her body being laid to rest?

"Arianna, what is it?"

"Nothing." I flinched. "Let us get this over with."

Before he could respond, I moved through the archway.

At the sight of her, I again halted. She was beautiful. A glistening glow surrounded her body as she lay on the bed. Thick curls of blonde highlighted her green eyes, and her skin was as smooth and white as porcelain.

Arianna. She smiled. Although I heard her words, her mouth did not speak them. *I am Shallendria of Maglavine.* She gave Darwynyen a slight nod. *The queen of our lands has watched over you for some time now.*

How? I thought.

Mystic in her ways, our queen holds great power, she replied. *She is able to see into the hearts of those who bear the same trait.*

As I accepted her words, I reflected on all that had happened in the past weeks.

I am sorry this room pains you. She slowly sat to face me, adjusting the sleeves on her white satin gown. *Madigan does not understand your emotions. It was not polite of me to take rest on your mother's bed.*

"There are no good impressions to be made through your influence of the mind," Darwynyen interjected. "Speak to her as you would any other of her kind!"

"Oh, Darwynyen." Shallendria rolled her eyes. "I was only seeing if she held the gift."

"Save your excuses," he snapped. "I see no need for your games."

For a moment she appeared angered but then calmed. "Sit with me, Arianna. We have much to discuss."

I caught the faint scent of flora as I sat.

"Our lady is proud of all you have done. Then her voice deepened, "Even so, she feels your journey is yet to find its end."

When I looked to Darwynyen, I felt her hand on mine. "Do not fear. Our queen, Aldraveena, will reveal everything to you in time."

Before I could respond, she put her fingers to her temples. "I must rest."

I stood. "You were not as I expected."

"Nothing in your future will be." She closed her eyes for a moment. "Assure me we will speak again soon." Her body fell to the bed. "I will seek you when I wake."

Unable to move, I held my breath. The magnificence of her presence overwhelmed me.

"Come." Darwynyen ushered me to the door.

As we descended the stair, I looked at him. "What happened to her? Why is she so weak?"

He led me through to the foyer. "Her powers diminished when she broke the spell on the portal."

"Will she be all right?"

"Yes," he replied halfheartedly. "But she needs rest to recover. That is why she was glowing. Magic draws out your inner being for a time."

Before I could question him further, he halted. "How is your friend doing?"

"He is all right," I answered in suspicion. "Why do you inquire?"

"Because we have yet to question him," he replied. "What if he—"

"He is not," I interjected. "Do you think my judgment is so poor?"

"No." He looked away for a moment. "It is your kind heart that troubles me."

"Can you not trust me as I have trusted you?"

"Until he is proven worthy, you cannot ask me to embrace him as you have." He sighed and continued his pace. "If you have no objections, I plan to see him later."

"He would probably welcome that." I took his arm, fearful of my next words. "Does it bother you that I stayed with him last night?"

"No." He stiffened. "Of course not."

I tightened my hold to reassure him. "Please do not take my act of kindness as—"

"We have other things to focus on." He again halted. "I sensed fear in you earlier. Do not let your impression of Shallendria sway you. The queen only seeks you out as a means to find your father."

"But I know little of him," I insisted. "If she has watched over me, she must know that most of my life was spent with my mother in Hoverdire." The pain from the memory resurfaced.

He embraced me. "Do not fight your emotions."

To conceal my weakness, I pulled from him. "Thank you for your comfort, but I am in desperate need of a bath." I turned. "I will leave you in search of Edina. Shall I save the water for you when I am finished?"

"Thank you, but no," he replied. "A few of us jumped in the stream this morning." I felt his hand graze my hair, "I will take some rest in a while if you care to join me."

"I will find you when I can." I left the question open. Despite the urge to concede to his wantings, I had my own agenda.

He nodded and left in the direction of the stables.

As I watched him leave, I felt deceitful. I shook the thought. There were things that needed doing. With that in mind, I made way to the study. If Shallendria was right, I wanted to be prepared for the next leg of my journey.

Lost in thought, I did not notice Madigan's presence upon entering the study.

"Arianna." He turned from the window as I lifted one of the metal boxes from a shelf next to the door. "Why are you here?"

By the look on his face, it was obvious I had interrupted him. "I apologize for disturbing you." I returned the box to the shelf. "I came here in search of—"

"Would it be these?" He revealed my sai upon a cloth of satin. "By your previous words at the den, I assumed them to be yours." He appeared intrigued. "These weapons would not be a common choice for men in these regions. In fact, they have only been seen in the distant South."

I nodded as I took hold of them. "My uncle gave them to me. We had many travelers in Hoverdire. To protect ourselves, we had no choice but to learn how to use them."

My eyes darted the room. "Did you not find the sheaths?"

"No." He shook his head. "They were found wrapped in this cloth."

He raised his brow. "Assuming your life to be meager in Hoverdire, I can only guess that your uncle spent his life's savings on these." His hand caressed the metal, "This metal has been folded several times, making them the strongest I have ever seen."

"How do you know such things?" I questioned. In the back of my mind, I thought of the sheaths. There were only a few things I still held from my uncle. Where had they gotten to? Perhaps my father had them destroyed. My heart sunk at the thought.

"Are you surprised?" Before I could respond, he continued with keenness in his eyes. "They have grown dull. Allow me to sharpen them. I wish to test your skill in the arena."

I looked at him with apprehension. "What is your interest in my skill?"

"Have you killed a man before?"

"No." I sunk back in an uncomfortable manner. "I have not yet had the need."

"Then let us hope you will not be faced with the decision." His stance stiffened. "Even so, we must make sure you are prepared."

"But I am," I countered.

"Then prove it." He put his fist to his chest. "Meet me to spar!"

"I am not ready." I turned. "Perhaps, I will find you later. If I am soon to make my way to Maglavine, I will need appropriate clothing."

"So, Darwynyen has spoken to you of the coming journey then?"

"Yes." I nodded. "He and I will set out once I have said good-bye to my mother." My heart skipped a beat, stunned that I was able to speak her name without hesitation.

"You are full of surprises, Arianna. Your strength has not gone unnoticed." He crossed his arms. "I will expect you in the arena this afternoon."

My mouth fell open. "But I told you I was not ready."

"You will never be ready," he stated emphatically: "If nothing else, your time with me will leave you better equipped."

"Then I shall be there." I was about to retreat when I caught a glimmer of sadness in his eyes.

"Madigan, is there something that troubles you?"

He looked down. "Thank you, but you need not concern yourself."

"Please." I took his hand. "I promise you my confidence."

He took a heavy breath in his response, "I am troubled by the people's disregard to my warnings." There was hesitation in his voice. "Perhaps I do not understand the way of the common folk. Is it that I have been in hiding for so long that I have forgotten how to embrace them?"

Sensing his pain, I squeezed his hand. "Tell me of your life? I mean—"

"Do not worry." His eyes met mine. "I hold no blame to you. We have both lived in the shadow of your father's deceit."

I looked deep into his green eyes. "You are a wonderful man, Madigan. I am so grateful to have met you."

"As am I." He looked to the window. "To answer your question, I was raised by a Guardian. He plucked me from the arms of my dead parents and took me as his own." He leaned on the ledge. "Although he was stern in his way, he was honorable. He put me in charge of his horse and armor and led me to lands afar. As I grew in age, I was instructed in the way of the sword." His paused for a moment. "When his health began to fail, we settled in Tayri. That is where I met Shallendria." He smiled. "Our relationship was troubled at first. They are different from us. In time, she showed me how to love again."

"How did you get involved with the Men of Moya?"

"There is a vast library in Maglavine," he replied. "After studying all I could of my heritage, I found information about the stones. When Morglafenn learned of my bloodline, he introduced me to its keepers."

"You have lived an amazing life," I gasped. "I mean after—"

He interrupted, "Everything happens for a reason. Although the death of my family was heart wrenching, I had to move on."

I struggled to hold back the tears. "Then so shall I."

"Do not fear, Arianna." He smiled. "All will be as it should."

"I will try to trust in your words." I looked away. "That is, if my father's will does not defeat us."

"Do not let him concern you now." He ushered me to the door. "He will be found soon enough."

I managed a smile as I moved through the threshold. "I will see you soon."

"Yes." He took hold of my sai, raising them above his head. "This afternoon in the arena."

"Please." I reached for them desperately.

"Do not fret." He took a step back. "You will not be without them for long."

"Very well." I conceded halfheartedly. "I will find you in the arena."

CHAPTER 18:

VELDER⊕N

Scouts were on his path, he could feel them. Despite his urge to wait on the Crone, he could no longer sense her. Was she ... could that evil bastard of an Elf seen to the death of her? He shook his head. She probably only conceals herself.

"Velderon." A Troll approached and bowed as his companions gathered around him. "We should move on." He looked to the sky through the filtering trees.

"Corbett has yet to arrive," he snapped. "We must wait on him."

"I fear the general has met his death." The creature winced. "Perhaps your daughter's cleverness is greater than you have allowed yourself to believe."

"You give her acclaim she does not deserve," Velderon snapped.

When the surrounding Trolls began to cackle, he stood. "Leave me! I wish to be alone."

As they disappeared through the shrubbery, he thought of her, Arianna. He could only see her survival as the reason for his missing companions. Part of him wanted her alive. In an odd way, he was almost proud of her strengths. Vexed by the emotion, he shook his head. There was only deceit in her. Even so, he was drawn to her, his only flesh and blood.

"Velderon." A Troll had appeared next to a neighboring boulder. "Scouts have been spotted in the distance."

"Very well. Let us move on." He tore a twig from a branch and trudged his way through the trees.

Chapter 19:

A Break in the Stream

As I made my way to my quarters, I found Evelyn in the ballroom, kneeling by my mother's box. Sobbing into a cloth, she did not hear my approach.

"Evelyn?"

When she turned, I rushed to embrace her. "Thank you. Thank you for aiding in my rescue," I cried.

"There is no need." She welcomed my hold. "I was not to leave you at the hands of your father as I had done your mother. If only I had acted sooner …"

I wiped a tear that escaped her cheek. "It was beyond your control. No one but my father can accept the blame."

She pulled away, closing the drapery. "I have spoken with Madigan, and though it is not tradition, he has agreed to hold her service at the mainstay. I hope you do not mind." Her eyes widened. "I only thought that your mother, being committed to her duties, would have wanted it that way." I put my sleeve across my mouth as she continued; the stench of death was getting to me. "What kind of ceremony would you like, my dear?"

Unsure, I looked at her blankly. "Perhaps her life should end in a celebration," I said, recalling the words of Darwynyen. "As you said, she loved her duties. She would want to be remembered for them."

"Oh," she replied, "that is a wonderful idea. Still, she will have to be burned according to custom."

"Of course." I stood; the putrid smell was becoming unbearable. "Is there anything else you would ask of me?"

"Have you prepared your words?"

"No." I shook my head.

"Then that will be the last of my requests." She smiled sincerely. "You have enough burdens to bear, for it is you the people will look to for strength."

Struck yet again by the deathly odor, my stomach began to weaken. "Evelyn?"

"Go child. You have not used oregano oil to conceal the smell."

I wavered in my step. "Thank you. I will see you later."

When I returned to the abode above the keep, I was surprised to find Edina at the wardrobe.

"Arianna." She smiled. "The king has given me permission to move your belongings. He does not expect you to reside in your prior quarters after all that has happened."

"Thank you." I threw my cloak to the bed. "That room no longer holds value to me." I moved to grab a bucket near the bathing tub. "Now that my life is moving in a different direction, I wish to leave the past behind."

"Are you to bathe?"

"Yes." I nodded. "I have been in need of one for days."

"I was soon to be on my way to the stream." She paused. "Perhaps you would like to join me."

I dropped the bucket. "Yes, of course! Nothing would please me more." I hesitated when I thought of the boys who used to follow me in Hoverdire. "But what if someone sees us?"

"The chances are few," she replied. "I know of the perfect place."

"All right." I tensed with anticipation. "Then let us go!"

At my response, she grabbed some drying cloths.

She led me to an area in the eastern part of the lea. Sheltered by trees, I felt confident we would go unnoticed. As we undressed, I inhaled the fresh aroma that escaped from the neighboring lilies.

"What are you waiting for?" She leapt into the water.

"Nothing." I threw my dress aside. "I was only enjoying the peace of the day."

When she rolled her eyes, I jumped into the water. "Wow!" I allowed myself a moment to adjust to the sudden drop in temperature. "This is most invigorating!"

"So." She dipped her head into the current. "Tell me of this man you have been keeping company with."

I could feel my cheeks as they warmed. "There is not much to tell."

"I do not believe you." Her eyes narrowed in a playful manner. "I would guess him to be the one you spoke of."

"How did you know?" I asked, bracing my feet on a small boulder.

"By the way he looked upon you." She raised her brow.

"You are right." My body shivered. "He is the one."

"Why did you not tell me?" she questioned. "Do you not trust me?"

"Of course, I trust you." I returned her stare. "Tell me again of your gentleman. Are you soon to see him?"

"I believe so." She twirled in the water. "At Madigan's succession, he announced the return of our outer armies. If his words are true, I expect him any day."

"Trust in his words," I assured her. "Madigan is an honorable man."

"Well, if nothing else, he is a ... " She paused. "Oh, Arianna, I did not mean—"

"I wish everyone would stop with their fussing." I shook my head. "It is sending me over the edge."

"It was not my intention to upset you." She looked down.

"You have done nothing of the sort." I released a heavy breath. "I am only frustrated. How can I move on if people will not allow me?"

"You are right." I felt her hand on my shoulder. "I will tread softly no longer."

"Thank you." I placed my hand on hers. "It will be best for all concerned if I am able to get on with my life."

When the sun broke through the trees, I realized the hour and made way for the bank. "I must go if I am to find Marion."

"What is it you require?" She puckered her brow. "I know all too well the gowns you possess."

"I wish her to craft me some trousers." I climbed from the stream. "With all the uncertainty, I wish to have proper attire should I need to defend myself."

"Trousers are for men," she snickered.

"I am not bothered by others' opinions."

"Oh." She blinked. "I all but forgot that you possess skills with weaponry. Would you teach me one day?"

"Yes, of course." I squeezed the water from my hair. "If you would like to join me, I am to meet with Madigan this afternoon. He has insisted on testing my skill."

She bit her lip. "Have you ever killed anyone before?"

"No." I looked to the water. "Even so, I fear soon I will not be given the option. By the words of the Elf mistress, it seems my troubles are far from over."

"The Elf mistress? Who is she?"

"She is the one Darwynyen and Madigan spoke of in the kitchen yesterday. Her name is Shallendria. She arrived from Maglavine this morn to breach the portal."

"The portal? What did she learn?"

"I cannot say." I pulled my dress over my head. "Darwynyen did not mention her findings." I turned. "Are you not coming?"

"No." She splashed back in the current. "I think I will stay on a little longer, if you do not mind."

"Take your time." I wiped my brow.

"Before you go." She hesitated. "There is something I forgot to tell you."

"What is it?" I replied with concern.

"Darwynyen appeared at my door last night."

"Whatever for?" I asked.

"He was in search of you." She paused. "Flustered by his tone, I blurted only that you were in another man's quarters. I am so sorry." She looked away. "I hope I did not cause you any trouble."

I looked at her and laughed. "I now understand the jealousy in his eyes when I awoke to him." I grabbed a drying cloth. "Please, do not trouble yourself with worry." Before she could respond, I disappeared through the bushes.

As I ran through the courtyard, I heard my name. Slowing my pace, I found Madigan near the stables. "What is it?" I rushed over.

"I am afraid we will have to postpone our sparring until tomorrow." He looked away. "Something has come up."

I squeezed the remaining water from my hair. "I have not been able to see to my chores yet either." I was about to turn when I realized that my mother's service was tomorrow. "I think it best we meet the day after tomorrow. My mother's—"

"Of course." He nodded. "Forgive me. I have had much on my mind."

"There is nothing to forgive." I managed a smile.

"How are you?" he asked.

"I would be a lot better if people would stop asking me."

"People ask because they care." He took hold of my chin.

"I know." I took a step back. "Your concern is greatly appreciated." I turned to make way for the door.

"Do not worry," he warned. "I *will* find you when the time comes."

"I am sure you will." I replied with an undertone of sarcasm.

Despite my frustration in Madigan's insistence, I kept focused, making my way to Marion's quarters. There was no doubt my idea for new attire would not be welcomed. Even so, I had to do what I felt was best.

When I arrived, I found the door slightly ajar. In recollection of my last visit, I knocked lightly as not to annoy her.

"Who goes there?" she yelled.

"It is I." I peered through the opening. "Arianna."

The door opened with haste. "My lady." Unlike my previous visit, her tone was comforting. "What a pleasant surprise. Is there something you are in need of?"

Confused, I cleared my throat. "May I come in?"

She extended her hand. "Please."

"Thank you." I entered timidly, unsure what to expect.

She shut the door behind me. "So, what is it you need, my dear?"

"I require some attire." My eyes darted around the room in search of appropriate material. "Attire that is not of a usual kind for a lady."

"What exactly do you mean?" she questioned. "I do not understand."

I stilled my breath. "I require trousers, though not of a common sort. They must hold a slit in the front, baring the knee. I am skilled with the sai. For me to utilize these weapons, I need easy access to them."

She thought to herself for a moment and then shrugged. "I suppose you will require something for the top as well."

"Yes." I spoke freely, encouraged by her compliance. "They too must bear slits that extend halfway up the forearm so that I may wear wrist guards, and it must not be constricted in any manner as I am familiar with archery as well." I closed my eyes for a moment, remembering I no longer had my bow, having had to leave it with a village hunter on our departure from Hoverdire.

"That will be no problem." She nodded. "I will craft them for you out of deer hide." She paused and looked at me with curiosity. "In return, you must tell me of your skills."

"Agreed." I smiled.

"Then let us get started." She ushered me to a stool.

It had taken well over an hour, and my legs had grown tired. Determined to see the outcome, I kept my stance.

"I am almost finished, my dear," Marion said, pulling a pin from her mouth.

"May I ask you something?" I lifted my arms when she put her hands to my waist.

"Of course, child. Speak." She helped me from the stool.

"You seem more relaxed than my last visit." I followed her to the mending table. "Has something happened to ease your mood?"

"Your father was evil in more ways than one, my dear."

"What do you speak of?" I asked with concern.

"I should probably not tell you this." She hesitated. "But perhaps it would lessen my burden."

"What did he do?"

"By no request of mine," she spoke sternly, "your father would see his way into my quarters."

When her eyes began to tear, I tried to comfort her, "Please, Marion, I did not mean to upset you."

She wiped her eyes. "Your father was alone and yearned for company of a personal nature." Her eyes narrowed. "I am glad to know I will never have to see his face again."

Sickened by her words, I looked down. "How could he do such things?"

"It is over." She nodded. "I can move on now."

I followed her to the window. "Marion, if you ever need to talk, please come to me."

"Thank you, child." She managed a smile. "I will have your outfit ready before long. In the meantime, you should visit the armory. If you require a new quiver and bow, that is where you will find them."

"How did you know?" I frowned.

She simply smiled and ushered me to the door.

"Thank you, Marion. I will return later." I shut the door behind me.

† † †

As I walked the corridor to the defense area, I noticed that it had been tended to. No longer did cobwebs cling to the stone walls, and the bronze on the torch mounts had been polished. I smiled, realizing Madigan had already begun to restore the castle to its previous glory.

When I reached the small foyer, I darted past the opening to the dungeon, feeling guilt ridden by Gin's torture. Beyond two wooden doors, several pieces of armor hung on the walls. Torches lit the room to the right, which was devoid of any windows.

I was about to continue, when I heard a commotion from one of the adjacent corridors. Curious, I made way. When I reached the archway at its end, I peered inside.

Madigan and Darwynyen, among others, were seated at a long wooden table in the center of the room. They appeared to be in a heated discussion. Maps were laid out along with measuring devices and charcoal. When they caught sight of me, the room fell silent.

"What are you doing here?" Darwynyen snapped.

"I was—" I stiffened my stance. "What are *you* doing here?"

"We are making battle plans." Dregby chuckled, "No ramblings that would interest you."

I looked to Madigan. "Is this why you postponed our engagement?"

Madigan nodded. "Shallendria found a map when she entered the portal. The Hynd are preparing for an attack."

"What engagement?" Darwynyen eyed Madigan.

"Why was I not alerted," I huffed.

"We thought not to trouble you," Madigan replied.

Insulted, I spoke harshly, "Well, are you going to tell me what you are discussing?"

Although hesitant, Madigan conceded, "We are trying to figure out where to send the troops." He looked to the others. "Because our men have not stood together for many years, we fear they may fight amongst themselves if we are not careful."

"Why would they do that when we hold the same purpose?"

"It is complicated." Dregby raised his brow. "You would not understand."

I shook the urge to confront him. "Perhaps if you would take a minute to explain, I might have something to offer."

A few of the men rolled their eyes.

"It is a delicate situation with many sides," Madigan replied, "a bit petty, if you will. Prior to the last war, the people of Man's Blood assisted in the protection of the bordering regions, being we had the most men to offer."

An Elf who stood next to Darwynyen interjected, "That is because you have no caution in your mating, thus overwhelming the rest of us with your kind!"

A few men laughed at his remark, but Madigan countered, "I fear you speak because your men do not know how to please a woman. Why else would your populations falter? Even your Elf mistress has turned to our kind!"

Flustered by his words, the Elf looked to the floor. Madigan continued with impatience, "Will you let me finish?"

In the silence that followed, he took a deep breath. "It was many years ago, so I can only tell you what I know." He nodded to the men. "When the war over the stones ended, people began to forget in the union. With no one to fight, they were left to bicker amongst themselves. First, it was over land regions, then gold and magic. Not long after, a rift emerged." His tone deepened, "To make things worse, the Amberseed went missing from Tayri." Madigan looked to Morglafenn. "Despite its location, the seed had no rightful heir."

I interrupted, "Amberseed?"

"Yes," Dregby concurred. "It is a treasure that far succeeds the value of the stone."

"When the Amberseed was discovered near Tayri, many feared it." Madigan leaned on the back of a chair. "Because of that, our trusted leaders agreed that no one would ever use it. To keep it safe, it would stay under the protection of the Elves. If it was to get into the wrong hands …" He hesitated.

"How did they know of the Amberseed's power?" I asked.

Darwynyen responded, "Scriptures were found with the seed. In the translation, it was learned that whoever consumed the resin would obtain powers far surpassing anything we have seen."

Taken aback by his potent words, I turned to Madigan. "Please, you must tell me more of this seed?"

"We do not have the time to get into detail," he replied, "but I can tell you that if the seed is found, the Stones of Moya will be the least of our concerns."

I nodded as he finished. Overwhelmed, I looked to the others. It was apparent from their stares that my presence was not welcome. Undaunted, I paid little heed. It was my father, after all, who had set this wheel in motion.

"You see." Madigan gripped the back of his chair. "From that time, isolation from one another was inevitable."

I again interrupted, "Who do you believe stole the Amberseed?"

Madigan looked to the others in his response. "To this day, it is not known. Most speculate that when the Stones of Moya are joined, their powers will lead their keeper to where the Amberseed lies. We believe that is what the Hynd seek now." He led his hand across the room as a gesture. "That is why we assemble our armies in haste. There is no time to spare."

"Now is not the time to concern ourselves with the seed." I raised my hands. "We must focus on the stones, nothing more!" When the men began to nod, I continued. "In light of your words, I think it best that the troops work intermingled, and it should be done so immediately. Not only will their different skills make for a grand army, but they will instill fear in the Sorcerers who would no doubt dread such a union. Moreover, it will allow the men to settle their differences while time is still in our favor."

When the room began to stir, I turned. "I hope my words have helped." Before they could respond, I left the room.

As I walked the corridor, I was struck with the staggering realization that my father was only part of this never-ending puzzle. The notion brought shivers to my skin. How could we move forward knowing so much was at stake? Unable to contend with my thoughts, I took notice of the armory that opened on the opposite side of the hall.

Stepping through the threshold, I noticed this room, unlike the others, had yet to be tended to. Cobwebs clung to the weapons, and sheets of dust formed into makeshift blankets. My nose itched as I inhaled the filth. I paid little notice as I delved deep into the clutter.

The swords were the first items that caught my attention. Not the ones that lay in piles on the floor, but the ones secured to the walls. Adorned with intricate engravings, they stood proud beside their scabbards. Because I was not skilled in such a weapon, I took my direction elsewhere.

At the end of the room, I found several uniforms upon wooden mannequins. Black undercloth provided contrast to display them proudly. I brushed the dust from one of the breastplates. The steel shimmered in the glow of the light. I was about to turn when I caught a glimpse of a quiver on the far wall. I had found what I was looking for.

In anticipation, I approached the bows with haste. Searching the wall, one quiver seemed to call out to me. It hung proudly above the others, and I grabbed it eagerly. Its case was made from dark leather with etchings of horses around the edges. When I reached for the bow, I realized it was longer than the one I had grown accustomed to. Intimidated, I assured myself that I would adapt to its length quickly. As I tested the tension, I thought of my engagement with Madigan. Thankfully, we were only to spar with the sai.

If only my mother could see me now, strong and in charge of my life. The pain resurfaced, though only mildly this time. It seemed that, with all the distractions, my grief was finally subsiding.

"Excuse me."

I turned to find an Elf at the threshold. "Can I help you with something?" I asked.

"Yes." He looked relieved. "The mistress has sent me in search of a girl named Arianna. She said I would find her in the defense area."

"I am Arianna," I giggled. "I will make my way to her now."

He looked at me oddly. "Shall I escort you?"

"No." I brushed past him. "I know the way."

Before entering my mother's quarters, I hid my new bow and quiver under the drapery of a table near the door. Not only was it none of her business, I was not yet willing to share my intentions. With that in mind, I made way through the opening.

I found Shallendria sitting on one of the settees. "You asked for me?"

"Yes." She smiled. "I thought we could continue our conversation now that I have rested."

She gestured for me to join her. "I apologize if I startled you earlier. I should have known it would have been awkward for you when I read your mind. I am not used to being around people of Man's Blood. You must excuse my ignorance."

Knowing the truth to be different, I raised my brow. "Except for Madigan, of course."

When a hint of anger appeared in her eyes, I stepped back. "I—"

"So you know about Madigan then?"

"Yes," I replied with caution. "I am sorry to have pried. It was not my place."

She smiled, as though to comfort me. "I do not wish to take on such a serious tone, but we must speak of what is to come."

"Darwynyen has already counseled me on what your queen seeks." I shrugged. "It is my intention to tell her all I know of my father."

"I see." Shallendria paused. "I hear you and Darwynyen have made a connection."

"I am not sure who has told you of this," I replied, sensing her disapproval. "But we have only just met."

"It is hard to bind a relationship when the other's blood differs from yours." She looked away. "I can only hope he does not break your heart."

My chest tightened. How could she be so disrespectful after she herself had taken a lover of my race?

"Please." She again motioned for me to sit. "It was not my intention to upset you. But you must understand that Madigan and I share a different kind of bond."

She reached for a glass of water. "Darwynyen is my cousin. I know him well." She took a sip. "He has been, for lack of another word, *troubled* over the years. I am not sure he is ready for a commitment."

I stiffened my stance. Not only was I distraught, I did not like the fact that she felt she could peer into my mind whenever she felt the need to. When she smirked, my anger boiled over. To avoid further words, I turned to leave. From the corridor I could hear her call after me.

I ignored her and continued my pace. I did not care about her wantings.

Chapter 20:

Forewarning

Undaunted by Arianna's mannerisms, Shallendria stood to look out the window.

Shallendria. A stern melodic voice struck her hard. *Do not be so cruel. She is only a child by our years.*

"My Queen," Shallendria uttered. *My only intention was to save her from the pain of Darwynyen's indecision when it comes to matters of the heart. You know as well as I that he is unable to commit.*

You have not seen the future as I, the queen countered. *We need her strong and abiding for the coming months, not weak and insecure!* Her voice took on a warning tone, *Do not make me contact you again!*

Before Shallendria could respond, the connection severed.

Stunned by the queens words, Shallendria looked deep into her soul. She knew compassion abided there somewhere.

Chapter 21:

To Seek the Comfort of Another

I clung to the wall in shock. It seemed surreal that I would be summoned to my mother's quarters in a time of grief only to have an overbearing Elf mistress meddle with my desires. Was she truly that cruel, or was she right? Uncertain, I began to question Darwynyen's intent. It frightened me that we still knew so little of each other.

Struggling with my thoughts, I stumbled up the stair. At the third level, I made way to seek Gin in hopes that he would comfort me.

I knocked lightly on the door as I pushed it open. "Gin, are you awake?" When I saw movement, I entered.

"Hi there." He smiled. "I was wondering when you would return."

I smiled when I noticed the color had returned to his lightly freckled face. "I will assume you are feeling better."

"Yes, much!" he replied. "I was able to take a short walk before your arrival."

"You should not push yourself," I warned.

He shook his head. "I will not."

After an uncomfortable silence, he continued, Your friends stopped by earlier." He put his hand to his chin. "One was called

Madigan and the other Darwynyen. They appeared anxious and asked me several questions."

"Oh?" I searched his eyes, taking notice of what remained of the previous swelling. "Were they convinced of your answers?"

"I believe so." Then his expression wilted. "They told me your mother's service is tomorrow. If you do not mind, I would like to attend."

"Yes, of course." I tested his brow with my hand. "If you are able, that is."

"I am." He slid his body upward. "It is you I am worried for."

"Why?" I huffed. "I can assure you my wounds have begun to heal."

"I am glad." He fixed his pillow. "I am sure your mother would have wanted it that way."

"I suppose you are right." I sat on the bed.

He placed his hand on mine. "There is something else." He paused. "I do not mean to pry, but your friend Darwynyen—"

"What?"

When he hesitated, I looked at him with annoyance. "Well? What did he say?"

"He wanted to know of my health. Why I needed attention, day and night."

I turned away in embarrassment.

"Did I say something wrong?"

"No, of course not." I sighed.

"Please," he begged, "tell me what is troubling you?"

With no one else to turn to, I decided to confide in him. "I am unsure of Darwynyen." I took a moment to find the words. "Although in many ways he is still a stranger to me, this has not been our first meeting."

"How could that be?" He puckered his brow. "Did you not spend most of your life in Hoverdire?"

"That is where I met him." I recoiled shyly.

He sat forward. "You must not stop there."

"Another time." I stood. "The past is irrelevant. It is now that I worry on. You see." I cleared my throat. "Through all that has happened, we have somehow made a connection."

"I see." He looked away for a moment. "If your future lies with him, then so be it. Even so, there is no need to rush things, Arianna."

"You are right." I nodded with conviction. "I will not look past tomorrow until I am certain."

"Good," he replied. "You are strong. Time will see you through this. Besides." His hands fell open. "For now you should be focusing on nothing more than your coming role as queen."

I blinked, realizing he was not aware of Madigan's succession. "Have you not been told?"

"Told what?"

"I have given the charge to Madigan."

"But why? I thought you were …" He searched my eyes. "What are you not telling me?"

I took a moment before responding, "If I tell you, I need you to swear you will never breathe a word of it."

"What is it?" he asked, clearly distressed.

"Swear to me first."

"All right, I swear!" He shook his head.

Anticipating his shock, I spoke with caution, "I no longer believe my father to be an impostor."

"Impostor? Who told you—"

"The Men of Moya," I interrupted. "They do not believe him to be who he claims."

"How would they know?" he retorted bluntly.

"They have had many suspicions to sustain them."

Gin nodded. "What has led you to conclude otherwise?"

"My father showed me a pendant." I half shrugged. "He said it proved who he was."

"Then why have you said nothing?"

"I do not know." I sighed. "But I think it is best to leave things as they are. Madigan is a true leader. His will demands it, unlike me, who shudders at the thought."

He bore a look of disappointment. "Because you have sworn me to secrecy, I will take no action, even though I doubt your decision. I can only hope you have not made a mistake."

I looked to the floor. Was he right? Had I made the wrong decision? No. "What is done is done." I took a step back. "Thank you for your confidence."

"Wait!" He threw the covers aside as if to follow me. "Now that you have given away your charge, what will you do?"

"I will stay on at the castle," I replied, returning to cover him. "Despite everything, Madigan has embraced me as a sister."

When he managed a smile, I secured the covers around his body and then left the room.

CHAPTER 22:

A Moment to Meddle

Despite the ongoing deliberations, Darwynyen stood up from the table. "My cousin calls for me." He nodded to Madigan and then to his Elvish companions. "I will return when I can."

When the men nodded, he made way to Shallendria's quarters.

"You asked for me?" he asked as he entered her room.

Shallendria turned from the window to meet his stare, keeping silent.

"I see you have recovered." When she did not respond, he grew impatient. "What is it you need?"

Again she kept silent.

Annoyed, Darwynyen moved to the door.

"I wish to discuss Arianna."

Darwynyen turned. "I do not wish to share my feelings with you!"

"Why?" she demanded.

"Because you will not understand." He put his hand to his brow. "I do not understand myself. Moreover, I need not your mocking. I love you, my cousin, but now is not the time."

Her voice softened, "You care for her then."

"Yes," he responded with certainty. "In fact, my heart desires her greatly."

"Then what holds you back?"

Darwynyen began to pace the room. "Nothing. It is only that we know so little of each other."

"I thought you cared not for those of Man's Blood!" She said with a scowl.

"Never say such a thing again!" Anger bore through him. "As I have just told you to the contrary!"

She responded with derision, "What of all your female friends at home? Arianna will surely learn of them on your return."

"I am glad you are enjoying this," Darwynyen huffed. "It seems to me that you have grown bored with your powers and in their place have learned to take pleasure in hurting others." He shook his head. "You are not the cousin I remember."

"Oh, Darwynyen." Shallendria moved to embrace him. "I am sorry. Perhaps you are right. I will leave the conversation for now."

She changed the subject. "Please, let us find Madigan. We need to discuss the days ahead."

"Agreed," Darwynyen replied, and he escorted her from the room.

CHAPTER 23:

NEW BEGINNINGS

After a long and wearisome walk along the stream, I returned to the castle. When I reached the landing, I saw Darwynyen and Shallendria descending the stair from her quarters. To avoid a confrontation, I hid in the ballroom as they made their passing.

At the bottom of the lower rise they turned toward the defense area. The nerve, I thought. How could they include her in the battle plans when it was made clear that I was not welcome?

I shook the thought when Shallendria glanced over her shoulder with a smirk. Again, she had read my mind.

"Arianna." Marion appeared, breathing heavily. "I have been looking for you all over." She wiped her brow of the sweat, making it obvious that moving around the castle had become tiresome at her age.

"What is it?" I tried to manage a smile. "Do you need more measurements?"

"No." Her eyes brightened. "I have one of your outfits ready. Please." She beckoned. "You must come and see."

Conceding, I allowed her to take me in the direction of her quarters. When we entered the room, I stood in awe.

"Oh my!"

"Then it has met your approval?"

"Yes," I gasped, taken aback. It was far more than I had expected. Somehow, she had managed to keep the design feminine, yet strong.

"Let us see it on you." She began to remove the clothing from the mannequin.

The soft leather felt like satin. "Do not be fooled by its delicacy." She raised her brow. "The hide is strong, I assure you."

As promised, the sleeves bore slits up the forearm that were stitched with a heavy leather rim. The legs too held the slit I had requested that would allow me to obtain my sai more easily. Overwhelmed, I looked to her with gratitude. "How did you finish so quickly?"

"If, my child, you are not already aware, I am the best at my line of work. Besides," she shrugged, "There was not much intricacy." Her eyes brightened. "Will you not try it on?"

I nodded at her request and quickly undressed.

"It fits perfectly!" I tested the elbows.

She handed me the trousers. "You must see the outfit complete."

As I pulled them to my waist, I took notice of the braided leather on each side. "These will make for easy work." I tightened the laces.

"These straps will be of assistance as well." She tugged at loops of leather along the waist. "If you wish to stow extra weaponry."

As I admired her work, she moved to the wardrobe. "Here." She handed me two wrist guards.

"They are beautiful." I examined the engravings.

As though to avoid the moment, she ushered me to the mirror. "You look grand, my dear."

I was shocked by my appearance. My slender figure held nicely in the garments. "I cannot find the words to thank you." I danced in my reflection. "May I leave these garments with you until the day past tomorrow?"

Her eyes wilted. "Forgive me. I forgot your mother's—"

"No." I pulled the shirt from over my head. "You misunderstand. I wish to keep them secret until I am to face Madigan in the arena."

"Are you to spar with him, the king?" She crinkled her brow.

"Yes." I nodded. "He has insisted on testing my skill."

"Say no more," she smirked. "Your secret is safe with me."

"Thank you." I paused, realizing I had forgotten my new bow and quiver under the table outside my mother's quarters. "I must make way. By your direction, I did find what I was looking for in the armory. It is now that I must retrieve it."

She nodded as she placed my outfit in her wardrobe.

"Will I see you tomorrow?" I asked.

"I will send you my strength through the crowd." She looked down. "I hope the day will pass quickly for you."

Unsure how to respond, I released a heavy breath as I left the room.

CHAPTER 24:

DOUBT

When the meeting adjourned, Shallendria and the others left Madigan and Darwynyen to speak in private.

Still lingering on the outcome, Madigan looked to Darwynyen with doubt. "I am certain they will alter their plans now that we have used the eye against them." His voice tightened. "If only Shallendria had gone unnoticed."

"Things are as they should be," Darwynyen replied with assurance. "If nothing else, we have brought fear to toil with their reason."

"Perhaps." Madigan stood.

"What concerns you?"

"I am not sure." Madigan hesitated. "It is only a feeling."

Darwynyen's eyes darted around the room. "I too hold a feeling."

"In regard to what?" Madigan returned to his seat.

"Arianna."

"Why?" Madigan frowned.

"Because she is naïve," Darwynyen replied. "She trusts too easily."

Madigan broke out in laughter. "You are jealous of Gin! I can see it in your eyes!"

"I am not!" Darwynyen snapped.

Madigan regained his composure. "Then what is it?"

"I hold concern over our visit to Maglavine. I feel …"

"Darwynyen." Madigan rolled his eyes. "Tell me what is really bothering you or speak no further."

"I do not understand my actions when she approached earlier." Darwynyen paused. "Why was I angered by her presence?"

"Is it conceivable that you were taken aback by her fervor?" Madigan questioned. "It is obvious to many that she carries a great will."

Darwynyen looked at the table. "She is most definitely not the girl I once rescued in the forest. Her innocence has been lost."

Madigan sat back. "Is that a bad thing?"

"I am not certain." Darwynyen shrugged.

"What of her gives you certainty?"

Darwynyen bit his lip. "The thought of being without her."

"Then you will have to see that it does not happen."

When Darwynyen nodded, Madigan stood, "I will leave you with your thoughts." He turned before leaving. "Try not to be so hard on yourself."

Darwynyen closed his eyes. When he opened them again, Madigan was gone.

Chapter 25:

His Return

The creaking hinges on the cottage door awoke me. "Darwynyen?" My eyes fought to secure his outline. "Is that you?"

"Yes."

My body tensed. "Have you come to check on me?"

"I have come to rest with you." He lit a lantern. "Do you mind?"

"No." I thought to Shallendria. "I am glad you are here."

He began to disrobe. Unsure of his intentions, I slid to the other side of the bed. "You must be exhausted."

"Words could not describe …"

Despite my urge to reach out to him, I pulled the blankets tightly around me. "Then let us get some rest."

As he slipped under the covers, he reached out for me. "I apologize for the way I treated you in the defense room." I felt his arm around my waist. "I cannot explain my actions."

"Why did you deny me?" I sat to face him. "If it concerns my father and his conspirators do I not have the right to participate?"

"I will make a better effort in future." He released a yawn. "What were you doing there anyway?"

"It is not important." I began to fluff my pillow. "My only concern is the growing tension between us."

"I …" He hesitated. "Do you want me to leave?"

I shook my head at the thought. "Forgive me. Perhaps my emotions have strayed."

"For what reason?"

"Your cousin." I clenched my fists.

"Forget her," he growled. "Her words are poison."

"But—"

"No buts." He took hold of my chin. "I will not let her come between us."

The tension in my body eased. "I do not know what to say."

"Say nothing." He extinguished the lantern and then fell back on the bed. "By the way, you did well today."

"I do not understand."

"Your suggestions were not taken lightly," he replied. "Before long, our troops will be reunited."

"Do you speak the truth?"

"Yes." He yawned again. "You were right in your words."

"I cannot believe it!" I gasped.

"Believe it." He repositioned his pillow.

"Thank you." I rested my head on his chest.

"There is no need." He led his fingers through my hair. "It was not my doing—it was yours."

When his breath began to slow, I looked at him through the moonlight. Secure in his hold, I felt guilty of my suspicion. I should have never allowed Shallendria to influence me. Despite our differences, Darwynyen had not once given me a reason to distrust him. In actuality, he had done nothing but reassure me with an honor I had grown to admire. Secure in my thoughts, it seemed for once that rest would come easy.

† † †

The day I had dreaded was finally upon us, a day many had not anticipated for years. As I made my way to the royal coach,

I noticed the congregation that was to follow. Beyond the royal ensemble, who were dressed in their finest military uniforms, hundreds of common people stood patiently awaiting my arrival. Before us, my mother's box was set upon a wagon, adorned in an array of spring blossoms.

"Arianna." An old man with thinning gray hair approached with caution. "May I?" He took the place of the herald and opened the door.

"Who are you?" I asked, suspiciously scanning his face.

"I am your uncle." The man bowed his head. "You must forgive me; your mother and I were not close."

"Then why are you here?" I was finding it hard to comprehend the fact that she had never once mentioned him.

"I regret ..." He paused uncomfortably. "When she married your father, I refused her." His eyes began to water.

Sensing his pain, I conceded, taking my seat in the coach. "Under the circumstances, I will place my trust in you and not refuse you as you had done my mother." I gestured for him to join me.

"Thank you." He took a seat and closed the door behind him.

"What do they call you?" I put my hand to my necklace, the one my mother had given me.

"Beradin." He half smiled. "I am her eldest of kin."

I nodded in an awkward manner and sat forward when the heralds sounded their horns.

As the coach made its way through the city streets, the royal ensemble played a solemn hymn, one reserved for times such as this. The procession was held in the utmost grandeur. People threw flowers from the windows as we passed.

"She would be proud." Beradin wiped his face with a gentleman's cloth.

"Do you speak of my mother?" I asked.

"Yes." He met my stare. "Standing up to your father must have taken great courage." In many ways, he reminded me of the uncle I had grown up with in Hoverdire. "I would like to offer you a room in our cottage. With your family gone, I will not see you alone, especially now that you have relinquished your role as queen."

I was taken aback by his generous offer. "Thank you for your kindness, but …" I looked away for a moment. "I care deeply for a man who has in many ways saved me. I will join him. We go east to Maglavine in three days' time, where we will continue in our search for my father."

When he tried to interrupt, I persisted, "I assure you, I will not rest until I have righted his wrongs."

His eyes held a look of pride. "You carry the strength I once saw in your mother." He raised his brow. "May I ask of this man's identity?"

I was about to respond when the coached halted. The door opened to Darwynyen.

"Arianna," he said, extending his hand, "are you ready?"

"Yes." I took hold of him.

"You join with an Elf?"

"Yes." I turned with sharpness. "Is there an opinion you wish to share?"

"Who is this man?" Darwynyen sneered.

"He is the brother of my mother." I stepped from the coach. "Under the circumstance, I ask you to disregard his manner."

Darwynyen led me to an opening in the crowd. "Do you know him?"

"No." I shook my head. "But I have chosen to trust in his grief." When I looked over my shoulder, the man I would now call uncle followed my lead.

As I moved through to the main square, I admired those who had gathered. The pain on their faces gave me the assurance that I would not endure this alone. One by one, the vendors offered their reflections from a podium set up in front of my mother's box. In their words, I was able to find some solace as I gazed upon it.

"I would now like to welcome Arianna!"

When the Master Justice called my name, I looked to the crowd with apprehension. Darwynyen put his hand on my back. "Speak from your heart. Celebrate her."

I nodded to his words of encouragement.

Despite my efforts, the forgotten tears made their return. Even so, I stood at the podium and focused on the crowd with pride.

"I would first like to thank each of you for coming." I paused for a moment to wipe a tear. "My mother would be honored by your presence. I know this service is not one normally held for royalty. Because we spent many of our years in Hoverdire as commoners, I have chosen to celebrate Brianna, my mother, in a manner that would give her dedication a sense of purpose."

When the crowd murmured, I continued. "It is now, in this dark hour, that we must celebrate her life." Unable to control my emotions, I looked to Darwynyen. He nodded. "I will ask nothing more of you than to leave here with thoughts of joy, for my mother had shared joy with all of you."

At my words, the box was set ablaze. As flame consumed her, I realized that my father had stolen a part of me that day in the tower. To once again feel whole, I would not rest until I found the justice we all deserved.

As I bid good eve to those who remained, my uncle approached somberly. "I regret my prior words." He looked away uncomfortably. "I wish you the brightest of futures, Arianna."

"Thank you." I took his hand. "Perhaps, in time, I will call upon you. It would give me no greater joy than to hear your words of my mother."

"Of course." He nodded. "I will anticipate your return."

"You shall not wait long." I managed a smile.

He bowed his head before leaving.

I made my return to the castle without the company of Darwynyen. We did not want to further rumors until things had settled. As I stepped from the coach, I heard my name. When I turned, I saw Madigan at the stables.

"Arianna!" He raised his hand. "You must come."

Confused, I rushed over to meet him. "Has something happened?"

"My timing may be poor," he confessed, "but I have a surprise for you."

"What is it?" I puckered my brow.

He ushered to the stable boy. "Bring him!"

I was about to speak when he interrupted, "Close your eyes."

"Why?"

"Just do as I ask," he insisted.

When I conceded to his demands, I felt his hand on my face. "Do not peek."

"Please Madigan," I huffed. "The day has been—"

His hand lifted. "Look!"

I opened my eyes to find the most beautiful stallion. "Madigan?" I admired the beast. He was a tawny brown in color, and his black tail and mane shimmered in the afterglow of sunlight. I ran up and grabbed him by the muzzle.

"Where? How?"

"He is for you." He winked with a grin. "I thought he would prove a worthy companion on your trek to Maglavine."

"He is brilliant!" I shouted through my bliss. "What shall I call him?"

"His given name is Accolade, but you may change it if you choose."

"No," I uttered. "The name does him justice." I grabbed the reins. "May I take him for a ride?"

"Of course." Madigan laughed. "He is yours to do with as you please!"

As I absorbed his words, I mounted my new horse, Accolade. He fought my hold for a moment but soon resigned to my command. With zeal, I kicked him and made way to the lea.

Upon my return, I found Madigan addressing a few of his men. "Thank you, Madigan." I rushed over. "You have brought me elation in the most somber of hours." Before he could respond, I left to the kitchen.

"Evelyn." I brushed past her, darting through the area to the inner cold store. "You will not believe what Madigan has given me!"

"Slow down, child, before you give your heart a shock!" When I nodded, she smiled. "Now, what is it, my dear?"

"He has given me a horse!" I replied, reaching for a bundle of carrots.

"What goes on here?" Darwynyen entered the room. "Is everything all right?"

"Madigan has given me a horse!" I cried. "Quickly, come see for yourself!" Not waiting for a response, I ran back to the stables.

Madigan, having dismissed his companions, was awaiting me. "I am pleased that you have welcomed the surprise." He cleared his throat. "I worry on you … all you have been through. You do know I worry on you?"

"Of course." I gave the horse a carrot. "I worry on you as well." I paused. "In fact, I cannot imagine my life without you."

"As I." I felt his arms around me.

I took comfort in his embrace. "I will not forget this, Madigan."

Darwynyen approached. "Arianna?"

Madigan released me to address him. "To ease her burden, I have given Arianna this stallion. She will need him for your trek home to Maglavine." He hesitated, "You do not mind, do you?"

"Of course not," Darwynyen replied with little emotion. "It is a very generous gesture."

"His name is Accolade." I smiled. "Is he not magnificent?"

"He is indeed." Darwynyen looked to Madigan.

Madigan took the reins. "Let us take him to the pens."

I nodded and followed his lead.

Chapter 26:

Envy

Feeling numb, Darwynyen stood back while Arianna and Madigan led the horse to its dwelling. He could not understand why she shared her joy with Madigan alone. Things were not supposed to be this way. He knew he could not compete with such presents, nor did he want to.

To shake the ill-fated emotions, he made way to his own horse. He grabbed the brush, even though he had no intention of using it. As he caressed the bristles, he admired his own stallion.

"Myoway," he uttered, "you are the proudest of steeds."

Consumed with guilt, he glanced over to Arianna. As he watched her with Madigan, he tensed. He fought the emotion. He would not allow another to hinder his growing relationship with the girl. Instead, he would make an effort to stand by her, no matter who chose to meddle.

Satisfied with his thoughts, he decided to join her.

Chapter 27:

Time to Overcome

When Darwynyen approached from the paddocks, Madigan tensed. "I should be on my way."

His actions made it obvious that I was not the only one to sense Darwynyen's serious mood.

"Madigan." Darwynyen's tone was stern. "Would you mind?"

"Of course." Madigan nodded and then turned to leave. "Good night, Arianna."

"Good night." I raised my hand.

Darwynyen moved to take his place. "He is a beautiful stallion." He halfheartedly reached for the mane.

I smiled. "I have always desired my own horse."

When he did not respond, I looked to him. "What troubles you?"

"Nothing," he quickly replied. "I am pleased that Madigan has warmed to you. You are the closest he has to family."

The underlying sarcasm in his voice was undaunting in the moment. I wrapped my arms around the steed.

"I will be back for you in the morning, Accolade. If we are soon to travel, we must get to know one another."

Darwynyen looked to the ground. "Perhaps tomorrow, if you like, I can also share with you *my* steed."

"That would be nice." I took him by the arm. "Shall we retire?"

Without a response, he led me from the stables. We walked the corridors in silence. When we reached my room, I began to remove the braiding from my hair. After lighting the lantern near the bed, Darwynyen stood at the window. Worried about his mood, I placed the pins on the table.

"Darwynyen, is everything all right?"

"Will you sit with me?" He ushered me to the bed.

Hearing the seriousness in his tone, I began to panic. Thoughts of Shallendria flew through my mind. Was he going to leave me? I could not bear it.

"How about we make way for one of the towers?" I turned. "I am not yet ready to retire. Besides, there is not a cloud in the sky, and I love to gaze into the twilight."

"That would be nice." He followed with reluctance.

When we reached the top of the northwest tower, I halted. "Look at the stars." I smiled with enthusiasm to engage him. "Are they not brilliant?"

"Arianna." He pulled me to face him. "I do not know what to say other than that I am sorry for the way I have been treating you. I know we shared words last night, but no longer do I feel settled."

"Darwynyen." I tried to ease him. "Let us not worry on the past. Our only focus should be on the future." I paused. "Perhaps we should take this time to learn more of one another. How about you tell me of your life in Maglavine?"

"Why do you ask?" He stiffened. "Did Shallendria speak ill of me?"

"No." I looked at him blankly to conceal the truth. "I am only trying to get to know you better."

"Good," he sighed in relief. "I would not want you to hear of my life through my cousin. Although I love her, her ill-fated intentions on this matter have already been proven."

"You speak as though you have something to hide."

"I kept with several women in our sanctuary," he said, his eyes straying to the distance. "It was not my intention to betray them, only I could not accept my true emotions. After our brief encounter in Hoverdire, I was in desperate search for a means to fill the void."

Disappointed, I looked down, for I, unlike him, had not been with another.

"Did I upset you?"

Thoughts raced through my mind. Was my reaction unreasonable? He was an Elf, after all. With time as no hindrance, he could live his life as he pleased with little repercussion. I, on the other hand, did not have that luxury.

"I am fine," I uttered. "You were not bound to me for those years. You were free to do as you pleased."

"To the contrary," he countered, "I felt imprisoned."

"Imprisoned?" I frowned.

"Yes." He nodded. "Despite my attempts, all I could see was your face." He sighed. "It was only when my desires began to settle that you once again appeared."

"I was not expecting to see you again either." I bit my lip before I could further accuse him.

"I will never forget that moment." He chuckled. "There you were, sitting at that table. You had no idea what you had gotten yourself into."

Despite his previous words, I needed further assurance. "Then why were you so cold when your eyes fell upon me?"

"What was I to do?" He spoke assertively. "Did you expect me to pick up where we had left off, in front of the watchful eyes of my companions?" He continued before I could respond, "Moreover, I was in shock. It took me several moments to accept the fact that it was really you."

"Say no more." I blinked. "I understand."

"Are you disappointed?"

"There is no need to be." I put my arms around him in an attempt to persuade him. "You have lived many lives, and I have only the one."

I tugged at his collar. "How old are you anyway?"

He appeared hesitant. "I am to the year of one hundred and eighty-three, still considered quite young in my region."

I laughed, having forgotten the previous subject. "Wow, what can I say to that?"

"Nothing," he replied. "How old are you?"

"I am almost embarrassed to say." I recoiled.

"Do not be, please," he begged. "Tell me before I start guessing and anger you."

"I too am considered quite young in terms of my people." I sneered in a playful manner. "I have only lived eighteen years of *my* life."

His eyes widened. "I guess I would have thought you to be older."

I stepped back. "Should I be insulted?"

"No." He reached for me. "It makes no difference, I assure you."

Not waiting for a response, he directed me to the stair. "Let us make our way back. I do not want you to get a chill."

Once we had settled in for the night, dressed in our underclothes, Darwynyen turned to face me on the bed. "I must again apologize. In future, I will do my best to respect you as you deserve."

I smiled at his gesture. "I will make an effort to do the same."

When my body gave way to a yawn, he extinguished the lantern. "May your sleep be peaceful." He smiled through the moonlight.

"And so may yours." I pulled the covers.

He kissed me on the brow before turning.

Although I was still uncomfortable with his revelation, I felt for the first time that we were finally getting to know one another, and I promised myself that I would not hold his past over him and that I would try to be more patient. Secure in my decision, I slid next to him. When he felt my presence, he pulled my arm around him. In the warmth of his body, I quickly fell asleep.

† † †

It was early when I awoke. It must have rained during the night, for the morning cloud was still breaking up across the skyline. After a stretch, I turned to embrace Darwynyen. To my surprise, he was already gone. He must have gotten up early and chosen not to wake me. Undaunted, I leapt from the bed.

As I ran a brush through my hair, I thought of Edina. I had not seen her since my mother's service. I decided that my first stop of the day would be to her quarters.

When I reached her door, I hesitated. It did not sound as though she was alone. "Edina?" I tapped lightly. "Are you there?"

Moments later, she appeared in a state of disarray. "Arianna!" She tried to straighten the mess that had become of her hair. "I apologize for my tardiness. Is there something you require?"

"Did I come at a bad time?" I peered over her shoulder.

"No, of course not." She slid through the opening and pulled the door closed behind her. "My fiancé, Stuart, returned last night. We have been inseparable ever since."

"Oh, Edina!" I smiled. "I am so happy for you." Before she could respond, I turned. "Please, I will bother you no further. Fetch me when you both have settled."

"No, wait," she beckoned. "What is it you need?"

"Nothing." I smiled again. "To be honest, I was only looking to share in your company."

She took me by the hand. "There is something that troubles you."

It was not my intention to steal her from her happiness. To sway her concern, I spoke with conviction, "Do not worry on me. Please, enjoy your time together."

"And we will indeed!" A man appeared at the threshold.

"Stuart!" Edina glared. "You must not speak in such a tone. It is lady Arianna that stands before you."

"Forgive me, my lady." He bowed his head.

I held back my laughter to better observe him. His short curly locks were a mess. The buttons, misplaced on his shirt, clung to his lengthy torso. Like Edina, he too bore a long nose, which made them look well suited.

"There is no need." I half smiled. "It is I who have interrupted."

He nodded and stepped back into the room.

Edina led me down the hall. "I will send Stuart on his way. He has yet to visit with his family, and if he does not do so soon, I will for certain take the blame." Before I could respond, she continued, "As your friend, I will ask that you do not fight me. I have wanted to visit with you."

She slowly backed away. "Wait on me by the castle doors. I will not be a minute."

"Very well," I conceded.

It felt like an eternity as I waited for her. "Where could she be?" I grumbled. Annoyed, I began to trudge up the stair.

"I am here!" She smiled from the landing. "I apologize if I kept you waiting."

"What took you?" I growled. "I do not have the day to wait!"

"Arianna." She took me by the arms. "What is it? I can tell something is troubling you?"

"It is nothing." I looked away. "I only worry on Darwynyen. I am not sure how ..."

"Why? What happened?" She searched my eyes. "I have seen the way he looks upon you, so it must not be caused by your relationship."

"You misunderstand." I took a moment to find the words. "It was when I found you with Stuart that I realized I would also share a bed in such a manner, only I know nothing of the deeds."

"Oh, Arianna," she sighed. "You two share a bond. He will lead you in that direction when you are ready."

Then her brow crinkled. "Not to pry, but if I am not mistaken, have you not been sharing—"

"Not like that!" I stammered. "It is not proper—" I broke off my words. "I meant no disrespect."

"Do not look down on me, Arianna. Stuart and I have shared a life together. If he had not been called away, we would have been married already. As for last night, I could not—"

"How did you know," I questioned. "How will I?"

"Only you can answer that." Her hand grazed my cheek. "Try not to rush things. Take this time to better get to know one another."

I released a heavy breath. "I feel silly for even asking."

"No." She shook her head. "It proves your trust in me. Now come," she insisted, "let me tend to your hair."

I nodded and followed her back up the stair. When we reached my room, she had me sit at the desk, being there was no dressing table in my new abode. As I awaited her, she grabbed a straw basket next to my wardrobe that held my brush and comb as well as an assortment of clips and pins.

"Ouch!" I cringed when I felt the bristles on my scalp. "Why are you pulling so hard?"

"Stop fussing." She jerked at my tangled locks. "We have little time. Are you not to meet Madigan in the arena today?"

"Oh." I closed my eyes for a moment. "I had almost forgotten."

"Word has traveled. Many speak about it." She giggled. "Are you nervous?"

When she applied the final pin to my hair, I turned. "How could I have agreed to such a thing?"

"You must not cancel." She nudged me from the chair. "The disappointment will be far reaching."

"Are you saying there will be spectators?"

"Only those who work within the castle walls." She directed me to the mirror. "I braided your hair and knotted it at the back. I would not want you to be hindered in any manner."

"Thank you." I grabbed my cloak. "I must find Marion. She has my new wardrobe."

"She has agreed to assist you then?"

"Yes." I moved to the door. "Will you join me? Your opinion would be most appreciated."

"I will find you shortly." Her eyes began to wander, "I first have a quick deed, but I should not be long."

I looked at her with suspicion. "What have you been doing that warrants such secrecy?"

"Nothing of interest." She began to fidget with a smirk. "I promise. I will not keep you waiting this time."

Despite my urge to confront her, I nodded and took my leave.

† † †

Under the mounting tension, I forgot to knock on Marion's door before entering.

"Arianna?" She turned from the mending table.

I halted. "Please," I begged, "forgive the intrusion. I do not know where I have left my manners."

"Do not fret, child." She moved to close the door. "Are you ready, my dear?"

"Not really." I began to disrobe.

"Do not give into fear," she warned, "for it will prove to be your greatest weakness." She handed me the outfit from her wardrobe.

"I can make no promises." I pulled the trousers to my waist.

"Here." She unfolded the top. "There is no doubt this outfit will complement your strengths, should you choose to use them."

"I will." I thought to Darwynyen and wondered how he would accept these changes. Perhaps I should have told him. It mattered little now. What was done, was done. I would not stay submissive for him.

I moved to the mirror.

"Do you like what you see?" Marion made the final adjustments to my wrist guards.

"I no longer recognize myself," I admitted. For the first time, my inner strengths would be seen on the outside.

"Your life takes on a new path, my dear." A tear escaped from her eye. "I am so very proud of you."

"Thank you," I uttered. As my eyes began to water I embraced her. In many ways, she had taken on the role of a mother, a role that had never really been filled by my real one and now never would be. Guilt from this emotion led me back to the mirror. I wiped the tears and turned in a circular motion. As I came about, I noticed she held another garment in her hands.

"Here is your second outfit, my dear. Upon your return, I will have more."

I smiled at her generosity. "I will never be able to repay you for your kindness."

"Arianna?" A knock came to the door.

"Who goes there?" Marion stiffened her stance.

"It is Edina." I moved to unlatch the door. "I hope you do not mind, but I have asked for her."

"Of course." She bowed her head.

"Oh my," Edina gasped when I came into view.

"Is it too much?"

"No." Her eyes ran the course of my body. "I have not once in my life seen a woman so grand."

"You had best be on your way." Marion winked.

"Yes." Edina took my hand. "The king awaits you!"

Before leaving, I turned back to Marion. "Forgive me, Marion. Would you care to join us?"

"No, no," she replied. "I am too old for such things. No, I will watch from afar." She ushered me through the door. "Now go! I bid you good luck!"

As we made our way down the corridor, I again thought of Darwynyen. I could only hope he would not be angered by my new appearance. In our descent to the main foyer, the front doors burst open. To my surprise, Darwynyen appeared, along with several of his companions. Still wet from their bathing, they were full of laughter.

I froze in fear of his reaction.

"Arianna?" Darwynyen's eyes widened. "What ... what are you doing?"

It was plain to see that he was stunned. To ease him, I spoke lightly. "I was just on my way to meet Madigan. He wishes to test my skills in the arena."

With those words, I remembered my bow and quiver. Before he could respond, I turned to Edina and whispered, "Will you please find your way back to my quarters? I may need my bow and quiver. They are hidden under the bed."

She nodded and rushed up the stair.

Darwynyen turned to his companions. "I will see you later."

Without words, the men took their leave.

Although apprehensive, I made way to meet him.

He grabbed me by the hand, lifting it to get a full view of the outfit. "What is this?"

"I had the seamstress, Marion, craft it," I replied. "If we are soon to make our journey to Maglavine, I want to be prepared should we fall to danger."

"There is no need." Disappointment filled his eyes. "I can and will protect you."

"I know you can." I smiled. "But what if you are not around?"

"Are you doing this to punish me?"

Shocked by his selfishness, I angered. "This has nothing to do with you! This is about me and who I have become!" I took a step back. "I thought you would be proud of my strengths."

His expression of dissatisfaction did not change. To avoid an argument, I decided it best to leave. "I must go. I am late!"

When the door struck the latch, I halted. Tears filled my eyes. I wanted to return to him, to mend his ill sentiment. The underlying anger between us was slowly killing me inside. If we could not see to reason, how could we grow to love one another as I thought we were destined to do?

"Oh, thank the gods." Gin stumbled over from the stables. "I thought I had missed the beginning."

"Beginning of what?" I discreetly dried my eyes.

"Are you not to meet the king in the arena?"

"Forgive me." I met him at the bottom of the edifice. "I was only just—"

"Never mind your worries. You will be fine" He took my arm. "What is this new outfit you wear?"

I stiffened my shoulders. "I had the seamstress, Marion, craft it."

"You look amazing." He felt the leather on my sleeve before turning toward the arena.

Stunned by his reaction, I said nothing to his response and followed his lead.

When we entered the arena, I halted in astonishment. I had seen it before, but only from the balcony. It was far more intimidating from within. Putting my hand to my brow to deflect the sunlight, I took notice of the two grandstands that faced the open field on opposite sides. The one to my right had a décor meant for royalty. The other was left to open air with few comforts. Along the ledge of the royal stand stood many spectators. Some had even taken rest on the benches, making it obvious that the pretence of this assembly was under no regal authority.

"Why do you linger?"

Shaken from my thoughts, I smiled. "Come. Let us proceed."

"No pressure." He winked. "But you had better win!" He left to join those who had already gathered on the benches. "All my money has been placed on you!"

Taken aback by his comment, I raised my brow. "You must be joking."

"Arianna!"

When I turned, I found Madigan by a stand filled with weapons. At my approach, he held out my newly sharpened sai.

"Thank you." I took them with caution.

"Be careful," he warned. "They are sharp!"

"Yes, I can see." I led my finger down the flat of the blade.

"Here." He pulled off the cover of a box. "I want to give you these."

I took a step back when I saw the most beautifully decorated sheaths. "Your gift is far too generous!"

"You will need them for your travels." He held the box forward. "I am certain you will find them to your liking. I had them crafted for you yesterday."

I hesitated at the thought of my uncle and the missing sheaths. "Perhaps I could make use of them until I find the ones my uncle gave me."

"Of course." He nodded.

"They *are* beautiful."

"And so are you."

When I looked at him with widened eyes, he continued, "I mean … in your new outfit, that is." He looked to the others. "It is not only I who sees it!"

Stunned, I looked to the crowd. They were staring with anticipation. The stress left a pit to form in my stomach.

"Where is Darwynyen?" He asked in a concerned voice.

"I cannot say." I placed the box on the ground near the stand. "Shall we get started?"

"I thought you would never ask." He handed me a pair of wooden daggers. They were well used, with dents and scratches along the blades and grips. "We do not use real weapons when training."

As I took the makeshift weapons, the crowd grew silent. Madigan grabbed his set of wooden blades. They were identical to mine. "Do not worry," he said, twirling his weapons. "I will not go hard on you."

Aggravated by his remark, I narrowed my eyes. "It is I who shall go easy on you!"

The crowd began to murmur, inching forward to gain a better view.

"What are we waiting for?" I urged him.

He extended his arm. "After you, my dear."

We proceeded to the middle of the arena where we started to move around each other in a circular motion. From the corner of my eye, I noticed Edina. She held up my bow with a gesture. I motioned to her with a slight nod. When Madigan followed my stare, I took the opportunity to side kick him in the stomach. Taken by surprise, he rolled to the ground.

The crowd murmured again.

He quickly resumed his position. "I will not fall for that one again!"

"We will have to see about that," I smirked. "I am not finished with you yet!"

Annoyed by my response, he swung at me. When he overextended his torso, I knelt to grab his shins and pulled his feet from under him. With nothing to brace his fall, he hit the ground hard.

I laughed. "Not too quick on your feet, are you?"

The crowd began to laugh.

"So you are serious then?" He sat up. "If that is the case, let us see what you are made of!"

I nodded and extended my hand in courtesy. He took it. Locked in his grasp, he pulled me down. Before I knew it, he was on top of me and holding his blade tightly to my neck.

"Never aid your victim, no matter how hard he pleads!"

Stunned from the fall, I took a moment to collect my thoughts. He loosened the tension and gazed deep into my eyes. When I returned his stare, I lost my breath. The moment was intense, far more than I had anticipated. Could it be I was attracted to him, or moreover, was he attracted to me? No, I shook the thought from my mind.

In the awkwardness that followed, I shifted. "If you do not remove yourself, how shall I defeat you?"

He jumped to his feet and extended his hand. As he lifted me, I pulled the same move on him, only I kicked out his feet instead.

As I knelt upon him, I smirked smugly.

When I raised my hands to rally the crowd, he changed our positions with haste. "Are we going to muck around on the ground all day?" he asked.

I wiped the smile from my face. We had broken even in our sparring. In agreement, we both raised ourselves from the ground on our own accord.

Keeping aggressive while conservative in our posture, we again began to circle one another. I blocked his strikes with vigor, holding what would be the sharp of my wooden blade to my forearm. Every second swing, he stood back. I made note of this weakness and waited for him to do it again. When he lowered his arms to pull away, I struck him in the face, to my immediate regret. Rage appeared in his eyes.

"You are a quick one; I will give you that. But not quick enough for me!"

Annoyed by his taunting, I went for his neck with a backswing. As I overextended, he grabbed my arm. Tight in his embrace, he dug his blade into my side. "Have you had enough?"

I could feel his breath on my neck. "Never!" I stomped on his foot.

Staggered by the blow, he loosed his hold enough for me to break free.

"I am surprised you fell for that one." I used my sleeve to remove the sweat from my brow.

Furious, he lunged at me with full force. I hopped to the right, kicking him on the backside. Unprepared, he again fell to the ground.

As he recovered from his fall, we broke out in laughter.

"Arianna, I must say …"

"Say nothing." I put my hand to my chest. "Not to be bold, but it seems my uncle has taught me well."

He looked to the crowd. "Forget your wagers! We are finished here!" Before I could protest, he moved to the table and grabbed a wooden sword.

"Does anyone else care to spar?"

Many men came forward. They were no rivals for Madigan. With little effort, he quickly defeated them. As though bored, he began to challenge two or more at a time. I wanted to join in. Even so, I felt certain by his current disposition that our match was by far a fair one.

Once he tired completely, he walked to me and bowed. When I smiled, he turned to the others. "That is all for today. Make way!"

When they began to disperse, he wiped the sweat from his neck. "I can see now that I need not worry about you."

"But the other men …" I began. "It was plain to see you went easy on me."

He took some water from a canteen. "Men will never fight a woman as they do each other." Then his voice deepened, "But trolls Will. To stay sharp, you must keep up with your training." I felt his hand on my back. "Take heed to my words. Keep to your strength. You are a strong woman." I could feel my cheeks warm.

When he saw my blush, he changed the subject. "So, what other skills do you possess?"

Surprised by his interest, I spoke freely, "Well, I have learned the skill of archery. I found a—"

"Come!" he shouted to two Elves sitting on the ledge of the grandstand. "Since you are in no hurry to leave, this lady would like to challenge your skills in archery."

I took a step back.

"There would be no contest," one replied. "She is of Man's Blood."

Angered by his comment, I interjected, "Do you decline because you are afraid?" I was not to walk away without a fight.

The Elf snickered, "If it is your will to lose, I see no harm."

The other shrugged. "Let us make way to the stables. There is a target mannequin there."

"Agreed," I replied.

When I turned, Madigan stopped me. "I apologize. I should have asked you first."

"It is all right." I shrugged. "But if there is any wagering to be had, do not bet on me!"

He rolled his eyes and ushered me forward.

Chapter 28:

The Presence

"She is stronger than I first thought." Darwynyen looked to his cousin. When Shallendria did not respond, he moved from the gallery to get a better view of the arena. "I am finding it hard to accept her strengths." His hands fell to the ledge of the balcony. "She has changed so much from the time I first met her."

Shallendria joined him. "Will you tell me how you met?"

Annoyed by her prying, he looked down. "That is something I do not wish to share with you. It will only give you the ammunition you crave to destroy our bond."

"If that is how you feel." She backed away. "I will ask no further."

Guilt ridden, Darwynyen stood forward. "I am the one who should apologize. Perhaps I am not yet ready to speak of the past."

Shallendria decided to change the subject. "There is something I have been meaning to discuss with you."

"What is it?" Darwynyen asked with interest.

When she hesitated, he took her hand in support. "What is troubling you?"

"I have felt a presence from the time of my arrival." Her tone deepened, "A presence of evil."

He shook his head, assuming her insinuation was meant for Arianna.

"Hear me out, please!" she pleaded. "I am not claiming that your precious Arianna is evil."

"I would hope not." Darwynyen calmed. "Please, continue."

"The presence is very faint, well hidden from my powers, but it is here. I am certain."

"What should we do?"

"Nothing." She looked to him with an insistent resolve. "We can only wait. If we are patient, this person will soon reveal themselves."

He looked to the arena. "In the meantime, I will keep a closer eye on Arianna. She is naïve in such matters."

Before she could respond, he turned. "I must go. I will speak with you later."

Chapter 29:

A Gesture

When I looked to the crowd that had assembled in the stable area, Darwynyen was nowhere to be found. Through my disappointment, I grew angry. Although I feared his presence, I yearned for his support. Why was he being so bitter?

I broke from thought when I felt a tap on my back. I turned to find Edina with my quiver and bow.

"Here you go." She smiled. "Good luck. You were terrific out there!"

Madigan glared in her direction.

With the slightest of shrugs, she rushed off.

"Where did you get this?" Madigan took the bow from my hand.

"I borrowed it from the armory." I looked to the ground. "I hope you do not mind?"

"No." He shook his head. "What is mine is yours." His brow rose. "But I now know why you were in the defense area the other day."

I nodded, taking my bow from his grasp.

One of the Elves carved a line into the ground with his bow. "We shall use this as our starting point."

"Very good." I gave Madigan a fleeting look. "What should I call you, sir?" I discreetly admired his bow.

The shorter one standing next to him stood forward with confidence. "I am Elster. My companion's name is Kendrick."

I nodded and took a step back to allow them their space. "Shall we begin?"

When Kendrick stood forward to aim, I could not help but notice him. He was broad in the shoulders, and his auburn locks danced on his chest. He appeared strong and menacing in his way.

"You are a friend to Darwynyen?" I asked.

"Yes, but I do not believe he is coming." He began to pull back his bow but then paused. "Perhaps you should go first."

"I—" When the crowds began to murmur, I stiffened my stance. "Certainly."

As Kendrick cleared the path, I tested the tension on my bow. It was far more comfortable than my last. I aimed with ease. When I allowed the arrow its freedom, it glided directly into the mannequins' head. Thrilled, I jumped in my place.

Kendrick ignored me and looked to the servants' entrance.

I followed his stare to find Darwynyen. "You are good," he said and slowly began to clap his hands.

"You are right." Kendrick stepped back, acknowledging his presence. "I see no need to continue." He began to disperse the crowd.

Darwynyen approached. "Where did you learn this skill?"

"I took instruction shortly after our first encounter." I continued when his eyes narrowed. "After noting your bow and quiver, I was determined to learn the skill for myself."

"I had no idea I held that effect over you."

"You did," I uttered.

He led me toward the lea, avoiding those who still lingered. "There are obviously many things about you to be told. Although I am pleased by your strength, you are no longer the innocent girl I once met in the forest."

I looked down. Throughout our time together, I never once assumed that he was still holding onto the young girl who once needed him. "You should be relieved by my independence. I would not wish to be a burden."

"A burden?" He kissed my brow. "Not ever have I thought of you as a burden, nor will I." I felt his fingers down my back," Would you care to practice more? Not to be impolite, but I am guessing your last contest was won by chance."

"You have guessed right." I raised my bow. "Still, it feels as though this bow has always belonged to me."

"Then you have found the one you should carry always." He pulled a strand of hair from my brow. "Be sure not to lose it."

I nodded and returned to the stable to retake my stance in front of the target. Darwynyen followed.

My first three shots missed. It was hard to concentrate in his presence. I was about to give up when he took hold of me from behind.

"I want you to follow my stance and memorize it," he directed. "You are not standing correctly."

I practiced his posture to keep him near. He moved my limbs around until satisfied. "How does this feel?"

I pulled back on the string. To my surprise, I was getting better gain when extending. With confidence, I grabbed another arrow. Placing it along the bow, I took aim. When I let go, it sped into the thatch head.

"Wow!" I jumped in elation. "That felt great!"

"You have done well." He took my bow. "Well enough to have worked up an appetite?"

"To be truthful, I am famished."

"Let us find Madigan. That is, if he wishes to be found." He chuckled. "I do not believe he was expecting such a skilled opponent."

Startled by his remark, I halted. "Did you watch the match then?"

"Yes." He smiled. "But only from afar. I needed to speak with my cousin."

"Oh." I hid the ill sentiment. "Should I ask for your opinion?" I searched his face for approval.

"Your training has proved you worthy." His eyes grew serious. "But you must remember that today was in fun. It will not be so easy when you are faced with death."

"I know." I broke from his stare. "I have toiled with such feelings as of late."

He embraced me. "It was not my intention to frighten you."

"You did nothing of the sort." I held him tightly. His hold comforted my worries, even if it only lasted for a moment before he pulled away.

"Come." He took me by the hand. "Let us make way."

When we reached the dining hall, he ushered me inside. To my surprise, the room was full of people. "What is going on?" I looked to Madigan who stood waiting by the door.

Shallendria followed my stare.

"Ask the Elf next to you." He winked. "This is his work."

Darwynyen nodded. "I thought it would be nice for you to spend some time with your companions before we embark on our journey to Maglavine in a few days."

I turned to Edina, who sat patiently at the table. "Is this why you kept disappearing on me?"

"Yes." She nodded, putting her arm around Stuart. "Are you pleased?"

"Of course." I glanced back to Darwynyen with a smile.

"I am also pleased." Gin shifted in his chair. "You won me much money today."

"I said to forget the wagers!" Madigan sneered.

Kendrick lifted his goblet. "A toast to the victor!"

The men began to chuckle.

"Do what you will." Madigan took his seat at the end of the table, in the throne my father once used. Shallendria took the seat next to him, my mother's.

Darwynyen directed me to a chair on the opposite side. "Let us eat."

"Wait for me. Wait for me!" Dregby appeared at the main door. "Sorry I am late." He moved to an open setting, one without a chair.

"Everyone," Madigan said, taking hold of his goblet, "raise your glasses. We have much to celebrate. Not only has Shallendria revealed to us the Hynd's plans, but our armies will now join as one." He took a drink. "I have a good feeling for our future!"

As the others took their measures of wine, I hesitated.

"Arianna." Madigan frowned. "Why do you not join us?"

"My mother," I uttered. "She told me that spirits would poison my mind."

The room broke out in laughter.

"Arianna." He held his goblet to mine. "You must not deny me. It will bring about an omen of bad luck!"

Although reluctant, I nodded. "I suppose it would not hurt this one time."

Madigan looked to the others. "Again, we will drink to our future!"

When they followed his lead, I slowly raised my glass.

The burning sensation made me to choke. Desperately, I reached for some water.

"She speaks the truth," Shallendria snickered. "Not once has she tested the spirits."

Embarrassed, my eyes fell to the table.

"It is good that she does not dabble in the nectars." Madigan spoke in my defense. "They only make you weak!" When he felt my stare, he quickly countered his words. "Do not worry. You have to drink plenty to lose your way."

Darwynyen took my hand and squeezed it from under the table while changing the subject to idle conversation.

When I had finished with my meal, I decided to indulge in the array of fresh fruits that decorated a table near the wall.

Morglafenn joined me. "Blackberry does wonders for the palate," he said as he reached for one.

"I could not agree more." I took another. "In Hoverdire, we always had to search for our berries. Many a time I was too tired to eat them on my return."

He smiled.

Uncomfortable, I continued. "Where is it you are from?" I blinked, realizing my blunder. "What I mean is … do you live in Tayri or Maglavine?"

"Both." He met my stare. "I go where I am needed. Because a loch breaks the region, communication between our people is minimal. Not only has the queen given me the responsibility of governing both cities, but I am the only healer as well."

"So." I puckered my brow. "Are you saying you are gifted in the magic?"

"No, my dear." He reached for another berry. "Although it involves the skill, I only focus on the aspects of healing."

"Come." I felt Darwynyen's hand on my back. "The king awaits us."

Confused by his remark, I looked to the others who had begun to take their leave, "Where?"

"You will see soon enough." He took my hand.

I turned back to Morglafenn with an awkward smile as I was led from the room. When we reached the ballroom, I halted. The room was overflowing with people. In the corner, musicians assembled their instruments. Near the colored glass windows, a makeshift bar was erected where men filled their mugs in merriment.

"What is this?"

"We rally to celebrate the coming of your troops," Darwynyen replied.

"Announcing the king!" a herald bellowed.

The room went silent. One by one, men and women bowed as Madigan passed. "No formalities tonight!" Madigan shouted from the foot of the stair. "While time is at hand, let us rejoice in each other's company!"

When the music began, he ushered Darwynyen and me further into the room. "Arianna." He paused. "I know we have just—"

"Do not worry, Madigan. It is the people who need your strength, not me. A celebration such as this is an honor many will not forget." Before he could respond, I made way for the stair.

"Wait!" Darwynyen followed. "Where are you going?"

"To our quarters." I continued my ascent. "I will not be gone for long."

Unable to find a suitable gown, I began to tear apart my wardrobe. "There must be something!"

"May I be of assistance?"

I turned to find Edina. "I do not know what to wear!"

Without hesitation, she grabbed my copper dress. "You should wear this one. If I am not mistaken, it is the color of the one you wore when you first met Darwynyen."

"How did you know?"

"You mentioned it once in idle chatter," she replied.

"Clever you are." I began to disrobe.

As she tightened the lacing, I looked at her through the mirrored reflection. "I see you still wear your work attire."

"Is it not suitable?"

"Not if you wish to sweep Stuart off his feet." I winked. "Please, you must take a gown of mine."

"Although your gesture is generous, it is not necessary." She recoiled. "I know my place."

"Your place is with me," I said decidedly. "Besides, I will be gone the day past tomorrow. If nothing more, let us share this last evening together as sisters."

Her eyes began to water. "Thank you, Arianna." Like a shy girl, she moved to the wardrobe.

"I have always liked this one." She pulled out a purple gown that I had never worn.

"Yes." I smiled. "The color will enhance the blue in your eyes."

"Thank you again, Arianna." She removed the gown from its hanger and began to undress.

When we reached the level of her quarters, she took my arm. "Come, I have the perfect thing to finish off your outfit."

Curious, I followed her direction. Once in the room, she pulled some white buttercups from her vase.

"Allow me to put these in your hair."

I smiled, remembering the floral crown I had made on my way to the falls of Dean.

After placing several flowers within my braids, she turned me to face her. "The aura around you is magnificent. Go to him. See where your feelings take you."

A tear left my eye. As though sensing my worry, she embraced me. "Do not fret. Everything will be fine."

As we descended the stair, she began to fidget. "Before we proceed, you must know that Madigan labored over the idea of having this celebration. He worried on whether or not it was too soon."

"I know," I replied. "We have already addressed the matter." Before she could continue, I halted. "Do I look all right?"

"Yes, of course. Do I?

"You look extravagant." I shuffled the crinoline in her dress.

She blushed and took my arm in laughter.

At our approach, people turned to stare. Through the crowd, I searched for Darwynyen.

"I must find Stuart." Edina gave my hand a squeeze before leaving.

"Arianna."

Recognizing the voice, I turned awkwardly, sensing the heat filtering through my cheeks.

To my relief, he seemed to share the same discomfort.

"You ..." he uttered, "you look as you did the day we first met."

My heart skipped a beat at his words. We shared a moment lost in time. He put his hand to the nape of my neck. "You have awoken several memories from the past."

Shallendria appeared from behind us, startling me. "May I have a word, Darwynyen?" She pulled him away.

Madigan took his place, appearing as handsome as ever. "Would you like to dance, Arianna?"

"Yes." I glanced over my shoulder, half expecting Darwynyen to protest. He was nowhere in sight. "I would love to."

He turned to the band. "Play the song of hope!" I felt his hand under mine. "Shall we?"

I allowed him to escort me to the center of the room as I admired his strength and honor. For the first time, he seemed comfortable in his new role as king, something I had hoped for from the time of his succession. Taking notice, the people stood aside, the men in proper posture while the woman curtsied in their gowns. When the music began, I placed my free hand on his shoulder. He put his tightly around my lower back. The sensation caused me to shiver. With the thought of Darwynyen, I tried to ignore the sensation.

"Do not take much heed of them," Madigan offered. "Elves do not enjoy our dance or music. They have their own traditions."

By his remark, I realized my look of disappointment must have been far more noticeable than I first thought. To sway his concern, I smiled sincerely. "Forget them. Nothing will ruin this evening for me."

He raised his brow. "Good!" Not waiting for a response, he twirled me to the chorus of the music.

CHAPTER 30:

AN ILL-FATED INTERRUPTION

When they reached the mezzanine that overlooked the main foyer, away from prying ears, Darwynyen spoke in anger, "What is it Shallendria?" His eyes narrowed, "How dare you drag me away from Arianna like that!"

She drew back in disdain. "I thought I was saving you. No more than I do you enjoy the dances of the Man's Blood."

"Still." Darwynyen crossed his arms. "I would not have denied her."

Shallendria laughed audaciously. "Do not be ridiculous. You do not even know their dances!"

Infuriated by her callousness, he took a moment to regain his composure. "Do not push me, Shallendria. I warn you now!"

When she looked at him blankly, he stomped back into the ballroom.

CHAPTER 31:

NIGHT TURNS

While I endured the conversation and fare in the ballroom, Darwynyen did not return to me. Was it out of guilt or was it just his nature? Because I knew little of his people, I tried not to judge him by his actions. Even so, I could not help myself.

"May I have a mug of ale?" I leaned at a bar that was erected near the colored glass windows at the back of the room. After swallowing most of the measure, I asked for another.

"You will regret your behavior in the morning." Madigan took the mug from the barman. "Arianna, you must start slowly with these things."

Annoyed, I snatched the mug from his grasp. "Leave me be, Madigan. I will be fine."

"If it is your will, then so be it." He stomped off, shaking his head.

Swallowing the last of the measure, I began to feel woozy. I ignored the sensation. If nothing else, the spirits gave me a sense of confidence, enough so that I began to mingle with whomever crossed my path.

"Are you enjoying the evening?" Morglafenn said at my side.

"Most certainly." I tried to conceal my disappointment. "I love social gatherings."

"Give not your attention to Darwynyen." He took a mug of ale. "These feelings you share are new to him. In time, they will be realized."

My legs began to waver. "Thank you for your concern, but these excuses are not yours to make. His years far outweigh mine. If there were any reason for this madness, I should be the one holding back, not he."

"That is why it is you who must see this relationship through." He placed his hand to mine. "You must not give up unless you are certain."

Disheartened, I looked away. Not once had the thought occurred to me. "Oh, I have no intention of giving up." I hiccupped. "He has been in my heart for so long, I cannot imagine my life without him."

"Then with him you shall be." He squeezed my hand.

When I again hiccupped, he released me. "I must retire. Good evening, Arianna."

"Good evening." I began to search the room for Darwynyen.

Minutes later, I found him near the stage, engulfed in laughter and surrounded by his companions. Enraged, the words of Morglafenn were instantly forgotten. I took hold of the nearest gentleman.

"Shall we dance?"

"I would be honored," the man said with a bow.

CHAPTER 32:

CONCERNED

Madigan approached Darwynyen with caution when he saw him leave his companions abruptly to stand on a step near the stage. "Why is it you deny her?" he asked, following Darwynyen's stare to find Arianna dancing in the arms of another.

Darwynyen turned with narrowed eyes. "What do you mean?"

"Well, my friend, if you let her go, she might find another." He paused. "I know it is not your way to be with a woman of Man's Blood, but—"

"As you know, I have felt jealousy in the past days, something—" He broke off his words. "I will not have it anymore, not even for her!"

"So you admit to your jealousy." Madigan raised his brow. "Why now?"

"It is not important." Darwynyen released the tension in his shoulders.

"Either way, your actions bewilder me." Madigan again looked to Arianna. "There is no doubt she carries love for you. I have seen it in her eyes."

"That is what frightens me," Darwynyen replied. "I have never held such feelings before."

250

"Do I need to reiterate my previous words?"

"No." Darwynyen scowled. "I will go to her soon."

"Do as you wish." Madigan turned to leave, not waiting for a response.

CHAPTER 33:

ᛖIDERS

In need of some fresh air, I made my way to the balcony. The air was crisp. To keep warm, I crossed my arms. When I looked to the sky, the stars were dancing in the blanket of night. My stomach began to turn, a consequence of the spirits. I had taken too much ale.

"Are you enjoying the evening?" a voice asked from behind me.

Knowing it to be Darwynyen, I replied coldly, "Yes."

He released a heavy breath. "I apologize. I just …" I felt his hands on my back. "I have no excuse for leaving you. If only I understood your ways."

Unable to deny him, I turned. "What is it your people do for enjoyment?"

"We enjoy pleasures as you," he replied. "Only they are of a lighter nature."

"Do you share in dance?"

"Yes." His eyes wandered to the ballroom.

"Will you show me?"

"Of course." He took my hands. "Forget the music you hear now. Follow my lead." When I nodded, he pulled away. I did the same. We rejoined as we turned. Halting, he circled me in my place. Upon his return, he pulled me to him. Holding me tight, he led my hand down the back of his neck. The moment grew tense. Caught in his gaze, I felt a prickling sensation on my skin. I closed my eyes, desperate for him to take me.

"Darwynyen!" Madigan shouted. "Come! You are needed."

Darwynyen pulled away. "Needed for what?" he growled.

"There is no time to waste! The Mider troops have arrived." Madigan disappeared.

"Forgive me, Arianna." He ran after him. "I must go."

Gin soon appeared in his place. "Arianna! Have you been told?"

"Yes." I put my fingers to my temples. "I should retire for the evening. My head has begun to burn."

"I suppose your mind is spoiled by the spirits." He rolled his eyes.

I nodded stumbling away.

"You cannot go now," he beckoned. "You have to see this!"

"Can you not see that I am ill?"

"Forget your ailments," he replied. "You are about to witness something our people have not seen for hundreds of years!"

He sparked my curiosity. "What is it you speak of?"

"Look." Gin pointed to the fields aloft, those below the mountains of Vidorr. "Give your eyes a minute to adjust, then look to the land below the mountains."

When I claimed view, I took a step back. "How many are there?"

"Thousands," he uttered. "Is it not amazing?"

"Yes." The pain in my head resurfaced. "I must make way. I do not feel well."

"Can you not wait?" His eyes widened. "Before long, the land will begin to tremble. It will be enough to reinvigorate you, I am certain."

"I have seen enough." I turned.

"Shall I walk you?"

"No, thank you," I replied, not having the patience to wait on him in his weakened state.

"Why?" He seemed disappointed.

"Stay." I pinched his cheek with a smile. "Enjoy the moment."

Before he could respond, I pushed my way through the gathering crowd.

† † †

I awoke to the remnants of a headache that had thankfully worn off in the night. Darwynyen was nowhere to be found, nor did I expect him. Sick to my stomach, I slowly crawled from the bed, guarding my eyes from the sunlight that had begun to break through the windows. My first instinct was to get some food and then I would take a ride to clear my head.

After grabbing some bread and cheese from the kitchen, I made way to the stables. I found Accolade where I had left him. Unable to cope with the gear, I asked the stable boy to prepare him while I ate.

The boy approached as I swallowed the last of the bread. "My lady, your horse awaits you."

"Thank you." I tried to clear my throat as I dismissed him.

Desperate for the wind on my face, I quickly mounted the stallion and made way to the gates. A tour around the city streets would no doubt ease my mood.

"Halt!" A guard blocked my path. "Where goes Your Highness?"

"I leave to the city!" I snapped.

"My lady." He put his fist to his chest. "You cannot leave the castle on your own."

Annoyed, I replied in anger, "Why not?"

As though confounded by my question, he stood for a moment and then stepped to the side as he ushered me through.

CHAPTER 34:

PREPARATIONS

Darwynyen spent the remainder of the night in the eastern courtyard where they prepared the fields for the coming troops. To avoid any expected animosity between the different regional accompaniments, they had no choice but to divide the land equally.

The sun was well into the sky when he finished flagging the last of the trees. Exhausted, he chose to retire and hoped that he would soon fall into the arms of Arianna.

When Darwynyen reached the abode above the keep, Arianna was nowhere to be found. Although disappointed, he did not think much of it. She was probably well rested and off with Edina, preparing for their departure to Maglavine tomorrow. He was looking forward to his return, despite the ill-fated memories of the place that often seemed to plague him.

As he lay on the bed, he thought of Arianna and how he desired her. Delicate and naïve in her ways, she left him with an overwhelming urge to share his love with her completely.

He gave way to a yawn, and slumber soon followed.

CHAPTER 35:

EDRIC

When I arrived at the mainstay, I took notice of the fountain and immediately thought of Edric. I had not seen him since before the rebellion. To thank him for his efforts, I made way to the inn.

I left Accolade with the establishment's stable hand and rushed inside. The pub was quiet in comparison to the last time I had visited, and I did not see Edric anywhere.

I approached the barman. "Where is Edric? I wish to speak with him."

The man set his drying cloth down in a somber manner. "My lady." His voice broke under the tension. "Edric died in the rebellion."

Unable to comprehend his words, I turned away. "No." I closed my eyes. "Not him."

"My lady, if it is …" His voice was lost to the echoes in my head. Unaware of my steps, I found myself on the outside of the building. Children began to gather around me, expecting money. I had none to offer, nor, if only for a moment, did I care about their needs.

Nudging them aside, I staggered into the stables where I began to cry.

"My lady." The stable hand directed me to Accolade. "Forgive me, but is everything all right?"

"Leave me." I took hold of the reins. "I wish to be alone."

He nodded and left me to give his focus to awaiting patrons.

As I made my way back to the castle, several vendors waved in passing. Not to disappoint them, I raised my hand in gratitude. It would not be in the people's best interest if I were to show weakness when our people were preparing for war, a war with many uncertainties.

When I reached the blacksmith's repository that opened off the mainstay, I pulled the reins, distracted by the clanking of steel. Men labored to complete their weapons, adding them to a large stack outside the establishment. The smell of heated metal and fire filled the air. As I watched them, I soon realized that, despite my efforts, there was little I could do to settle the fears of what was to come in the inevitable battle.

I was about to move forward when the ground around me began to rumble. Uneasy, Accolade began to stir.

"Giants!" a woman screamed. "We are under attack!"

"Stay calm!" a guard shouted from the wall walk. "There is nothing for you to fear!"

Horns sounded from the barbican. As they bellowed through the air, I realized their intent. They were announcing the arrival of the Miders.

"Make way!" I kicked my horse with anticipation.

Finding my way through the gathering crowd proved difficult. When I arrived at the barbican, I steadied Accolade. In the distance, I could see the approaching battalions.

"Amazing," I uttered. There must have been thousands of them.

Heavily armed, the Miders were decorated in their finest military uniforms. On foot, the pounding of their hooves was in complete synchronization. Miniature horses were used to pull the wagons that followed. Despite the Miders' short measure, their demeanors were intimidating. With pride on their faces, they paid no attention to those around them.

They halted at the gates as though waiting for some sort of acknowledgment. Through the confusion, I rode up to the portcullis. "Where is the king?" Chaos seemed inevitable without direction.

I looked to the Miders when they began to grumble.

"Keep calm, my lady." A guard stood forward. "The king is on route."

Annoyed by Madigan's tardiness, I made haste to the stables, certain I would find him there or somewhere along the path.

"Madigan!" I pulled the reins when I reached the stable gate. "Why do you delay?"

"He must." Dregby replied. "It is a demonstration of strength."

Madigan mounted his steed. "Let us make way."

Dregby put his hand to his chest, "After you, my lord."

"Where is Darwynyen?" I dismounted.

"He seeks you now." Madigan placed his helmet over his head. "You will find him in the study."

I nodded, handing Accolade's reins over to the stable boy.

When I reached the study, I found Darwynyen half asleep at the table. "Darwynyen?"

He stood in a startled manner. "Where have you been?"

"I took leave to the city." I reached for his hand. "There is something you must know."

"Do not worry." He yawned. "The grounds have been prepared for the Miders' arrival."

"That is not what I speak of." My eyes began to tear. "I went to the tavern today. Upon my arrival … Edric did not make it through the rebellion."

"I know." He released a heavy breath. "We found his body in the caverns."

"Why did you not tell me?"

"I thought you had been through enough. I was going to wait until …" He did not finish his words. "There was another."

"Who?" I asked with apprehension.

"The guard, the one at the gatehouse, I do not recall his name."

"Kalvern?" I thought of Evelyn. "Do you speak of Kalvern?"

"Yes." He embraced me. "Do not mourn them. Give them honor, for they did not die in vain."

In the silence that followed, I thought of Edric. Although the pain was not as deep as it was for my mother, I owed him much. Not only did he lead me to the truth, he led me to the one I loved. Because of that, I would never forget him. Kalvern had also changed my fate. If Darwynyen and his men had been unable to breach the castle, the general would have for certain had his way with me.

I pulled away, taking notice of an open book on the table. "What are you reading?"

"It is nothing." He pulled out a chair. "Will you sit with me?"

"Is that my father's handwriting?" I stiffened.

"No." He took hold of the book. "It is a journal written by his Crone."

"What does it say?" I blinked. "Are there any writings of me?"

He shook his head. "I found nothing of a personal nature."

"Then what did you find?"

"A detailed account of your father's studies," he replied. "To our misfortune, it seems he has grown very powerful."

"How powerful?"

"Here." He flipped through the pages. "This tells us he has learned to summon the creatures of night." He paused with a look of concern. "Are you sure you want me to continue?"

"Yes," I insisted. "I want to know all there is about him."

"Very well." He flipped to another page. "This section covers his influence over the elements. He has found a way to manipulate the clouds and thunder."

I frowned. "If he is as powerful as you claim, why did he not use these spells the night he fled?"

"Because they take hours to conjure," he replied.

I looked down, embarrassed by my naïveté. "What do you know of the magic? I mean, can you …"

I felt his hand on the back of my neck. "What do you want to know?"

"I am not sure." I sat forward, distracted by his touch. "Are you skilled? Can you conjure spells?"

"A few." He nodded. "To be truthful, I have never held the interest."

"But still you learned. Why?"

"The reason is not important," he replied bluntly.

Knowing not to push him, I stood. "May I look inside the secret room?"

He raised his brow. "Of course. You do not need to ask."

Although a part of me feared what lay inside, I slowly stepped through the doorway. The room, to my surprise, was not how I had expected. One small table stood between me and a narrow bed that was set halfway into what looked to be an old fireplace. Jars filled with various herbs sat upon a shelf near the door. Forgotten candle wax covered the protruding stones that riddled the walls. In the corner—

"Darwynyen!"

"What is it?" He rushed to my side.

I pointed to an iron encasement on the wall.

"It is the portal of forbidden eyes." He pulled me to face him.

"But …" I hesitated, glancing over my shoulder. "It really is eyes!"

"Yes." He tried to distract me. "They are preserved in an emulsion that allows them to be called upon with magic."

"Who did they belong to?" I cringed.

"Come." He led me from the room.

"Arianna, I am pleased to have found you."

Startled, I turned to find Shallendria at the threshold.

"Has Darwynyen made you aware of our plans?"

I gave him a fleeting look. "Why? Has something changed?"

"I will now accompany you on the first leg of your journey," she replied.

My mouth fell open in disbelief.

"She is to join us through to the woodlands of Maglavine where she will take her leave north to meet with the council of Tayri."

Certain she was reading my mind, I smiled. "I shall look forward to our time together then."

"As will I." She winked at Darwynyen before leaving.

Darwynyen took my hand. "You still appear bothered by her. Why? Is there something you have yet to tell me?"

"She …" I paused to choose my words carefully. "That night you asked if she spoke ill of you. Well—"

"What did she say?"

"She told me that you were soon to break my heart. That you were not ready for a commitment."

The veins in his forehead began to bulge. "I must go."

"No, Darwynyen! Please, it is not worth the effort," I pleaded. "Her words are no longer poison now that I have spoken them. It is you I believe in, no other."

"Do not listen to her, Arianna." He embraced me with vigor. "She has done nothing but stir trouble from her arrival."

"No one will tear us apart." I put my hand to his face. "If only she did not have the gift of reading minds."

"She is not as powerful as you believe." His brow crinkled. "That skill was only acquired recently."

"It matters, nonetheless." I sighed. "She still has the ability."

"Forget her." He moved to the window. "She will not be in our company for long."

When I joined him, I could not help but notice the Mider troops in the lea who had set out in preparing their camps. Tents, smaller than those used by the Man's Blood, were erected in small circles instead of the neatly lined rows of men that I had once witnessed in Hoverdire during a small battle when I was a child. Smoke filtered from the coal pots that were scattered within the area. Around them, Miders were stacking the supplies they had brought by wagon.

"There are so many," I gasped.

"Yes," Darwynyen replied. "Still, this is only a small portion of the armies that are soon to gather."

"If more are to come, how will we accommodate them?"

"There is no need." He looked to the horizon. "The others will wait for us in Biddenwayde."

"Biddenwayde? Why Biddenwayde?" I questioned. "It will take us several weeks of travel to get there."

"Unfortunately, our options are few." He shrugged. "It is the only region that borders Cessdorn."

"If north is our destination, why did Dregby have his armies gather here?"

"There was no other road for them to travel," he replied.

"I see." I rested my head on his shoulder. "And what of your armies?"

"There is not one to speak of. To the contrary of what you may believe, our people are not vast in population." He paused as though the subject pained him. "Elves are a dying breed."

"What do you mean?" I asked.

"It is complicated." He put his hand to my chin. "Do not fret. You will be impressed by what we have to offer."

"If only we could leave now!" I took a step back, frightened by my zeal. It was almost as though I was looking forward to the coming war. Disturbed by my thoughts, I quickly pushed them aside.

"I should probably pack my belongings."

"I will join you shortly." He walked me through the door. "I must first check on the men."

I nodded and motioned for him to proceed ahead of me.

Chapter 36:

To Confront

After leaving Arianna, Darwynyen made way to the eastern courtyard where the Miders continued preparation of their camps. Searching the area, he quickly found Dregby and approached.

"Dregby!" He raised his hand. "Is there anything I can do?"

"No, Darwynyen." Dregby tapped him on the back in a fatherly manner. "The time will come when you will need to tend to your own men. Do not trouble yourself with mine."

Darwynyen nodded. "How many more are expected?"

"At least three times this many, but, like you, I will not send for them as of yet."

Darwynyen again nodded. "Do you think this will work? I mean, the joining of our troops. It has been many years since our people have stood together."

Lost for words, Dregby met his stare. "Only time will tell, my friend."

"I will leave you to your work." Darwynyen turned.

Ascending the stair to the northern balcony, he came across Shallendria, sitting on a bench near the gated passage to the dining hall.

"Just who I was looking for," he huffed.

She smiled. "Darwynyen."

He moved to meet her. "I would like to ask you of Arianna?"

"What is it?" Her face soured.

Darwynyen halted, startled by her sudden change of mood. "What is wrong with you? You have carried nothing but anger since your arrival."

Shallendria's face softened. "I do not understand why Madigan is so protective over her. It bothers me."

When Darwynyen broke into laughter, she grew angry. "What is so humorous?"

"You are experiencing jealousy," he replied. "It was new to me as well."

"Jealousy," she scoffed. "Impossible! I have never had it before."

"That is because your relationship with Madigan has always been in our region."

"Yes, but—"

Darwynyen spoke to enlighten her, "Over the past days I have learned that the people of Man's Blood do not hold their feelings back. They turn to one another to seek comfort. I believe we find unease in this because of our lifespan. It has done little more than lead us to solitude."

He paused. "It may be in our interest to embrace their culture, to embrace what we have forgotten."

His hand stroked his chin. "I must admit, I too was wondering of Madigan's intentions. But I see now that he only takes Arianna as a sister."

"Perhaps, you are right." Shallendria took a moment to absorb his words. "Forgive me. I will trouble you no further."

"Darwynyen!" Madigan yelled, waving from one of the encampments in the courtyard. To his right stood Gin. "I need to speak with you!" He and Gin began to approach.

Darwynyen met them at the crest of the stair. "What is it?"

"I wanted to advise you of Gin's upcoming charge." He put his hand on Gin's shoulder. "I have given him control of my second battalion. His knowledge of Velderon's army will give us the advantage should any impostors try to infiltrate our forces."

Concealing his suspicion, Darwynyen offered his hand to Gin. "Congratulations." When Gin pulled from his grasp, he looked back to Madigan. "May I have a word?"

"Yes, of course." He nodded.

"I meant in private!"

Gin immediately excused himself and returned to the courtyard.

"Are you certain of your decision?" Darwynyen directed Madigan to the ledge. "You have only just met him. He may be an impostor himself!"

Madigan spoke in exasperation, "Do you speak out of concern, or do your words stem from Arianna's friendship with the lad?"

Darwynyen rebelled in anger. "I do not like what you are implying!"

"Both of you!" Shallendria leaped from the bench. "Calm yourselves before you find regret in your words!"

She looked at Madigan. "Darwynyen was right to question you. You know little of this man!"

"I have heard enough." Madigan looked around as if searching for the quickest escape.

Shallendria crossed her arms. "Is that all you have to say?"

"Have you forgotten who you are speaking with?" He stiffened his stance. "As king, I am the one bound by the consequences of my decisions, not you."

Shallendria stomped off.

Madigan closed his eyes for a moment and then took after her.

Darwynyen watched them, shaking his head.

CHAPTER 37:

A Moment

"I see Shallendria is not the *only* mind reader in this castle."

When I looked up from the chopping board, Darwynyen winked. "How did you know I was famished?"

"I thought that while I awaited you," I replied as I cut the last of the bread and placed the knife in a basin near the stove, "I would prepare us a snack."

"Should I find us a bottle of wine?"

"Sure." I bit my lip.

"If you would prefer some water instead, I—"

"No." I smiled. "Wine will be fine."

When he returned from the cellar with a bottle and two glasses, I gathered the food. "Are we to share a quiet evening together? Or are you too busy?"

"I am never too busy for you." He ushered me into the hall that connected the main foyer to the kitchen.

"Give any free beds to the commanders!" Dregby appeared through the servants' entrance. He was followed by several Mider companions. "We are safe behind the city walls. There is no need for them to stay outside when there is plenty of room in here."

He ignored us, leading those behind him into the kitchen. "The king has hired extra kitchen staff." He pointed to the boiling pots of stew near the back. "If you need anything, see to the House Master, Evelyn. *Do not take advantage of the hospitality;* keep to your troop kitchens as much as possible!" As though we were invisible, he left through the outer door adjacent to the livestock hold.

I looked to Darwynyen. "It seems this place is soon to be bustling with activity."

"Then we had better take advantage," he smirked. "Let us get out of here before someone finds us!"

"Agreed." I glanced over my shoulder as we made way for the stair.

When we reached my quarters, I left the tray on the table. "Shall we first have some wine?"

He took hold of the bottle and moved toward the window to take in the last of the waning sunlight. "Time seems to pass unnoticed."

I approached him from behind. At my touch, he turned. Before I could speak he startled me with a curious question, "What led you to the Falls of Dean that morning?"

I had to think back to my motives. "If I remember correctly, I was feeling a bit rebellious. My mother and uncle rarely let me out of their sight. As for the falls, I was always intrigued by them. I cannot explain the reasons."

He nodded. "I have often thought back to that day. From the moment I set eyes on you, your presence overwhelmed me."

"I too have held to that day." I embraced him. "You have brought forth emotions from me I never knew existed."

"It is a wonder how I stumbled across you." He sighed. "I rarely took leave to that region, though somehow I was drawn there that day. Fate seemed to guide me."

I pulled his long dark locks to the back. "Then it is a fate you and I both share."

In the passing hours, we continued our discussion in an attempt to learn more of one another. To my amazement, I found we shared a passion for many things. Peace was of mutual importance. Adventure was something that kept us alive. Our favorite color was green. We both loved the water, especially tranquil streams. He did not like horses as much as me, stating he preferred to feel the ground in his pace. Tulips were our flower of choice, though his appreciation of nature far surpassed mine.

When I asked of his family, he would only say that they were gone and that his wounds were still deep. Magic was another topic he declined to discuss. Because both subjects seemed painful, I wondered if the two were somehow intertwined. Before I could pry further, he changed the subject to the times he and Madigan had shared in the woodlands of Tayri. His words gave me a better understanding of the bond they now shared.

In comparison, my life proved quite boring. Even so, he listened attentively when I share with him my childhood, leaving me thankful of his interest.

Finished with the last of my stories, I sat up from the bed to tickle his chest.

Unresponsive, he frowned. "What do you think you are doing?"

I smiled, taking hold of a pillow. "I am only playing."

He watched me in confusion. Without hesitation, I hit him on the head with the pillow.

His eyes widened. "What was that for?"

"It is my weapon." I hit him again. "For I wish to fight you!"

Consenting to my ploy, he grabbed another pillow. "If it is an opponent you seek, you shall find one in me," he smirked."

After smothering him several times, he tried to bind me down. I was not to give in. Resisting his every move, we began to roll over one another. On the third turn, we lost our balance, falling to the floor. I bore the brunt of the misadventure.

"Are you all right?" He put his hand to my head.

"I am fine." I nudged at him playfully.

At my response, he began to tickle me. Forced into laughter, I tried to break free. He took my arms, holding them above my head. When our eyes met, the mood intensified.

The connection was undeniable. His lips brushed mine. Nervous, I closed my eyes. Fire raced through my body, setting my heart aflame. It was astonishing. It felt as though we were one. When he drew back, I knew our kiss was not to end there. He quickly stood, taking me with him. I could feel his lips as they caressed my neck. In our fervor he began to pull at the strings on my gown.

A knock came to the door.

"Go away!" he shouted.

"I cannot!" the voice of Morglafenn replied.

Darwynyen took a heavy breath. "I apologize for his timing." He kissed me on the brow.

"There is no need." I moved to the door.

I smiled at the look on Morglafenn's face. It was in a twisted grin of embarrassment.

"I regret my interruption." He scanned the room. "I have come with a warning from our queen. She wishes you to depart now. Danger lies near. She has sensed the Grackens. Their beasts encroach on our territory as we speak!"

Puzzled by his words, I looked at him blankly. "What are Grackens?"

Darwynyen was about to respond, but Morglafenn silenced him. "They are soulless beings of evil, trackers if you will. Never let your guard down. They seek out those who are weak, sensing their fear."

"What are the beasts?" I cringed.

"They have sensed the coming war," Darwynyen interjected, ignoring my question with a look of realization. "That is why they dare to tread among us! He pulled me inside the room. "Enough talk. We must prepare!"

"Darwynyen," I cried. "What does this mean? Perhaps we should wait, leave another day?"

"Too much time has already been lost." He began to gather his belongings. "We need the queen's wisdom before more is compromised."

"I am frightened." I stumbled back toward the door, as though rehearsing my escape.

"Do not be." He secured his quiver on his back. "We will be fine."

Trusting in his words, I nodded. I took hold of my new warrior attire, for it was now that I would need to make use of it.

"Excuse me." I stepped behind the open door of the wardrobe to change.

He ignored me, securing his daggers in his waist belt.

After gathering what we could, we met with Shallendria and Madigan at the stables. "Have you got all you need?" Madigan questioned.

"All but the food." Darwynyen looked over the saddlebags.

"I have already seen to that." Shallendria mounted her steed. "We must depart now, while night is still in our favor!"

Nodding in agreement, Darwynyen looked to Madigan. Without words, we mounted our horses and started for the courtyard.

Morglafenn appeared at the stair. "Be on your guard! Ride swiftly!"

Shallendria raised her hand in acknowledgment.

† † †

Storm clouds had taken what remained of the evening light. We would have to find our way through the darkness. Even so, Darwynyen and Shallendria seemed to be having little trouble with their direction. The breeze, holding the essence of a chill, befitted the circumstance, a circumstance filled with dread. Even so, I would place my trust in Darwynyen, knowing he would do what he could to protect me.

When we reached the castle gates, I pulled the hood on my cloak over my head. Our anonymity was imperative. The people would not understand my sudden departure.

To my relief, the cobblestone streets were abandoned. It seemed the hour was far later than I had first thought. Darwynyen and I must have gotten lost in each other's company. At the thought of our kiss, I looked to him with the shyness of a young girl.

"Do not worry." He smiled as though to assure me. "Everything will be all right."

I nodded to his gesture. Unsure what to say, I looked onward.

Free of the city, we proceeded south down a narrow ravine. Old oaks accompanied the surrounding countryside. Shielding the undergrowth beneath them, the shrubbery was lush and plentiful. A lurid eeriness held to the land. Uneasy, I scanned the shadows. There was no underestimating our rivals. Darwynyen and Shallendria, undaunted by the landscape, guided me through with swiftness. Before long, we were in the fields and making way in an eastward direction.

Hours passed. When the horses began to tire, we halted at an abandoned farmhouse near the towering forest of Maglavine.

"We should rest here." Darwynyen scanned the horizon. "The sun is soon to rise. We will need her light to guide us through the woodlands."

"If we must." Shallendria glanced over her shoulder. "It is not in our interest to linger."

I looked to Darwynyen with worry.

"What have you felt?" he asked, following her stare.

"I am not certain." Once on the ground, she again glanced over her shoulder. "After we have rested, we should move on."

Darwynyen nodded as he assisted me from my horse. "Are you cold?"

"No, I will be fine." I did not want to appear weak in front of Shallendria.

He looked at me in disbelief. "If you are not, then I am sure you are the only one."

Shallendria led us to the main residence, an old farmhouse adjacent to the barn. "We should go unnoticed in here."

"Go inside." Darwynyen turned. "I will return in a few minutes."

"Where are you going?"

"I need to find some stones." He pulled up the hood on his cloak. "Shallendria will summon the heat from them with her magic."

Before I could protest, he retreated into the night, leaving Shallendria and me alone for the first time since she had spoken ill to me.

"Come." She ushered me through the archway. "Let us find something to sit on."

I nodded, evading her stare.

"Arianna." She released a heavy breath as though sensing the tension. "I wanted to—"

"If we have little time, we should split up." I interrupted, circling the foyer. "As you can see, this dwelling contains many rooms."

"Very well." She made her way to the far side of the sitting room. "Should you need anything, call out to me."

I ignored her as I glanced over the surrounding area. It was filthy. The accumulation of dust and cobwebs made the room daunting. Time had worn away at its foundation, leaving the floor to slant in an eastward direction.

In a room to the right, I found an assortment of furniture covered in a blanket of dust and webs. Most appeared rotten. Reaching out for a chair, I lost my footing. To my relief, an old wooden table next to the chair held my weight despite its weakened legs.

Taking a moment to find my path, I took hold of the chair and dragged it from the room to an old stone fireplace in the main quarters.

"Arianna!" Shallendria called from one of the rooms in the back.

"What have you found?" I followed her voice.

"I need your assistance!"

Careful in my steps, I made my way down the corridor. It opened to a wing at the back. The windows to the west were missing. Winds of the past had left an array of dead foliage on the floor.

"Here." She motioned to a bench. "Help me carry this into the main room."

I stumbled through the darkness to meet her.

"Arianna," she said, again trying to open the conversation, "would I be mistaken to assume you are still bothered by my previous words?" Before I could respond, she continued, "If you are, you must allow me to apologize."

I narrowed my eyes in suspicion. "Why now?"

"My cousin, it is obvious he needs you." Her eyes widened. "In light of my gesture, I am hoping you will allow me to embrace you as a sister."

"Should we not take things as they come?" I questioned. "That way neither of us will be disappointed?"

"I understand." She tried to manage a smile. "At the very least, we will be given the opportunity to better discern our differences while on this journey."

I nodded, leading her through the corridor.

When we put the bench to the opposite side of the fireplace, I was caught by a wisp of wind that spiraled through the broken roofline, causing me to shiver.

"Are you afraid?" she asked condescendingly.

When I gave her a look of warning, she quickly countered, "I mean ... I know it is intimidating in here. Try not to worry. Darwynyen and I will protect you."

"Where is he?"

She glanced to the front door. "Stay here."

I took her by the arm. "I am going with you."

"There is no need," she huffed. "I will only be gone a minute."

"Still," I insisted, "you will not go alone."

"Then keep silent and follow," she demanded. "Do nothing unless you are told."

I nodded obediently, regardless of her overbearing attitude.

She opened the main door with caution, making her way quietly along the front of the residence.

I followed. "Where are we going?"

"You will see soon enough." She peered around the corner. I did the same. In the distance, I caught view of the barn. Darwynyen was nowhere in sight.

She grabbed my hand, pulling me out into the open.

Overwrought with stress, I fought her hold. "Where are we going?"

"Quiet!" she demanded.

When we reached the end of the barn, she halted. "This is where the farmers are most likely to store the stones they find in their fields."

"Then where is Darwynyen?" I began to panic.

"Do not worry." She turned to face me. "We will find him."

"Find who?" Darwynyen chuckled.

"Where have you been?" I crossed my arms.

"I left the horses some water." He pointed to a well. "When I searched the barn for buckets, I noticed a secret room below the floorboards." He looked to Shallendria. "We should take our rest there."

She nodded, following his direction.

He led us down a narrow set of stairs to a room below the surface of the barn. The air was dank, almost musty. Through the waning candlelight, it was hard to see. "Come." He extended his hand. "I have set the stones in the corner."

"I will join you in a moment." I scanned the area. Several cots were built into the walls. Chairs were strewn around a table that held the remnants of a forgotten dinner. Cobwebs covered the plates and utensils. "What is the purpose of this room?" I asked.

"I believe it was used to hide the family who once lived here." Darwynyen eyed the wall behind the stair. "It seems they were in some sort of trouble."

When I followed his stare, I saw the weapons. "Who ... what?"

"Do not worry. Whatever happened here happened a long time ago."

He rubbed his hands together. "Work your magic, my cousin. I have a chill."

"I will get started immediately." She made her way to one of the chairs.

Curious, I sat next to her. "Do you mind if I watch?"

"Of course not," She remove three small packages from her waist belt. "Keep your eyes on the powder." She began to sprinkle a fine granular mixture over the stones.

I sat forward with anticipation.

After mixing two other powders, she blew them from her fingers. Tiny sparks flickered in the air. The smell was potent, reminding me of the times my uncle and I had burned moldy shrubbery in the fields.

It took several moments for the flickers to cease. Soon after, the stone began to glow from within.

Shallendria held out her hands. "Ovhelanty, ovhelenty!" At her words, the glow from the stones began to emanate, heating the area around us.

"That was amazing!" I gasped. "Where did you learn such things?"

"She is being groomed to take over," Darwynyen replied. "In a time, not far off, our queen will return to her roots and become mortal."

"Why?" I asked. "I thought your people lived forever."

"We may possess eternal life, but when one seeks the magic, as our queen has done, they become overwhelmed by its power.

They can no longer abide it." He put his hand to Shallendria's. "Living forever has its boundaries."

I looked to her with disbelief. "Why would you follow such a path?"

Her eyes began to water. "The decision was not mine to make."

Rather than place judgment, I chose to find compassion in the depth of her complexities. Perhaps the nature of her upbringing put cause to her actions.

With no other display of emotion, Shallendria wiped her eyes and took comfort from the heat.

When we left the barn, the amber skyline struck the horizon with perfection, allowing the sentinels of Maglavine to stand proud. The majestic tress reminded me of the woodlands in Hoverdire. Morning's breath was soon to be upon us.

"Quiet!" Darwynyen searched the area.

Shallendria put her hand to her chest. "Darwynyen."

It was as though she felt something.

"Quickly." He ushered me to the horses. "Stay with Shallendria."

"But what—" He disappeared before I could finish.

The hairs on my neck were standing on end. "What is happening?"

"Listen!" Shallendria brought forward her bow.

I was about to respond when I heard the crying of a beast. It was charging through the brush from behind.

She turned her horse. "Prepare yourself!"

I nodded, searching for my bow.

When Darwynyen's stallion skipped a gait, I reached for its reins.

"Leave him." She anchored her weapon, testing the tension. "He will make his return when this is over."

Accolade fought to break free. As I restrained him, I slid an arrow from my quiver. Through the shrubbery, I caught view of the beast from behind. Its figure was revealed by the fragments of trickling light. At a glance, it could have mistaken it for a boar, only larger.

Shallendria released an arrow, striking it directly in the head. Jumping back, it frantically pawed at the flange. "Hurry! You must turn!" She kicked her horse to the side, allowing me to maneuver Accolade. "You are defenseless in that direction!"

I strained to control Accolade, using my legs to force him into position. While doing so, Shallendria released another arrow, perforating the beast's upper chest. From behind, she sped another arrow, piercing it in the hind. Despite its injuries, the beast did not falter as it closed the distance between us.

Unable to concentrate, I missed my mark completely. When I looked to Shallendria with dread, she fired yet another arrow, striking it in the eye. The fatal wound left the beast rolling to a halt on the ground.

"Who are you to kill my seeker?" a raspy voice demanded.

From the dense shrubbery, a horseman appeared. It was a Gracken, I was certain. From the hood of his cloak, his amber eyes bore through me. Twisted horns protruded from his sunken brow.

"It was I!" Shallendria drew her sword.

Darwynyen jumped from one of the neighboring trees. In readiness, he let off an arrow, embedding it in the creature's neck.

"Your attempts will prove futile," he wheezed, snapping the arrow in two as he pulled it from his hardened flesh.

Shallendria sent the next arrow into the creature's face. To my dismay, he again pulled it out, throwing it to the ground.

Darwynyen took another shot, striking the Gracken in the shoulder as his horse picked up speed. He dismissed it with little more than a grunt.

"Over here!" Shallendria kicked my horse to the side, directing her sword to charge him.

The Gracken raised his sword to her challenge.

The first pass was to no one's success. The horseman turned and looked at me alone. It was as though he could sense my fear.

Darwynyen flung his dagger. The force threw the creature to the ground.

Although weakened, he fought to stand. Shallendria sped forward, decapitating him on her pass. To my relief, he fell motionless to the ground.

"Are you all right?" She asking, riding back over to me.

"Yes." I sat forward in an attempt to still the beating of my heart.

"Come." Darwynyen whistled for his horse. "We will ride hard until we reach the forest."

† † †

As we maneuvered through the towering trees of Maglavine, I kept silent. The attack was still in the foreground of my mind. Why had I reacted in such a manner? Did it stem from my lack of skill, or was I nothing more than a coward? I looked to both Darwynyen and Shallendria, wondering of their thoughts. Behind their composed demeanors, could it be they were more disappointed than me?

When we reached a bluff, Shallendria pulled some bread from her satchel. She brought her horse to my side. "Here. We must eat to keep our strength."

"Thank you." I took it greedily.

"We should allow the horses some water." Darwynyen led his stallion to an open pool near the winding stream that we had been following.

As I dismounted, I tried to release the tension in my legs.

"We should ride until midday." He yawned, directing his focus to his cousin. "Take rest at that old lookout point."

Shallendria gave me a fleeting look. "Whatever you think is best."

"Do not let me hinder your plans." I put my hand to Accolade. "We will not falter."

Darwynyen approached. "There was no insinuation in our words." His hand grazed my cheek. "We are only concerned. The Gracken brought great fear to us all."

Unable to control my emotions, I looked down. "I apologize. My actions were inexcusable."

"Do not give way to guilt." He sighed. "These experiences are new to you."

"Yes, but ..." I thought I was going to cry. When I put my hands to my face, he embraced me.

"Say no more." His hold tightened. "If it were up to me, you would not be faced with such things."

"It is not up to you." I pulled away.

"I know." He met my stare. "You have made your feelings clear when it comes to your father."

Unable to continue in the conversation, I joined Shallendria at the stream.

Despite my need to take rest in our ongoing journey, I kept my promise and did not falter. Shallendria, sensing my weakness, constantly looked back at me, but not in the way I had grown used to. Could it be she was sincere in her previous words?

"We are here!" Darwynyen leapt from his horse.

Confused, I searched the surrounding area. There was no sign of an encampment *or* a lookout point.

"Come." He beckoned. "Let us stow our horses and get some rest."

When my feet hit the ground, I stretched my exhausted body and wondered where we were to take our rest with no visible shelter in sight.

"Darwynyen loves this place." Shallendria winked. "We used to play here as children."

"Somehow." I paused, forgetting my search. "I cannot imagine you as children."

"Curious." She lightly slapped her horse on the hind. "It seems the myths of our people are far grander than the truth." Her eyes brightened with a smirk. "I cannot imagine why."

I could not help but chuckle. Although our conversation was brief, I was beginning to see a side of her I could identify with.

Darwynyen took my hand and led me downward between the roots of a gigantic tree. "In our region, we use what the land has given us." He pushed aside some foliage. "We take shelter in its foundation."

As I caught view of an opening below the surface, I lost my footing.

He caught me in his strong arms before I could fall. "Careful. Some of the roots are entangled."

When I nodded, he opened a makeshift door, forcing a hidden mechanism into action. Seconds later, the inner parts of the room began to glow.

"We use small mirrors to capture light from the sun." Shallendria smiled.

"Where are they." I frowned.

"You will not find them," Darwynyen challenged. "They are built within the tree."

To prove him wrong, I began to inspect the area. The dwelling was circular and contained several hammocks for beds that hung idle around the core. The outer rim was filled with an assortment of furniture, some carved out of the trunk. Shelves, free of any items, riddled the walls in what appeared to be a narrow kitchen.

"See to your comfort." He put his hand to my back, directing me to one of the hammocks. "I will join you shortly."

As I climbed onto the makeshift bed, its swaying motion brought me a sense of ease. I could have easily fallen asleep. Instead, I chose to eavesdrop on their conversation, which they had chosen to engage in on the opposite side of the room near the kitchen.

"I see no need to push forward tonight," he whispered. "Arianna needs her rest."

Despite my urge to interject, I kept silent.

"Agreed," Shallendria replied. "Rest or not, it would be a waste of time trying to navigate this forest in the dark."

"How much food do we have?"

"Enough." I heard Shallendria open one of her satchels.

"Before you retire." He unbuckled his quiver. "There is something I must ask."

"What is it?" she spoke in a dulling tone.

"Aldraveena—I have begun to wonder of her motives when it comes to Arianna."

"Why would you ask me of such things?" I could sense the distress in her voice. "You know she senses everything!"

The room went quiet for a moment.

"Forget I spoke." He released a heavy breath. "It was not my intention to upset you."

"Try not to worry, Darwynyen." I heard her disarm. "The future path has already been set. Despite Aldraveena's intentions, there is nothing you nor she can do about it."

"How can you be—"

She interrupted, "Let us get some rest." A hammock began to creak as it swayed. "I will wake you in the morn."

"Very well." I could hear him make his way toward me.

She yawned. "Good rest, my cousin."

"And you," he replied.

When I felt Darwynyen's arm around me, I did not stir. Because of the peculiar nature of their words, I decided to wait for a more appropriate time to question them.

† † †

I awoke to a sensation on my face. At first I thought it was Darwynyen, but when something scurried up my cheek, I sat up, flinging what appeared to be a bug to the ground.

"It was only a dream," Darwynyen mumbled. "Go back to sleep."

"No." I cringed in disgust. "It was a bug!"

"A bug?" He tried to hold back his laughter. "Do not fear. They are our friends, enriching the soil around us."

Shallendria shifted in her sleep.

"Do not worry on her." He tried to embrace me.

Still aware of my surroundings, I pushed him aside.

"Did I do something wrong?"

"No." I continued to scan the shadows.

"Then go back to sleep." I felt his hand caress my cheek. "Our journey tomorrow will be a long one."

"If we are not to rest," Shallendria said, sitting up from her hammock, "perhaps we should eat."

Darwynyen sat up as well. "Shallendria, "I apologize. We did not mean to wake you."

"It is of no bother." She stretched her limbs. "Are either of you hungry?"

"Yes." I slid from the hammock.

"I am as well." She reached for her satchel.

After we consumed the last of the rations, Shallendria stood. "Now that the sun's light is upon us." She eyed a small window in the door. "We should ready the horses."

"If we must." Darwynyen sighed.

I nodded, taking hold of my belongings.

"I will join you shortly." He began to lace his boots.

When we reached the crest of the stair, I scanned the area. Shallendria took my arm. "Do not fear the woodlands of Maglavine. They are safe, I assure you."

"Perhaps." I tensed, remembering their previous words.

"I sense concern in you." She hesitated. "May I ask why?"

I met her stare. "Your queen, can you tell me of her intentions?"

"You assume too much." She looked away. "I do not have the answers you seek."

Deciding it best not to push her, I made way for Accolade who had strayed to a neighboring tree. "It is of no bother. We are soon to be in Maglavine anyway."

"May I ask a question of you?" She knelt to the stream to fill her canteen.

"What is it you want to know?"

"Will you tell me of your first encounter with my cousin?"

"He saved my life." I closed my eyes in thought of the day. "Nothing more. When I twisted my ankle on moss-covered stone, he carried me back to my village in Hoverdire. Despite our differences, he insisted on ensuring my safety."

"Were you not to see him again?"

"Not until recently." I tensed in anticipation of her reaction.

"Arianna." She smiled. "I carry no ill feelings toward you. I am only taken aback."

"Why?"

"Your words have explained many of his actions over the years."

Darwynyen appeared from within the tree. "Are we ready?"

Although I wanted to continue the conversation with Shallendria, I mounted Accolade. "As ready as I will ever be."

Darwynyen nodded, looking to Shallendria for a moment before making his way to his stallion.

Shallendria, well rested, took to leading our direction. We stopped several times to inhale the abounding fragrance that emanated from the forest riches.

In a constant ascent up a hill that seemed to have no end, the landscape began to change. Robust vines of blue had broken through the soil, weaving their way around the bulk of the trees. Morning dew left them to shimmer in the sun's glow. Birds mingled among the tresses in search of their breakfast, while waterfowl bathed in the idle pools, shedding themselves of the evening dust.

At the crest of the next bluff, we halted for a moment's rest. "You should fill your canteens." Shallendria leapt from her horse. "We will follow this stream no further."

As I knelt to the waters, Darwynyen took Shallendria aside. "You must not delay. You are needed in Tayri."

"I suppose you are right." She glanced over her shoulder. "I should find the northern passage while light is still in our favor."

"Ride hard." He directed her to her horse.

"Do not worry on me, my cousin." She winked. "You know my horse is the best."

"It is not your horse I worry on." He rolled his eyes.

"Arianna." She mounted her steed, guiding it to me. "I will see you again, in Aarrondirth, should both our journeys prove favorable. Until then, take care. Enjoy your time in Maglavine."

When I grabbed the harness to her horse, I could not help but notice a peculiar hump on its brow. "I will look forward to seeing you once again in Aarrondirth ..." I paused with curiosity. "Your horse—"

"I must make way." She looked to Darwynyen. "Tell the queen I will connect to her once I have gathered the assembly."

"Consider it done." He put his hand to his chest.

As I watched her ride away, I was struck with an odd sense of sadness. Despite all that had happened, it seemed I could no longer deny the bond that had been growing between us.

"She will be fine." Darwynyen mounted his steed. "We should get moving."

I secured the lid to my canteen and returned to Accolade. "How much farther are we to travel?"

He kicked his horse. "If we keep our pace, we should be there long before nightfall." Not waiting for a response, he made his way up another incline.

As I matched his stride, I tried to further the conversation, "Will you tell me of Shallendria's horse? He seems different somehow."

"Did you notice the slight protrusion on his brow?" he asked.

"Yes." I bit my lip in hesitation. "Is he deformed?"

"No." He chuckled. "Not in the least. Within his veins, he carries the last blood of the Unicorn."

"Unicorn?"

"It is a breed of horse that no longer graces our land. It is known by a horn that protrudes from above the eyes. It was hunted to extinction long before you were born. After most had given up hope on its existence, a lone mare was found near the shores of Tayri. When the Elves mated it with a stallion, a colt was born. He was of great strength. To acknowledge Shallendria's commitment, he was presented to her on her fiftieth year from birth."

I looked at him in awe. "So, the hump is a remnant from a horse your people call a Unicorn."

"Yes." He smiled. "Because of their uniqueness, the bond he and Shallendria share is strong."

I took a moment to absorb his words. The thought of the Unicorn's demise was almost tragic. Even so, it was comforting to know the creatures' bloodline would persevere in another.

"Arianna, fall back." He took hold of my reins. "The land here is rugged. Allow me to lead you through."

Without question, I did as he asked.

The ascent was again steep and winding. My taut muscles began to burn. Dead branches from old shrubbery broke the rugged path. Darwynyen snapped what he could in passing. What remained caught on my cloak, forcing me to slow.

At the top of the bluff, he turned. "Are you all right?"

To conceal the pain, I leaned to stroke Accolade on the neck. "Do not worry on us."

"We are almost at the peak." He eyed the narrow path ahead of us. "From there, our travels will come with ease." Before I could respond, he sped up the incline.

"Wait!" I kicked my horse to approach his rear. "You have yet to explain Shallendria's purpose in Tayri."

"She goes on behalf of our queen, to rally the leaders." He slowed his horse. "Some have chosen to resist the allegiance. It seems in their years of solitude they have grown wary of foreigners."

"Wary?"

"Yes." His eyes wandered. "As you know, Tayri was the city where the Amberseed was stolen from."

"What does that have to do with the allegiance?"

"They came under attack when it went missing," he replied, "by those of the different regions, including those of Man's Blood."

"Why?"

He blinked. "Because it was said that no one could break the twenty-one spells cast to bind it, except, of course, those who had conjured them, leaving suspicion to fall to the Elves."

"Who do *you* believe took it?"

"I do not know." He shrugged. "No one will, for its keeper chose not to use its power."

"I see." I rode up beside him. "Well, I hope—"

"Look!" He pointed. "The gates of Maglavine!"

My mouth fell open when I saw two trees covered in glittering crystals.

"I would not have expected such things," I uttered. Reaching for the sky, the intricate braiding of the branches had created a perfect teardrop opening. At the foot of the trees, stone archers aimed their arrows in readiness. Beyond the threshold, lush flora bloomed as far as the eye could see.

"Do not be fooled by its splendor," Darwynyen warned. "It is meant to entice."

"What do you mean?"

"Are you able to see the pool of water on the other side of the threshold?"

I stood in my stirrups. "Yes, I see it." Small pillars broke through the mirrored reflection. "Those pillars, are they steps?"

He nodded. "When these borders were guarded, strangers would have to pass over them. If they were not worthy, the pillars would sink."

"What would happen to the person?"

"The water was alive with magic and would devour them in an instant."

"Would there be no grounds for judgment?" I questioned.

"Not in those times." He leapt from his horse. "Shall we take rest here for a while?"

I stretched my sore muscles. "To be honest, there is nothing I would desire more."

"Nothing?" He winked.

When my cheeks became flush, he removed his riding blanket, placing it between the roots of a tree. "Come." He held out his hand. "Lie with me."

Gathering the remainder of my strength, I jumped from Accolade to join him.

Entranced by the landscape, I found it impossible to sleep. Cotton-like fluff drifted through the air, dancing upon the crystal-lined branches. The faint whisper of flora flirted with my senses. Desperate to further explore my surroundings, I slipped from Darwynyen's grasp.

As I stood, I noticed a small ravine. Water from the gated pond slowly trickled through the roots and broken branches. Near the narrow of the cleft, a fallen tree had formed a makeshift bridge.

To claim a better view, I stood upon it. Although the area had a sense of abandonment, it was majestic nonetheless. Taken away in the moment, I felt like a queen on a pedestal.

"Do you not wish to sleep?"

Startled by Darwynyen's sudden presence, I nearly lost my footing.

"I do." I took his hands as he neared. "Only this place ... not once have I witnessed more beauty."

He put his hands to my face. "There is only one beauty I see here."

With the shyness of a girl, I looked down. He put his finger to my chin. As I met his stare, he placed his lips to mine. I thought I was going to faint.

Lost for breath, I drew back.

"Arianna, I—" His eyes grew serious.

I stiffened. "Have I done something that displeases you?

"Why would you ask such things?"

I again looked down. "It was not my intention to refuse you ... only, I felt weak. These feelings I have for you frighten me."

"Frighten you!" he replied lightheartedly.

I did not find humor in his words. "I just ..." I paused. "I worry that I might lose you. There is no telling what the future may bring."

"You will never lose me." He took me by the shoulders. "We are bound together—forever."

"Forever," I uttered. "Promise?"

"Promise." He kissed my brow.

"Was ..." I again paused. "Was there something you wanted to say to me?"

"It can wait." He looked to the treeline. "It is time for us to continue our journey."

Although I wanted to push him further, I nodded and followed him to our horses.

As we passed along the outer rim of the gate, I was overcome by the aroma of flora. It was hard to breathe. "Darwynyen." I sneezed. "These flowers are very potent."

"They are called Hellum's Dew." He returned to take my reins. "Like the water, they are enhanced by magic. Their scent is used to ward off evil. Trolls find them unbearable, even in the coolest of winter's breath."

"Then perhaps there is Troll in me!" I sneezed again.

"Not likely." He chuckled. "I will lead you through."

I nodded and covered my nose and mouth with my sleeve.

It was hours into our journey when a barrier materialized before us. Beyond it, the landscape was distorted.

"Darwynyen, there is something ahead, through the trees."

"Yes," he replied. "You witness a wall of water."

A slight breeze carried ripples across the transparent surface.

"What is its purpose?"

"It is a ring wall, comparable to a wall walk. The only difference being that it is made through magic. If an intruder penetrates its barrier, it glows amber. The residue dwindles for hours, following the person's every step. No intruders will go unnoticed here."

"How does it know?" I asked.

"All good can sense evil." He smiled. "Did you not carry immediate suspicion of your father?"

"I suppose." In many ways his words made sense.

"Come." He broke through the ripples that formed the barrier. "We are close!"

I kicked my horse to follow.

When I reached the wall, I pulled the reins. "Darwynyen, I do not ..."

"Trust me." His hand broke through the barrier. "You have nothing to fear."

I took a deep breath and took hold of him. After a moment of deafening silence, I was on the other side and as dry as I had been before I entered it. My heart skipped a beat. "Am I to glow?"

"No," he smirked. "Well, maybe just a little."

I looked at my arms and found no essence of the amber. "You are a cruel one to tease me, Darwynyen."

"You left me no choice." He chuckled. "I told you it was safe."

"Who goes there?" an Elf dressed in warrior's attire shouted from one of the upper limbs of a tree. "Announce yourself!"

Seconds later the guard's companions emerged from the undergrowth. Their arrows were pointed in readiness.

"It is I," Darwynyen shouted. "Put down your weapons!"

"It is Darwynyen," one gasped. "He has returned!"

"Darwynyen!" The Elf from above slid down a vine to greet him. "My friend, I am most grateful to see you."

"As I am you." Darwynyen dismounted his horse and took hold of the Elf's shoulders.

They bowed their heads for a moment before he turned to me. "I would like to introduce you to Sikes. He is like a brother to me."

When I nodded, he nudged Darwynyen. "Is this the one our lady seeks?"

"Yes," he replied. "Her name is Arianna."

"Will you tell us why one of the Man's Blood has been summoned?" A stern-looking Elf approached.

"Mind your business," Darwynyen snapped. "It is of no concern to you!"

The Elf stepped back with a stare of suspicion.

Darwynyen mounted his horse. "Sikes, I will seek you out later."

Sikes was about to respond but then rolled his eyes. "We have company."

Through the trees appeared a mass of shimmering bugs. Before I could discern them, they sped past. "What are they?" I cringed.

The buzz spooked Accolade. Securing his reins, I spoke harshly, "What are they?"

The Elf guards began to laugh.

"Do not worry." Darwynyen searched the area. "They will not hurt you!"

"Yes, but—" Just then one of the creatures flew to my face. To my surprise, it was a person, a tiny person with wings. Hovering in its iridescent glow, it giggled.

"What are you?" I held out my hand.

It landed on my fingers. Its skin glistened radiantly with speckles of gold and silver. Wings as delicate as the breeze reflected the waning sunlight.

"Are you a fairy?" I asked.

Without a word, it spun into the air, gathering its companions.

"Be gone!" Sikes demanded.

In a taunting manner, they flew around his head before leaving us in an eastward direction.

Darwynyen kicked his horse. "Come, Arianna."

Ecstatic, I forgot the guardsmen as I rode up next to him. "Was that a fairy?"

"Yes." He smiled as though enjoying my reaction. "They are, if nothing else, loyal to our queen."

"Why did you not communicate with them?"

"Because they are nothing more than a nuisance." He shrugged. "Like I said, they are loyal to our queen. They do nothing more than meddle on her behalf. Do not be fooled by their size. They are clever and will misguide you. Trust me when I say that no good ever came from a fairy."

"I did not get that impression," I countered. "To the contrary, they seemed quite friendly."

"Give it a few days," he huffed.

I nodded and followed his lead.

† † †

When we arrived at a large encompassing hedge, Darwynyen guided me through to a gated passage.

"Welcome to Maglavine, Arianna."

Stunned by the mystic realm, I took a moment to better observe my surroundings. Trees, larger than any I had ever seen, held what appeared to be their dwellings. Carved from within the trunks, staircases led to several doors and extended upward as far as the eye could see. In the higher reaches, bridges connected the thicker limbs like an elaborate puzzle.

A rich smell escaped from the flowers that broke through the dense shrubbery, leaving me to wonder how they grew so readily in the pale shelter of the forest. Among the growth were several openings that were similar to the shelter we had stayed at near the border, only larger.

Lyrical notes echoed through the trees. A cascade of gentle voices like Shallendria's sung in a choir, so solemnly that it almost broke my heart.

"You hear the song of honor." Darwynyen smiled. "Our Elf maidens sing in their work."

Unable to speak, I bit my lip. There was no doubt the splendor of this place would stay with me forever. Before I could give way to tears, I thought of my father, being he was the most shattering of distractions.

Darwynyen dismounted near an open paddock. "Arianna, what is it? Are you disappointed?"

"No." I wiped my eyes. "Nothing about this place could leave me disappointed."

"I was hoping you would feel that way." He turned. "Over here!"

When a stable hand approached from the neighboring paddock, he assisted me from my horse. "Come. Let us get some rest."

The path we took led us to a small lagoon. Pallid light caused the algae to shimmer like newly shined gems. Toads, lost in slumber, clung to an array of water lilies that had accumulated near the center.

Distracted by whispering voices, I glanced over my shoulder. To my dismay, several Elves had stopped in their chores to stare.

"Darwynyen!" The older female Elf waved from one of the circular staircases. "Welcome home!"

"It is good to be back." He smiled. "I will come see you once we have settled."

"Very good, my boy." She gestured to the others to take their leave.

"Who were those people?" I again glanced back. "Why were they staring?"

"Take no heed." He winked. "They are only curious."

I nodded, following him over a narrow stone bridge.

At the bridge's end, the path split in two. We took our direction east along the stream. "How many Elves live here?" I asked.

"Not many." He looked to the trees. "Maglavine is a sanctuary, created for our queen."

"Where is she?"

"You will meet her soon enough." He halted and extended his hand. "We are here at last. Arianna, I offer you my home."

The tree before me was unlike the others, holding but a single residence. To the right, a gentle waterfall opened to an isolated pool shrouded by an array of climbing foliage. Above and in the distance, I caught view of an odd-looking structure that appeared to be made out of vine. Trickling through the leaves was a glow similar to the one I had seen around Shallendria.

"What is that structure over there." I pointed.

"It is the realm of our queen," he replied.

"Are we to make our way there now?"

"No." He began to remove the vines of ivy that had grown over the vestibule in his absence. "She will summon you when she is ready." Tiny white flowers bloomed from the vine's luscious green veins. The aroma was intoxicating.

"Shall I carry you through?" He released the latch.

"There is no need." I brushed past him.

The room was large and circular. A bed hung from the ceiling to the left. Alongside it was a wardrobe and small desk. To the right was an old stone fireplace that finished off the narrow dining area. Beyond it, two doors opened to a balcony. Curious, I made way to investigate.

When I stepped out, I immediately took notice of the beautiful waterfall I had seen moments before. Mist filtered through the air and danced around the ferns that clung to the embankment. Parched, I reached out to captures some of the moisture. In doing so, I felt him embrace me from behind.

"Arianna, reassure me. Do you speak the truth when you say you like it here?"

Unable to comprehend my surroundings, I closed my eyes as I responded, "Not even in my dreams could I have imagined such a place."

"It brings me great joy to hear you say that." He released me. "Get some rest. I will return shortly with some food."

"Are you to leave me here on my own?"

"You will be fine. The queen will not call upon you until later. After the two of you have spoken, we will take an early night." He kissed my brow before leaving the room.

As I awaited him, I splashed my face with some stilled water I had found in an open basin. Although the journey had been shorter than I had first expected, the steady uphill climb had taken its toll.

Welcome to the realm of Maglavine, Arianna. A melodic voice seemed to surround me. *As the queen of this land, it pleases me that you are here.*

I searched the room for a moment before realizing that, like Shallendria, she had entered my mind.

Come to me when the sun has departed. There are things we must discuss.

"Should I bring Darwynyen?" I asked.

No. My words are for you alone!

When the connection severed, I felt ill at ease.

Do not fear me Arianna. The queen's presence had returned. *For I have seen into your future. My only intention is to guide you.*

The door opened from behind. Unsure who it was, I turned abruptly.

"I have rabbit, bread, and—" He broke off his words when he saw me and placed the food on the table. "Did something happen while I was away?"

"Your queen," I replied, releasing a heavy breath. "She has summoned me. I must go to her realm when the sun has set."

"I see." Darwynyen paused. "Do not fear her, Arianna. She is wise in her ways."

"Shall we eat?" I mustered a smile. "I am famished."

"Of course." He pulled out a seat.

Unable to finish my meal, I stood on the balcony. There were many thoughts within me that I could not settle.

"How about we bathe in the pond?"

Uncomfortable with the idea, I stiffened. "I cannot bathe with you!"

He smiled cunningly. "Why not?"

I took on a demanding tone to disguise my fear. "Because it would not be proper!" I noticed a stack of books by his bed. "Perhaps I will read while you are gone."

"Those books are not for reading; they are of magic, a present from my mother."

"Oh." I bit my lip. "Will you not even allow me a glimpse?"

"There is no point." He stepped onto the balcony. "They are written in Elvish."

Disappointed, I returned to my seat.

"If it is your wish." He unlaced his boots. "You may go after me. That way you will have your privacy."

I glanced at his chest when he removed his shirt. Perfectly lean, his muscles bulged from his elegant skin. I wanted to touch him.

"Are you certain you do not wish to join me," he smirked, tossing his clothing over the ledge of the balcony.

Embarrassed, I turned. Moments later, I heard a splash.

"Arianna, can I not persuade you? I will not look, I promise!"

My decision was already made. How could I refuse him? When I peered over the ledge, he awaited me with a flower in his mouth.

"I will, but I will not jump from here. Tell me where your drying cloths are and I will make my way down the stair."

"They are beneath the bed," he replied. "Hurry!"

As I descended the stair, I noticed I was clenching tightly to the drying cloths. Fighting my fear, I tossed them to a boulder. There was no need to be nervous, even though this would be the first time I would unclothe in front of another—another being a man, that is.

"Arianna, are you coming?"

When I neared the bank, I narrowed my eyes. "No peeking! You promised!"

"If it is your wish." He turned.

I watched his movements carefully as I undressed. Once naked, I quickly ran in.

The water was invigorating, soothing my sore muscles.

He swam to meet me. "Could you ask for anything more?" He gently took me by the waist, picking up my legs. As he swung me in a circular motion, he looked deep into my eyes. "Arianna, there is something I must share with you."

Before I could respond, I was struck by the force of the waterfall. Lost for breath, I began to kick.

He released his hold, leaving me to recover on my own.

Taking refuge on one of the neighboring boulders, I wiped the droplets of water from my eyes. "How could you?"

It was too late, he had already started laughing.

Seeking my revenge, I moved to try and push him under.

He was too strong, tossing me aside.

Unable to match his strength, I began to splash.

In the chaos to follow, he pulled my feet from under me. When I broke through to the surface, I glared. "I *suppose* you are enjoying this."

"How could I not?" He shrugged with a devious grin.

I began to pout, knowing it had always worked on my uncle. "Please, Darwynyen," I whined, "I am too tired for this."

As I expected, his smugness gave way to guilt. "Here." He placed me on a boulder. "Let me rub your shoulders." I felt his hands on my back when he shifted my hair. "Do not fear, Arianna. I will take care of you."

"I know." My head fell forward in compliance.

His fingers were strong. It was not long before my muscles began to loosen. I faced him, intending to return his gesture.

"Shall I do the same for you?"

"That would be most welcome." He kissed me on the brow.

Before I could move, I was pushed off the boulder. Once again, I fell to the water. Annoyed, I recovered with haste. "Would you like a rub or not?"

He held out his hands in exclamation. "I was—"

I took his arm. "Take your place, Darwynyen, before I change my mind!"

As though lost for words, he sat obediently.

Pulling his hair to the side, I noticed a scar on his left shoulder. "What is this wound you carry?" I rubbed the area.

"I was struck by a poisonous arrow," he replied.

"By whom?" I examined the area further.

"By a creature called the Rinjeed." His shoulders tightened. "We were ambushed on the trail to Tayri when I was a child."

"Who would attack a child!" I gasped. "What are these Rinjeed?"

"They are mind killers," he replied solemnly. "Their blood consists of both Elf and Man. They originated in the slave colonies up north." He rose from the water, exposing his upper torso.

"Come. The sun has begun its descent. The queen is soon to summon you."

I ignored him, trapped by his words. If they were true, if this creature turned evil by carrying both our blood, what would happen to our children should I choose to bear them?

"What is it?"

"These creatures." I recoiled. "I fear them. If they carry both our blood, what would happen should I—"

"Save your fear." I felt his hold. "I would die before I let one of them hurt you."

"I know, but—"

"Arianna." He pulled away, looking down at me through the rippling water. "I … if only—"

"Darwynyen! Darwynyen, where are you!" a man's voice beckoned.

I tensed at the shouting.

He shielded me with his body. "Come no further!"

"I need to see you!" the voice called.

"I will be there in a minute!" He turned. "I must go. You may dress once we are gone."

"How long will you be?"

"Not long." He reached for his clothing.

I nodded, admiring his body as he dressed.

When he finished, he turned with a wink. "See you soon!"

When I was certain they were gone, I reached for my drying cloth and secured it tightly around me. After grabbing my belongings, I made way for his dwelling.

As I climbed the stair, I halted. The door was ajar, not the way I had left it. When I looked through the opening, I saw several fairies hovering over the bed. Unsure what to do, I stepped inside. Sensing my presence, they sped through the window before I could question them.

On the bed lay a gown. Upon it was a note with my name written on the fold.

> Arianna,
>
> As this note was written with my very hand, I once again welcome you to the land of Maglavine. As a gesture of my goodwill, I leave you this gown. In return, I ask that you wear it in my presence.
>
> I will call upon you soon.
>
> Aldraveena, the Lady of Maglavine

I dropped the note to pick up the gown. It was extravagant. As I slid it on, I could not help but notice the fabric. Softer than silk, it clung to my skin like morning dew on a blossoming flower. The color reminded me of a perfect snowfall in the mildest of winters. Several folds fell to the back. Weaved into the shoulder, they extended to a narrow hem that gathered on the floor around my ankles.

When I turned in search of a mirror, I felt her presence.

We do not take pleasure in our reflections. Vanity does not lie in our path.

As I absorbed her words, I felt droplets of water on my back. I had little time before we were to meet. I grabbed a comb from one of my satchels. As I pulled it through the knots, I thought of Darwynyen and wondered if we were soon to share our love. The fear I had once carried seemed to have vanished in the passing hours. Morglafenn had been right; time was the only boundary between us when it came to securing the bond that only he and I could share.

Come to me now! the melodic voice commanded.

My stomach tensed with anticipation. She was waiting for me, waiting to share with me a future I could only hope I was willing to face.

Follow my voice and you will find me.

Unable to resist her command, I made way for the door.

Follow the path, the one lit by the setting sun. I am waiting for you there.

When I neared a bridge on the opposite side of Darwynyen's dwelling, she returned.

Do not hesitate. It is your destiny. Should you get lost, I will summon my fairies to guide you.

The other side of the bridge was overgrown with dense shrubbery. I pulled up my gown. Thorns tore at my bare skin, reminding me of the demper vine in Hoverdire.

"Where are you?" I cried. "My feet will not outlast this burden."

From behind me, the fairies appeared. "Follow us!"

Before I could respond, they disappeared through the thicket. Frustrated, I paused for a moment's rest.

"You must not keep her waiting!" One flew to my face. "She does not like to be kept waiting!"

"I am doing the best I can," I huffed.

When it giggled, I felt the desire to swat it to the ground. Darwynyen's forewarning had begun to make sense.

"Over here!" It sped through the air. "You are not far now."

At the crest of an embankment, I found an archway. Beyond it, the path was unhindered. I followed it around several trees before coming to the structure I had seen earlier. In my approach, I realized that there was no visible entrance, nor could I see through the leafy intertwined vine that concealed the inner side of the realm.

"You must say the words." The fairy reappeared from over my shoulder.

"What words?" I snapped.

"In your language, it translates to, 'If I am bound by truth, I shall enter.'"

When I repeated the words, the vine moved, creating a perfect teardrop opening like the one I had seen at the gates.

I entered with caution. The aroma was of a lurid sweetness. Sparrows danced around the outer rim as the vine sealed the entrance behind me. I was about to step forward when I noticed a pool of water similar to the one Darwynyen had warned me about at the gates.

Follow the lighted pillars, Arianna. A stream of light materialized from the water.

Near the center of the pool, I came to a large flat stone. As I leaped to the next pillar, I noticed that the center opened to a staircase that led deep into the land. Candles lit the narrow downward path that appeared almost forlorn in its isolation.

That is my sanctum, Arianna. Not there will you find me.

I looked to a lone tree protruding from the water. A narrow set of stairs led to a plateau with several unlit torches.

You look where you will not find me!

"Then where will I find you?" I spoke harshly, annoyed by her elusiveness.

I heard the vine move behind me. *I am here, Arianna.*

When I turned, I found her sitting upon a throne. She was dressed in a long, white satin gown, similar to one Shallendria had worn on our first encounter. Her ivory hair flirted ever so lightly with the breeze. Skin, as pure as the lilies, gave her an appearance of youth I had not expected. In many ways, she seemed familiar, only her beauty could not to be mistaken for another.

Come to me, Arianna. Her emerald green eyes met my stare. *There is much we need to discuss.*

Although hesitant, I slowly made my way across the slate rock face that connected to the outer part of the throne to meet her.

Arianna. She smiled. *You are a child in many ways, and yet still you are very brave.* She gestured for me to take a seat before her. *Despite all you have been through, I fear your journey has not yet found its end.*

"How is it you know these things?"

"My powers go well beyond most," she replied gently. "With them comes foresight."

When I nodded, she extended her hand. A small broken pebble lay in the middle. She closed her palm as she continued, *Do not fear the magic. Fear only what is evil.* She reopened her hand. *You see?* A butterfly had taken the pebble's place. *There is much good to come, even if it is hidden in the most unlikely of places.*

I could feel her searching my mind.

"Curious." Her eyes narrowed. "Would you share with me your first suspicions of your father?"

"Why?" I frowned. "I thought I was here for you to speak of my future?"

"Will you not answer me?"

I released a heavy breath. "His ill sentiment was obvious from the moment we first met."

"Did you sense deceit in him?"

"Not in the beginning." I shook my head.

"Tell me of Madigan." Her eyes darkened. "Why did you relinquish your charge?"

"Because my father was an impostor!" I stammered.

"You lie." She resumed in my mind, *I know what you have given up, but that is not the way it is to be!*

"What are you asking of me?" I looked to her with dread. "There is nothing you can say that will make me resume my command of the throne. Besides, Madigan will make a far better king than I would ever make as queen."

"And king he will rightfully stay. Even so, you must stand with him, regardless of your doubts. Do not fear. He will abide by you. Your strength will carry many."

She looked deep into my eyes. "In your heart, you know he cares for you deeply. We have both seen the way he looks upon you!"

'No." I stood in contempt, or denial. "He looks upon me as a brother looks to a sister, nothing more!"

"It was not my intention to upset you." Her eyes lightened. "Perhaps we should continue when you have rested. When you are clearer in your thoughts."

She paused. "Before you go, I must ask you of these feelings you carry for Darwynyen."

"Darwynyen." I looked away. "If you are to warn me of him, I do not wish to hear it."

"It is now, in his attempt to reassure you, that he will try to give you his ring of eternal life." Her eyes again darkened, but this time with greater intensity. "It is you who will be faced with the decision of whether or not to accept it."

"I do not understand."

"Go to him now." She sat back in a commanding pose. *Speak nothing of my words!*

303

Although many questions still lingered, I nodded and took my leave.

As I stumbled down the path, I thought of Madigan. Was it true? Were there feelings in him greater than those we had shared in kinship? For that matter, did I nurture them as well? No. The love in my heart was for one alone. At the thought of Darwynyen, I hastened my pace.

Halfway up the stair, I hesitated. What would I tell him? Nothing. I did not want to be the cause of a rift between him and Madigan.

"You have returned." He appeared at the door with Aldraveena's note in his hand. "Did you speak with her?"

Unsure what to say, I made way for the balcony.

"Were her words to upset you?" He came to my side.

"Forgive me." I looked away. "She has asked that I not yet reveal them."

"Oh." He embraced me. "It is all right. I understand."

When I pulled away, he looked deep into my eyes. I was about to speak, but he silenced me with his finger.

"I trust you, Arianna. In that, you must carry no guilt."

"I ... I—" As I held out my hands, my dress fell from my shoulders. Insecure, I stepped back.

His eyes swept my body as he reached for me. "Your beauty overpowers me."

"Darwynyen." I began to pull at his buttons. No longer could I deny him. For a moment's time, I would forget the queen's words and give myself to him completely.

He pulled his shirt from over his head. "Arianna, I want you. I want you now, more than ever."

I allowed my dress to fall to my ankles. When he placed his hands on my skin, I shivered.

"I am yours, Darwynyen."

Without further words, he lifted me into his arms and took me to bed.

The passion of our love left me a different person. In many ways, I felt complete. As I watched him sleep, I knew in my heart I could never be with another. Desperate for his touch, I kissed his brow.

He awoke with a look of contentment. "For a moment, I thought I was dreaming." He turned to face me.

"Dreaming of what?" I ran my fingers through his hair.

"You." He closed his eyes for a moment. "Not once in my life have I felt closer to another."

"Nor I," I uttered.

"I love you, Arianna." A tear fell from his eye. "More than I thought possible."

"It is a love we both share." I could feel my chest tighten. "So much so, it frightens me."

"Why?" He took hold of my chin. "You must know by now that I would never leave you."

"Perhaps." I avoided his stare.

"What is it?" He sat up to face me.

"Nothing." I fell back on the bed.

"There is nothing to fear." He removed a plain gold band from his middle finger. I had seen it before but never took much notice of it. "Everything will happen as it must."

I tensed when the queen's words resurfaced in my mind. "What are you doing?"

"This ring." He held it to the air. "It binds me to a life I no longer desire. As a pledge of my eternal love, I give it to you."

"No." I shook my head. "You sacrifice too much!"

"Have you not heard a word I said?" He held forward the ring. "I do not wish to go on without you!"

"Then you must keep it!" I reached for my clothes. "I love you too much to allow you to give up your immortality, especially now, when the future is so clouded."

"There is no cause to refuse me," he growled. "I can assure you, the ending effect of its power will not consume me."

Although I was confused by his statement, I stood my ground. "How could you put this burden on me? Have you given any thought to how I would feel? Without the ring, you are weakened, unprotected by its strength!"

Before he could interject, I continued, "Do not pity me. It is your given right to live without the burdens that we of Man's Blood carry."

When I saw the hurt in his eyes, I calmed. "Please, Darwynyen, fight me no further. My decision—"

"Darwynyen!" A frantic knock came to the door. "You must come! It has started!"

"What do you speak of?" He gathered his clothes.

"Hurry!" the man beckoned. "You must see for yourself!"

"I am coming!" He began to dress.

"What is happening?" I cried.

"You ask me questions I cannot answer." He moved to the door. "We will continue this conversation later."

By his tone, I knew it was best not to argue, so I let him go.

Come to me now! the queen's voice resurfaced when the latch struck the door.

"Now is not the time," I replied with annoyance.

Ascend the stair to my altar, the one connected to the tree within my realm. I will await you there!

With a heavy breath, I began to dress in the outfit I had arrived in. Regardless of her wantings, I would not be returning to her in her chosen attire. She would have to suffer me as I am.

CHAPTER 38:

THE DRAGONS HOLD STRONG TO VENGEANCE

Darwynyen was led to a main lookout point at the crest of an outer tree. "Why have I been summoned?"

The gathering of Elves were taking turns peering through a looking glass. When they ignored him, Darwynyen pushed them aside. "What is out there?"

"Aarrondirth!" One of them pointed. "The city is under attack!"

Taking a turn at the lens, he caught view of the beasts that assailed the city.

"Dragons," he uttered. They were swarming near the landline. "The rumors have proven true. The beasts have returned to seek their vengeance."

"What should we do?" One of the younger Elves spoke. "Are we to be their next mark?"

"Sound the horn! We must prepare for an attack!" Darwynyen turned. "Find the others. Have them assemble at the outer towers!"

"We are no match for dragons!" another challenged

"Prepare your arrows with Hellum's Dew," he ordered. "In their blood, it will act as a poison!"

Before the Elf could respond, Darwynyen ran across a bridge that led to an adjacent tower. He found a group of Elves within.

"Prepare for battle! The dragons of Naksteed are soon to be upon us!"

When the men nodded, he descended the stair. He needed to get to Arianna and warn her of the looming danger.

Chapter 39:

Destiny

Aldraveena awaited me at the altar, the one I had seen on our first encounter, though this time the outer torches were lit. Standing at the center, her white gown danced in the open breeze.

"Has something happened?" I approached her with caution when she did not respond. She appeared to be in a daze. "Aldraveena?" I slowly reached out to her.

"Listen carefully to my words." She placed her hands to my temples, forcing me to my knees. "The future of many is soon to fall upon you!"

Her touch took me from my senses. It was as though I was no longer within my body. With speed, the land passed beneath me. First, I saw Hoverdire and then the mountains of Alcomeen.

Your journey has brought you far. The tone of her voice intensified. *Prepare yourself!*

I tensed with the sight of Aarrondirth. The city was under attack. Smoke billowed from the outer structures. Several of the towers were damaged. Sweltering heat escaped from the inner keep where the roofline was broken.

The dragons have returned to seek their vengeance, she warned. *The city of your birthplace is soon to lie in ruin.*

Dark shadows swept through the air. Despite their speed, I was able to discern the outline of their bodies. "Dragons," I uttered. Sleek and graceful, their wings carried them with swiftness, allowing their steel-like talons to shred through the stone on the wall walks and parapet with ease.

Before I could claim a better view, she led me north, to a place I did not recognize. At the end of a winding loch, the land became barren and cruel. Trees, empty of their leaves, dwindled into an encompassing desert. Far into its reaches, we came upon a stone structure. Its size was enormous. The structure was circular, and four arms with elongated hands reached for the skyline. In our quick descent through two of the forearms, I felt butterflies in my stomach. I ignored the sensation as I scanned over the area. In the center of the encasement stood a pedestal. Around it, several bowls and flasks were strewn about. Papers splattered with blood flirted with the gusts of wind.

You have been shown the way to Cessdorn. She led me back through the forearms and then further north. *Do not forget the path!*

Perched on a ridge stood the mightiest of castles. Enormous towers rose up over a sea of dark torrid water. A lone drawbridge connected its edifice to land. Everything was covered in soot. Mining operations were underway in the surrounding hillside.

Trolls, soon to be under the command of your father, work steadily in their preparation for battle.

Aldraveena! The coarse voice of a man called out the queen's name.

Before she could respond, we were struck with an invisible force.

How dare you cross into our lands!

I do not fear you! She broke us free of the force.

Be gone! the voice threatened, *before I turn you into a wingless pigeon!*

Save your threats! She pulled me in a southward direction.

"Who was that? Could it be they—" I winced, struck with an overwhelming pain in my temples.

Speak no further! Her voice was strained. *It weakens us both!*

I already knew the answer to my question: it was one of the Hynd.

When the loch returned to view, she directed us west. *I have one last place for you to see!* She hesitated. *Wait! What is this?*

I looked down to find my father. He was in the company of several Trolls. They made their way north through the thick of the forest. As though sensing our presence, he halted.

"No!" she shrieked.

Pulled from her vision, I fell to the floor. Cold and weak, I took a moment to regain my strength.

"Forgive me, Arianna." She knelt at my side. "It was imperative that he not see you."

"Why?" I found my footing.

"Because now is not the time for him to learn of our intentions." Her tone deepened, "Do not underestimate him. He has grown very powerful. I fear it will not be long before the Hynd succumb to his rule!"

Her presence intensified. *Do not be fooled by his previous actions. He is drawn to you in ways he does not understand. That is why you must go to Cessdorn!*

"Cessdorn?" I gasped. "If you speak the truth, you will need someone skilled in magic for such a task!"

"There is no magic to outlast him," she responded bluntly. "This charge falls to you alone. It is your destiny, Arianna. I have seen it! In the months ahead, your strengths will blossom. Courage will absorb the weakness."

I felt her hand on my shoulder. "My only concern lies with your ill-fated intentions. Forget them and follow the light. Revenge will only consume you and destroy your very soul!"

"What if I cannot resist him?"

"Do not put doubt in your bloodline. You carry the good that has been lost to your father. Your light gives balance to his darkness. Trust in that, and it will guide you."

She paused. "I understand that I leave you with a heavy burden, but in your mind you know that the truth has been spoken."

"I ..." I blinked. "The choice does not seem to be mine."

"Very good, my dear." Her eyes brightened for a moment. "From what we have witnessed, your father is soon to reach the Hynd. Only weeks stand between them. If he is swift, he will arrive before the next cycle of the moon. You will know of his success, should the sky turn dark to the north. Thereafter, it will only take two cycles before they are able to obtain the full power of the stones."

She looked to the horizon. "In this time, the people of the different regions must unite and make their stand in the north." Her eyes narrowed. "You must not let the union fail!"

She continued in my mind. *While they prepare, I have a quest for you.*

Overwhelmed, I tried to break the connection, but her will was too strong.

Choose four of those you trust, no less, no more. Lead them to the western shoreline by route of the loch, the loch you saw in my vision. Its currents will carry you to an enchanted sea. Beyond the mist, you will find a towering island where the shore bears a sand of copper. It is there where you will find a wizard who dwells in self-exile. His name is Archemese. He will assist you!

When she broke the connection, I spoke, "Your words are madness!"

A glow began to emanate around her. "It is you, Arianna, who must see this through. Take heed in my words. Share all you know with Darwynyen, even that of your bloodline. In turn, he will protect you."

Her glow dimmed. "If you fail, your father will set loose a force of inescapable terror, a force not even I could withstand." The aura around her extinguished.

Tears filled my eyes. "I ... there seems no way for me to refuse you."

She took my hands in hers. "But you refused Darwynyen's ring when he offered it to you."

"Yes." I blinked. "My love for him would not allow me to risk his life in what lies before us."

"Your gesture will not go unrewarded." She pulled a necklace from over her head. "Arianna, I give you this pendant. It is a gift of life and protection. You will need its power in the times to come. In its magic, you will be protected from fire; you will not burn. And protected from water; you will not drown." She placed it over my head. "This pendant carries my eternal life, the rest of which I leave to you."

"You cannot do this!" Darwynyen exclaimed.

I turned to find him at the crest of the stair where I had entered only moments earlier.

"Why would you give Arianna your pendant of life?"

"To keep her safe," she replied. "Is that not what you wanted?"

"Yes, but ..." he stammered. "You sacrifice too much, Mother!"

"Mother?" I took a step back. "She is your mother?"

"Be strong, Darwynyen." She closed her eyes for a moment. "Arianna will need you. It is—"

"Are you all right?" I took her by the arm. Her skin was changing. Silver veins had begun to appear beneath her skin.

"I must rest." She winced and her breath was ragged.

Before I could respond, she had vanished down the stair.

"What did she tell you?" Darwynyen took me by the arms.

"You will find no comfort in her counsel." I looked away with worry. "It was of my father. She has shown me the way to Cessdorn, where by her command, I must face him once again.

His powers grow stronger by the minute. Soon he will take over the Hynd. In doing so, the stones will no longer be beyond his reach."

"You!" He puckered his brow. "I do not understand! You are not skilled in the magic."

"That is why he will not perceive me as a threat," I explained.

When he did not respond, I looked to him for strength. "Darwynyen?"

"What else did she say?"

"She said that if he arrives before the next moon cycle, only two would have to pass thereafter before he obtained the full power of the stones." I again looked away. "While they work to succeed in their efforts, she has sent me on a quest. We must make our way to an island that lies off the western coast, to the realm of a forgotten wizard."

"The legend of Archemese?"

"She told me he would help us!"

"Perhaps." He paused. "If he is willing ..."

"What do you mean?"

"Come." He tensed. "We have no time for this! We are soon to be under attack!"

"The dragons?" I gasped. "Are they to come?"

"Yes." He dragged me to the stair.

When we reached his abode, he rushed through the door. "Quickly." He scanned the area. "Where is your bow?"

"Under the bed." I knelt to find it.

We have little time!" He handed me a small bottle from his pocket. "Dip your arrows in this potion. It carries a poison that will injure the beasts. Show no mercy! Aim your best! I will need to see to those at the lookout point. Once the attack has ceased, I will return for you!" He ran for the door.

"Darwynyen!" When he turned, I took a step back. "I ..."

"You will be fine." He winked. "You are stronger than you believe!"

In his absence, I released a heavy breath and pulled the cork from the bottle. The smell of the potion sickened me. It reminded me of the flora at the gates. Holding my breath, I dipped the arrowheads as Darwynyen had instructed. While doing so, a horn sounded.

"Prepare for battle!" a man's voiced echoed from the higher reaches.

With anticipation, I ran to the balcony. Through the treeline I caught view of the beasts circling above. Arrows began to whistle through the air. Seconds later came the familiar stench of smoke.

Holding my sleeve to my mouth, I made way for the door. I stepped out to find several trees set ablaze. As Elves leapt from their limbs, the trunks splintered and creaked from the sweltering heat.

An old woman appeared at the bottom of the stair. "Help us!"

"What can I do?" I rushed to meet her.

She handed me a bucket. "We need water from the stream!"

I nodded and made way toward the stream. As I knelt, the land began to rumble, and a gust of wind took hold of my hair. As I fought to secure it, I was pelted with twigs and tiny bits of debris. Rolling to the ground, I pulled an arrow.

A young boy, flailing his arms, jumped into the stream. I was about to aid him when I saw a dragon land on the opposite side of the embankment.

You! Its fiery eyes fell upon me.

Confused, I stumbled back. At my reaction, it pounced forward, thrashing its elongated tail through the neighboring shrubbery.

You! Heat rippled through its jagged teeth.

I pulled my bow. "Are you—"

"What are you waiting for?" An Elf appeared at my side.

Before I could stop him, he released an arrow, piercing the creature in the chest.

Falling backward, it dug its massive claws into the ground. *Soon it is you they will seek!*

When more Elves began to assemble, it extended its celadon wings. As it took to the air, it saturated the area with fire.

I crouched to a boulder when the flames drew near. The smell of burnt hair was all around me.

"Help him!" a young woman screamed, pointing to the stream.

I quickly searched the area for the beast before kneeling to the bank. The dragon was nowhere to be found. "Here," I reached out to the boy who appeared to be in shock. "Give me your hand."

He clung to me with desperation. "Mother!"

I cried out when I realized he was pointing to a burnt body on the ground. "Give him to me!" the young woman beckoned.

As I handed him over, my knees gave way. "Why is this happening?"

"Arianna!" I felt Darwynyen as he caught me. "Are you all right?"

I steadied my feet. "Please, tell me they are gone."

"Yes." He pulled me to face him. "What happened?"

"I am not sure," I uttered. "The dragon, I think it—"

"I thought I told you to stay out of sight!"

I looked down. "These people needed my help. Only I was too late and …"

"Forgive me." He embraced me with vigor. "Do not confuse my concern with anger."

"She is dead," I stammered at the sight of the woman, "because of my hesitation!"

"This is no fault of yours, Arianna; the beasts were to show no mercy."

Before I could respond, he took me by the arm. "Come, let us talk inside."

"Should we not help the others?"

"We take care of our own," he replied.

As we climbed the stair to his dwelling, I looked back to the sanctuary. Fires still burned in the higher reaches. People walked the grounds, searching for their loved ones. The devastation was severe. I had only observed a small part of the attack.

"Sit." He led me to a chair. "It seems you were caught in the breath of the dragon's fire."

"What do you mean?" I asked.

"Your hair." He lifted a few of the tresses. "I should never have left you."

I stood in panic. "Aarrondirth—we need to make our way back!"

"We will." He removed a blade from his boot. "After the necessary arrangements have been made here."

"How can you ask me to stay?"

"As you know, Aldraveena is not well. It is I who must speak in her place."

"Yes, but ..." I took hold of his wrist. "What about my people?"

"*Your* people?"

I looked away. "I mean Madigan's."

"Madigan is strong, strong enough to see those of Man's Blood through to victory," he countered. "Besides, if we arrive without the Elvish accompaniments, our attempts would prove futile should the dragons continue in their attacks."

Knowing his words to be true, I returned to my seat. "You are right. Forgive me."

He nodded and took hold of my hair. "Keep still while I cut away what is burnt."

After removing what he could, he set the blade to the table. "You did not lose much."

"Thank you." I put my hand to the pendant.

"You must never take that off," he warned. "Many will be angered that the queen has given it to you. No one other than an Elf has ever adorned it. Not only does it give eternal life, it protects the person who wears it. If you had not been ..." He broke off his words. "The thought itself is something I cannot bear."

"If there is truth in what you say, it seems I am already indebted to her."

I thought of the boy. "What of that child? Who will care for him?"

"Do not worry. He has many relatives here." His eyes softened. "As for the death of his mother ... that is something you will have to get used to, for I fear there will be many tragedies to face in the coming of this war."

I stood. "Darwynyen, where do you draw your courage from?"

"You forget the years I have lived."

"Yes, but—"

"But what?"

"Well." I hesitated. "Your will is that of no other I have seen."

"That is because I have been through much in my lifetime," he replied. "Most of which is too painful to speak of."

"Will you not share it with me?"

"Arianna." He slowly began to pace the room. "When you said *your* people ... I mean ... I know you have given up your charge." His stare met mine. "Is there something you have yet to share?"

My heart began to quicken. "To be truthful, it was my intention never to tell you, only your queen has insisted."

"What is it?" His eyes narrowed.

I took a step back in fear of his reaction. "My father, he had a pendant. He said it proved his bloodline to be that of King Alameed's."

"He is cunning," he said, resisting acknowledgment of what I had said. "How do you know he has not deceived you?"

"Your mother," I replied. "She confirmed his proclamation when she revealed to me my destiny."

"Why did you not tell me of this sooner?"

"Perhaps for the same reason you did not tell me that she was your mother!"

"I had my reasons," he snapped.

"As did I." I looked to him pleading. "If I was forced into my duty as queen, I would not be standing here with you now!"

He stiffened. "You will have to tell Madigan on our return."

"I know." I looked down. "If only things were different."

"Do not fear." I felt his touch. "You have been chosen for something of great importance. Give it time. When you are ready, we will face this evil together!"

"Your queen." I changed the subject. "What will happen to her?"

"She will continue her life as a mortal."

"Will that sustain her?" I asked.

"For a time." His eyes began to wander. "As I told you before, magic has its boundaries."

"What kind of boundaries?"

"Some, including those within my family, consider the gift of eternal youth to be a curse. In fact, many have chosen to deny its path, for once you are trapped in its bindings, you cannot survive without it, nor can you breed."

I took a moment to find the right words. "Is that why you said before that your people are a dying breed?"

"Yes." He nodded. "Our population has dwindled from its cause."

"But you ..." I spoke in realization, "you were to give me your ring. Why? Would that not have ended your life?"

"No." He shook his head. "I am still within the natural lifespan of our people. It would not have affected me as it does those who have outlasted it."

"Can you still breed?" I thought back to the Rinjeed, of how Darwynyen had spoken of offspring that turned evil from sharing the blood of our two races. "Will we ever have children?"

"To be truthful, I have not given it much thought." He shrugged. "Perhaps we should leave this conversation for another time, a time when war is no longer upon us."

"But—"

"No buts." He led me to the door. "Come. I must address my people."

I nodded and followed his lead, regardless of my desire for more answers.

Several hundred Elves had gathered in the inner realm at a staging area not too far from the main stables where we had first arrived. I presumed it was their area of commerce, even though there would be no trading today. Many carried a look of concern as they watched over those who had been wounded. The sanctuary was no longer a place of serenity; the dragons had stolen that in their attack.

As we approached, Darwynyen released my hand, making it obvious he was not yet ready to share knowledge of our commitment.

"Darwynyen!" A young girl emerged from the crowd. "You are back!"

He tensed when she flung her arms around his neck.

"I have missed you!" Her lips brushed his.

Sickened by the sight, I was about to turn.

"Wait." He pushed her aside.

She appeared confused by his actions. "What is it? I thought you would be pleased to see me."

"I have another with me." I felt his hand on my back. "Her name is Arianna."

"Oh!" She eyed me up and down. "Hello."

"This is Theisanna, she ..." He hesitated. "She is an old friend."

When her mouth fell open, he looked at her intensely, as though warning her with his stare.

"I ..." She backed away. "I should be going."

I took him by the arm. "Is she one of the women you spoke of?"

"Yes." He released a heavy breath.

"Why did you not tell me?" I said angrily. "I had no idea you were still with another."

"I am not," he replied. "I tried to tell her yesterday, only I could not find her."

I regained my composure when the Elves began to stare. "Your people await you. You must not keep them."

Despite the insistence in his eyes, he climbed upon a massive stump. I guessed it to be their staging area. "Has everyone gathered?"

"Why did the dragons attack?" an Elf asked. "Where is our queen?"

"Why does she not address us?" another questioned.

Uncomfortable, I put my hand to the pendant. In doing so, I felt their eyes upon me.

"What is this?" an older woman stood forward. "Do my eyes deceive me, or does this mortal wear the queen's pendant!" She turned to those around her with a look of disgust.

"Yes." Darwynyen stiffened his stance. "Our queen has given her pendant to the daughter of our enemy. Do not fear," he pleaded, "for it is she who shall destroy him."

"What will become of Shallendria?" a man interrupted. "Is it not her given right—"

"Forget your questions, my people." The echo of Aldraveena's voice filled the air.

The Elves, shaken, looked to one another.

"Through my foresight, I have seen the one." Her voice grew intense. "It is Arianna, the young girl that stands before you, who will lead us to victory."

A gust of wind swept through the trees. "Her father, Velderon, has sought out the Sorcerers of Morne, who in turn have released the Dragons of Naksteed. Now, with the beasts at their side, our enemy will stop at nothing to destroy us."

She paused. "We cannot let this be. Should they succeed, there will be no one to stop Velderon when he reunites the Stones of Moya."

When the crowd began to stir, she continued, "Arianna, with the power of my pendant, will seek him out, challenge him, and put his evil ambitions to rest. In the interim, this sanctuary must empty. Those who bear arms will follow Darwynyen to Aarrondirth. The remainder will make their way to Tayri to seek the protection of the council."

Her voice deepened, "As your queen, I warn you now to follow my command. Should you deceive me, you will not welcome the consequences."

The queen's fairies appeared with swiftness. "I shall watch over you, my people, from afar. Tonight, in honor of Maglavine, you will share in the joys this sanctum has given you, for tomorrow you will be gone!"

When her presence diminished, the people looked to Darwynyen.

"Our queen, Aldraveena, has spoken." He put his hand to his chest. "By her command, Maglavine must empty. Pack only what you must and make ready for tomorrow!"

As the Elves dispersed, several came to examine the pendant. Unsure what to do, I allowed them a moment.

A woman approached me in anger. "Who are you to come here with all your troubles?"

"Leave her!" Darwynyen jumped down from the stump. "She is not the cause of this!"

The woman backed down immediately. Darwynyen then turned to those around him. "Does anyone else wish to speak?"

At his words, those who had remained slowly began to take their leave, concealing their whispers.

"Darwynyen!" a tall lanky Elf called as he approached.

"Here!" Darwynyen raised his hand.

As the Elf neared, Sikes joined him. "What have you gotten us into this time?" The one I did not recognize chuckled.

"This is Falker," Darwynyen smirked. "You have already met Sikes." He put his hand to his chest. "Not only are they friends, both are commanders in our army."

I nodded, keeping silent.

"You are no friend." Falker rolled his eyes sarcastically. His strong demeanor commanded my attention, that and his height, being he was taller than most of the others.

"Take no heed in that woman's ranting," Falker continued. "She is a Venree, a clan who does not speak for the rest of us."

I again nodded. Unlike Sikes, he reminded me in many ways of Darwynyen. If I did not know better, I would assume them to be brothers.

"Is there somewhere we can talk?" Darwynyen glanced over his shoulder.

"Let us make way to my cottage." Sikes extended his hand. His mannerisms were gruff and left me somewhat intimidated. The scarring on his brow gave me the impression that he, more than the others, had seen his fair share of battle. Like Darwynyen and Falker, his locks were brown, a trait that seemed to hold true for most of their people. Although I wanted to query this new revelation, I decided to wait for another time.

As we ascended the stair to a tree on the outskirts of the inner realm, Sikes walked beside me. "I hope you are not bothered by heights. My cottage is the one at the top."

"Do not worry on me." I smiled. "I will manage."

"I hope you speak the truth." He winked. "This place is not always as it seems."

"What do you mean?" I asked with concern.

"Keep your story for another time." Falker sighed with a shake of his head. "I cannot bear to hear it again."

Darwynyen laughed. "Neither can I!"

"What?" Sikes frowned. "It is a good tale!"

"Then share it with Arianna another day." Darwynyen slowed to turn in his pace. "Tonight we have other things to discuss."

In the silence that followed, I looked over the sanctuary. The view was spectacular from this perspective. Several bridges spanned to adjacent trees that were comparable in height. Cottages filled the inner core of most. To the west, I could see what appeared to be the ocean caught in the thickest of mists. I longed to touch the salt water, if only time would allow …

At the stair's end, we reached a lone cottage. "Arianna." Sikes opened the door with a bow. "I welcome you to my humble abode."

I nodded and made my way inside. The interior was similar to Darwynyen's, only smaller, being the tree narrowed at its top. A small bed hung to the side of a neighboring kitchen. To the right, a table was positioned near a circular window and surrounded by chairs.

"We should speak about Aarrondirth." Darwynyen took a seat. "As you know, Maglavine was not the only region to fall under attack."

"What should we expect?" Sikes questioned.

"It is too soon to speculate, but if Velderon reaches the Hynd before the next moon cycle, I fear Aarrondirth will become crucial in the Hynd's vengeance."

"Why?" Falker frowned. "Would they not first seek out Biddenwayde?"

"No." Darwynyen shook his head. "To hinder us, they will look to toil with the morals of those with strength." He paused. "I fear they will seek to destroy the king of Aarrondirth."

"Madigan," I uttered.

Sikes nodded. "I understand he has taken up the charge of king."

"May I ask why you relinquished your role, Arianna?" Falker sat forward.

"My path lies elsewhere." I looked to Darwynyen.

"Have you given yourself to her?" Falker puckered his brow as he looked in Darwynyen's direction.

"Yes." Darwynyen took my hand. "I love her deeply."

"For once, you have left me at a loss for words, my friend." Falker gave Sikes a fleeting look. "I never thought I would see the day." He put his hand to his chest. "I wish you both the happiness you deserve. It inspires me to know that you have found love in a time of dread."

"Yes," Sikes spoke wryly. "You, Darwynyen, are *most* inspiring."

"Enough." Darwynyen released my hand. "If we are to leave tomorrow, plans must be made!"

Unable to contain my question any longer, I spoke, "Your people, they all seem to have locks of brown, except for Shallendria and the queen, of course. May I ask why?"

They looked to one another before Darwynyen responded, "Most of our people carry the brown. Few are born without it. Should they be, it is considered a sign. That is how Shallendria's and my mother's paths were chosen."

As I absorbed his words, I thought of Shallendria. Again, her actions became clear.

Falker met my stare. "Our queen, I know she sees much with her foresight. Even so, it is a wonder that she has turned to you."

Uncomfortable, I looked to Darwynyen.

"Do you not see?" His hands opened in exclamation. "Arianna is the perfect weapon. Not only is she his only living kin, he sees her as weak!"

As they began to deliberate on the plans for our forthcoming departure to Aarrondirth, I watched over them, wondering what, if anything, they would bring to our future.

"I will leave you to your work." I stood, having nothing further to contribute.

Darwynyen nodded. "I will meet you back at my cottage."

I turned to Falker and Sikes. "I look forward to our next meeting."

Sikes moved to open the door. "Then we shall see you at the falling of the sun."

"At the falling of the sun?"

"Yes." He glanced back to Darwynyen. "Tonight we will celebrate our coming departure."

When Darwynyen acknowledged his words with a nod, I left the room.

As I made my way down the path, I could hear a faint hum in the distance. "The fairies," I grumbled.

Seconds later, two of them approached. "What do you want?" I growled.

"We are here by the request of our queen," one of them replied. "Will you not give us a moment?"

"If I must." I observed its delicate body. It was clothed in nothing more than a waist garb, which allowed its speckled body to shimmer in the faltering light.

"Our queen has asked that we watch over you!" The other shot forward. "To accompany you back to Aarrondirth."

"But … why?"

"I am Teshna," the one I presumed to be female replied. "This is my brother, Zenley. With our guidance, I can assure you that your journey will not fall astray."

I nodded blankly.

At my reaction they flew out of reach. "We will join you in the latter part of the day, when we will seek your instruction!"

As fast as they had come, they were gone. Unable to comprehend the strange encounter, I searched the area. When I caught view of an Elf, I continued my pace. It was not in my interest to cause further distractions.

As I sat on the bed, I began to contemplate Aldraveena's intentions. Despite Zenley and Teshna's enthusiasm, what help could they possibly be? War, it seemed, was no place for a fairy.

At the thought of Aarrondirth, I tensed. What would we find upon our return? Was the city to be left in ruin? Moreover, how was Madigan coping with his newfound charge?

Unable to see through to the answers, I allowed my exhaustion its plea. As I began to drift into sleep, the door slowly opened.

"How are you doing?" Darwynyen smiled. "You have taken on much today."

I sat to face him. "I was not expecting you so soon."

"I accomplished what was needed." He pulled his shirt from over his head. "Enough talk, I wish to be with you again."

Even though I was not in the mood for passion, I was soon under his spell.

† † †

From within the darkness, I claim view of a wand of magic. My father, he is pointing it in my direction. There is no love in his eyes. Birds, birds of black, they fight to taste my flesh. Fire consumes them. A glowing orb, its power pulls the strength from my very soul.

I sat up in a state of panic. My skin was wet with moisture. When I turned, I saw that Darwynyen was gone. I could hear raised voices from outside the cottage.

Disorientated, I made way for the door, stumbling through what remained of the sunlight. I pulled the door open but a crack and saw him. He was standing at the foot of the stair with Theisanna. Her hands were on the rim of his pants. The conversation seemed heated. When she tried to flee, he grabbed her by the arm. As she fought, he embraced her. When she gave in, he kissed her gently on the brow.

Unable to accept what my eyes had witnessed, I stumbled backward. Moments later, the door slowly opened.

"Arianna?" Darwynyen seemed surprised to find me awake. "What did you hear?"

"I heard nothing," I stammered. "Your actions spoke loud enough!"

"You assume too much." He extended his hand.

"Do not touch me!" I recoiled.

"I told her it was over." He stiffened. "Nothing more!"

I could feel the tears as they fell from my cheeks. "How could you?"

"What is wrong with you?" He frowned. "You are not yourself!"

I shuddered at the thought of the dream. "No, it is you who is not himself," I snapped, avoiding the real reason for my outburst.

"What are you hiding?" He approached me with caution. "Something has happened."

"It was only a dream." I wiped the tears when the anger began to ease. "Nothing I wish to speak of."

"You are shaking." I felt his arms around me. "Calm yourself. You need not worry where I am concerned, for I love you and will never leave your side."

"Forgive me," I sobbed, "for overreacting."

He took a heavy breath. "Will you not tell me of this dream?"

"If I say it, it will become real!"

"Should you not let us decide on this together?"

Although reluctant, I conceded, "My father, he will show no mercy. In his greed for the stone, I fear he will see to the death of me."

"Do not let your thoughts lead you astray." He released me. "Dreams can never be trusted. Besides, Aldraveena would not send you to your death without first preparing you."

"No," I countered. "In preparing me, she would have only weakened my resolve."

"I refuse to believe that." He sighed. "In my heart, I know we have many years together."

"Perhaps you are right." I tried to smile. A part of me needed to see things as he did. "No longer will I carry this doubt."

"Good." He kissed my brow. "Now come. We must gather with the others."

I nodded, eager to leave the conversation, and made way for the door.

When we reached the inner realm, we found the Elves working steadily in preparation for our departure. Near the stables, two wheeled wagons were being filled with supplies and weaponry while others readied the horses. To the left, past the staging area, a group of women had gathered in a circle. Curious, I moved to better observe them.

"Where are you going?" Darwynyen took my arm.

"Over there," I pointed. "I would like to offer my help, should it be needed."

"I see," he responded with widened eyes, as though impressed by my enthusiasm. "I will join you shortly. First, I must find Sikes and Falker."

I smiled as I watched him go.

Because the situation was awkward, I approached the women in a guarded manner. "Is there anything I can do?" I glanced over their faces.

A young woman smiled. "If you like, you can assist us in making these arrows."

"She would not know of arrows," a somewhat older woman mumbled. I recognized her immediately. She was the one who had taken the boy from me after the attack.

"Then she can learn." The woman who had first addressed me stood. "I am Elisha. You may sit with me."

As I took my place on a stump, I caught a glimpse of fairies as they emerged through the shrubbery. It was Teshna and Zenley; they were flying in my direction. At first, I tried to ignore them, knowing the Elves did not welcome their company."

"Arianna!" Zenley flew to my face. "We are here to assist you! What can we do?"

The Elves gasped in awe.

"They speak to you!" Elisha said with surprise, rising to her feet.

"Yes." I gave Zenley a moment's glare. "Aldraveena has asked them to accompany me back to Aarrondirth."

The women looked to one another in disbelief.

"B-but they speak to no one," Elisha stuttered.

"They are here to help." I grew frustrated when the surrounding Elves began to gather. "Is there not some way for them to contribute?"

Elisha glanced over her shoulder for a moment and then seemed to yield. "I supposed we could use more feathers." She shrugged.

"We will bring you nothing but the best." Teshna twirled in the air.

Zenley tugged on my sleeve. I could tell he was uncomfortable. "Our intentions are honorable, I can assure you."

"I know." I sighed. "Only this situation seems a bit difficult."

"What goes on here?" Darwynyen fought his way through the crowd. When he saw the fairies, he shook his head. "What are *they* doing here?"

A man stood forward. "But *they* speak to her."

After a heated stare, he took me by the arm. "Come." He gestured to the fairies.

When we reached the stream, he halted.

Teshna flew to his face, "Why are you angered? We are only here to help!"

Before Darwynyen could respond, Zenley pulled at her hair.

"Ouch!" Teshna smacked him on the head. "That hurt!"

"Not as much as this will!" He pulled on her wings.

"Why you!" She pushed him.

"Both of you stop it now!" I ordered, looking at Darwynyen with worry.

"I am sorry." Teshna half smiled. Zenley flew to her side with a look of remorse.

"You should leave." I eyed them. "I need to speak with Darwynyen."

"But there is much to be done." Zenley flew forward. "If tomorrow our destination is Aarrondirth."

"I do not believe this!" Darwynyen broke into wry laughter. "Not only do you speak, you tell me your intention is to travel back to Aarrondirth with us." He scanned both their faces.

"I meant to tell you." I took a step back.

"Are their words true?"

"Yes," I uttered.

"I see." He paused for a moment, as though to gather his thoughts.

I looked to Teshna. "Are you certain of your decision? There are many dangers out there."

Zenley flew to my face. "Would you ask us to deny our queen?"

Darwynyen interjected, "How do you intend to assist us?"

"We are guides," Teshna replied. "We will scout out the land before you."

"Perhaps." Darwynyen blinked. "Skills such as yours would no doubt be needed."

Zenley flew to his face. "We will not let you down, son of Aldraveena."

"Then you should get to work," he huffed.

"Yes." I nodded. "Go gather the feathers as you have promised."

When they flew to the higher reaches, Darwynyen turned. "I am not angered with you. Still, your timing—"

"How can you say that?" I stood my ground. "Is it not plain to see that they only wish to help?"

"The Elves." He lowered his voice. "Many will find this unexpected union hard to accept. Until now, the fairies have taken little interest."

"I understand your concern. I put my hand to his shoulder. "Even so, they will need to adjust to these changes."

When he brushed the hair from around my ear, some of the Elves took notice.

A man approached with vigor. "You give yourself to her? One of Man's Blood!"

"My affairs are my own," Darwynyen replied with resolve. "If it is a—"

"Leave him be!" an older woman interjected. "Get back to your work!"

Although hesitant, the Elves returned to their stations.

"Do not mind them." The woman smiled. Her hair had grown white with age, reminding me of the village seamstress in Hoverdire who in many ways had been like a grandmother to me. "They are not usually this meddlesome."

I looked to Darwynyen.

He extended his hand. "I would like you to meet my grandmother, Mina."

"It is a pleasure to meet you, my dear." She opened her arms. "I understand you are soon to become—"

Darwynyen put his finger to his mouth to silence her. "Have you begun the preparations?"

"Yes." She drew back. "They are nearly complete."

Darwynyen moved to join her. "Arianna, there are things I need to see to. Will you wait on me for a while?"

"Of course." I glanced over the area in search of something to do.

"We will not be long." Mina gave Darwynyen a fleeting look.

"Arianna!"

When I turned, I saw Elisha.

"We are in need of your assistance," she called with a wave.

"Do not worry on me." I smiled to reassure Darwynyen. "I will be fine."

As they took their leave, I rushed to meet Elisha. "What can I do?"

"We need to get these tables over to the staging area." She wiped the sweat from her brow. "The celebration is soon to start. Should the food not be ready, there will be many men to grumble."

"I am yours to command." I bowed my head with a wink. "Shall we get started?"

With a look of brightened relief, she ushered me into our lengthy duties.

My fingers were stinging, having accomplished more than what was needed in our labor. As I watched the men empty the armory, I thought of Darwynyen.

"I should return to the cottage." I set the basket I was holding down on a banquet table.

"Do not fret; Darwynyen will find you when he is ready." Elisha took my hand and led me to an open area where the Elves had begun to gather. "Until then, we can share in the opening of this celebration together."

"Why do you call it a celebration?" I frowned.

"Because we gather to honor life," she replied. "It is a time to say good-bye to our loved ones, those whom we may never see again."

We both turned when we heard someone call her name. "Wait for me," she insisted. "I will only be a minute."

Before I could respond, she disappeared through the gathering crowd. In her absence, I watched the events unfold.

Near the stream, Elf maidens had begun to assemble. They were adorned in little attire, and flowers of white covered their breast and waistlines. Children bearing harps and flutes sat on the tree limbs around them. When the music began, the maidens formed a circle. As they danced to the music, a sweet fragrance filled the air.

"Arianna!" Sikes raised his hand as he neared. "Where is Darwynyen?"

"I am not sure." I searched the area. "Perhaps I should go and find him."

"That would be a waste of your time!" a man's voice offered.

When I turned, Falker stood there smiling. "He will be here shortly."

"Have you eaten?" Sikes eyed the open table. "Would you care to join us?"

Before I could refuse him, he took me by the arm. "Do not fear, there is plenty of food for us to share."

"I am a bit famished." I reached for a plate.

As we finished our meal, we were offered goblets from a half-empty tray carried by an Elf mistress in passing.

"What is this?" I asked, taking hold of one of the goblets.

"It is similar to what you call wine." Sikes winked.

I took the mug reluctantly, remembering the effects from the last time I had partaken.

"What is it?" Falker frowned.

"Nothing." I smiled, taking a sip.

"May I have this dance, Arianna?" Sikes bowed.

"I would love to." I could feel my cheeks blush. "Only, I do not know how."

Falker appeared from over his shoulder. "If you will allow me, I would be honored to show you."

"Find your own partner!" Sikes pushed him aside. "It is I who will be teaching her!"

"That is what worries me," Falker sniggered.

When I giggled, Sikes held out his hand. "You must not deny me, Arianna."

Unable to resist him, I conceded.

With a look of pride, he led me to a forming line where he joined my free hand with another Elf's. As we began to move forward, I looked to him and smiled, thankful to be taking part in such traditions.

Halfway through the song, I began to lose my balance. Before I could allow myself to fall, I broke from the chain. Following my lead, Sikes and I broke out in laughter.

"I see you are teaching Arianna your misplaced dance steps," Darwynyen huffed.

"Darwynyen." I stepped back, giving Sikes a fleeting look. "We were just—"

"Go find your own female!" Darwynyen took me in his arms. "As you already know, Arianna is mine."

"Curious," Sikes countered with a smirk. "Could it be you are threatened, my friend!"

Darwynyen rolled his eyes. "Not in the least."

Sikes took me by the wrist. "If you ever grow tired of him, you know where to find me."

"Not in your lifetime!" Darwynyen nudged him aside.

"We shall see." He looked to me with a nod before returning to the dance.

I turned to Darwynyen with a laugh. "If nothing else, he is bold."

"Very," he replied bluntly, taking my hand in his. "Did you want to stay or ..."

"What did you have in mind?"

"Darwynyen!" Falker approached. "Tell me you are not leaving?"

Although he seemed reluctant, Darwynyen took a mug of nectar from the table. "I suppose we can stay a little longer."

"Good." Falker cleared a path. "Sikes needs saving—saving *from himself!*"

With a chuckle, we followed him through the crowd.

We spent the remainder of the evening with his companions, who in many ways were starting to feel like friends to me.

"Darwynyen." Sikes took the last of his nectar. "Although you have claimed Arianna as your own, you have yet to share in a dance with her."

"He is right." I held out my hands. "Will you not show me?"

"Of course." He smiled somewhat reluctantly.

"He hates to dance you know," Falker snickered.

Darwynyen ignored him as he led me from their company. When the music softened, he took me in his arms.

Unsure what to do, I accidentally stepped on his foot. "Excuse my clumsiness." I blushed. "I am not accustomed to these—"

"Darwynyen!" Mina approached, sidestepping through the other couples. "Why are you still here?"

"I—"

"You must waste time and our work!" She insisted. "Why do you linger?"

"You are right." He tensed. "Forgive me. I was only—"

"There is nothing to forgive." She ushered us through the crowd.

When we reached the stream, I turned. She raised her hand and nodded, leaving me to wonder about their intentions.

As we ascended the stair to his dwelling, he covered my eyes. "No peeking."

Despite the curiosity within me, I did as he asked. As we stepped through the threshold, he released me.

Overcome, I nearly fell to my knees.

Petals of lily were strewn about the room. The aroma itself was intoxicating. Near the balcony, a barren circle was decorated with candles and vine.

He led me to its center.

"Darwynyen, I—"

"This is a ritual we share when we give ourselves to one another." He walked over to the table. Two goblets were positioned in a collage of flora and brushwood. Before he removed them, he spoke in Elvish.

My heart fluttered when his intentions became clear.

"Before we continue, we shall share in the nectar of a rare flower that lies off the coast." He pulled me to my knees. As I faced him, he lifted his goblet to my mouth.

When I consumed the resin, I could not help but notice the whisper of mint that reminded me of winter.

I was about to speak, but he silenced me, gesturing to my goblet. I brought it to his mouth. Consuming the nectar, he returned my stare.

Before addressing me, he again spoke in Elvish. A tear of joy trickled down my cheek. He set down his goblet and put his hand to his chest.

"It is now that I will plead to the gods and beg them to unite us for an eternity." His words once again turned to Elvish. The intensity of the moment stole my breath.

"I give my soul to you, Arianna. I pledge my eternal love. I swear to never look upon another as I look upon you." A tear fell from his eye. "It is now you must share in your commitment to me."

As I fought to speak, my body began to shiver. "I too give my soul, to you, Darwynyen. Not only do you hold my love, you hold my life. I will cherish every moment we share. I promise to love you for an eternity."

Taking the goblet from my hand, he let his fingers sweep through the nectar. With his free hand he placed the resin around my mouth. With a gentle kiss, we both took in the resin.

"Darwynyen." I held to the whisper of his essence. "I want you."

He lifted me to my feet, motioning for me to remove my shirt. "To sustain these vows, I give you the mark of my bloodline."

When I tossed my shirt to the floor, he poured resin onto my chest. Leading his finger across my torso, he drew a circle, completing it with two symbols. "From this moment on, you are mine."

He poured the last of the resin into my hand before removing his shirt. "Give me your hand."

He moved my resin-soaked fingers across his chest. After drawing a symbol similar to the one I wore, he lifted me into his arms and carried me to the bed.

"Now I am yours."

Unable to speak, I allowed him the desires we both undeniably shared.

CHAPTER 40

VEXED

Unable to sleep, Velderon took in the remaining warmth of the fire. He had been diligent in his studies and could not help but feel that he was nearing a breakthrough. If he conquered this feat, his powers would be endless, far surpassing those of the Hynd.

He chuckled at the notion. "If only those in Aarrondirth could see me now," he snickered.

At the thought of his daughter, his mood soured. "I wonder if she lives."

Memories of her had been plaguing him for days. He knew his time with her was not over, and the notion of seeing her again brought shivers to his skin.

Chapter 41:

The Dawning of Our Future

Darwynyen was gone when I awoke. In his place, I found a note.

> Arianna,
>
> You were amazing. I love you now more than ever...
>
> I have gone to make the final preparations. Once you are ready, meet me at the stables.
>
> Darwynyen

Tears filled my eyes as I held the note to my chest.

With little time to waste, I gathered my belongings. When I had stowed what I could, Darwynyen appeared at the door.

"What are you doing? I was expecting you some time ago."

I stood up from the bed. "Forgive me," I took hold of my bow. "I must have overslept."

"You are forgiven." He winked. "If I had it my way, we would never leave this place. Unfortunately, that option does not lie in our path."

"We are ready!" Teshna and Zenley flew through from the balcony.

"You are serious then." Darwynyen frowned.

"Of course we are, silly!" Teshna giggled.

Zenley flew to my face, "May we store our belongings with you?"

"What could you possibly have to bring," Darwynyen snickered.

"The magic of our queen," Zenley snapped.

"I see." He rolled his eyes.

Before they could argue, I took one of my satchels and emptied a pocket. "Will this do?"

"It will do fine." Teshna removed her shoulder bag, which was no greater in size than a thimble.

After buttoning the pocket, I looked to them. "Will you wait for us at the stables?" I wanted one final moment alone with Darwynyen.

"Of course." They giggled, making haste to the window. "Do not keep us waiting! There is much we need to discover!"

I could not help but sigh at their childlike manner.

Darwynyen joined me. "Shall we?"

"Not just yet." I took his hand. "I wish to spend one last moment with you before we leave."

He kissed my brow. "Come." I felt his arms around me. "Let us hold one another."

Safe in his embrace, I never wanted to let go.

"Arianna, we really need to be going."

"I know." I closed my eyes for a moment before releasing him.

Gathering the rest of my belongings, we made way for our horses. When we reached the inner realm, it was bustling with activity.

"Arianna!" Elisha rushed over. "I must apologize for leaving you on your own last night."

"There is no need." I embraced her. "Everything is as it should be."

"Move out!" Sikes shouted.

Darwynyen mounted his horse. "Are you ready?"

I nodded with apprehension.

Zenley and Teshna flew to my shoulders. "We are here for you, Arianna. Do not fear."

I smiled sincerely, before looking back to the sanctuary.

"Let us move out!" Darwynyen shouted.

At his words, the men and women began to assemble.

As we traveled into the forest deep, I thought of Aarrondirth and wondered what we would find upon our return. Despite the underlying sensation of dread, I would no longer look back. It was time for me to face my future.

END OF PART ONE.